FINDING JIMMY MORAN

CODICIL TO *THE CLAIRE TRILOGY*

TOM McCAFFREY

All the Best Lies
Are Wrapped Around
A Kernel of Truth

Black Rose Writing | Texas

ISBN: 978-1-68513-174-6 (Paperback); 978-1-68513-175-3 (Hardcover)
PUBLISHED BY BLACK ROSE WRITING www.blackrosewriting.com

Printed in the United States of America
Suggested Retail Price (SRP) $23.95 (Paperback); $28.95 (Hardcover)
Finding Jimmy Moran is printed in Garamond

Cover art by Richard Lamb of Inspired Lamb Design

*As a planet-friendly publisher, Black Rose Writing does its best to eliminate unnecessary waste to
reduce paper usage and energy costs, while never compromising the reading experience. As a result, the
final word count vs. page count may not meet common expectations.

This book is dedicated to my grandchildren, John Lucian, Scarlett Rose, Savanna Joy and Stella Anastasia, who all appear as characters in The Claire Trilogy, and to all of your future siblings and cousins who may follow you into this realm. The Dude and Nona love you forever. Never forget that there is magic in this world.

FINDING
JIMMY MORAN

PROLOGUE
(HINDSIGHT IS TWENTY-TWENTY)

They say that when you are dying, your whole life flashes before your eyes. That was true in my human form, where I actually died twice. The first time occurred when I was four human years and swallowed that damn copper penny – it got wedged in my throat and shut off my oxygen for the twenty minutes it took my frantic mother to get me to the emergency room of the closest hospital. That retrospective was a bit of a rip-off given there was not much to remember at the time – except Kathy Brown, her pigeons, and her delightful pecks. I guess that was enough. The second and last time I died as a human, I ingested copper in a different shape, when that 9mm bullet created a new opening in my body and pierced my heart. Turns out, that too was a rip-off, because while, by then, I had six decades of memories to draw upon, I was only playing the edited version of that life. The last thing I remembered then was my wife Gina. And that too, was enough. It still is.

But, as the last of the first group of Centaurian-Terran hybrids, I owe it to all those who have come after, and those humans and other mystical species on earth and other planets, including Claire, who all followed us into the Great Galactic War, to take this opportunity to get this one right, because this time is my last time. The twenty-four second clock has been turned off and I want that ball in my hands because I'm taking this last shot.

The good news is that the Centaurian evolutionary upgrade following my second human demise slowly restored that portion of my human memory that had been wiped clean, and I have had the last four-hundred and fifty years to get this straight. I've kept this recovered part of the first two decades of my human existence locked away from everyone, including Gina, and I'm sure I am going to have some explaining to do once I reach that other side of the veil.

I opened my eyes and gazed over at my two children, Stella and Apollo, the present rulers of Proxima b, who sat beside me stoically, absorbing my thoughts. They were beautiful.

So, I am sharing this memory with you both, to do with it whatever you think best.

01010100 01101000 01101001 01110011 00100000 01101001
01110011 00100000 01101101 01111001 00100000 01000100
01101001 01110010 01100101 01100011 01110100 01101111
01110010 00100111 01110011 00100000 01100011 01110101
01110100 00101110 00100000

This is my Director's cut.

01001001 01101110 00100000 01000101 01101110 01100111
01101100 01101001 01110011 01101000 00101100 00100000
01100110 01100001 01110100 01101000 01100101 01110010
00101100 00100000 01001001 00100000 01100100 01101111
01101110 00100111 01110100 00100000 01110111 01100001
01101110 01110100 00100000 01100001 01101110 01111001
01110100 01101000 01101001 01101110 01100111 00100000
01101100 01101111 01110011 01110100 00100000 01101001
01101110 00100000 01110100 01110010 01100001 01101110
01110011 01101100 01100001 01110100 01101001 01101111
01101110 00101110

In English, father, I don't want anything lost in translation.

Stella was indeed her mother, Petrichor's daughter. All business. No bullshit.

01000001 01101110 01100100 00100000 01001001 00100000
01110111 01100001 01101110 01110100 00100000 01111001
01101111 01110101 00100000 01110100 01101111 00100000
01110011 01100001 01111001 00100000 01101001 01110100
00100000 01101111 01110101 01110100 00100000 01101100
01101111 01110101 01100100 00101110 00100000 00100000
01001001 00100000 01110111 01100001 01101110 01110100
00100000 01110100 01101111 00100000 01101000 01100101
01100001 01110010 00100000 01111001 01101111 01110101

01110010 00100000 01110110 01101111 01101001 01100011
01100101 00100000 01110111 01101000 01100101 01101110
00100000 01001001 00100000 01110010 01100101 01101101
01100101 01101101 01100010 01100101 01110010 00100000
01101001 01110100 00101110 00100000
And I want you to say it out loud. I want to hear your voice when I remember it.

Apollo smiled, and for a moment I saw Gina in his face. I nodded.

"Make yourselves comfortable," I said softly, my voice a bit raspy from age and lack of use. "This may take a while."

"I got all the time in the Universe —" came a disembodied husky voice, followed by that Lurchy laugh.

A moment later my magnificent Mule, Claire, appeared before us in her holographic form. She nuzzled Stella and Apollo then reclined beside my chair and lay her large head across my lap.

I stroked her beautiful mane and thought for a moment of all of the adventures we had shared. She smiled as she read those thoughts.

"So let us begin. . . ."

CHAPTER ONE
(MOVING UPTOWN)

The last thing I remember about Gerard Avenue that morning in early January of 1960, as my father pulled his packed 1957 Chevy station wagon away from the curb, was staring out the car's back window at the large green eyes of Kathy Brown, who removed her right glove to wave as she watched the car take my family a short distance south before finally making a left and climbing 161st street towards the Grand Concourse. I caught one final look at the Old Yankee Stadium through the frost of my breath on the window as we made that turn north onto the Jewish Riviera and headed to our new home in the promised land. Riverdale.

The car was as cold inside as out, its Vintage Air heating system just powerful enough to de-ice the windshield and warm the legs of the passengers in the front seat. The rest of us had to rely on the body warmth from the close proximity of our nearest family member or pet. Thank God we had a decent number of bodies to keep the rest of us from freezing to death.

I never had been further north on this wide Bronx boulevard than Alexander's department store on Fordham Road, where my mother used to take the tribe to clothe us twice a year for Easter and Christmas. I remember its slogan: "You'll find Alexander's has what you're looking for; how lucky can you get?!" I guess that made us pretty lucky.

"Edgar Allan Poe lived there!" my mother exclaimed while pointing generally in the direction of a passing park on our right. My mother was a brilliant woman, who unfortunately had to sacrifice advancing to college once she married and started having children. Despite the lack of formal education, she, like her father before her, was a voracious reader. So, she was as smart as the Scarecrow in The Wizard of Oz, she just never got the paperwork to prove it.

At four years old, I hadn't a clue about Edgar Allan Poe and so I didn't bother looking. My older and only sister, Bonnie, who had a few years of grammar school at Christ the King under her belt, must have recognized the name, as she strained her neck to her right to catch sight of the top of the small cottage my mother was referring to. Bonnie was the perfect child, a parent's joy, until she later shed the limitations of our Catholic faith, in both doctrine and practice.

I was already bored, so I rolled over towards my next younger brother, The Ginger, caught his head between my two knees and gently tapped him on the nose with my fist. This always had the same effect. His freckled face scrunched up like the petals of a red rose and he started to wail uncontrollably.

I liked to think that I was doing my younger brother a favor back then. It toughened him up and when his Viking genes finally kicked in during his teenage years, it made him an absolute killer, the type that Led Zeppelin later sang about in its 1972 hit, "Immigrant Song." He gave Eric the Red a run for his money.

"What the fuck's going on back there?" my father shouted through the cloud of Marlboro smoke enveloping him in the driver's seat.

"Eddie, leave your brothers alone," my repeatedly pregnant mother shouted from the passenger seat beside her husband. Secondary smoke wasn't an issue back then.

"It was Jimmy," my older brother shouted back before rifling a right fist into my left shoulder, propelling me against the right back window and freeing the struggling Ginger, who quickly scooted from the cargo space over the back of the middle seat like a crab and into the protective arms of my sister Bonnie.

"You keep it up and I'm going to pull over and put you all out on the street." My father responded. "I'll rent your rooms in the new house to some of the neighborhood urchins."

My father was always threatening to put us out on the roadway whenever we acted up in the car. He really had no other hand to play given that the most troublesome of his children learned early on that riding prone in the storage section of all the station wagons he drove until he died meant that he could not reach us when he flailed blindly into the backseat behind him looking to strike one of the offenders. That frantic movement always set off the bursitis in his right shoulder, which led to a litany of curses I can still recite from memory. For my father, it was always safety first when he was driving. He never took his eyes off the roadway unless it was to light a cigarette.

By now we had reached the northernmost end of the Grand Concourse. I found this fascinating, because in my short life I had never come to the end of the road before. Turns out it was the first of many of such experiences both figuratively and literally.

Just one more end of the road in this lifetime.

Not even McCoombs park had as many trees as I saw lining the Mosholu Parkway, which formed the next leg of our journey towards the family forever home.

"Mosholu means 'hidden river' in some local Indian language" my mother announced, pointing at the road sign as we turned onto the roadway. "Our new house is on Mosholu Avenue."

It took us all a few tries, but we soon converted our first attempt at "Moshula" to "Mosholu" through group repetition led by Bonnie, who knew her calling early on and later became a teacher of the rich and mighty. I never got used to saying that word.

By then my father had followed the winding roadway through a large, forested area my mother identified as Van Cortlandt Park before we finally arrived at the exit sign number 22 for "254th Street and Riverdale Avenue." One more block and my father pulled in front of a large green and white, three-family house set up from and back off the sidewalk behind a retaining wall and a line of bushes.

"Home sweet home!" My dad shouted proudly, and he raced the station wagon through the narrow stone opening to the driveway like he had boat bumpers on the sides of his car.

At the end of a long driveway stood my paternal grandparents. Posie, whose given name was Rose, was a petite woman with that silver blue hair that was fashionable at that time and the most beautiful blue-gray eyes this side of heaven. I'm not sure she broke five feet in height or one hundred pounds. She was adorned with her chef's apron, which meant that she had arrived long enough before us to cook a full lunch for the family. She had a warm wool shawl tossed around her shoulders to temporarily ward off the January cold.

Since Posie had arrived in America from her home in Northern Ireland, she had worked as the cook for the wealthy titans of industry that lived in the doorman buildings and brownstones that dotted Manhattan's upper east side. Recently retired, she had agreed to join my parents in buying the Riverdale house, where she spent the rest of her days making sure that her grandchildren lived until adulthood. That was a full-time job.

Next to her stood my grandfather, Big Eddie, a moniker given to the eldest of the three generations of "Edward" in his family line. Within three years my yet to be born youngest brother would have mangled that name into "Spaghetti," which was quickly adopted by the entire neighborhood for as long as I lived there and I'm sure continuing as myth until this day.

Spaghetti was not particularly tall but had broad shoulders and massive forearms – like the cartoon character Popeye the Sailor Man - that were developed over his earlier life as a farmer and patriot in Northern Ireland, then as a steel laborer for many years in Todd's Shipyard in Brooklyn and finally as the superintendent for a row of tenements on 109th street. He was built like a large orangutan, and his appropriately ginger hair had long ago turned white.

There wasn't a piece of furniture or appliance that Spaghetti could not lift single handedly, and he could walk comfortably while carrying us all in his arms and hanging on his shoulders and back. He was the man the tenants in his buildings called when they needed something carried up the dark stairs of the tenement. For an elderly man he had amazingly quick fists, which he often unexpectedly delivered to the softest spots on his grandsons, just to toughen us up.

Spaghetti hadn't yet retired and held a coveted gig as the evening doorman of a luxury townhouse right by the Guggenheim Museum off Fifth Avenue in Manhattan. Irish doormen were *de rigueur* on the upper east side, as their innate bruteness guaranteed added security for the building's occupants. If you had a soft brogue it made the WASPs that lived there feel just a little more entitled as they passed you holding open their doors or umbrellas as you ferried them from the building to the waiting cab, or vis-a-versa. But Spaghetti never said a bad word about the people he served at his building. And they always tipped him well, especially around Christmas. He was the role model that taught his grandchildren how to suck it up and get on with living. It was his second job as a doorman, on top of his super's job, which allowed him to scrape together my grandparents' share of the down payment for this new Riverdale home.

Spaghetti was wearing a pair of gray wool slacks held up by suspenders stretched tightly over the massive shoulders of his upper long johns, both sleeves rolled up to the elbows. Spaghetti was impervious to the cold, although he wore one of those Canadian earflap hats to protect the top of his balding head and oversized ears from frostbite and winter sun.

Posie now threw opened the passenger side door of the car and after assisting my mother to her feet, called to Bonnie, who flew out of the car and wrapped her granny in a bear hug.

"Quick, come in before you catch your death of cold," Posie commanded.

The three women then turned on their heels and headed through the backyard and into the first-level back door.

My father grabbed a few suitcases out of the back of the station wagon and followed closely on their heels. As we boys tumbled out of the vehicle and went to race after them, hoping to get at that meal we could smell wafting from the kitchen, Spaghetti snatched Eddie and me by our coat collars and lifted us off our feet, while The Ginger scooted past him for want of a third arm. The Ginger mastered those same evasive skills over the years that followed, until one day, he didn't.

"Where do ya feckin' idjits think yer going?" He bellowed, steam firing out of both nostrils like a dragon.

Given that we were both being yoked by our collars, neither Eddie nor I were able to respond past the blobs of saliva now rolling off our extended tongues. I could feel mine freezing as we hung there.

"That's what I thought," he said, hurling us back in the direction of the station wagon like a couple of stuffed rabbits.

"Grab some of that gear and carry it inside." He said, giving me an extra boot in the pants for good measure. "There's no skivers in this family."

Eddie saw the writing on the wall, quickly grabbed as many of the bags as he could carry, and half dragged them in the direction of the house.

"But I'm only four!" I shouted back at my grandfather defiantly.

"And if yer want to see five, you'll do what yer told." He shouted back at me. I could see the ropelike muscles in his forearms begin to dance above his knotted fists.

I spit in silent protest to my involuntary servitude, and to jettison my frozen spittle, before grabbing a couple of the bags and dragging them after the others. Spaghetti playfully cuffed my ear as I passed him.

"That tongue is going to get yer in some serious trouble someday." He said with a laugh. "I hope I'm alive to see it."

Despite my facile wit, and the preternatural charm I developed shortly afterwards, once I swallowed that penny, I never won an argument with Spaghetti from that moment onward.

CHAPTER TWO
(THE GINGER'S FIRST IRISH EXIT)

I was raised in a Catholic household.

You've all studied Earth's great religions, even though it was just moments by binary download, so I won't bore you now with its dogma, which was recorded back in the day by a simple, patriarchal society. They did the best they could with what they had.

Understand that I believe that Jesus was a child of God, as I define a creator that is pure love and has unlimited power, and that all those millennia ago, this unique man evolved through his own efforts, and maybe a bit of divine intervention, to the highest of energy states. He transcended his humanity and fully harnessed the gifts our creator of all the stars and planets in the heavens has offered to all of those that believe in themselves, as the legacy of the creator. Luke 17:20-21 - "God's kingdom is coming, but not in a way that you will be able to see with your eyes. People will not say, 'Look, here it is!' or, 'There it is!' because God's kingdom is within you." Jesus knew his shit, he did it old school. No one had to zap him with the Hadron Distributor. The rest of the Terrans have all been playing catch-up for centuries.

That being said, my childhood was scheduled around my Catholicism. The Irish leapt from one feast day to the next, each a temporary pause in the struggles and misery of daily human existence. The Irish in particular enjoyed the pomp and circumstance that the Catholic church served up throughout each year on a regular basis. By keeping their eyes focused on that next big holy day, it was easier to ignore what was really happening around them on a day-to-day basis.

My concept of my religion was far less altruistic. I was not worried about redemption and did not believe that my creator put me on the earth just to suffer and repent over the pleasures I experienced in the body I was given. I do not believe that my creator would punish me with eternal damnation and hell fire because of failures caused by inherent defects in the tools I was provided with when I arrived on the earth. I still believe in the golden rule – treat others as you want to be treated – but after that, everything else is negotiable. Do your best with what you have.

Even now, as I await my passage across the veil, I do not fear retribution.

Well lucky for you there isn't any. Claire said. *Or you'd have some answering to do.* She winked at Stella and Apollo.

I chose to ignore her. I was on a roll.

Back in the day, I used to really enjoy Easter. Next to Christmas and Birthdays, it was the one day you woke up and there was a present waiting for you - an easter basket full of jelly beans, marshmallow peeps, and a giant chocolate bunny. There was always a stuffed toy rabbit with fake, and often colorful, fur in the basket, which each child then protected with his life.

I always felt that Easter basket grass was a static annoyance comparable to Christmas tinsel, it clung to you, got everywhere and some always ended up in your mouth.

During the lead up to the annual Easter feast day, our parents always took the children out to update our Sunday finery, with new suits and shoes, which were all put on display before the neighborhood at Easter Sunday High Mass. The mothers in the neighborhood all trotted out their new Easter bonnets, back when women wore hats to church. Young girls wore white paper or cloth doilies bobby-pinned to their hair. This was the early 1960s, at the time of the Tridentine Mass, when the Catholic High Mass - *Missa Cantata or Sung Mass* - was celebrated with all of its ostentatiousness.

High Mass on the Catholic holy days was the place the Irish Catholics wanted to be seen. There was always more than one priest on the altar, usually led by the Monsignor, and a ton of altar boys, the church having not yet evolved to sharing the altar with the feminine form.

My older brother and I were both tossed out of that altar boy cult on the same day, minutes apart, by the Monsignor – the purple priest: "Are you a champ or a chump?" were the last words the prick ever said to me. I would not have minded the summary dismissal if I hadn't sacrificed so many Saturday mornings, when I should have been watching cartoons, instead being drilled in Latin by my religiously imperious father - Confiteor Deo Omnipotenti - this was pre-Vatican 2.

Anyway, after my family first moved up to Riverdale from the Grand Concourse by Yankee Stadium, we spent the first few months living in the basement apartment of the family home while the Jewish family living on the top floor found a new apartment. Posie and Spaghetti lived on the first floor with my sister Bonnie, who had her own room. The rest of the children lived in steerage.

During the wee morning hours on our first Easter in Riverdale, a time before the older children were even enrolled in the local parish, St. Maggies Catholic School, my still wee little brother, The Ginger, wearing his footie pajamas, grabbed his new faux fur bunny, put on my mother's Easter bonnet, and toddled out the basement side door and into the unknown world, while the rest of the family dozed peacefully in their crowded bedrooms.

Now, that was the first time The Ginger made an Irish exit - *when a human leaves a place without saying goodbye to the people they are with* - a trick which later morphed into a coyote escape, when a now sober person with buyer's remorse will literally chew off their limb trapped under a pillow to escape a drunk one-night stand without waking their partner.

I am not being a sexist here, many a young man, including me when I was both young and a human man, has woken to find the severed arm left by a much prettier woman who sacrificed that appendage rather than face the snoring, farting bastard she woke up next to. Luckily, for both sexes, like a bearded dragon's tail, those limbs always grew back before the owner's next foray into bar dating. But I digress.

The Ginger ultimately mastered all forms of a magician's escape, without ever using magik. His cunning was pure genius.

Indeed, during our teenage years, we, The Ginger's siblings, called him "The Wind." He would always step away from a family table and excuse himself to go to the bathroom, which was in the hallway just outside and opposite the dining room. There was a closet in the same hallway that, when its door was open, would obscure that passage from my father's vantage point at the head of the dinner table. The Ginger always made a fuss about selecting some toiletry from that closet before he went into the bathroom, and always left the closet door open. By the time the sound of the toilet flush had run its course, The Ginger had vanished with the wind.

Anyway, back to that morning in 1960.

Like with most holidays, on Easter, the children woke up first so we could grab our respective baskets based on the name tags on the curved wicker handles.

My eldest sibling, Bonnie, would arbitrate all challenges with a sound thumping if there were any battles among her brothers over the size or amount of the contents of the baskets. She was the only one of us who could read at this time, and she was still bigger and stronger than all of the boys. Anyway, while we all sat around the living room chomping on jellybeans and chocolate, working on the bellyaches we would later suffer, my exhausted parents slept walked past us into the kitchen, and then returned moments later with their hot coffees to watch the Easter chaos from the comfort of the couch, still half asleep.

It was a good half hour before my slowly-waking, pregnant mother said, "Where's Bernie?"

My father looked over at The Ginger's basket, noticed the newest velveteen rabbit missing and responded, "He must have gone back to bed. I'll check on him."

My father then disappeared in the direction of the bedrooms. The next moment we heard my father's panicked, booming voice reverberating throughout the structure of the building. "Vvveeeerrrraaa, Bernie's not here!" My mother flew in the direction of the bedrooms where she began to shriek like a banshee.

Moments later the back door flew open and my grandfather, Spaghetti, rushed in, dressed in a pair of sail cloth long johns - with the two-button poop chute on the ass - his untied work boots and his beaten grey fedora. He was carrying his faithful hurley, a Celtic bladed wooden bat that could smack a small leather ball hundreds of feet and crack the skull of any man. Posie's head appeared from behind him. She was dressed in her nightgown and the fine netting she always wore to keep her silver-blue hairdo in check.

"Jeazus Christ!," Spaghetti bellowed, "Vera, you've woken the dead!"

At four years old, I wasn't sure in that moment whether Spaghetti was "the dead," or whether there were now a cluster of spirits floating around the apartment above us. Turns out, years later, it was both.

Posie pushed past her husband and raced into the bedrooms where my parents had by now overturned every bed and cleared every closet looking for The Ginger.

"He's not here!" my mother shrieked.

"Calm down Vera, you'll give yourself a heart attack," counseled Posie. "We'll find him."

"Are you all idjits!" Spaghetti shouted. "The side door is open!"

With that, all four of the adults rushed out through the side door onto the driveway and we could hear their voices, calling my brother's name, grow fainter as their searches expanded from the yard onto the surrounding block.

Seeing how Bonnie was distracted by the commotion, my older brother and I decided that if The Ginger didn't want his Easter candy, it was up for grabs. Of course, that led to one of our earliest Riverdale donnybrooks, as we both reached for his chocolate bunny at the same moment. Fists followed. I lost then, and in every rematch we ever had.

My older brother and I may have been still locked in that fight to the death, if it weren't for the annoying sound of a police siren rolling up our driveway. Bonnie, Eddie, and I raced out the side door and just got to the top of the cement stairway as the police cruiser, one of those iconic black and whites with the one flashing red cherry light on top, came to a stop at the top by the garage. Like a pack of dogs, the elder McCarthys came racing up the driveway in the cherry-top's wake, my mother with a look of horror on her face.

Two very tall policemen exited the front seats of the cruiser - I swear they looked like Toody and Muldoon from a popular television show at the time, Car 54 - and the Toody cop then opened the backdoor of the vehicle, crooked his finger, and a moment later, The Ginger, Easter Bonnet tilted back on his head and velveteen bunny in tow, slid out of the backseat and rushed into my mother's arms.

The Muldoon copper warily eyed Spaghetti, still in his long-johns and boots and reflexively waving his hurley menacingly.

"Is this boy yours?" Muldoon asked, with just a little trepidation in his voice.

"Yes officer, he's ours," my father said as he stepped forward and gave the officer a hearty handshake. "I'm sorry for the trouble."

Muldoon winced. Given the McCarthy code for handing out handshakes, I was surprised my father wasn't arrested for assault right then and there.

"Where did you find him?" Posie asked.

"We didn't." Toody responded. "A cab driver spotted him walking along Mosholu, right down the hill from your house. He picked him up and brought him to the 50th."

"We put him in the cruiser and figured we would drive around to see if anyone was looking for him." Muldoon added, still shaking blood back into his hand.

"The little bugger pointed to this house." Toody said.

By now the neighbors all started to appear at the foot of the driveway. That might have been the first of many times that the McCarthy household became the source of neighborhood entertainment.

Those were simpler but more practical times back then. Police were allowed to solve local problems as human beings and not as cogs in a bureaucracy. Today, The Ginger would have ended up in a stint with the local government's Child Services while my parents were put through their paces to get him back.

Anyway, their job done, the coppers left, the neighbors disbanded and the McCarthys got their shit together and attended High Mass in all of our Easter finery.

CHAPTER THREE
(A PENNY DROPS)

Before our move to Riverdale, I was not cognizant of the concept of personal property beyond the confines of the loosely drawn lines between what was individually owned or communally shared among my male siblings. Clothes were temporarily assigned based upon your size, and then passed on to the next in line. Toys often followed the same demarcation system, although that ownership never changed hands based on biology alone. The McCarthy boys hung onto their prized toys until it actually became too embarrassing to publicly assert ownership over the item.

My sister lived under a separate set of property rules. As the only girl in the family, she had her own room located on my grandparents' level of the house and whatever went into that room was hers. There were no hand me downs. Her bicycles were new, never used. If my parents couldn't afford something for her, Posie stepped in to make sure she had it.

And that was fine with her brothers. To begin with, Bonnie was the toughest of the siblings until the boys hit grammar school age and grew taller than her. As the shortest of the males, it might have taken me until second grade to catch up to her.

Until then, Bonnie had no problem throwing hands with her siblings, and given her favoring the McCarthy gene pool - she was built like a spark plug - it usually took only a handful of hair and a few well-placed blows to incapacitate her smaller and more slender brothers. In the odd chance one of the elders, like

Posie, came upon a cross-gender confrontation, the boys were always convicted without trial and summarily punished. Bonnie was untouchable.

So, the male siblings all learned early on that life was not fair, and that you either adapted or died.

But before we arrived in the house in Riverdale, I never realized that my parents had personal property beyond what they might have worn, drove or cooked with. As far as I was concerned, everything else was sacrificed for the good of the family.

Now I never really understood what my father did when he left the house each day, dressed in a suit and carrying a briefcase, beyond what my mother would explain as "Dad has gone to work."

I later learned that after his discharge from the Navy – we were all "leave" babies – my father had to sacrifice his dream of finishing college and going on to medical school, having been a top-rank medical corpsman during the Korean conflict. Turns out, he sold life insurance, which was an interesting choice, given how many of his comrades he had seen enter the insurance collection queue during combat..

And given that my father now had a lot of mouths to feed, that meant he had to sell a lot of insurance. So, we were no sooner in our new digs when he was back at work, leaving my mother and grandparents with sorting out the rest of it.

My older siblings were eventually enrolled in the local schools and were out of the house shortly after my dad each morning. In this age before preschool, I was still home, doing my best to get in the way of things, or convincing The Ginger to do it as my proxy.

Now The Ginger was still young enough to take an afternoon nap, so for that hour without his company, I was left to my own purposes to explore the parts of the house clearly off limits. That meant there were a lot of unpacked boxes lying around my parents' bedroom floor that needed investigating.

There was one particular, heavy, ebony wooden box with a copper catch on the front that sat on the floor in one corner of their bedroom. It was too heavy for my four-year old body to lift, so if I was ever going to get the chance to go through it, it would have to be in situ, when my mother was really distracted. That opportunity presented itself on the day Bridie "Nana" Burke arrived for a visit at her oldest daughter's new home.

So, after The Ginger went down for his afternoon nap, while the two Irish women sat around the kitchen table, drinking tea, and sharing my mother's dreams for her new home, I snuck off into my parents' bedroom and pried open the copper latch of the wooden box. It looked like one of those pirate's chests I saw in Bugs Bunny Cartoons. Inside was a treasure trove of all kinds of coins, some old, some new looking. Some were inserted in cardboard sheets and some lying loose in the numerous compartments in the box. With absolutely no understanding of what I was looking at, since I didn't understand the nature of money, I based my further inquiry upon how aesthetically pleasing these coins were.

Knowing that I would only have a limited time with my treasure, I selected a small coin that had some numbers and an Indian head on one side and a shield and some writing on its back. This coin was not the silvery color of some of the larger coins but still looked pretty new. I closed the box and was about to exit the room when my mother opened the door to show Nana her bedroom. Not knowing what else to do, I slipped the coin into my mouth with a little too much power. It skipped over the back of my tongue with the speed of a stone skipping across a still pond and I felt it strike my soft pallet before it disappeared down my throat. Never do things half-way.

My mother didn't seem to notice my instant distress, as she was too excited reciting her future plans while pointing around the large room. Nana on the other hand, stopped listening, and leaned over so her face was just a few inches from my own. By now the coin was safely lodged just behind my Adam's apple. Its placement paralyzed my tongue, although I still had the coin's strong metallic taste on my buds. I could feel the exposed pink tip drying out under my labored breath. I could not speak. In my mind's eye it felt like the coin's edges were pushing out the sides of my neck. My hands involuntarily rose up to my collar.

"Vera," Nana said in her Galway brogue, "your boy is choking."

I heard my mother's banshee shriek as Nana suddenly flew to my left, thanks to my mom's strong shove, and she landed safely on my parents' bed. Nana's eyes never broke from my own. Before I could look away, I felt my mother's powerful hand grab my right ankle and I was lifted into the air like a large bluefish in the hands of a Hunts Point fishmonger, tail skyward. The last thing I remember, I was staring at my mother's inverted waist while being spun clockwise with her left hand grasping my ankle, my right leg sticking out from my body at 45 degrees, like a garden sundial.

"Vera, don't –" Nana shouted.

The impact of my mother's right palm on my back forced what little air there was left in my lungs up through my windpipe with enough power to shift the coin, but not dislodge it. It now flipped from perpendicular to horizontal, shutting off my passageway completely, like the disk on a church organ. Full stop.

Then I heard Nana command *sábháil an buachaill,* and my mother respond with the fervor of her Sunday church voice, "Yes. Save the boy!"

Then blackness.

CHAPTER FOUR
(A MUSE MEANT IT)

This next recollection is the first of what I consider a recovered memory. It did not play in my highlight reel the night Dan Pearsall fired that 9mm shell through my chest. This and everything related to what I am about to tell you slowly returned as memory over the last few centuries, after the Great Galactic War. At first they arrived in faded snippets, but as my Centaurian genes continued to rise to dominance, my developing mind enhanced these recovered memories to such a point of cohesion and clarity that I now know them to be true.

I awoke on the side of a grassy knoll, beside a beautiful pond, with a mist rising off its still water. While I could not see the sun, the cloudless sky was bright and blue. I felt its warmth on my body, which was covered in a diaphanous tunic from my shoulders to mid-thigh. I was shoeless. And here's the thing, this was not my four-year-old body. This is what I looked like almost two decades later. But I didn't panic at the sight of the matured muscles and hair, I felt comfortable in my skin. I knew who I was.

I sat up and looked around. There was lush vegetation along the far edges of the pond and a healthy forest just off beyond that point. I saw a trout leap from the water by the bank closest to me, the light glistening off its colorful scales for that moment of its apex before it disappeared back below the mist.

Then a family of deer, led by the doe, followed by the fawn and finally the buck, appeared from the wood and began to drink. The fawn looked over in my direction but seemed totally unafraid.

Suddenly the air was filled with a floral fragrance, lavender, and, as I watched, beautiful flowers began to rise from the grasses around me, with the freedom of a dream state. And it all felt perfectly natural, until I heard the voice.

"It's beautiful, isn't it."

The voice was electrifying, and I actually shuddered at the sound of it. Goose bumps rose on my arms, and I could feel my hair follicles tighten and lift on both my body and my head. Yes, I had a beautiful thick head of hair that flowed to my shoulders, and I found this new version of me to have body hair as well.

I actually felt my testicles involuntarily lift as my penis did things that I had not yet experienced in my four years of life. For a moment I feared it would break. But I'd be lying if I said I didn't enjoy the experience.

My attention was again captured by the voice.

"Jimmy, turn around."

Now it is hard to compare the physical beauty among the many races I have encountered during my long existence, both male, and female. After all, it really is in the eye of the beholder.

Terrans seem to retain a broader genetic spectrum than on other planets, although I have noticed a growing homogeneity over the past few centuries, especially after the Great Galactic War. There has been more of a blending among my people, as they finally have accepted that they are really just varieties of one species among countless others in our vast Galaxy and beyond. However, I always appreciated the full range of beauty that was expressed through that diversity.

And, of course, Gina has always been my hallmark of beauty as we aged together as both human and hybrid. Right up to the end. I'm looking forward to seeing how she appears now on the other side of the veil.

The Centaurians, though a more advanced, homogenous, spectacular race, have had their own genetics aesthetically diversified over the last millennium by the introduction of the hybrid genes, including the browns and burgundy hair colors from our and other hybrid lines. *You, my children, know just how beautiful I think you are.*

But it is still easy enough to spot a Centaurian in a crowd if you know where to look. And Petrichor set an incredibly high standard.

My experience over the past few centuries with the other less humanoid races among the Galactic Federation, especially those that do not have distinct genders, have shown me that beauty must not be judged with just our eyes. It really comes from within. From our hearts and souls.

My cousin, Apples, the hysterical alien abductee that no one believed – how The Ginger loved to tease him when we were kids – helped the Greys create a whole new race from the most beautiful less-humanoid creatures, who saved the day, and the rest of us, in the final major battle in the Great Galactic War.

Yes Claire, you have always been beautiful to me.

And while it took me a half millennium to fully comprehend and appreciate the broad palette of beauty in this galaxy, I am a better man for it.

But when that strange dream-adult version of my four-year old self finally got the nerve to turn towards that voice, I was not prepared for the experience. I was breathless.

Indeed, I did not have the present spectrum of beauty I recognize now. I was pretty much limited at four years old in my visual aesthetic by the Celtic tribe I had been raised among for my short period on earth. Kathy Brown was the epitome. Fair skin, dark hair, and freckles with an upturned nose.

What appeared standing before me at that moment was, what I have since learned from classical Terran literature, the embodiment of a goddess, from the ancient Greek and Roman periods of human development. Flowing, shoulder length, Stygian hair, and matching eyes that pulled you in with the gravitational force of the largest black hole. Flawless olive skin that retains its glow through the longest of winters.

And while my four-year old mind didn't consciously appreciate it, she had the perfect body, easily apparent through her matching diaphanous tunic that ended just below her ample hips. Given my seated perspective, three distinct diamond-shaped spaces formed at the peak, knee, and ankle levels between her legs, as she stood before me at attention, as if inspecting me. However, I was obviously subconsciously returning the favor, taking her all in, because that wonderfully strange feeling returned to my genitals as I tried to rise to my feet.

She laughed, which made my heart flutter even more. I was confused by my physical reaction, and felt embarrassed that the tunic did nothing to hide it.

"My name is Erato, Jimmy." That melodious voice again distracting me.

"I am a muse, one of the original nine sisters that once walked among your kind."

When she reached over and took my hand, I gasped, and almost pulled free, her touch was equally electrifying. But in a moment, that energy fused me to her, and I would have rather lost the hand then voluntarily released her grip. She gently led me towards the pond, never looking at me. But I couldn't take my eyes off of her. I could see she was as tall as that dream form of me.

"Someone on the other side must love you dearly," Erato whispered as she walked. "I'm not often called upon to intercede."

I had no idea what she was talking about. And I didn't care. I would have happily listened to that voice read my death warrant at my execution. We had reached the side of the pond.

She released my hand, turned towards me, and moved closer. I had that strange physical reaction again and was afraid that if she took another step towards me I would poke her.

"Now is the time you must make a choice, Jimmy."

"Choose?" I was surprised at the deep tenor of my voice.

"Choose what?" I repeated haltingly.

"To move on to be with your ancestors, or to return to your family?"

My confusion was increasing, I didn't know what was going on in this crazy dream. I didn't even know what "ancestors" meant. But then I thought of my mother, and the horror in her face just before I passed out, my hand rose to my throat, as I remembered the penny. I missed my mother.

Erato gazed into my eyes, like she was searching for something, and then her own eyes half blinked in recognition. She had found what she was looking for.

"I will send you back then." She whispered. I could feel her warm breath on my chin. There was that lavender fragrance. Right on cue, there was my physical reaction, but this time I didn't care.

"But I will give you my mark, a touch of my power, as a parting gift, so I will always know where you are."

Her hands reached up, captured my face and with amazing strength pulled our lips together. As I try to remember that feeling now, I cannot properly describe the explosion of energy and thoughts, few of them my own, that raced through me in that moment. Everything blended, every sensation one could experience happening all at once, even pain. I thought I would pass out.

She broke our embrace and held me at arms-length by my shoulders, while I fought to recover my breath. She smiled once more, the tip of her tongue sliding sensually across her upper lip, as she gazed at me with half closed eyes.

"I will see you again." She whispered.

I wanted to pull myself back towards her and repeat that experience, but before I could move she tossed me through the air and into the pond, where I sank like a stone. Again, blackness.

CHAPTER FIVE
(JUST WHAT THE DOCTOR ORDERED)

"Well, we know he's not dead," came that first disembodied voice through the darkness.

"Not at all. In fact, he's quite healthy, the little dear," came another. "He's got wood!"

Both voices laughed. It was sweet laughter.

"See how red his lips are?" returned that first voice. "I've never seen that before."

"Possibly a reaction to the anesthetic," the second voice responded. "Look," the second voice added. "He's stirring. Go get Doctor Goldberg."

My eyes opened just a crack, and I saw the back of one woman in a white uniform exit the beige room through a doorway, while another approached the bed I was in. She also wore the same uniform with a tiny white plastic hat on her head. She reached down and grasped my left wrist with her right hand, which was much tanner than my own, and grasped a small clock that was pinned to her chest with her left. She stared at the clock intently for a little bit while she gently pressed my wrist between two of her fingers and thumb.

She was a young woman. Her jet-black hair and large dark eyes reminded me of something. Someone. She was pretty. She had kind eyes.

"Your pulse is a little high," the second voice woman said to me. Her voice had an accent, not soft, like the Irish, more musical, with a faster beat. "Not surprising. Who knows what dreams you've been up to under sedation?" She gestured with her head towards the lower part of the small bed. There, under the bedsheet, was a smaller version of the cloth tent I had in my dream.

I felt myself blush. I really had no control over my body.

"I want my mom." My voice rasped. My throat felt dry, my tongue thick in my mouth. When I tried to swallow, it felt like a thousand shards of glass were passing down my windpipe. I noticeably winced. But my tent went away.

At the sound of my voice, the woman's face softened. I had her full attention.

"Your poor mother was here all night." Said the woman. "But don't worry, she's just gone home to shower. She'll be right back."

She reached down below the side of my bed and must have been turning something because the head of my bed started to slowly rise until my body was almost sitting up.

"There you go, that's better."

I tried to say, "thank you, " but my voice was hoarse and my throat sore, so I gave up after the first word. But I could tell this woman heard me, because at that one sound she suddenly smiled, showing me a beautiful set of perfect white teeth. I had never seen a set like that among the Irish. She looked like she was blushing.

"My name is Nurse Torres," the woman said. "But you can call me Annie."

I nodded and smiled back at her but said nothing. I didn't want to set my throat back on fire.

At that moment an older man came into the room. He was wearing a long white coat, but I could see he had the same kind of tie and slacks my Dad wore to work underneath.

"How is our young patient, Nurse Torres?" He asked. He had a kind voice.

"His BP is a little elevated, and his throat is definitely sore, but otherwise he seems in good shape." I thought I saw her glance where my tent used to be.

"I'm Doctor Goldberg," the man said. He walked to the foot of my bed and removed a clip board from a slot there. He studied whatever was on the clip board for a moment and then slid it back into place. He approached and sat on the edge of the bed, removing something rubber from around his neck and pulling down the neck of the gown I was wearing. He placed the rubber tips of the curved metal tubes at one end of his contraption into his ears and placed the round disk on its other end onto my chest right above my heart. It was cold and I caught my breath, my throat ached.

"Sorry." He removed the disk, cupped it in his hands and blew hard on it. He breath smelled like the cleaning fluids my mom scrubbed the kitchen with. Then he placed it back on my chest. Much warmer.

He closed his eyes and listened for a moment, moving the disks in a small circle to spots around my chest.

"Cough for me."

I did, softly, so as to not awaken the dragon in my throat. I still winced.

He removed the rubber disk thing and swung it back around his neck.

"His lungs are clear and his heart sounds strong as horse." He declared. "Let's see what your throat looks like."

He took a small pen light out of his white coat.

"Open up," he commanded. I was hesitant, but finally complied. He shined the light down my throat and peered carefully. His eyes were the greenest I had ever seen.

"Say aaahhhhh." He instructed.

I refused.

"So, the cat's got your tongue?" he said, and then smiled. "That's all right, I've seen all I need to."

Satisfied, he shut off the penlight and slid it back in his coat pocket. He tapped my chin to signal I could close my mouth.

He stood up, walked back to where the clip board waited, and scribbled a few lines on it.

"Never mind a horse, this little Mick is as strong as a mule." He declared to Nurse Annie. "You can send him home this morning."

He looked back at me and studied me a moment longer. Then his eyes brightened as if he remembered something. He reached into his coat pocket and removed a small clear container for me to see. Inside was that copper penny.

"This little fellow gave me quite the hard time." He said as he stared at the penny proudly. "It was wedged in there down your larynx. I had to use the five-and-a-half-inch forceps to reach the bugger."

He thought for a moment more while continuing to stare at the penny and then whispered to himself. "I thought we lost you for a moment. Quite miraculous."

I couldn't tell if he was talking about the penny.

I wish I could go back there now and read his mind.

"Normally, I would put this up on my wall with all the other crazy items you kids like to swallow," he said. "But this is a valuable penny, and I'm sure your folks want it back."

He handed the penny to Nurse Annie. "Make sure his parents get that."

"Yes, Doctor," she replied, but he had already turned and exited the room.

CHAPTER SIX
(BIRDS, BEES & BLARNEY)

From my earliest conscious memories, I have always appreciated the differences in the sexes. I did not fully understand those differences and never compared their respective biological or emotional traits for purposes of ranking one against the other. I never saw it as a competition. That's just as well because given my limited experiences as a child, the men in my family repeatedly fell a distant second to the women.

Despite the physical prowess handed down through our family's male XY chromosomes, it was the females – with their double X chromosomes - that dominated our Clan. The McCarthy's were a matriarchal society. My grandmother, Posie, ran the show. Spaghetti was only her feared enforcer. The Queen's Hand.

You didn't have to be blood to inherit the matriarch title. It fell upon the shoulders of the woman who bore the surname – displayed or not - through blood or marriage, who was most likely to withstand the pressures of leadership. Even on my mother's side, it was mystical Bridie Burke that called the shots for her Clan.

That worked out fine, because the males in my family seemed more interested in adventure than leadership. We are naturally selfish, play the short game, and have a tough enough time being responsible for ourselves, never mind others, including our siblings. Don't misunderstand, the males in my family are extremely loyal to the Clan and when called upon will blindly defend its members to the death. No one gets to hit a McCarthy except another McCarthy. My brothers' pugnaciousness was more for the sport of it, the lust for battle. Any excuse to throw down. But without the wisdom and guidance of the women, who always played the long game, most of us would never reach our adulthood. Fact.

Indeed, after Posie passed, in the absence of the mystical matriarchal guidance of my sister Bonnie during her self-banishment across the pond, the Clan itself devolved into an attenuated series of separate families whose women fought desperately to keep my brothers and I from foundering on the rocks of life's stormy seas. I had already left what was to become the McCarthy family construction business and after a few false starts pursued a legal career that took me right into the heart and soul of another kind of family altogether. There was nothing matriarchal about that family.

We all know how that turned out.

And maybe that is why - as far back as Kathy Brown on Gerard Avenue - I have always been so attracted to strong women. It was a subliminal, innate desire for self-preservation – from myself

As the hidden memories concerning Erato have returned over this last part of my five centuries of existence, I realize that Fate may have played a stronger hand in the outcome than I ever thought possible. Erato's kiss gave me an edge I didn't deserve, and ultimately couldn't help me. But I would be lying if I suggested that the gift that she transferred between our lips in that dream, and afterwards, did not come in handy along the way.

Relatively speaking, I grew up an average human male. In school yard parlance, I was never the captain of any team, never the fastest, the strongest or the most talented. But I was always picked to play. I was good enough.

Even among my siblings, I had the least to offer genetically. Eddie and The Ginger sprouted into semblances of their Viking blood lines and lusts. Their size and temperament assured their success, especially in the New York construction industry. My youngest brother, John, got the sweetness and looks that the Irish families always seemed to save for their baby. As if by design, my parents were going to give their last shot at procreation their best. John was the family politician, the wisest among the males, but don't let that magnanimity fool you. Even John had the McCarthy temper and would go red-eyed if sufficiently provoked. He became the face of the brothers' family business. Unfortunately, none of their talents could keep them from being vaporized in an explosion the night Ty Valachi and his family were rounded up in that federal RICO bust. And that's on me.

In addition to her hidden fraternal proclivities, which may have explained her ability to whip all of our asses when we were younger, my sister Bonnie also had the advantage of everything positive from her double X chromosomes. Plus, it turns out, she received the bonus magical qualities genetically bequeathed by Bridie Burke, that only descended through the female line. Growing up there was nothing Bonnie couldn't do. In my parents' eyes, she was the perfect child, until she wasn't. But until her sapphic fall from family grace, her brothers didn't even try to compete with her.

And I didn't try to compete with any of them. My brothers grew into leaders and captains on their athletic teams, got the accolades, and filled the family shelves with trophies, medals, and MVP awards. Bonnie won all of the academic awards. The nuns at St. Maggie's loved her.

Athletically, I was the family journeyman, the utility player who got the team trophies when I was lucky enough to play on one of my siblings' championship teams. Never the all-star. I was probably second in the siblings to Bonnie academically, but not because of my intellectual prowess. As my mother always bragged, my siblings got their collective brilliance from her side of the family. With me, it was far less grey matter and far more intuition, the answers I needed seemed to present themselves just when I needed them, and never stuck around a moment extra.

The only way I can explain how my human mind worked is by drawing an analogy to Terran original computer software. You open up the computer screen and the RAM software kicks in. The more powerful the RAM processor, the more issues it can juggle and problems it can solve. But the moment the computer is shut down, the RAM's issue juggling and problem-solving stops. So, if you don't have an equally impressive hard drive on which to save all of the RAM's impressive work, it's gone forever. My human mind was all RAM and no hard drive.

And looking back, I am okay with that, because I got the blarney. Although I did not know it back then.

Now every Irishman in the Celtic diaspora knows that the Blarney Stone is set in ramparts of the Blarney Castle in County Cork, Ireland. Millions of humans have made the pilgrimage to its resting place and leaned backwards over the abyss to quickly kiss the stone with the hope of drawing upon its power. Like most Celtic history, we are terrible written record keepers, so the origin of the Blarney stone has many variations. Some say it was delivered to Ireland by the prophet Jeremiah, others say it was the spoil of war with our Scottish Celtic cousins, and others say it was Jacob's pillow brought to Cork from the Holy Land after the crusades.

My favorite version is the story about the castle's builder, Cormac Laidir MacCarthy, a possible ancestor, who fell out with the British monarch Elizabeth and was in danger of losing his lands, and possibly his head. Cormac entreated the Celtic goddess, Clíodhna, for salvation. She instructed the chieftain to kiss the first stone he saw when he woke up the next morning. Being a good Irishman, he did exactly what the woman told him, and as a result, manifested enough blarney to convince the Red Queen to allow him to keep his lands and head.

However, whatever its source, all Irish will agree that by kissing the Blarney stone you receive the gift of persuasiveness. We are rightfully a superstitious people. For good reason.

Now I have kissed a lot of things, but not that stone. And yet I still had a good natural dose of blarney.

Looking back over my human lifetime, whatever its source, that natural blarney talked me out of a whole lot of trouble, talked me into some more, including the trappings of any professional success I may have had, and even talked me into my last professional gig as a consigliere for a mafia boss. My natural blarney consistently talked life's luck into breaking in my direction.

And while I didn't kiss the blarney stone, my lips still played a part in my story. It turns out that ethereal kiss I shared with Erato endowed me with a variation of the mystical blarney on steroids. Of course, I didn't know any of this until Erato took her gift back with one last kiss and then wiped my memory of her clean. But I don't want to get ahead of myself.

If I hadn't been zapped with the Hadron Distributor over four centuries ago, that secret would have remained buried, and my human life would have remained that interesting series of coincidences, many you already know.

Now here's the thing. Turns out there are no magic words or incantations to Erato's blarney. Generally speaking, I could literally repeat the very same words to any female, that another person immediately before me just spoke with no effect. But in my case, for some reason, the female always responded, amorously. And the effectiveness of my erotic blarney clearly correlated with the intensity of my passion or desire. So, for example, the Latina in the bodega near the construction site where my brothers and I worked wasn't going to leap over the counter after me just because I asked for cream in my coffee. But, if she was cute enough to register on my toxically male radar, and I swear it was never intentional, her number may have ended up on one of the napkins at the bottom of the brown paper bag. Drove my brothers crazy.

In hindsight, this recovered Erato experience also explained a lot about my history with the opposite sex. It made it easy for me to attract any woman I really set my heart on but given that it really was just a transient parlor trick, it never took much longer than a few days apart for any young woman to come to their senses and dump me. Quickly, sometimes through a friend, most often by phone. You just can't magic your way into love. And when I finally found love, Erato's blarney had nothing to do with it.

I didn't know any of this at the time. And while the gift brought me lots of physical pleasure, it broke my heart more times than I would like to admit.

But let's not get ahead of ourselves.

CHAPTER SEVEN
(ANTS GO MARCHING)

The only memories I have from kindergarten at P.S. 81 both involved tears. I cried my first day because I thought my mother brought me there late. Turns out, I was in the afternoon session, and we had actually arrived early, so all of those children I saw happily playing behind that locked door were the morning session. My mother operated on Irish time, which meant that, given her primary role of herding five children to various events over the years, she got things done on her own time, and if we were a little late for things, so be it. In fact, the reason I was in the afternoon session, when all my local friends attended the morning session, was that my mother signed me up late.

The second, and far more traumatic memory, was the caterpillar incident.

It was still Indian summer that Friday in early September. The children were outside at afternoon recess, when the teachers allowed the class to stretch our legs for fifteen minutes in the school yard. I hadn't really bonded with any of the children yet, most of whom arrived on Yellow School buses from all over the Riverdale area of the Bronx, so I explored the large industrial school yard that I would later learn was referred to by Riverdalians as "The Courts." Half of this school yard was devoted to one full court basketball court and three more half courts. The asphalt plain was surrounded by twelve-foot-high fences that bordered the community baseball field and park to the north and the Riverdale Neighborhood House, a community gathering spot with a large pool that became the area social hub each summer, to the east. The west and southern flanks of this space were protected by a three-story L shaped building that looked very much like the prisons where I used to visit clients during my later tenure as Valachi's lawyer. Along the base of the northern fence line were a row of benches, with uniform concrete bases and wooden slats. None of the school children ever used these benches, but after school they were filled with the local teens that took over the area in the afternoons and evenings.

The most incongruous item in The Courts was a monolithic Maple tree that rose out of its center and offered an oasis of shade under its thick canopy. The tree was almost as tall as the school building and its branches extended twenty feet from its trunk. The tree was so large that it had its own gravitational energy, and most kids entering The Courts tossed their school bags around its base while they played during recess and before school was called to order each morning. The children felt that their belongings were safe there.

That particular afternoon I was drawn to the base of this large tree because I spotted large white triangles in its branches. They looked like diaphanous tents, fluttering in the gentle fall breeze. When I arrived underneath the boughs I could see little bugs crawling along the outside of the white pockets. One slipped off its tent and floated down towards me.

What turned out to be a furry caterpillar landed at the base of the tree among its large extending roots that reminded me of the varicose veins on Spaghetti's powerful calves. The creature didn't move, so I reached down and picked it up. I had never held a caterpillar before and felt that a dead one was a good place to start. I was fascinated by its many tiny legs and its ample fur coat. I carried it back to the benches by the ball field and studied it.

While I was sitting there petting its fur as it lay quietly in the palm of my hand, I noticed that some of its legs started to move. It righted itself and started to crawl around my hand, its body undulating like a Slinky. I sat there for the next five minutes playing with this new friend, allowing it to circle my fists and passing it between both hands. It tickled.

When the recess bell chimed, my classmates all lined up, two by two, in front of the entrance door closest to our classroom. I waited until everyone else had assembled and then joined at the end of the line. A girl named Leslie Romani was standing there next to me and spotted the caterpillar crawling around my hands. I liked Leslie; she was quite an athlete, could throw a ball as well as any boy and was the first girl that was willing to play tag with the boys in the class.

"Can I hold it?" she asked.

I extended my fist, and she placed her knuckles interlocked with mine so Fred, the name I had given the caterpillar, could safely crawl onto her fist. By now the front of the line started to advance forward and into the school. Both of the kindergarten teachers were standing on either side of the doorway counting heads as the children entered.

"Here, you better take this," Leslie said, extending her palm. It took me a moment to corral Fred, and by then the last of the line in front of us had proceeded forward, leaving just the two of us standing there, laughing as I tried to capture the wiggling caterpillar.

"What are you two up to?" called Mrs. Benson, the head teacher.

By now I had recovered Fred and held him in my closed palm behind my back. Leslie trotted into the school after the others.

"What do you have in your hand, Jimmy?"

I showed her my empty hand.

"The other one."

Fred did a circle around my now open palm.

"You can't take that into school." She said softly but firmly.

"Then I'll stay out here," I responded and started to pet Fred.

Now Mrs. Benson was an older woman, from what I could tell, about the same age as my mother. I wasn't the first recalcitrant child she had to deal with. She studied me for a moment, assessing my resolve.

"Okay," she said, "what if you give me the caterpillar and I'll put it a safe place until school ends."

I thought about it for a moment, and when she extended her palm, I decided that if she was willing to allow Fred to crawl on her, I could trust her. I slid Fred onto her palm.

"Go inside, and I'll take care of this."

I cannot remember how I passed the next forty-five minutes until dismissal, I'm sure it involved finger painting or making clay ashtrays, but just as the bell went off, Mrs. Benson came over to me, took my hand and led me out through the doors onto The Courts.

She pointed over to the corner of the fence by the baseball field. "There, in the orange juice can."

I ran over to where the can rested, slightly obscured by the demarcation of dark shade and the afternoon sun disappearing over the school rooftop. The can looked a little darker than it should.

When I got closer I saw that the darkness was actually a stream of black ants scaling the orange juice container's walls and spilling into the can. The bottom of the can was an inch deep with ants that were already finishing the last of Fred's carcass. I didn't know if it was the smell of the orange juice or Fred that drew them from their colony in right field, but it didn't matter. I kicked that can about thirty feet through the air, sending it sailing over the eastern fence and into the RNH pool. I could hear it clanging around the pool's empty cement foundation. I then stomped on the remaining army of ants circling where the can's base once sat. When I was satisfied that I had avenged Fred's death, I turned back towards Mrs. Benson, who stood watching me, a look of horror on her face.

I didn't know if her look was based on her own hand in Fred's death, or in witnessing my reaction.

At that moment my mother appeared, appropriately late. I tried to maintain my anger, but when our eyes met I burst into tears and ran into her arms, blubbering about how my teacher had killed my pet caterpillar. My mother lifted me up and shot Mrs. Benson the closest thing to an Irish evil eye, then turned on her heels and carried me out of The Courts and along the next block to our house.

My mother made sure to sign me up for first grade in the neighborhood Catholic School the following Monday morning. I may have been the first in next year's class to enroll.

Over the centuries, I've made my peace with the ants, I mean, they were just doing what ants do. But I never trusted a teacher again, even the nice ones.

CHAPTER EIGHT
(SPAGHETTI)

By the time I entered first grade – the first level of education where humans attempt any actual learning - my siblings and I had already collected a core group of friends from the families on our block. There were the two German protestant brothers, Larry and Eddie, the youngest of their larger brood closest to our ages, whose father was a mechanical engineer, who taught his brood how to build anything they set their minds to and gave them free access to all of his tools to do it. They lived in the house directly to the south of our own. Martin, the only child of two brilliant and cultured Czech emigrants, whose sole goal was to raise their only son to be the brilliant doctor he ultimately became, was my age and lived a few houses directly to our north. An Irish American family with an equal number of children of comparable ages lived right around the corner, and our parents became good friends. There were other children in the area as well, but if you had to cross a street to get to them, they might as well have lived on the other side of an ocean. There was a geographic exception provided for kids coming from a close by dead end which could be considered a separate block, if they could reach each other's homes cutting through neighbors' yards.

The neighborhood parents' rule was that their children were allowed to explore and play on the block without adult supervision within shouting distance. This was the time before milk cartons began to remind the Terrans that we lived in a dangerous world. But childhood gangs made up of sibling subsets of close but different ages offered enough protection back in the day.

You must not forget that most Terrans could not communicate telepathically, and our technology was forty years away from providing us the interconnectivity of cell phones.

When anyone's parents wanted their legacies to return home, they would just throw open one of the windows of their house and start shouting names, most often in reverse chronological order. The larger the brood, the more likely one of them would hear the call and alert the others that it was time to return to their nest. If a non-family member heard the names of one of their friends carrying across the wind, they were duty bound to alert that friend, so they would not get into trouble for ignoring it. If enough of a kiddie cluster were syphoned away from an active group at play in that fashion, the survivors would often just call it a day and return to their own homes.

When we weren't in school, these recalls would most often occur around meal time – lunch and dinner – so the McCarthy's large Irish ears were tweaked for greater receptivity during those hours, like radar disks. However, Martin was an exception. He had other obligations.

The eastern European mother of our future Renaissance man had the most beautiful voice – she was a beautiful woman with the aging genes of a Vampire - and would exercise her vocal cords every afternoon in her native tongue around two o'clock, to call her son back home for one of his many extracurricular activities, sometimes foreign linguistics, but most often piano lessons.

Now the more Martin hung around with our Irish family, the more rebellious he became - it's in our Celtic genes and quite communicable - and so there were times when we would be playing guns or building forts or chasing the Junkie when "Martinco" heard his call to prayer. He would try to resist these siren songs by racing to the front of his home and responding forcefully from the street with a plaintiff litany in a matching staccato foreign tongue, fired at his patient but resolute mother, who was still hanging out her upper window. It always began in English, with "But Ma-Ma—" before shifting into the Czech vernacular.

We didn't understand the exchange that followed, since there were no subtitles and we couldn't really read yet anyway, but we started to figure the gist of it contextually, since Martin, soul crushed, would always end with a no-look wave goodbye to his friends and, head hung low, he would march towards his home and through its front door. Moments later we would hear the most beautiful piano sonatas by what we learned later were Haydn, Beethoven and Lidtz, floating through the same upper window vacated by Martin's mother.

This brilliant woman soon decided that if she were going to raise Martin into the success he was destined to become, she had to find a way to separate him from the revolutionary influence of the local urchins, at least for his formative years. So, when the time for first grade arrived, Martin was shuttled off to Elizabeth Seton Academy, just outside the parish, instead of attending St. Maggie's with the rest of the Irish and Italian Catholic children. Best thing she ever did for him.

By the time I followed my older sister and brother through the huge red arching doors of St. Maggie's Old School building, The Ginger was closing in on four years of age and tiny John, the youngest of my brothers, had reached the age of two.

And that is when my grandfather became the infamous Spaghetti.

It was one Saturday afternoon in September, right around John's second birthday.

Since my grandfather worked nightshift at his job as a doorman on the upper east side, he slept each day until around noon, and then spent a few hours fixing or painting something around the house before leaving for work in Manhattan. The man had to stay busy and did so right up until his last breath.

My grandfather was always working around the outside of the family home in the afternoons. Sometimes he did interior maintenance as well. The home boiler was my grandfather's latter-life archnemesis, a hulking inanimate creature that loved to expire every winter holiday morning. Each time, like an old-school doctor, my grandfather would grab his tool bag, light up a pipe full of Prince Albert and storm into the boiler room cursing a blue streak. Behind that closed metal safety door echoed the sounds of a blacksmith shop as my grandfather beat that metallic monster into submission, and we all breathed a collective sigh of relief when we again heard the pounding of the steam again rushing through the house's black pipe arteries. Patient revived.

Each fall my grandfather liked to perform preventive maintenance on the black metal beast, replacing a pipe, or valve, or switch, before the boiler used it as its excuse to expire like clockwork on Christmas morning. But there were a lot of pipes, valves, and switches to that old boiler, so no matter how strategic my grandfather's maintenance plan appeared, the boiler – maintaining its title as his truly "arch" nemesis - always attempted to stymy him on the coldest day of the year.

Now my siblings loved when my grandfather was embroiled in a major interior project, because that meant he wasn't outside to prevent us from getting into mischief around the property. When my parents went off to do the weekly shopping, or any of the other errands required to keep the family functioning, my grandfather protected "his" property with the blind passion of a bridge troll. He would threaten his blood relatives and any of our friends with the worst physical consequences if he caught us doing anything he considered an afront to his absolute rule over the property. His weapon of choice was his manual hedge shears, which looked like an oversized scissor with long sharp blades and round wooden handles. They not only made quick work of any branch that fell within the closing arc, but my grandfather honed them to such an edge that they could slice paper.

One of our favorite mischiefs was to scale the back side of the steep shingled roof of the garage that anchored the back of our property. There was a tall stone wall on an adjoining back property a few feet from the bottom edge of the back of the garage roof. We could get to the top of the wall by climbing the fence behind the garage. Then, with a bit of a running start, we could leap onto the garage roof, making sure to flip on our asses as we landed so we could lay down as much of our rubber sneakers souls flat as possible to catch hold of the gritty shingles and keep us from sliding off. Once our feet successfully adhered to the shingles, arresting any slide, we could flip back over and, using just the front balls of the sneakers, scale the rest of the way to the peak on all fours. There we would survey most of the world, as we knew it at those tender years, from its lofty perch. The view was relatively spectacular.

Why did we do it? We were bored kids in the Bronx and Everest wasn't available.

One time my cousin Apples tried to make the garage roof leap wearing his leather souled, cockroach killer shoes, a style named after its sharp toe that allowed its wearers to crush the escaping vermin in the tightest corners. Every kid in Manhattan had a pair. The fear in Apple's eyes as he disappeared off the edge of the shingled rooftop that day was palpable. But he never made a sound. Apples always took what was coming to him without complaint.

If it were not for the fact that there were years of rotting vegetation piled in the small alley behind the garage, he may not have survived the fall with more than a few bruises and a broken pair of glasses. Of course, science was turned on its head that day as it was Apples, and not Newton, that again proved the theory of gravity.

As a matter of fact, Apples' involuntary descent was the reason all further attempts at scaling the garage were banned by my grandfather.

Well, this one September Saturday afternoon, while my parents, Posie and our sister Bonnie were attending a family wedding – family always left the boys off those invitations for some reason – Bozzy MacDootz, another local kid who was the youngest of his small Irish family that lived further north on Liebig Avenue, was hanging with our sibling crew for the first time. He had heard from someone in my first-grade class at St. Maggie's that only the coolest kids got to the top of the McCarthy garage, so he was all in. Once my grandfather was fully involved with his boiler repair, we sent The Ginger and my youngest brother to the side door of the basement to keep watch and to let us know if Spaghetti was coming outside.

Now The Ginger was a natural for the role of watching for inherently dangerous adults and sat on the side of the driveway, eyes-glued on the basement side door for any sign of movement. Looking back on it now, how was he to know that my grandfather had decided to clean one of the mucky boiler valves in the basement kitchen sink at the back of the house. The Ginger could not have guessed that the old man had already walked to the back door for a better look at his handiwork, and just happened to glance up at the garage roof just as five pair of hands reached over its peak. The Ginger could not have anticipated our grandfather's next movements, as he flew out of the back door, across the yard to the end of the driveway, and through the garage door to retrieve his trusty hedge clippers.

Finally, The Ginger could not have surmised that, at that moment, tiny John would make family history, when, not having the concentration of The Ginger, his eyes wandered to the peak of the garage as well, to watch our hands appear at the summit, and then drop down to street level just as my grandfather reached its double-door entry. In that moment, the wee lad did all he could do and shouted, "Big Eddie!"

At least that's what he attempted to shout. What actually came out of his two-year-old mouth was the soft cry, "Es-Getty!."

MacDootz was hanging next to me, first in line on the peak of the garage roof at its most dangerous northern end overlooking nothing but a concrete cushion. After me came my brother Eddie, Martin, and the next-door protestant Eddie, in that order, when we all heard the cry.

MacDootz stammered nervously, "Did someone just say Spaghetti?"

At that moment we heard my grandfather's bellow like a Minotaur from the back alley behind the garage.

"I'm going to ring all yer feckin necks when I get ya."

To demonstrate he meant it, the tips of the hedge shears appeared above the lowest edge of the roof and snapped shut with that meshing metal blade sound.

MacDootz was the furthest away from the southern edge of the rooftop closest to the neighbor's access wall. He watched helplessly as Martin and the other two Eddies nimbly scramble off that edge and high tailed it through the neighbor's yard towards the dead-end street behind us. Every man for himself.

By now my grandfather had reached that spot by the exit wall, cutting off our escape.

When I heard the second air snip of the hedge shears, I shouted, "Come on," and hauled myself over the roof peak and hurled myself down the front of the garage, more sliding than scrambling.

MacDootz was just a second behind me but where I just hit the bottom edge, leapt, and took my chances with the hard two-foot landing on the driveway cement, no doubt destroying the growth plates in my knees and ensuring a lifetime of being the shortest of the male siblings, he hesitated for just a moment, before following me into the abyss.

That hesitation gave my grandfather just enough time to circle back around the front of the garage, where he was waiting with his clippers as MacDootz landed before its large wooden doors.

By then, I had hobbled down the driveway on two very sore legs away from the garage towards the street. If my grandfather was going to kill me I wanted witnesses among the passing traffic. Then I spotted The Ginger and tiny John staring past me with looks of absolute horror on their faces.

I heard my grandfather behind me shout "You thought you'd get away, you little bastard!"

I turned back just in time to see my grandfather shove his open shears forward, trapping MacDootz head in the wide-open triangle formed by the two blades against the garage door behind him, their tips wedging into the wood. And that's when MacDootz leaned back against the garage door and fainted, his eyes rolling back in his head, which then slipped through the triangle as his body went limp and dropped to the ground.

My grandfather left the shears firmly wedged in the wood, reached down, and lifted MacDootz's lifeless body from its laundry pile to its feet with one hand and gave both of boy's cheeks a firm slap with the other. The terrified boy came to enough for my grandfather to assess that he was still breathing. "Wake up you young welp, you ain't dead yet."

My grandfather released MacDootz and then ripped the shears from the garage door, eying the two chips in its wood for a moment before saying to MacDootz, "I oughtta make you paint that."

Then my grandfather laughed and headed back towards the basement door, his trusty shears slung victoriously over his right shoulder. He called out for good measure to all of the eyes and ears he knew were watching, "If I catch any more of you up on that garage, I'll hit you between the lug and the horn."

To this day, I have no idea where that death spot is on my anatomy, and I don't want to know.

When my younger brothers and I reached the now recovering MacDootz, all he could do was point after my grandfather and ask, repeatedly, his voice trembling, "Was that Spaghetti?"

The recounting of that event rapidly coursed through the streets of Riverdale, in every shop, at the back of every mass, and through every classroom by the following Monday afternoon. It remains mythic to this day.

Every neighborhood man, woman, or child, who met my grandfather from that day until his death in his mid-eighties, addressed the man respectfully as Spaghetti.

And none of the local urchins ever risked a deed that could result in a rendezvous with Spaghetti's garden shears.

CHAPTER NINE
(EAST COAST COWBOYS)

The only cowboys I ever recall seeing in my first five years of human existence were those appearing in John Wayne movies and Marlboro Man ads. The reason I only recall the John Wayne cowboys in movies is that my mother was such a die-hard John Wayne fan that she once – when I was seven or eight and able to read - made me post a fan letter to him at the Riverdale Post Office. It was hidden among a stack of bill payments she had rubber banded together, and which I immediately went through during the three-block walk to their government-controlled destination. When I came home and asked her about it, she blushed and commanded me to never mention it again. That explained why whenever one of The Duke's movies appeared on the Million Dollar Movies series on WOR Channel 9 in New York, my mother was watching it.

The visual cues to the Marlboro Man were far more ubiquitous. The red and white cardboard boxes containing the cigarettes he represented could be found everywhere throughout our household. And I cannot to this day recall a time when there wasn't one of those boxes in my father's hands, in his dress shirt chest pocket or rolled up in the left sleeve of one of his white t-shirts. He was a two-pack a day man. So, it was completely understandable that my eyes were drawn to any magazine or television advertisement that featured those cigarettes. And the actors portraying the Marlboro Man over the years were always tough looking cowboys with a Marlboro cigarette hanging nonchalantly from their lips as they performed some macho cowboy deed from the saddle of their horses.

My father never wore the Cattleman cowboy hat or rode a horse, but he chain-smoked the cigarette hanging from their lips. That made him tough enough for me. There's no coincidence that those cigarettes ultimately took the lives of five of those actors as well as my father.

It's no surprise why Marlboro was my cigarette of choice, when I first lit up with Joe Marrero in fourth grade. Marlboros, the Golden Gloves, and, later on, my male pattern baldness were the only common traits I shared with my father. But I don't want to get ahead of myself.

I saw my first live cowboy the summer after first grade. At least, that is what they wanted me to think.

When we first moved to Riverdale it took all of the family's finances and adult income to cover the down payment, mortgage, and monthly bills for the large house we lived in. In those early years the McCarthys could not afford the membership to the neighborhood pool. So, my parents used to walk us as a caravan down Mosholu Avenue, across Broadway, and into Van Cortlandt Park to fill our Saturdays. Sometimes Posie and Spaghetti would come along, because Spaghetti used to love to dig up some of the bushes he found in the thick woods to add to his collection around our property.

Always the family tour guide, I remember my mother reciting some of the interesting facts about the park as she led the family though its miles of back trails, like it was over a thousand acres in size and was formed by glaciers. Of course, at five years old I had no idea what an acre or glacier was. It was named after its original owner, Jacobus Van Cortlandt, who used slave labor to construct the large lake and the Mansion that anchored the southern ends of his massive property. Along with the squirrels and pigeons I had been used to in McCoombs park by Yankee Stadium, Vanny Woods, as we came to call it, had all kinds of other animals like hawks, owls, and raccoons. If you were lucky, you could spot a coyote making its way north along the abandoned train tracks. The lake had fish like bass, blue gill, and crappies, and you could find cranes fishing along some of its tributaries and shallows.

There were natural caves, where the rare homeless person would find shelter, and a giant staircase that led up a steep hill to nowhere. Probably the coolest monument in the park was on the southern end of the park, across the bridge that traversed the Saw Mill River Parkway that connected the west side of Manhattan though the Bronx to Westchester and beyond. The abandoned family cemetery sat up on the hill overlooking the parade grounds, where the Lenape

Indigenous people once cultivated their crops. The large iron gate had rotted away leaving the thirty square-foot walled cemetery left to the elements, their ghosts long forgotten. I could feel them every time my brothers and I raced ahead of the adults and ran among its toppled and cracked headstones, the names long since worn away.

Our weekend trips through Vanny were not all educational. My father taught his children how to throw baseballs and footballs on the large field near its Mosholu Avenue entrance, and Spaghetti taught us how to kick "real footballs" without ever touching them with your hands. My mother and Posie would sit over in the shade of the trees by the large wool picnic blanket they bought with them and lay out food and drink for the rest of us.

But the highlight for me was when the adults took the kids for pony rides.

There had always been a stable in Vanny Park to cater to the last of blue bloods that lived on Fieldstone Road or along the scenic parts of the Hudson River, by Wave Hill. It was easier to board your thoroughbred there than in the stables in Central Park or Westchester. The horses kept there were beautiful, and large. We would sometimes pass a couple of riders when we walked the back trails on the weekend. Most riders didn't even notice our existence as they cantered past us, tucked away along the side of the trails in whatever gaps or crevices we could slide into upon hearing their approach. They were more likely to notice the squirrels or birds closer to their eye levels. During those early years, I'm quite certain I could have easily walked directly below the bellies of their standing steeds without ducking my head.

My only experience with equines at that point in my life was the large old mule that used to draw the wooden wagon around the neighborhood on garbage days to collect anything its owner, a little elf of a man we called Junkie, thought could bring salvage money. My friends and I used to torment man and beast whenever we saw them riding by, until Spaghetti gave me the word – in no uncertain terms - that Junkie was untouchable. Turns out Junkie's undecipherable rants and threats towards the street urchins were actually Irish, and Spaghetti made sure no one ever fucked with him again.

But there was another breed of equines to be found in Vanny Park.

The city had rented a small circular track and six open stalls to a small carnival crew who tried to look like cowboys. They were from somewhere up north in Yonkers, which was way more like the tougher parts of the Bronx than the posh Westchester county it fell within. They weren't the heroic types that you saw riding with John Wayne across the western prairies. These characters looked like the type that always rode with the villains. They all had cigarettes permanently jutting out of their mouths like toothpicks.

The oldest among them seemed to be the boss. I thought I heard one of the others call him Angel, which stuck in my mind, because based on what I'd been hearing from priests on Sundays, he looked like he played for the other team. He took the money from the parents who wanted to give their child a ride, fifteen cents for once around the track and a quarter for twice. He never smiled.

There was nothing warm and fuzzy coming from his crew either, who looked, to the man, like the last thing they wanted to be doing was to be ferrying a bunch of kids around a circular track on the backs of ponies that had seen far better days.

When my turn in line came, a tall skinny teenager, the only one without a cheap cowboy hat, looked over at his boss, who held up one finger. The teen hoisted me up into the worn leather saddle and, after wrapping a leather strap around my waist and tying it off on the horn of the saddle, he snapped a single clothes pin onto the leather belt, lit his Winston cigarette, and led the pony to the entrance to the outer ring of the wooden chutes.

Sitting in that saddle gave me a brand-new perspective in life. I was clearly taller than six feet in the saddle, a height I would never reach on my own, despite my brothers all crossing that barrier. I could see the cars passing on Broadway in the distance to the west. And directly below me, as he led me to the chute, I could see that my cowboy's greasy black pompadour was doing a lousy job of covering the beginnings of a bald spot on the crown of his head. There were also clusters of parents and children waiting at spots along the perimeter of the ring to wave with more excitement than warranted at their passing charges.

Pompadour gave the pony a tap on its haunches, which started it on its slow walk around the ring.

The pony I was riding was all black. The coolest looking of the bunch. He slow walked me around the outer ring, coming up beside a painted pony who had come to a halt on the inner ring, which caused the four-year old girl sitting in its saddle to begin to cry. My pony snorted and leaned across the low wooden barrier as it came up beside the paint and gave that pony a small nuzzle with it nose, which started its recalcitrant cousin back in motion.

As I got to the far end of the ring, I spotted a cute brown-haired girl, leaning against the outer ring, who I recognized from recess periods in St. Maggie's school yard. She was a few classes above me. She wore her hair in a short bob that seemed from the television commercials to be in fashion at the time. She had large brown doe eyes, and porcelain skin, not a freckle to be seen. So, I knew she couldn't be Irish.

She wore blue jeans and a t-shirt, and I could see from the slight curves that she had the beginnings of a body that was certainly not a boy. It's amazing what a Catholic school uniform can hide.

As I came up beside the girl, she smiled and waved, although she avoided making eye contact with me. I hesitantly waved back in her direction and could begin to feel the blush rising above my shirt collar. I wanted to look back, but I didn't have the nerve.

When my pony reached the end of the road, another one of the teens removed the clothes pin and led us to a spot away from the ring, where he unfastened the leather and lifted me clear of the pony, sending me on my way towards the exit as he led the black pony to the line of kids still waiting for their rides.

Since my younger brothers were just entering the ring on their ponies, and my parents and grandparents were anxiously watching from the other side of the ring, I knew I had a few moments to kill. I raced clockwise around the outside of the ring until I found the cute girl, still waiting at its apex. She was staring at something in the ring.

When I came up beside her, I leaned against the wooden rail and said, "You go to St. Maggie's, don't ya?"

She took a moment to turn to me, and a moment more before she seemed to acknowledge me.

"Oh hi," she responded before turning back to the ring. "Yeah, I'm in Sister Florence's class."

Then she turned back towards me and looked like she had just really noticed me.

"Do I know you?" She asked, smiling for the first time. She had a nice smile.

"I thought so," I replied, now feeling a bit sheepish, "You just waved at me as I passed."

She scrunched up her face as she tried to remember the event.

"I just went by on the black pony." I offered, trying to jog her memory.

"Oh," she said. "No, I wasn't waving at you, silly, I was waving at Snoopy."

She saw the confusion in my eyes and followed up. "The black pony. His name is Snoopy, he's my favorite."

As if on cue, the black pony now passed carrying another unappreciative child, and the girl called out, "Hi Snoopy!" The pony turned to the girl, snorted, and tossed its head, causing its mane to flutter.

"My name's Karen." The girl said. "Karen Anderson." She held out her hand and I shook it. It was soft and warm. She held onto mine for an extra moment, "And you are?"

For some reason it took me a second to recall my own name. Finally, it came to me, "Jimmy. I'm Jimmy McCarthy."

She smiled and slowly released her grip. She turned back towards the ring. "So, what brings you down to the ponies, Jimmy?"

"I'm here with my family." I said pointing to where my parents were now meeting my brothers at the ring's exit. I then pointed to my grandparents, standing at a spot along the perimeter next to my sister. Spaghetti was working on a small cumulus cloud of Prince Albert coming from his pipe.

"Is that your sister?" Karen asked with a tone of recognition. "I think she's in my brother George's class." I nodded.

"What about you," I asked, "are you here with your family?"

She thought about the question for a moment before answering. Her face looked a little sad.

"No," she said, "I just stopped by on my way home from the stables, pointing across the field in its direction by the edge of the woods. "I muck out the stalls there, in exchange for riding lessons."

I had no idea what mucking out a stall meant, but I nodded knowingly. Given that the ponies seemed to know what they were doing, I couldn't grasp what lessons their riders needed to ride them.

"I'm going to be a cowboy someday." Karen whispered to no one in particular and turned back to the pony ring. She looked over at me through the corner of her eye and added. "You know, I've never told anyone that."

"Jjjjiiiimmmmyyyy!" I heard my sister call from her position by my grandparents on the far side of the ring. As I looked over in her direction, she pointed at me and then crooked her finger in the universal sign for *let's go*. Bonnie always seemed to know exactly where I was at all times. She could track me in any crowd, like radar.

I turned back to Karen, who had been watching the exchange.

"Gotta go." I said, a bit forlornly. I held out my hand. Karen took it, pulled me closer and gave me a quick peck on the cheek, then she giggled.

"I don't know why I just did that." She said, this time matching her facial blush to my own.

"Jjjjjiiiiimmmmmyyyyy, c'mon, we're leaving." I heard my sister call.

I did a half-wave and then turned and ran towards my sister, who waited for me while my grandparents headed off to find the rest of the family.

"Is that Karen Beck?" Bonnie asked as I arrived at her side.

"No, Karen Anderson." I replied, touching the spot on my cheek where her lips had just touched.

"Well, she's George Beck's sister." Bonnie proclaimed. "He's in my class and I see them walking home together after school."

Bonnie took my hand and led me to where the family was waiting, and we all headed off for the long walk back up Mosholu to our home, Spaghetti in the lead.

I never spoke with Karen again until we were much older and hung out as part of a larger group of cross-pollinating teens partying in the woods together.

During the years between those times, I had learned that Karen and George were foster siblings who loved one another as much as any blood sibling could. What's in a name, anyway?

By then, Karen was going by her nickname, "Cruiser."

Before she turned twenty, Karen packed her bags, headed west, and became the Bronx cowboy she always wanted to be. She never gave up on her dream.

CHAPTER TEN
(ST. MAGGIE'S)

Fourth grade in the local Catholic School was a lot of firsts for me. In school, it was the first time we got to use cartridge pens for cursive writing. It was the first time the students were responsible for reading actual classic literature and doing reports on those books. If you were an altar boy, by fourth grade you had graduated from Patent Bearer to at least Second Server, or you had already washed out. You could participate in the intermural sports offered by the school and started getting chosen for pick-up teams for those same sports in the school yard by your peers. Hierarchies began to shape. Reputations, good and bad, started to be established. In biblical terms, the wheat began to separate from the chaff. It was the beginning of a transition that led me to where I am now. But there were a few highlights beforehand that may be worth mentioning.

The few things I recall with any clarity from those first three years at St. Maggie's was that in first grade one of our more interesting classmates was taken out of our classroom weeping and was never heard from again. Rumor had it that the young man, a tiny Irish kid who resembled a wizened old man with a continuous stream of snot always flowing from his nose, had been subjected to and succumbed to the apocryphal "spanking machine" that was allegedly kept in a back room off the principal's office. One of my other classmates tragically lost an eye to a bb gun sniper who fired into the new schoolyard from a wooded area across Delafield Avenue. He had been walking in tandem with two other first graders, as the middle man of the trio, locked together at the shoulders singing some silly song when the bb struck. Three on a match is unlucky for one of them. They never caught the shooter. I met Sister Peter in first grade. In my memory she will always remind me of Sally Field playing the Flying Nun. She had kind eyes and nice smile. Never once did she administer corporal punishment. I'm almost certain she came to her senses and left her order.

In second grade I had my first lay teacher, Mrs. Lynch. She was great because she was the right mix of teacher and mother who had two of her children attending the school at the time. She lived only a half block away from me, so I had to be on my best behavior or chance a visit to my home. She taught me how to really read books for comprehension. Other than that, the only other moment that stood out from that second year was that our country's first Irish Catholic president, JFK, was assassinated. I didn't fully appreciate the tragedy at the time beyond the fact that my parents and grandparents remained glued to the television and radio and the official photo that hung in the family's home was draped with black crepe from that moment on. The only visual I recall was the riderless black steed with the empty boots fixed backward in its stirrups during the televised funeral procession. The students got a couple of days off for our troubles.

Third grade connected me with Sister Florence. She wore the same habit and wimple as Sister Peter – all black ensembles with the kind of black funnel around their faces you see on male dogs after getting the snip – so they can't lick their empty sack. Sister Florence told me that those wimples gave the nuns the ability to hear the softest whispers from the furthest corners of the class room. The funnel shape captured the sound. Must be true because they always heard mine. Sister Florence was far older than Sister Peter. However, Sister Florence was the only older nun I ever met that hadn't turned into a crusading harpy whose sole purpose in life was to convince the girls in their charge to join their order and punish the young boys on this earth who could lead them astray, while shepherding the incorrigible males toward their inevitable rewards in hell. I developed a theory back then that nuns never really die. They are just taken out every few hundred years for a new coat of paint, given a new name and posted in a new school. Sister Florence was that strange exception to the harpy rule who convinced me that I wasn't all bad and had a shot at redemption.

Sister Florence was also the nun who inadvertently showed me that they had human bodily functions just like the rest of us. One Saturday I was serving a few hours of morning detention – yes I was an early starter – for talking one of my classmates into biting into a cracker ball firework on the pretense that it was a jawbreaker candy. What was the most interesting part was that I talked the young man into first stealing the cracker ball off of Sister Florence's desk, where it sat in plain view after she had relieved me of it before I could detonate it during recess in the school yard. His mouth puffed out just as you would expect in any cartoon, followed by a wisp of smoke and trickle of blood. Luckily, there was no serious damage to his teeth, but I do believe he was left back that year. Anyway, having performed all of my janitorial tasks around the new school building, I returned to my classroom so I could be officially released from detention.

But there was no Sister Florence to be found. Knowing I could not leave detention without her official approval and realizing that every moment past the required termination time of 11 a.m., was an involuntary relinquishment of another moment of a precious Saturday, I searched all of the classrooms on both floors of the building, hoping to find her. When that came up empty, I became desperately creative and decided to peek into the girl's bathroom. I mean, after all, I was actually beginning to worry about the nice old nun.

Now there are very few Catholic males from the 1960s who could honestly say that they ever crossed the threshold of a girl's bathroom in a catholic school, and probably only a handful that have lived to talk about it. But that late spring Saturday morning I slowly pushed the door inward just enough so I could get the lay of the land and see if I could spot the old nun lying dead on the floor.

The first thing that registered was that there were far more toilet stalls and no wall urinals. Made sense. It was also a lot cleaner than any boy's bathroom I had ever been in.

Not seeing any bodies on the open area of the floor, I was about to slip back outside when I heard that sound that has haunted me over these past five centuries. It sounded like the approaching rolling thunder I later heard coming over the mountains in Colorado during those hot summer nights. To my eight-year-old human mind, it was ominous. Then I heard Sister Florence clear her throat in the trademark fashion she was known for. But there was no sign of her.

I dropped to my knees to get a look at the only area not visible at normal eye level and peaked below the foot space of the stall doors. Below the fourth stall, closest to the windows, I saw the pair of black sensible boots that kind of looked like Spaghetti's, with black hosiery continuing up the legs out of sight beyond the stall doors. I heard the scratching fluttering sound of the industrial toilet roll and a moment later, the shoes and feet disappear under the rapidly descending bottom of a black habit. Luckily, I was able to make my escape under the cover of the loud flushing sound that followed.

I could never look Sister Florence, or any nun for that matter, in the eyes again. That wasn't the last time I was subjected to detention, or its more advanced version of J.U.G. – Justice Under God - but this one made the most lasting impression on me.

But I digress.

CHAPTER ELEVEN
(FOURTH GRADE)

Outside of school, fourth grade offered a number of other firsts that I found far more interesting, as they all somehow related to my lips – first kiss, first beer and first cigarette. Turned out, I had a natural affinity for all three. Given what I know now, I might have stolen all three as well.

I shared the experience of my first beer and cigarette with Joe Marrero. Turns out, he also played a role in my first kiss.

I had known Joe since first grade. He seemed to draw the attention of the nuns and teachers in the school, not because he was the only Puerto Rican in St. Maggie's in the 1960s, but because, like me, he had a hard time respecting their authority, or anyone else's for that matter. Joe was also the class clown – a real natural - and, again like me, he showed an early interest in girls. He used his comedic talents to get the girls' attention. It seemed to work out for the both of us.

In catholic school, the sexes kept to themselves. While they may have been equally interspersed among the seating in the classroom, always under the careful watch of the nuns and their direct boss, God, they herded together along gender lines in the schoolyard, during recess and lunch breaks. For the first three years you would swear that neither the boys nor the girls knew the other sex was present in the same school yard. We were invisible to each other.

By fourth grade, something started to change. Hierarchies started to form as the more dominant personalities in each gender began to surface and rise. You would expect that the natural athletes would have been the natural leaders, and at least among the boys that was true. But you would be surprised how terrible those pure athletes were at extending their reach beyond the athletic fields and courts, at least until sixth grade, when the dominant players on the St. Maggie's basketball teams started to pair off with the cute girls on the cheerleading squads. Junior Varsity pairings ultimately moved up to Varsity. Familiarity breeds relationships and school royalty tended to engage with their genetic equals.

Back in the sixties the coolest snack around that you could make at home in the evenings with your family was Jiffy pop. It came prepackaged in this flat tin foil pan with a metal wire handle. You could place the pan on top of your stove and, by shaking the handle over the open fire, the artificially buttered and salted kernels inside would start to pop, and a large tinfoil blister would start to grow on the top of the pan.

It was a primal interactive experience decades before that word came into existence in our world.

There was always that first pop to start the show. While its distinct sound, like a muted firecracker, always startled you to the point that most people would back away from the stove for a moment, it signified that the magic was beginning to happen somewhere out of view. The excitement of you and everyone around you increased in a direct correlation with the size of the expanding tin foil blister and the increased rapidity of the popping sounds coming from within. The person handling the pan usually increased the tempo of the circling or shake of the pan over the fire. Something cool was happening. Looking back on it now, it was a metaphor for sex.

Kids are like popcorn kernels. Even though they are all exposed to the same heat of life while first sitting in the pan, some start to pop earlier than others. And like the Jiffy pop pan, when it was all said and done, there was always some duds and burned kernels left in its bottom.

When it came to girls, I was more sensitive to the heat than most of the other boys in my class. But I wasn't the first kernel to pop. That was Joe Marrero.

Joe masked his blooming interest in the opposite sex through physical comedy. At first it was by walking up alongside a cluster of girls – who for some reason always gathered in inward facing circles - and flipping up their skirts and then running for his life back to the safety of a cluster of boys. That usually resulted in the shriek of the surprised recipient, and laughter from the insensitive males.

But by fourth grade, hierarchies for both sexes had taken shape, and some of the girls started to develop in new and wonderous ways, that, along with their aesthetic prowess, resulted in some of them being much taller and more physically powerful than their slower blossoming counterparts. Those early risers that grew up in families with brothers, suddenly stepped into the breech and became protectors of their sex.

Patty Perata and Mary Jane McGuinness were two of the first female enforcers to strike terror in the boys of our class. Both cracked the five-foot height mark years before any of the males' voices or testicles dropped. And Mary Jane had other things going for her, besides her height and awakening body. Her long muscular legs made her the fastest creature in the St. Maggie's schoolyard and her equally muscular arms gave her a herculean grip in her large, though well-appointed hands.

Patty Peralta was the other early Amazon in our class. You could tell from the size of her older brother, who once spun me around like a track-and-field hammer and tossed me across the schoolyard like I was a sack of laundry – I had it coming - that the family must have descended from giants. And her road towards physical maturity peaked by fifth grade, when she could have passed for a senior in high school. She was the grown woman in the room of little boys, and with her family size, strength, and temper she had no trouble taking out the testosterone delayed members of the weaker sex.

Luckily, Joe was very fast. So much so that he could do a few laps around and among the shrieking girls – a highly contagious phenomena - before racing back to the safety of his now laughing peers. That worked perfectly for Joe until that one warm spring afternoon towards the end of fourth grade.

Joe was entering the schoolyard through the Old School exit from the basement lunchroom. As usual, the girls were all collecting in their circle in a small alleyway formed where the new and old schools connected. The boys in our class were gathered about twenty-five yards away over by the basketball court closest to the fence of the gas station, directly south of the schoolyard, where, when the wind was right, we could inhale the enticing smell of the then leaded vapors as adults would fill up their cars. I'm sure the residual lead in our cell structure accounted for some of our conduct as we got older.

Someone in the boys' group spotted Joe approaching nonchalantly towards the circle of girls and passed the alert through a continuous chain of thighnuggies to the boy to their immediate left until the entire group now had all eyes on Joe.

Looking back on it now, I may have been witnessing the expiration of the first of Joe's nine lives.

Satisfied that he had captured our rapt attention, Joe began to drift towards the closest circumference of the females in the alleyway, walking like Charlie Chaplin while miming an exaggerated whistle and cane twirl as he waddled along. But just as Joe reached for the edge of the skirt of Nanette Walters, the circle wall cracked just enough for Mary Jane's powerful hand to reach out and intercept Joe's own at its wrist. Joe was then pulled into the circle with the speed of a Jackson Chameleon's tongue. He was gone in an instant, but we could hear him screaming before the fissure snapped shut.

The only thing that saved Joe that day was the ringing of the recess bell, signaling for all students to assemble onto their class lines for a return to the school building. Most of the boys in our group obediently headed off to our class line, while some of the girls started peeling off from their circle to do the same.

I couldn't take my eyes off the cluster of girls and when Nanette broke from their ranks I could see through the gap that Mary Jane was holding Joe's arms behind his back while Patty pummeled him into submission. It was brutal. As the second recess bell rang, Nina Calvani, a future cheerleader and one of the rising leaders of the group, pulled Patty away and signaled for Mary Jane to release him. Joe dropped to the ground like he was dead.

I ran over past the last of the dispersing girls, accidently bumping into Nina's rising number two, Chrissy Dosela, who everyone thought was Italian because of her long black hair and eyes, and darker skin. The vowel at the end of her last name sealed the deal. Turns out, I was soon to learn that she was actually a First Nation Apache. But in that moment all I could do was look into those eyes and stutter an apology. Her fleeting smile almost caused me to forget about Joe. Luckily she broke gaze first and returned to the end of our class line just as it disappeared through the entrance way.

Joe was now stirring, and I helped him to his feet. His clothes were in total disarray and his face had the making of a new fat lip. As I dragged him towards the doorway that we had to enter before the schoolyard monitor sealed it and imposed another day of detention, Joe moaned, and then whispered,

"Jimmy, I think I'm in love."

CHAPTER TWELVE
(WASTED ON THE YOUNG)

When I was young, I could not wait to get older. In Riverdale, your age defined where you could hang out and who you could hang with. Since this part of the story gets a little complicated, I need you to hang with me here.

During grammar school there was a seasonal migration where everyone who had not yet graduated from St. Maggie's would hang after school in the old and new schoolyards throughout the fall through spring months. The odd thing about that schoolyard nomenclature was that the "Old School Yard" was actually off the beige bricked more modern "New School" that housed the lower classes. The "New School Yard" was off the ancient flag stone building that housed the upper classes, the gym, the lunchroom, the administration, and the nuns' convent at the very top of the four-story fortress, so they could be closer to God. The convent had its own entranceway off the New Schoolyard with its own elevator, and I'm quite certain Mr. Otis himself had installed it.

The New Schoolyard was created when the Old Church building that sat adjacent to the Old School was torn down and its ruins plowed over with enough asphalt to field numerous parking spaces, a full court basketball court, and two more side courts that the younger kids ran as a lateral full court. A New Church building then went up across 260th Street, adjacent to and just north of the rectory that housed the purple frocked Monsignor and his supporting cast of priests. The entire school watched the tall crane carefully lower into place a very modern cross on the pinnacle of its spire. A week later my then third grade class was the first to receive its confirmation. At that holy event, I took on my fourth name, Anthony, once the Bishop slapped my cheek, because St. Anthony was my mother's favorite Saint. I may have been the first McCarthy in the history of the Clan to ever don an Italian appellation.

The controversial New Church was very modern, with a sharply pointed ceiling from which lights meant to represent the crown of thorns, but which actually looked like spiked dog collars worn around necks in the best of S&M dungeons, hung perilously from long rods above the pews. Everything from the New Church's statues to its Stations of the Cross looked disconcertingly different from anything my parents and grandparents had ever seen in a house of God on either side of the pond.

To me, the most interesting feature of the New Church was the large triangular wall directly behind the altar, which now faced the people, and consisted of a close-set pattern of black and brown ridges that ran perpendicularly from floor to ceiling. They were so closely set together that if you stared at it for more than a second it caused a cognitive distortion making the lines appear to wiggle and wave. It was a great distraction during the extended high masses and prepared us all for future "highs" in life. I learned that it also provided an easy exit from all of the holy day masses during the school year that the nuns used to force us to attend during school hours.

One of my friends from school, Matty Burns, had a strange form of epilepsy that was triggered by those wall lines each mass before the Offertory Prayers could be said. This caused him to flop around wildly in the pew for a few seconds like a hooked fish in the bottom of a boat, before he finally collapsed on the kneelers. He always woke up a few moments later not knowing what had happened. I'll not lie, the first time he did it freaked me out, as I thought he was having a religious experience. But once the rest of us learned that the nuns always asked the boys closest to him to help assist him out of the church and back to the classroom, there was always a battle to try and land a spot sitting beside him in church.

Rumor had it that Matty always had a pack of cigarettes in his pocket that he regularly stole from his older sister Katy, and being a good Christian, was always willing to share one in the below ground level alleyway on the back side of the Old School after each religious epiphany. As there was only a few Holy Days of Obligation left in the school year after our confirmation, I didn't get in on that action until late in fourth grade.

You see, cigarettes were the 1960's school boys' skeleton key to unlock entrance into anything that required us to be older than we were.

Okay, let me stop you there, Jimmy. Cigarettes are disgusting. Claire interrupted. *Stella and Apollo don't be fooled, there is nothing good to come out of smoking.*

If you would just let me finish Claire, of course cigarettes are disgusting, they killed my father, but I was young, human, and stupid. And had I not evolved into a Centauri, who knows what would have happened to my human body. But I have a story to tell, warts and all. Now, can I go on?

Proceed. She scratched her chin on my thigh and then lay her head back in its resting spot on my lap. I started to scratch her ears, which she folded back on her neck.

Now where was I?

Skeleton key! Apollo answered. *And what is that exactly?*

Go ahead Pop. Ignore him. I'm over four hundred years old. I'm not going start any new bad habits now, especially human, assuming I felt like traveling back in time just to find one of those cigarettes. Stella added. *You were talking about cigarettes.*

And skeleton keys, Apollo added.

Got it. Okay, so I first learned of this skeleton key to the big leagues from Joe Marrero, who learned it from his older brother, Steve, who was in the same class as Bonnie in St. Maggie's.

Anyway, one day in September, after we spent an extra hour cleaning chalkboards in detention, Joe and I were walking down 260th Street towards Liebig Avenue, where Joe would head north and me south towards our respective homes.

"You ever try one of these?" Joe asked, looking furtively around us to make sure none of the nosey neighbors were watching out their windows.

Riverdale had less privacy than the most CCTV laden sections of London in the twenty-second century. In the 1960s, women had yet to fully engage in the workforce, so most spent their time within walking distance from their homes, doing daily circuits to shops and schools and parks and play grounds. Everybody knew everybody. So, if you were doing something wrong while on a Riverdale street, odds favored you being spotted by one of these constant patrols who would get right on the next land line phone – and if it was particularly heinous, the next pay phone they came to - either directly to your family, or to someone in those six degrees of snoopiness chain that would pass it on to the appropriate adult that would get it to your family. The worst part about the gender of these daily patrols, were that women are far more observant than the average male, and more likely to smell bullshit when the excuses flew.

Finally, most families were multigenerational. No one went to a nursing home if a younger generation existed, so, there was always a chance a retired grandparent was looking out the front window or doing something around their property at just the wrong time to catch you in the act.

The major neighborhood party central was the woods whose entrance was right across Mosholu from my home, and Spaghetti liked to make a daily circuit around the park, where The Courts, rocks, and smaller woods where we also partied were located, with his favorite border collie, Pepper. So, my grandfather often spotted my brothers, friends and acquaintances doing the wrong thing. However, Spaghetti wasn't a grasser. Plus, I never saw him with a telephone in his hand. He hated all technology. He was more likely to grab hold of the errant boy and give him a hard boot in the ass with a follow-up threat of a more dire punishment if he caught them again.

In the rare occasion it was a female acting up, Spaghetti would bellow in his thick Northern Ireland brogue, "I know your grandparents, Lassie. Get your ass home and don't let me catch you doing that again." Most of the girls couldn't understand him but were sufficiently frightened by the spectacle that it had the desired effect.

If Spaghetti spotted any of his blood descendants in the mix, we got a good smacking with a litany of Irish blasphemies soundtrack from him when we returned home. But he never ratted us out to our parents.

In all situations, we did our best to avoid passing within Spaghetti's radar in the future.

Now this one particular afternoon, Joe ended his question by lifting a pack of Newport cigarettes from the sweater pocket closest to me. There was the grey packet with what looked like the white swoosh that appeared forty years later on all Nike Athletic gear. While it wasn't as familiar to me as my father's Marlboro Reds, I had seen enough commercials on television to recognize it as the leading menthol brand being touted among the networks, including in iambic pentameter by "a Jackhammer Jockey named Jake."

"Got these from my brother," he added.

I shoved his hand back down in his pocket and looked around to see if I spotted any movement among the second story curtains or blinds along the street.

"What are you doing with those?"

"Going to smoke them."

"What, here?" There was real panic in my voice. I took another look around.

"No, Saturday, in the woods."

"Which woods? Vannie?

"No,"

"Mush?"

"No."

"Above the rocks?"

"No," he said impatiently, "in the Mosholu woods at the fort."

Now there was only one "fort" of any renown in the neighborhood. It had been built by Matty Burns from scrap wood stolen on weekends by different crews of boys from various houses that were being built in the area. He had built a prototype in the lot by his house down on Huxley Avenue. It was so advanced in design and comfort that it had electricity via extension cord so that five of his closest friends could cram into it comfortably and read interesting stories in Playboy magazine while listening to AM radio. Matty had the craftsman skills that would match any magical dwarf in legend or history, which was fitting, given he was one of the shorter members of our class, and the rumor was that smoking had probably stunted his growth.

When Matty built the fort in the Mosholu woods, up on the plateau above the Mosholu library, he raised his game to a whole new stage by dropping the fort below ground level. Like the great Egyptian architect Hemiunu who designed the pyramids—

I heard rumor the grays helped the Egyptians with that. Apollo chimed in.

—Matty designed the fort to last for eternity, so it was built to withstand the weight of a solid, four-inch layer of dirt and stones and brush that hid it from the unsuspecting humans – including police – that may walk above it. He bolted a hollow stump over its trap door. It would still be there to this day if the Russian government had not bought the land from the City and built their Russian Mission there in its place. They probably used Matty's fort as the keystone to its prefabricated foundation.

"So, are you in?" Joe asked. "Four p.m., just before dusk."

I hesitated.

Joe called my bluff.

"Okay," Joe said, "suit yourself." He shoved his cigarette crammed hand deep into his pocket and turned towards home.

"I heard some of the girls from class may come by to check out the fort." He called over his shoulder. "Nina, Pee Wee, ... and Chrissy Dosela."

"Okay," I shouted after him, "I'll come."

"Good," Joe responded without looking back. "Bring your own ciggies."

I wonder if Joe ever kissed Erato.

CHAPTER THIRTEEN
(SATURDAY SOUL SEARCHING)

Saturdays were always busy in the McCarthy household.

By the fall of 1965, the Second Vatican Council had decided that in order to make the Church more accessible during those turbulent times of the Beatles and Rolling Stones, the centuries old Latin Mass could be performed in the vernacular of the parishioners of the Church where it was located. altar boys had been contributing to the Latin Mass since the Synod of Mainz in the year 859, freeing the true religious acolytes from the more menial tasks and allow them to proceed with actually learning how to be priests. Indeed, altar boys even had their own patron, St. Tarcisius, who died defending the holy Eucharist from a bunch of thugs. Some altar boys, like Paddy O'Rourke, stayed with the process and ultimately became a priest, but Satan later convinced him to leave the order and join his team. Paddy made a fine lawyer.

When my older brother, Eddie, and I returned from our family's summer vacation in Maine, the first August Saturday found us back at altar boy practice, held each week in St. Maggie's gym. We were instantly amazed that my father's years of tortuous, early morning Latin lessons had finally taken hold, as everything coming from the lips of the new third grade patent bearers sounded just like English to us.

The Dempsey brothers, Franky, and Timmy, who ran the altar boys like the mob, soon set us straight about the seismic shift in the Church's ecumenical direction. But it was quite apparent right from the start, that our historic religion would never be the same.

Part of the altar boys duties was training the younger boys in the intricacies of our defined roles during the mass. So, the older altar boys would take the newbies over to the Church and walk them through a mock mass with one of the Dempsey's playing the priest while the other put the boys through their paces and timing.

The entry level altar boy was the paten bearer. His one role was to stay on his kneeler at one side of the altar until Holy Communion, when he would remove his trusty paten, a golden stick with a slightly concave disc at its end, from its purple cloth sack, and then follow beside the priest and place the disk under the chins of the waiting devotees while the priest placed a small barely dissolvable host – the body of Christ - on each of their protruding tongues. There was a lot of pressure to this role, because God forbid one of those hosts missed their mark, it was the paten bearers sacred duty to catch it before it hit the floor or face the fate of eternal damnation.

The servers, or *Ceremonieri*, were the next step up. They worked the bells that were rung during the mass. They also brought over the sacred items like the back-up chalices, where the sacred hosts taken from the main chalice in the tabernacle are distributed, and the water and wine cruets when the priest was about to consecrate the hosts. One server poured the water over the fingers of the priest into a bowl and handed the priest the purificator, a small towel used to dry their lips and fingers, while the other server poured the wine into the chalice over the hundreds of now consecrated hosts.

Back in the Latin days, during High Mass, servers also included the *Thurife*, who carried the thurible used for incensing, and the *Navicularius*, who carried the incense boat from which the priest would shift some incense into the thurible to smoke out his parishioners. Then there were the *Ceroferari* who carried the tall candles during most formal processions and placed them carefully at their appropriate spots on the altar.

The final rung in the altar boy ladder was the reader or lector, who was assigned to the care of the missal and the lectionary, which is the large book containing passages from Holy Scriptures. It was his job to make sure that the lectionary was opened on the altar to the right page for that particular mass for the priest to read from. It was also his job to cue the audience to know when to stand, sit or kneel. During school masses, he was assisted by Sister Rosalind, who had this strange metal clicker she would use to train us like puppies. One click to sit, two to stand. It took me half of each summer listening to the crickets at night to desensitize to this Pavlovian response. Finally, it was the reader's job to make sure that none of the other altar boys fucked up. He would also collect any donations from families after weddings or funerals and distribute an arbitrary share to the other servers. Trickle-down economics at its best. Paten bearers never got a piece of the action. They hadn't earned their keep.

But after the Second Vatican Council, all hell broke loose among the altar boys. A number of us started to participate in things like pew racing wherein four altar boys would start at the back of the church and all race forward towards the front along the top of the pews. Success came down to knowing your stride and not trying to overextend yourself. Better to go the slower route, knees up, and hit the tops of all of the pews than to try to stretch it out and fall short of an alternate pew top. That continued until Packy Harrington missed a step and broke his clavicle. But that was after I was gone.

Some of the more religiously daring would go back into the sacristy and swipe some unconsecrated hosts, popping them into their mouths like chips and then washing it down with some of the altar wine. I was too superstitious to cross that line. In the end, I really hope the nuns and priests were wrong and that their Catholic God has a sense of humor.

My days as an altar boy were numbered anyway, because by the Fourth Grade first quarter report card, I had garnered a D on the back of the card next to the final entry, "Courtesy and Cooperation." I always believed that that particular entry was far too arbitrary to mean anything.

Monsignor Fitzmorris, an ex-Marine chaplain who had blessed the dead eyes of many American soldiers in "Vet-Nam," ran the entire parish, including the school, and did not suffer fools easily. He stood straight and tall, about six feet in height, with broad shoulders and no signs of softness under the purple piping black cassock he always wore. From my vantage point in the first-row troublemaker seat closest to the teacher's desk, I could literally see my reflection in the shine of the tips of his black shoes. His only physical surrender to his age was his thick white hair, worn cropped short on his head and his round spectacles, which made him look like Teddy Roosevelt.

When he handed out the report cards, as he did for every class in the school, he would stand at attention and ask in an imperious tone if the student standing before him was "a champ or a chump?"

Without waiting for an answer, he would slide the cardboard report card out of its gray paper sleeve, examine the numerical grades on the front of the card and then flip it over with the dexterous fingers of one hand and review the letter entries on its back side.

"McCarthy," he said as he studied the back side of my report card that day, "aren't you an altar boy?"

"Yes Monsignor," I replied, nervously.

"Not anymore," he said sternly. "No chumps allowed."

It was a bad day for the McCarthy boys. Fifteen minutes later, Monsignor Fitzmorris summarily dismissed my older brother from the same pseudo-religious organization on the pretense that Eddie was intentionally distracting him by playing with an ink cartridge on his desk while the Monsignor was addressing the class. My mother's hopes for a cleric in the family died that day, as my younger brothers refused to join the altar boys in protest.

Confiteor Deo omnipoténti

But this particular Saturday, I did have altar boys practice and then afternoon chores around the house under the supervision of Spaghetti. The foliage from the four-story tulip tree that anchored the back fence along our property was beginning to drop *en mass* from its host's umbrella-like canopy. That meant broomstick blisters on our hands as my older brother and I swept nature's detritus from the corners of the yard into large piles in its center. My younger brothers then stuffed the leaves into special string mesh bags that Spaghetti would then hoist upon his back and carry across the street to dump deep within the lower section of the Mosholu woods. He resembled Santa Clause, as his ubiquitous pipe pumped balls of Prince Albert smoke above his head like a steam engine in cadence with his powerful strides. This was a time before plastic garbage bags were in wide use. Spaghetti was way ahead on the recycling curve.

At that moment, my mother was in the house cleaning and Posie was preparing the evening family meal. My sister was sitting at Posie's kitchen table reading one of her Nancy Drew mysteries.

My father was stashed away in his tiny windowless study right off his second-floor bedroom working on one of his many get rich schemes that he hoped one day would free him from the soul killing service of selling people, who could not afford it, insurance they didn't need. With everyone caught up in their own worlds, it was easy enough for me to tell my brothers I needed to take a piss break, sneak into the upstairs kitchen, and swipe a pack of Marlboro Reds from one of the three open cartons that my father kept stashed on top of the cabinet over the sink. My father was a two-pack a day man and left open packs for convenience around his favorite spots in the house, so he would never miss one pack.

Cigarettes safely tucked into the pocket of my sweatshirt, I snuck down the front stairway, hid by the front door and waited until my Grandfather returned across Mosholu with his empty leaf bag. As soon as he was safely up the driveway, I bolted across the street and entered the woods right where he had exited. It was time to grow up.

CHAPTER FOURTEEN
(MANIFESTING A MUSE)

There were two ways to get to Matty's fort from the Mosholu Avenue entrance to the woods. The first was a straight path just off the northern fence line of the Public Library. You then had to scale a very tall set of two large boulders that glaciers had carved from what was now the Hudson River, and stacked on top of each other a half mile away. Those rocks ran sixty feet to their pinnacle at a sixty-degree angle. The other option was to take the long and more circuitous path that rose at a more attainable forty-five degrees and arrived at the same hilltop from the south. This winding path led past various clearings along the street level of the woods, just off the interior incline. Each were naturally created by large fallen tree trunks that served as makeshift seating and tables for the partying kids. All were set deep enough into the trees that a passerby could not spot the campfires or hear the music from whatever hand radio one of the kids had brought along with them.

The Mosholu Woods was the largest isolated remnant of the thick coniferous forest that used to stretch over the entire northern Bronx and that can only still be found in Van Cortlandt Park. It was approximately thirty acres in size and was bordered by Mosholu on the West, the poorer end of the winding Fieldstone Road on its North and East, and by the Saw Mill River Parkway to its South. The trees along its Mosholu border were wide and as tall as the top of its interior hill, rising a good sixty feet above the rest of North Riverdale. Centuries of rotting vegetation left the trails thickly carpeted enough to mute the sounds of any passage unless one stepped on a dry twig, so you could travel quite silently through those woods if you chose to.

The high broad limb of one of those trees served as the anchor for a thick old rope swing that one of the prior groups of teenagers had installed years before. Its arc passed from a small ledge forty feet up on the boulders for fifty feet over the direct path by the Public Library. B.J. Delaney, who had already established his adventurous reputation among the neighborhood hooligans, was the only one crazy enough to try that swing and ended up with a cast on his arm for his troubles when he slipped from its bottom knot at the apex of its arc and fell forty feet. But that wasn't the fall that killed him.

The interior of the Mosholu Woods was always dusky even on the brightest sunny day and got dark long before the surrounding streets of Riverdale. It was a great place to party because the cops at the 50th Precinct never wanted to chase any of the kids into it and would never venture into it on their own volition more than a few feet without putting on their flashlights. Their bright beams provided the young partiers plenty of time to escape over the hill and out the opening on the Fieldstone Road end of the woods, which had its own precipitous thirty-foot drop with protruding hundred-year-old tree roots. The young people could easily ascend or descend them as a natural ladder but they would give way under the weight of an adult human.

If Peter Pan was an American, he would have hidden the Lost Boys in the Mosholu woods.

As I wound my way into the wood's recesses that particular Saturday afternoon, I came upon one of the party clearings. My eyes were drawn to a small campfire burning in its center, whose faint light made the surrounding woods seem that much darker in comparison. I saw a lone figure sitting on a small log by the fire. As I drew closer I could see it was a girl.

She was gazing into the circular flame at her feet. She had long, thick black hair, parted in the middle, which flowed over the shoulders of her short black leather jacket and extended down its front midway to her waist, where faded blue jeans that ran into black leather boots completed her ensemble.

I couldn't tell just how old she was, but I knew she didn't attend St. Maggie's. I had recently begun to really notice the features of my developing female schoolmates and found that Mediterranean and Latin features were more aesthetically attractive to me. Dark hair, eyes and skin registered as more exotic when you come from a race with porcelain skin and blue peepers. For example,

Denise Di Nome, one of twelve perfect Italian American siblings who all attended St. Maggie's, and who was in my older brother's class a year ahead of me, was at that point the exemplar of physical beauty in my limited experience.

This girl knocked Denise right off the aesthetic pedestal. I instinctively knew someone like her would never be sitting anywhere alone, never mind in the Mosholu Woods, so I stopped and looked around to see if some very large boyfriend was relieving himself among the surrounding trees. When that came up empty, I studied her surroundings, looking for an unmanned fresh beer bottle or burning cigarette suggesting another's presence, but other than the small campfire, and the girl herself, there was nothing.

She sat staring at the flames at her feet with such intensity, that I didn't want to disturb her. Just when I made up my mind to double back along the path and enter the woods from Fieldstone Road, the girl tapped the log beside her with her left hand and, without looking up, said.

"Come Jimmy, sit beside me."

CHAPTER FIFTEEN
(ENGAGING ENERGY)

That was the first time any young woman ever asked me to sit next to her. Any juxtaposition beside a female that wasn't family up until that point, had occurred through assigned seating at St. Maggie's or just by chance, as in filling the only open seat on a bus or in a movie theater.

During these gradual initial social interactions among the sexes in grade school, like the one I was headed for, boys and girls tended to travel in packs along with their own gender. While they may have arrived by design at a common location to meet with the opposite sex, they still tended to operate as two distinct organisms engaging across a common boundary. The alphas in each gender's group tended to do all the arranging for these interactions and remained the conduits for most communication between the two groups.

The two alphas in our fourth-grade class were Nina Calvani and Robbie Maclaren. Strangely enough, they were recent imports from other parishes, he from the Fordham Road area off the Grand Concourse and she from the northeast Italian section over by Allerton Avenue. They both stepped into their respective roles riding the momentum of their transfers into St. Maggie's, interrupting the slower natural evolution of social pecking orders developing among our classes from first grade. They were the latest flavor of the month. The shiny new pennies. It didn't hurt that they were both innately attractive since birth and didn't have to evolve into something more appealing as they got older. Given that none of the original parishioners wanted the job just yet, we were all happy to ride the alphas' coattails and see where it got us. All the heavy lifting was done, the rest of us just had to show up.

"Come on Jimmy, don't be shy."

The girl's voice sounded so familiar. I racked my brain to place it but came up empty. But the sensation the voice caused felt familiar as well and I moved behind the closest tree to adjust my jeans for comfort. When I stepped back into the path, the girl was now standing right there beside me, and I felt my face flushing from her close proximity. I had not seen her move.

"My name here is Eleni," she said, matter-of-factly, and then looked me over like she was checking for something. Her eyes finally returned to my face and squinted half closed, locking onto mine. And then she smiled, and my knees weakened. I thought I was going to pass out.

She took my hand and led me back to the log. I could not have resisted her if I wanted to.

"Sit," she said, pointing towards the log. "I want to talk to you."

I did as instructed but didn't want to let go of her hand. My heart was racing, and the flush still hadn't left my face. I stared down at the fire hoping its heat would mask the redness in my cheeks.

"Jimmy," she said softly, adding her second hand to the one I was holding. "Look at me."

I turned to face her and gazed into eyes so black I could not distinguish the irises from their pupils. I felt like I was being drawn into their darkness and then everything started to spin.

The next moment I was in a fugue state, sitting by a pond on the lush grass. I was back in my older body, dressed in a diaphanous tunic. It all felt so familiar, and yet I remained disoriented, like in an uncontrollable dream. Someone beside me was holding my hand.

"Jimmy," it was that girl's voice again. When I turned towards it, she was no longer a young girl but a woman. She shared the physical traits of the young girl but raised them to their adult physical perfection. I must have looked startled, I certainly felt it.

"You're safe," the woman cooed, gently caressing my face with one of her hands while still holding my hand with the other. "I'm Erato." She studied my face for some recognition. "You don't remember, do you?"

There was that déjà vu feeling again, something in my memory, just out of reach. I shook my head in frustration.

"Relax," her sensuous voice counselled. "You're all right. I just wanted to check on you."

"What is this place?" I asked, again surprised at the deepened timber of my voice. "How did I get here?" Despite what I looked like physically, my pre-teen human perspective could not process it.

"I will explain it all to you," she responded, "I promise. Later. When you are ready."

I could not take my eyes off this woman, and I did not know why. But I didn't care. I just wanted to be in her presence.

She then stood with the effortless grace of a ballerina, and gently lifted me by the hand she still clutched, to my feet. I never felt such strength from a woman, and I was raised in a house of strong women. She gently started to lead me towards the pond. I would have followed her anywhere.

"You need to go back now," she said, a hint of sadness in her voice.

"Why?" I asked, my own voice breaking on that one word.

"Because you have a life to live and a lot to learn." She stopped when we came to the edge of the pond.

"Can you come back with me?" I whispered, taking her free hand with my own.

"No," she said, removing both of her hands from mine, her own discomfort starting to show. "But I will come visit you from time to time, as Eleni. You will remember her."

I could feel tears forming on my eyelids, and one brimmed over and trickled down my cheek. She reached up and wiped it gently with her fingertips.

"I wish I could prevent all of the tears you will cry," she whispered. "I will let you remember one thing from here," she added, leaning into my chest – her firm breasts pressing against me - I could feel the warmth of her breath on my earlobe. "Nothing that comes easy for you will last."

She pulled back just enough so that her face was so close to my own that her chin was brushing against my adult form beard.

"Let this imprint of my gift help you to know true love when you find it, because, in the end, that is the only thing that can save you."

With that, she leaned forward and kissed my lips so gently, it felt like the fluttering of a butterfly's wings, and I could smell lavender on her breath.

As I tried to inhale it, I was back in the water, and then darkness.

CHAPTER SIXTEEN (SMOKES AND SUDS)

"Jimmy. . . .Jimmy, wake up."

Someone had grasped my shoulders and was shaking me. As my eyes slowly opened, the fuzzy face of Robbie Maclaren started to come into focus. It really wasn't fair to the rest of us boys that we had to compete with this newcomer. His whole family was good looking. Both his parents looked like they descended from the Celtic Brahman in Hyannis Port. His younger sister, Fiona, had all the earmarks of the future beauty she became, and for a long while she dated The Ginger. Robbie's youngest brother, Trevor, bucked the Celtic genes with platinum blond hair, and was better to have around than a puppy if you wanted to attract the cute girls. And what really sucked was that the entire family was nice, so you couldn't even hate them for their genetic privilege.

I sat up with a start and tried to get my bearings. I was next to the log I had been sitting on and once I realized that I had been laying on the same spot as the small campfire, I rolled hard and started to crawl away.

"Are you okay?" Robbie asked.

After I got far enough away, I looked back at the spot I just vacated but there was no sign of a fire.

There was no sign of Eleni either.

"Where's that girl?" I stammered.

"What girl?"

"The pretty girl. . . Eleni. . . She was just here with me."

Robbie stared at me like I was crazy.

"Are you on drugs?" he asked, extending his hand.

Despite the fact that no one in my class had actually taken drugs, yet, this was the sixties and there were plenty of mind-altering chemicals available in the neighborhood, should we feel the inclination. Some of the crazier St. Maggie's boys a few years ahead of us – like Demo and Woody - had dabbled, with some unexpected results, so that question became the go to line when any of us acted a little weird.

"No," I said, grasping his hand and letting him lift me to my feet. The movement triggered the edge of a memory, but it was gone in a moment.

"So why were you out cold on the ground?"

I didn't respond, but kept looking around, expecting Eleni to pop out from behind some tree. I toed the earth where the camp fire had been burning with the end of my sneaker. There was no warmth coming from the ground. Nor were there any of the stones that had surrounded Eleni's campfire.

"C'mon," Robbie said, dusting off my sweater. "Everyone's up at the fort. Joe sent me down to stop by your house and see if you were coming."

That made a lot of sense because, after Bozzy MacDootz's near brush with death a few years earlier at the end of my grandfather's garden shears, Joe Marrero was terrified of Spaghetti and would not set foot on our property unless my parents were in plain sight. Robbie hadn't caught up on the neighborhood gossip just yet.

Robbie looked down towards the spot I was staring at and then back at me. "You sure you're okay?"

"Yeah, sure," I responded. "I must be more tired than I thought. Weekend chores. Sat down on the log for a second and nodded off. Dreamed about some girl."

"Good," he said, as convinced as he needed to be and suddenly excited by more pressing news. "Come on, let's get up there. Matty stole a case of beer from his dad's stock in the basement. It's warm but beggars can't be choosers."

Now I may be of Irish descent, but I never had a beer in my ten years on earth. However, if I was willing to have my first cigarette, I might as well go to hell in a handbasket with my first beer as well.

As we approached the plateau, I could hear young voices, some louder than others, as well as the sound of Matty's portable radio tuned to Cousin Brucie on

77 WABC. *Sugar Pie Honeybunch* by the Four Tops was playing. I also heard some female voices, some of them singing along. Things were looking up.

As we entered the clearing I could see about a dozen of my classmates milling around a flat area beneath which Matty's fort was located. It was strategically set among large boulders around its circumference, which helped conceal its entrance. A number of my classmates were sitting on the boulders in groups by gender, chatting, laughing, and doing their early interpretation of flirting, which appeared to be one of the boys shouting something obnoxious to tease one of girls, and draw a laugh from the crowd, which lead the girl to chase the boy around the area, while the rest of the group egged both on. The trick for both kids was not to allow the boy to be caught, because neither one really knew how to close the deal, except through maybe a friendly hair pull and some blushing.

* * * * *

It's a wonder humans procreate at all. Claire interjected.

We managed. I responded.

Stella and Apollo both laughed. I couldn't help but feel uncomfortable making sexual references in front my children, even though they were both over four hundred years old and had long ago paired off with mates and successfully sired their own family lines that extended for many generations. I guess you never lose the Irish repression. But if I was going to tell the whole story, I couldn't escape the sex.

But let's not get ahead of ourselves.

* * * * *

The fort's trap door was open with its cover stump tilted over on its side. The stump looked like a flat-topped Octopus, with its roots reaching beyond the four edges of the hidden door underneath. Some of those roots had been blunted on the side where the hinges were, so the door could be opened. Matty thought of everything.

Suddenly, Joe's head appeared like a meerkat from the fort's entrance. True to his word, there was a burning Newport hanging from his lips, its tip pulsing as he sucked in some smoke and released it through his nostrils. It was true, it did make him look older. It also made him look a bit devilish. He hoisted up a couple of kerosine lamps, stolen from a local road construction project, through the opening. Danny Mo, Matty's best friend, and soon to be St. Maggie's legend, took them from Joe, lit them with a Ronson lighter, and placed one on the closest boulders on either side of the opening. The timing was perfect, as dusk was now deepening into darkness.

Robbie was quickly absorbed into the group, slapping hands with each of the boys he passed and waving at the cluster of girls, some of whom were singing along to *I Got You Babe* by Sonny and Cher. I always wondered how the girls memorized all of the lyrics to the top hits on the radio, and then I learned that there was some weekly magazine that printed the lyrics for just that purpose.

I admired Robbie's confidence and watched as he walked right over to where Nina Calvani was holding court and slid up on the rock right beside her. None of the girls in my class had started wearing makeup, but Nina still stood out in her natural state.

At that moment, Joe lifted himself effortlessly out of the entrance, and winked at some of the girls, who all giggled nervously. This kid had Latin charm before it became a thing.

"Evening ladies!" he called out past his cigarette with a flourishing bow. "Glad you could make it."

By now, Danny Mo was cobbling together a camp fire by a nearby downed log. Some of the other boys were gathering kindling and some of the girls used this as an opportunity to commandeer seats on the log closest to the fire. I studied the line-up against the flickering light to see if any of them looked like Eleni.

Joe spotted me and waved me over.

"Matty," Joe called me through the fort's opening, "two beers." His voice seemed to deepen as he said it.

I couldn't help glancing around to make sure there were no adults in the area. Luckily, the only structures in Riverdale tall enough to spot our hilltop gathering were the three Skyview buildings to the west. At twenty-one stories each, at the time they were the tallest buildings in the Bronx. But those monoliths sat a quarter mile away on the high ridge overlooking the Hudson River. So, unless someone was peering through binoculars, there was no way they could identify the ant size creatures milling about in the woods this Saturday night.

Over time, I came to hate those buildings for a whole different reason.

Matty Burns appeared in the portal holding two bottles of Schaefer beer.

"Hey, Jimmy," he called out when he spotted me. "One of these for you? Joe looked at me. "Well?"

I hesitated. It felt like every set of eyes were now on me. So, I nodded, and Matty – who thought of everything - snapped the tops off both beers using the wall can-opener he had screwed into the underside of the entry door. Then he handed them up to Joe. Joe passed me one of the beers and then tapped the glass neck of his own against mine.

"*Slainté*, my Irish brother." Joe toasted with a pronunciation that would have made Spaghetti proud.

"No going back now," I said in response.

Turns out I was right.

CHAPTER SEVENTEEN
(IT'S NOT THE FROG, IT'S THE KISS)

Growing up is a lot harder than it looks.

Now there is nothing inherently appealing in a warm beer. Even cold beer is an acquired taste. But my peers were watching, and I was on the spot. I wasn't sure how much I should drink in one shot, so I just continued gulping until I saw Joe lower his bottle. I really should have eaten something.

"Did you bring your cigs?" Joe asked, removing his pack of Newport from his sweatshirt pocket, and tapping the heal of the pack on the palm of his hand. Like magic the filter of a single cigarette rose a quarter inch out of the opening at the top of the pack. He retrieved it with his lips without ever touching it with his fingers, which left them free to fish out his lighter from his pants pocket.

I was feeling the sudden rush of the effervescent alcohol and not at all sure I was enjoying it. Joe lit his cigarette and began projecting the coolest series of smoke rings in my direction. Now I had lived in a haze filled house of Marlboro and Prince Albert smoke but had never smelled the minty fragrance that came off the first of Joe's smoke rings that reached my face.

"What's that smell?"

"Menthol," Joe replied, expelling the rest of the smoke through his nose. "Keeps my breath smelling fresh for the ladies."

He glanced over at the cluster of girls on the closest boulder, but they seemed distracted by the sound of The Dave Clark Five's *Catch Us If You Can* coming from Matty's radio.

I placed my beer gently down on the ground by my feet and removed the now slightly crushed pack of Marlboro from my pocket. I realized that since it was the hard cardboard packaging with a fold over top, I wasn't going to be able to match Joe's coolness in the way I retrieved one. In fact, I fumbled with the thin pull tape on the covering cellophane for so long that Joe finished his cigarette and flicked its butt, end over end like a tiny sparkler, into the now surrounding darkness. He took the pack from my hands and smacked it hard between his palms which caused the cellophane to blow open at the top, which he then easily peeled off and handed me back the pack.

By the time I had retrieved one of the cigarettes from the box, Joe had his ignited lighter waiting before my face. It created a small bright circle around us, and I felt like an actor standing on stage in the spotlight. I clasped the butt of the cigarette between my teeth, the way I had seen my father do a thousand times, closed the seal around it with my lips, and started to pull in the smoke with my cheeks while its tip ignited in a bright red ball.

"Now inhale," Joe instructed with the tone of the most devoted athletic coach.

Joe had the benefit of older siblings that could teach him the ways of the world. My older sister was well on her way towards Irish Sainthood, until she fell from grace much later, and my older brother Eddie had not yet crossed any moral lines with the family. If I was going to be the family black sheep, I had to learn my lessons on the street.

I'd love to say that I looked every bit as cool as the Marlboro cowboy, but the truth was that the first inhalation of smoke burned my throat and forced me into a violent and uncontrollable coughing fit. I dropped the cigarette when I doubled over, just before the half bottle of warm Schaefer projected up from my stomach and out through my mouth and nose and all over Joe's new black Converse All Stars.

"Fucking Smokey, my sneaks!" Joe bellowed as he leapt back from the second salvo of smoke and suds that came barreling out of my mouth. My head was spinning, and I really needed to sit down.

After a few more dry heaves, my stomach stopped seizing. By then Joe had abandoned me and was wiping my vomit off his sneakers with a brown paper bag, while Matty poured a little RC Cola over the infected area. Matty was one of the first to fully appreciate the cleansing agent qualities of the colas we drank by the gallon each day. He swore that he had witnessed some spilled soda strip the paint off of the front panel of his oldest brother's car.

Robbie Maclaren was now by my side and guiding me back to the boulder he had been sharing with Nina. And they weren't alone. Chrissy Dosela was sitting next to Nina sipping from a can of Seven Up through a straw. Neither girl took their eyes off me. I was a walking mess.

"That was some performance." Nina announced as I arrived. I wanted the ground to open and swallow me as all of my friends within hearing distance joined her in laughter. Everyone except Chrissy, who just sat there, staring at me, sipping her soda. I was about to wipe my face full of tears, snot, and vomit on the sleeve of my sweater when Chrissy produced a purse-sized packet of Kleenex from her pocket.

"Here," she offered. Unlike Nina, there was no judgment in her voice.

"Thank you," I replied, taking the pack from her. I walked off into the darkness and did the best I could to clean myself up before returning a few minutes later and offering Chrissy her packet with the last wipe in it. She waved me off, "Keep it." I slipped it into my sweatshirt pocket, right next to the cursed Marlboros.

She now held out her Seven-Up can. "Here, you may want to rinse your mouth out."

While I was off performing a rigorous rinse and spit, as the bubbly sweet nectar washed the last of the smoke and vomit from my teeth, I heard the sound of a guitar playing. I looked over and spotted Joe sitting on the log by Danny Mo's campfire, strumming away as he worked himself into some pattern of a melody. I didn't recognize the music or the lyrics – that had to do with some poor bastard having no balls at all—and was pleasantly surprised by both Joe's playing and his singing voice, as he accompanied the chords he was strumming. He was a natural troubadour.

He then went into the chorus which had everyone around him laughing. But it soon faded into the background, as I was more interested in returning to the rock and Chrissy Dosela.

Robbie and Nina had left the boulder and joined the crew over by the camp fire. I could see in the shadows that Chrissy was now alone. I checked my breath with my cupped palm over my mouth and nose, and all I could smell was the refreshing soft drink. I walked back over and tried to look as confident as I could, given the circumstances, as I hoisted myself up on to a spot right next to her.

She seemed to be focused on Joe's song and the laughter accompanying it.

"That was some show you put on." She finally said without looking over at me.

I wanted to die.

"I've seen worse," she added. "My older brother spent a whole night bent over the toilet the first time he drank beer."

She turned to me and smiled. She had perfect, beautiful, white teeth.

I couldn't tell if it was the flicker of the glow from the distant campfire, but her skin appeared reddish, and her face was flawed only by a small half-moon crescent scar by the outside corner of her left eye. It was pleasant to look at.

"You're really quite nice," was all I could come up with.

Surprisingly, her smile intensified, and her brown eyes seemed to sparkle.

By now Joe's voice and playing was intensifying and I could tell he must be reaching the end of the song. Matty and Danny Mo were now accompanying him in horrific harmony.

What happened next will forever stand out in my memory. Chrissy leaned into me and gently pressed her lips against mine. I was thrilled with the softness of her full lips as I subtly tried to turn my head and move my nose out of the way of this pleasant experience. I don't know where the taste of Seven Up was coming from, and I didn't care. It really only lasted a second, but given the range of emotions it inspired, it felt much longer.

She pulled back, smiled again, hopped off the rock and was now standing before me.

"That was nicer than I expected," she offered. "Gotta go."

She turned and walked over to where Nina was sitting on the log next to Robbie. A moment later they were both heading out of the clearing and off in the direction of the exit to the woods. Chrissy turned back towards me and did a little finger wave.

And then, as if on cue, the guitar playing stopped while Joe bellowed one final line of the chorus, slow, solo and a cappella.

"Jimmy McCarthy has no balls at all!"

CHAPTER EIGHTEEN
(INDIAN SUMMER)

Over the next couple of years, I worked hard on expanding my new repertoire. I became pretty adept at smoking, drinking, and kissing. I never surpassed Joe in the first two events, but I broke all records when it came to the last.

I did not realize it while it was happening. I certainly did not understand it until hundreds of years later, as my human mind continued to evolve into its Centaurian form, when I started to recover my memories of Erato, that I never once had to initiate a first kiss, with one exception, the last one.

Despite our first kiss, and a few random others far enough apart to technically count as booster first kisses during the year that followed, Chrissy Dosela didn't become my first "steady" girlfriend until sometime in fifth grade. It seems that my relationship with Chrissy provided an initial pattern, a template, that consistently repeated itself as I got older. Despite my obvious averageness, girls were interested in me while in my presence, and all it took was oral discourse. It didn't happen all the time and with all girls. It did require a focused interest and intent on my part. So, it wasn't like random women or, worse, female members of my family were lining up to throw themselves at me just because I was reading a newspaper out loud.

But, if I was attracted to a girl, and managed to get a moment alone where I could engage them in a sustained conversation, about any topic whatsoever, that's usually all it took. They always made the first move. And the older I got, the easier it became. And once puberty hit, that chess game was played until there were no more pieces on the board.

But here's the other pattern that also developed right from those very first years. The girl's attraction to me was always as temporary as it was spontaneous. I was able to have relationships, where I interacted with that girl on a daily basis. However, if I was out of sight, I was out of mind. If more than a day passed without a direct physical contact, the relationship usually ended.

As I look back at it now, I understand why. Their attraction was never real. It was a conjuring. But in the moment, when it inevitably ended, always as abruptly as it started, it appeared to me to be repeated cases of buyer's remorse. And while I was a young kid, who didn't understand what was happening, that put a lot of scars on my heart, hardening it. After a while, I took it for granted that I would never find true love. So, as I grew older, I adapted, and made the best of as many good things as possible.

And on the rare chance I was able to sustain a relationship through daily physical contact, there was always a divine intervention. *Deus ex machina.*

But in fifth grade, I got to see Chrissy Dosela on a daily basis. She sat behind me, in the last desk in the first row, against the wall, in one of the two fifth grade classes in the old school building of St, Maggie's. After school, I always walked her to within a couple of blocks of her home, leaving that physical buffer to avoid running into Chrissy's crazy and extremely over protective older brother, Mickey. He had graduated St. Maggie's the year before, so I didn't have to worry about running into him on school grounds, but he remembered me from our shared time on the altar boys, and we never really hit it off back then. When he learned through the grapevine that Chrissy and I were an item, he literally threatened to take my scalp. And I believed him.

On weekends, I used to meet Chrissy in the early afternoons down by Vanny Park, or on Saturday night we would hang out with the rest of our crew up by Mush Park or Matty's fort. When she was selected for the school's Varsity Cheerleading Squad, I got to walk her home after the games. And I always got that kiss. That was more than enough. I mean we were just kids trying to figure it all out.

We had a great run, until the day that Sister Carter punched my lights out.

Our regular teacher, Mrs. Fitzpatrick, had a mild heart attack during the spring of fifth grade. As was the general rule, whenever one of her full-time teachers went down, the school principal, Sister Rosalind, would sub in one of the ancient nuns that haunted the convent at the top floor of St. Maggie's old school building. On this particular rotation, we got the oldest nun of all.

Sister Carter was shorter than even the shortest fifth grade boy, lucky if she broke five feet in height. She was as wide as she was tall. She wore the conical wimple as part of her all-black ensemble, but it didn't seem to help with her hearing. Neither did the hearing aids that rested on the desk most of the days. She really didn't need them, given that she was usually asleep at the desk within five minutes of the morning bell. And that was just fine with us

Most of the students didn't care if the substitute teacher actually taught us anything. Mrs. Fitzpatrick had already completed the year's curriculum by working the students to death, which is probably what drove her into cardiac arrest. I didn't care one way or the other, because I never studied anyway. I never understood at the time, but either my subconscious retained enough from just listening to a teacher for me to get a decent grade, or someone else was feeding me the answers from the ether. It never mattered where those answers came from, as long as they showed up when I needed them.

So, my class made the most of our sleeping policeman by whispering to each other and passing notes *via* folded airplanes across the room. Every once in a while a loud fart resounded from underneath the black tent in front of us which sent the class into hysterics and woke the old nun from her slumber. Her go to move was to grab something on her desk and hurl it blindly at the class and then immediately fall back to sleep. She almost took Phil McGrath's eye out with one of those set square triangular shaped rulers. She had some right arm. As I was soon to discover.

Some of the better-behaved kids sat in the front of the class and reviewed their text books or read novels to kill the time, while the more confident boys flirted with the prettier girls and the incorrigibles sat in the back and planned after school or weekend parties.

Joe Marrero and Matty Burns liked to tempt fate by meeting up by the last window at the back of the room and sharing a cigarette, while blowing the smoke discreetly out of the crack at the bottom of the window. Both boys could blow perfect smoke rings through that crack, much to the amusement of the rest of the class who watched the rings float out into the sunshine and then dissolve into the breeze. Given that the classroom faced a quiet Delafield Avenue, no one noticed the streams of smoke billowing out the second-floor window.

Matty was fearless because he knew he had immunity from prosecution. His mother was one of the most senior and well-respected lay teachers in St. Maggie's. He could get away with anything short of murder. Plus, given his regular epileptic fits during high mass, the nuns were always afraid that there was some religious influence and did not want to make him a martyr. Joe, on the other hand, would have been expelled in a heartbeat if the Administration could catch him doing anything wrong. And he did it anyway.

Nina Calvani sat in the last seat directly behind Robbie Maclaren, who was now her steady boyfriend. They were in the second row, right next to Chrissy and me. Robbie and I had become best friends over the past year, so we all spent a lot of time milling about the neighborhood afterschool as a foursome.

This one Friday afternoon in May of that year, while the black blob snored and farted up front, there came a loud knock on the classroom door. After repeating the knock multiple times for about thirty seconds, Matty Burn's older sister Katy opened the classroom door and walked confidently over to the sleeping nun and gently shook her awake.

Katy was even more fearless than Matty, as she was not only protected by her mother, but was smart and pretty, and the most popular girl in her class. All of Matty's friends had a not-so-secret crush on her. She was also the captain of the St. Maggie's Varsity Cheerleading Squad. In short, she was untouchable.

When the nun reached consciousness, Katy respectfully explained that she was there to notify the girls that there had been a change in the time for Cheerleading practice scheduled for that Sunday morning. The very excited Chrissy couldn't control herself and called over to Nina quite audibly, "That's us!" In fact, Chrissy shouted it so loud that the deaf old bat heard her.

The nun was incensed that any student in her class would have the audacity to call out like that and was immediately on her feet pointing that triangular ruler towards our general direction.

"Who dared call out?" The nun demanded with such anger that her false teeth literally flew out of her mouth and onto the desk. At that point the class erupted into laughter, which only further enraged the nun, as she slipped her choppers back into place.

"Who said that?" She again demanded, this time a little more carefully. When no one responded she pulled out her trusty Kelly Book and read down the class list until she came upon my name.

"Master McCarthy," she bellowed. "Come to the front of the room."

Now I did have a reputation with some of my teachers, so I wondered if there was some notation by my Kelly card that listed me as a "usual suspect," to be rounded up to answer for all crimes real and imagined. Another old nun did catch me kissing Elaine Staltare that one time behind the rectory, and they loved to gossip, but that came later. However, I did what I was programmed to do by five years of catholic school and slowly made my way to the front of the room. Dead man walking.

"Why were you calling out just now?" She demanded.

"I didn't, Sister."

"Don't be impertinent, young man."

"I'm not." I responded, defensively, not knowing what "impertinent" meant. "I'm not on the girls' varsity cheerleaders."

I never saw her right jab leave her rosary belt, but a moment later my head snapped back. My eyes instantly watered and my mouth filled with blood from my busted lips. She had caught me square in the teeth.

"Now go back to your seat."

I don't even think her knuckles were bruised.

It would have probably ended right there and then with the severe corporal punishment if I didn't spit the mouthful of blood onto the floor, and on the nun's black shoes, and if the words "Mother Fucker" didn't leap out of my mouth.

* * * * *

When I returned to class from my week-long suspension, during which I was "grounded" by my parents, complete lockdown with no phone privileges, my spot had been moved to the first seat in the middle row, directly in front of the desk of the false-tooth, flatulent, forty-wink, black silhouette. To add insult to the injury of being within that gaseous hypocenter for the remainder of the school year, the spell on my first girlfriend had been broken. This was evidenced by the handwritten note that Nina Calvani dropped on my desk as she made her way to the back of the room. It was written in Chrissy's perfect cursive penmanship and simply said. "I'm breaking up." Chrissy was sick that day. We never had a direct conversation again.

CHAPTER NINETEEN
(PUBERTY CALLS)

My human physical maturation started with a scare during the summer break before sixth grade. My nipples became hardened and sensitive. First the right and then the left. And they were sore. I thought I had cancer. Being Irish, of course I never said a word to my family. I just accepted my fate and waited for the worst. Given that these signs of bodily rebellion began on either side of my still broken heart, I considered it just one more insult to the injury of being jettisoned by my first girlfriend. I didn't really notice the rest of the changes that were occurring.

I wasn't the only one suffering the changes. Other members of both genders of my St. Maggie's class were beginning to mature, some faster than others. And once you expanded the gene pool to incorporate the rest of the kids in the neighborhood, there was even a broader variation.

Lara and Xavier Anzara were a sister and brother who lived with their divorced mother in Netherland Gardens, the oldest apartment complex in Riverdale. Someone once told me they were Basque, and that their last name meant "goose" in their father's native language. Xavier was my age, and Lara a year younger. Given that they both attended P.S. 81, the only regular neighborhood overlap I shared with them during the school year was playing against Xavier on the North Riverdale Baseball League each spring. After fourth grade, we all swam together on the local summer competitive team, now that our family finances could finally afford the annual group membership fees for the Riverdale Neighborhood House pool.

I was a self-taught, natural swimmer and despite a terrible form, could usually place in the top three of whatever age group I was assigned to. I was a utility player, who was always going to bring in some team points. The Anzaras, on the other hand, were purebred standouts from an early age. They mastered and dominated all four competitive strokes – freestyle, backstroke, butterfly, and breaststroke – blowing away all competition. They only took home the gold trophies. They were royalty on the RNH team.

Now the thing about swim teams is that the team suits were always the nylon and close-fitting Speedo brand, which gave the swimmer the competitive edge with less drag as their bodies passed through the water.

On pre-pubescent boys, these bathing suits were affectionately referred to as "penis pinchers." Post puberty they were called "banana hammocks." The boys in either group always made sure they went right for their closely hung towels the moment they exited the cold water so as not to be judged either way. I was on my way to banana status.

But the girls always matured faster than the boys.

Thank God the water was always cold.

There was an older set of siblings on the swim team named Bolton. Linda and Lisa were in seventh and eighth grade, respectively, at St. Maggie's. They were blond and beautiful, long before I really understood what beautiful meant. Watching them work out at practice made our own arduous training so much more bearable. The younger boys would gladly suffer the cooler evening hours of practice where the jacked-up chlorine caused auras in your vision when you gazed at the overhead night lights, and the water bleached your fingers white and wrinkly. A small price to pay for stolen moments of voyeuristic pleasure.

With this kind of competition, the younger girls never garnished much notice. But each summer's garden brought new blooms.

The summer after fifth grade was Lara's time to shine. She was always tall and athletic, with long muscular legs, a trim waist and powerful chest and shoulders. In prior years Lara always wore her dirty blond hair short, which gave her an androgynous look. After a summer of sun and chlorine bleaching, it was almost platinum, which popped against her deep end of summer tan.

Given that Xavier was her brother, none of us ever considered Lara a girl. She had "little sister" status, which psychologically rendered her off limits to any lustful thoughts.

Swim team try-outs were in early June, and they were only held for the new kids looking to make the team. Once on the squad, you were there as long as you could compete.

The actual team practices began in mid-June, usually weekdays around dusk, after the pool closed to the public at five p.m. In the Bronx, June evenings were still cool enough to sleep through without a fan, given that no one in the neighborhood had yet traded up to air conditioners in the 1960s.

That meant that all of the swim team members were cold from the moment we showed up pool side, after showering the day's sweat off our bodies, until the moment we again hit the showers to wash off the chlorine. This was especially true as we stood in line at the pool's edge waiting between our practice laps.

That first day of practice, most of us had been hanging out at the pool beforehand, sitting on the sundeck slathered in enough baby oil to guaranty skin cancer in our later years, and talking shit as boys of our age often did. We watched with a strange sense of entitlement, as some of our older friends who were the lifeguards made sure the regular mothers packed up their kids and exited the pool at closing time. It was like herding cats.

We counted heads as some of the other talented core members of the team started to arrive, including the returning high schoolers, like the Nugent brothers, Gene and Brendan Kearney, and Ross Goldberg. Xavier and Lara finally showed up, climbing the stairs to the sun deck together in lock step. They resembled fraternal twins, as she was as tall as he was, both now a few inches taller than me. But that day there was something about Lara that seemed different. All was revealed moments later when Lara removed the long towel from around her shoulders and grabbed her spot on a chase lounge beside me. Xavier's warning glare at the rest of us made it clear our eyes were to remain only on him.

I'm pretty certain I strained my peripheral vision that day, trying to sneak glances at Lara without turning my head notably in her direction. She suddenly had curves where she never had before. Surprisingly, the modifications in her body didn't impact her athletic performance in the slightest, as she still blew by anyone in the other lanes in the pool, including Xavier.

At this point late in that first practice, I was sitting on the large cement block in the middle lane of the pool, just having finished a hundred yards of free style.

Lara was performing the second of two laps of butterfly in the first lane. She moved like a porpoise undulating along the surface of the water as her powerful two-handed strokes and dolphin kicks propelled her effortlessly forward. When she flip-turned at the far end of the pool, her legs threw a wave of water over the ledge that reached the chairs on the lower deck and would have made Shamu proud. She covered the ten second closing sprint to the nine-foot end of the pool and disappeared below the surface about five feet away from the wall. A moment later she shot out of the water like a breaching orca, catching herself on the ledge with her hands and lifting her glistening form over the side with continuous momentum. Even if Xavier was standing right in front of me, with the wet end of a twisted towel poised to snap me right in the nuts, I could not have avoided staring as she shook the water off her arms, shoulders and legs and then trotted over to grab her towel from the nearby fence. Lara's little sister status evaporated in those moments like the last drops of water off my unusually warm body.

At the end of practice, when Xavier invited some of us to stop by his mom's apartment the next day for a few beers, I didn't hesitate to accept.

CHAPTER TWENTY
(MAKING MONEY)

I only had one real responsibility the summer after fifth grade. My father decided that my older brother and I should start to earn our own pocket money. He asked around the neighborhood and learned from like-minded fathers that the only kind of employment not yet banned by child labor laws for children of such tender years, was being paperboys.

If you are going to continuously block me from searching your mind for definitions for these colloquial human terms, father, you are going to have to take the time to explain what you mean, even if it has to be in English. Apollo interrupted. *Or you could just save yourself and us any more trouble and just download everything to us in seconds in binary.*

Apollo stop it. Stella commanded. *You know how Father likes to digress. Be patient for once in your life.*

Proceed, Jimmy. Claire responded. She raised her head from my lap and gazed knowingly into my eyes. *We got as much time as you need.*

Back in my youth, I continued, with a wink at Claire, *humans received their general information about events that happened outside of their direct experience through primitive means of radio transmission, television transmission and the slowest manner available, printed paper transmission. I won't waste your time reviewing the crude external technology that they used, suffice it to say that the first machine is comparable to me telepathically sending you thoughts — words alone - with no accompanying images. The second adds the images to those thoughts. Like I am doing now — with images of early radio and television receivers. Only the most exceptional humans back then had anything close to the telepathic abilities that*

Centaurians have relied on for millennia. Paper transmission was the slowest communication process of all, but it offered the most information available each day and could be consumed by the humans at their leisure.

"Good enough?" I asked, aurally. My children nodded, and Claire returned her head to my lap and nuzzled my hand as her signal for me to return to scratching her ears. "Let's continue."

Now the real hustlers among the neighborhood were the latest immigrants, a German family named Armstrong, who had recently moved into a large house in Riverdale with two other equally large families of cousins. They immediately sent their more industrious children out to snap up the highest paying paper-boy routes for the major New York papers like the *New York Post* and *Daily News* before any of the more established Riverdale families realized they could exploit their kids before they were old enough for working papers. Those routes paid more money each week because they were numerically superior and geographically concentrated as they covered the series of apartment buildings on the western edge of Riverdale that ran from 246th street to 263rd including the three tallest buildings in the Bronx, Skyview. Bobby Armstrong was the paperboy of record on all routes, and oversaw the family operation, but the entire Clan pitched in delivering those papers with the efficiency and strategy of an ant colony. Once the bundles of papers were delivered to the predesigned street corners by large trucks, the Armstrong Clan broke them down according to their subscribers by building. Each paper was then given their three-layer origami fold to decrease its size and enhance their aerodynamics and weight and placed into large sacks that were carried into each building along the route. They were then distributed from top floor to lobby by hurling them against the recipient's door with a loud thud, so the consumer knew that their paper had arrived. It is no wonder the entire Armstrong Clan went on to becomes captains of industry.

Given the McCarthys were the last to the paperboy dance, we were only able to snag a couple of the smaller routes for the regional newspaper called *The Herald Statesman*. Unfortunately, those routes were spread out along larger geographic areas of private houses among the many side streets. So, at the same time it took the Armstrong enterprise to deliver three hundred papers, I delivered 40 along the lower stretch of Fieldstone Road and Vales Avenue. If Bobby Armstrong hadn't been kind enough to teach me how to fold those papers tightly so I could hurl them from the street to the relevant porches, it would have taken me twice as long to finish each day.

I was very thankful for that Armstrong time-tip the day I was going to head up to Xavier and Lara's apartment for the beer party.

In our neighborhood the only places for kids to party, that looked too young to go to bars, were various outdoor wooded areas that were passed on from one age group to the next over the decades. Those places were strategically located to be as close to a source of alcohol as possible, so as to lessen the chances of getting spotted on the street with beer or booze during transport by nosey neighbors, or worse, the cops. Being picked up by the latter had far more serious repercussions, given that our crew used to stock our parties using the five-finger discount. We shoplifted.

Like anything else in Riverdale, this skill set was handed down from one age group to the next. The older kids knew that younger kids were more likely to receive just a store ban if they were caught shoplifting, while the older kids could end up waiting for their parents to retrieve them from the 50th precinct if they got caught, and if caught more than once, a JD card. Having a child adjudged a Juvenile Delinquent in the New York Court system had caused more than one Riverdale family to move out of the neighborhood out of embarrassment.

Matty Burns was the first in our group to realize that working for the older kids for the occasional cigarette or beer with the added bragging rights of sharing them with the older group was a complete rip-off and organized our crew to go into business for ourselves. We didn't realize it then, but Matty's dad was a major player in the NYPD and so, like with his mother in St. Maggie's, Matty's dad's position offered him immunity from the repercussions of his illegal acts. The good news was that if you were ever caught in one of Matty's illegal enterprises, his immunity also trickled down to you.

Matty's fort was based deep in the woods that sat behind a core stretch of stores that ran along Mosholu Avenue. So, those stores became our most available resource for all things party related.

Junior's Corner was a neighborhood malt shop on the corner of Fieldstone and Mosholu, run by two Israeli brothers, who we only knew as Nathan and Sol. Their thick Hebrew accents made Gaelic sound like it was articulated by Professor Henry Higgins. Those brothers were protected from our collective pilfering because a couple of the crew's members, Poofy and Ray-Ray Johnson, got to work off the books behind their counter after school and they allowed the Herald Statesman's paperboys to wait in their store for the daily delivery truck during winters and inclement weather. We loved to go into Junior's and order egg creams – seltzer, milk, and chocolate syrup - and listen to "Sergeant Nathan of the Israeli Border Patrol" tell us his stories of how he and his brother Sol, single handedly established the Jewish State in an otherwise hostile territory. They told us that they now had to work in the United States under assumed names because there was a bounty on their heads from every Arab state in the Middle East. I remember thinking I would never like to be in their position. Funny that.

I'll always remember one time when we were all sitting at the counter and Poofy came out of the bathroom towards the back of the store. Nathan looked over at Poofy and shouted with his heavy accent, "PPppeeeeddddaaaaa, you eat like a pig, and you sheet like a horse."

Nathan knew how to turn a phrase.

However, there was a grocery store one store up from Junior's that made the mistake of placing their individual packs of cigarettes in a rack in one of the aisles and stacking cases of their beer right inside the entranceway. And that worked out just fine for us.

Strategically, it was rather simple. One of the crew would go inside and buy a soda. A second member would walk into the back of the store and wait. Then Joe Marrero or someone who was as humanly fast as Joe would wait to the far side of the large front window and watch until the person buying the soda was at the one working counter. Once that person had engaged the girl behind the counter, Joe would pull open the door, grab the top case of beer from the stack and run down Mosholu, past Junior's and around the corner to where the rest of us would be waiting. We'd grab the four six packs from the cardboard case, race up the tree roots and then disappear into the woods. During the commotion that ensued, in which the responding, very fat manager did his best to run down Mosholu after Joe, the crew member waiting at the back of the store would walk into the appropriate aisle, snatch a few packs of cigarettes, stuff them under his shirt and calmly walk out the store and up Mosholu in the opposite direction from where Joe had run, thereby missing the manager, who was, at this point, standing at the foot of the woods cursing in some foreign language at the miscreants. Since everyone knew that the cops would never climb the tree roots to get up to the high entrance of the woods, the manager didn't even bother calling them.

This method worked about three separate times that summer until Moose Murphy decided to go rogue and pull a solo beer heist without any back up. As his name suggested, Moose was a big boy who was as strong as his namesake, but as slow as a turtle. On the day in question, some of us were up at Matty's fort when Danny Mo came flying into the clearing, shouting that Moose had been pinched right in front of Junior's Corner when he tried to make off with three cases of beer but could not outrun the fat foreign manager who finally bagged his thief. Danny was heading to the woods entrance when he spotted Moose being taken out of the grocery store by the cops in handcuffs. To give Moose his due, he never ratted on the rest of the crew, and after some tap dancing by his father, who was a lawyer, and accepting a life time ban from the store, Moose dodged what was certainly looking to be a JD card.

So, on the day of the Xavier and Lara beer party, after I finished my paper route, I stopped up at the fort and grabbed a six-pack of Rheingold, placed it in my canvas shoulder bag beneath one of the extra copies of that day's paper, and headed off in search of excitement to Netherland Gardens.

CHAPTER TWENTY-ONE
(MAKING OUT)

There was one more place in Riverdale where underage kids could party without any interference from nosey neighbors or the authorities – the homes of kids during extended periods where the adults were absent. Once we all started to hit our human teenage years, these opportunities flourished as parents were more willing to leave their kids alone for a night out, and sometimes even for an overnight given that they now had convinced themselves that they had raised their children to be responsible, law-abiding citizens. But while we were younger, the only time this opportunity presented itself was in the case of a single parent household, where the only adult had to go out and earn a living to keep a roof over their family's head.

Xavier and Lara came from just such a household.

When I arrived outside their apartment door at around two p.m., I could hear a Yankee game blasting from the television somewhere inside. Joey Pepitone had just hit a homerun and, according to the announcer, the Stadium was on their feet. It took a few buzzes on the doorbell before anyone responded. I heard the peephole disk slide open and closed and then the door flew open. It was Lara.

She was wearing tight lowcut bell bottoms and a cropped tie-dyed t-shirt which disclosed a very flat tanned stomach with a cute outie bellybutton. When I looked up to her face I may have hesitated a moment too long where the newly acquired attributes that had so readily caught my eye the day before at swim practice were now lifting the front of her t-shirt a few inches off her stomach.

When my eyes finally made their way to her corresponding peepers, she winked, and I could feel the flush rise to my eyebrows.

"Xavier," she called out over her shoulder without breaking eye contact, "it's Jimmy McCarthy."

Her brother arrived at the door behind her and, pulling her aside, waved me through the doorway, taking a quick look around the hallway before closing the door behind me.

I removed the Rheingold six pack from my paperboy sack and handed it to him. He removed a can from the plastic ring, handed it back to me and carried the remainder over to the living room area where he distributed them to some of the other boys watching the game. Like most of the professional athletes in the sixties, most of the best swimmers on our swim team drank and smoked cigarettes, so there was a haze of smoke collecting over the couch in that area.

"Going to watch the game?" Lara asked.

I looked over at the guys and then back at Lara. The 66 Yankees were struggling in tenth place, so I looked back at Lara and shook my head.

"Good," she said, and took my arm. "I just got the Beatles compilation album – *Yesterday and Today* - and I'm dying to listen to it. I hear the British version of *Yesterday* is better than the U.S. version."

I followed Lara into her room and, at her direction, sat at the end of her bed while she lifted the album from its sleeve in a wooden milk crate that sat by her desk and gently placed it on the turntable of her portable record player.

Can you at least give us a visual to help us follow a little better? Apollo interjected impatiently.

I flashed a quick visual of my memory of the moment then blacked it out.

She's tall like Petrichor, Stella added.

You were supposed to be focusing on the record player. I responded. I had never gotten used to Stella referring to her mother by her first name. But when Stella explained that once the family had been reunited on Centauri, she found it difficult to call both Petrichor and Gina "mother," and since Petrichor didn't seem to mind, Stella just went with it.

Go on Jimmy, Claire said. *This is getting good.*

Now up until this point, my entire human experience with girls had been limited to the occasional one-off kisses shared from the standing position from my one-off girlfriend, Chrissy Dosela. And given that I never had to initiate those kisses, I wasn't sure how to do that now. Lara slid onto the bed next to me as the hissing from the album converted into songs, and I quickly chugged a few gulps of Rheingold for some Dutch courage. As "Nowhere Man" began to play we both turned to each other and said, "I like this song." As social norms demanded whenever the same words are simultaneously uttered by two people, she shouted "jinx" before I could, which meant that I was unable to speak unless released from the bond by calling out the names of five cigarette brands and whistling. Given my intentions, that was not going to work for me.

I sat through one more forgettable song before deciding to free myself.

"Marlboro, Lark, Kool, Kent, Raleigh." I shouted just as the beginning guitar chords of "Yesterday" came from the mono speakers on her desk.

As I puckered my lips to whistle, I turned towards Lara and was met lips to lips with her own pucker. Sensing my capitulation, she continued to push forward until we were both lying on her bed, her on top of me, without once breaking lip contact. But the icing on the cake was feeling those latest additions now pressed closely to my own chest. There was no hiding the fact in this clinch that my banana had ripened.

I'm not sure either of us took a breath for the next few songs, and I don't even remember the songs, but just as I heard the beginning of "We Can Work It Out" start to play, I then heard an interesting second verse that sounded quite off key, "What the fuck is going on here?"

Neither Lara nor I had noticed the bedroom door opening or her brother standing there. I'm not sure either of us would have noticed a bomb going off.

"What are you doing with my sister?" he shouted as we both sprang up to a sitting position.

Given that I thought our situation was self-explanatory, and that his question must be rhetorical, all I could do was shrug my shoulders.

"Xavi," Lara shouted, "get outta my room!"

"I'll get out of your room, as soon as Jimmy gets out of your room!" Xavier shouted back.

I had been raised to believe that discretion is truly the better part of valor, and I realized that I had indefensibly broken the "don't touch my little sister" bro code, so, I stood up to make my exit from the room. Of course, that then disclosed the lingering tell-tale sign of my obvious enjoyment to both siblings, drawing a smile from Lara and a grimace from Xavier. As I fled from the room, embarrassed as all hell, I heard Lara shout, "Call me," before I reached the apartment door.

The Yanks must have lost another one, because the television was off, and the rest of the guys were now all facing in my direction, grinning at me as I waved and then slammed the door behind me. Always leave them laughing.

Despite Xavier's best efforts, for the next three weeks Lara and I managed to continue our make-out sessions after every swim team practice, and otherwise sat with each other for parts of every day at the RNH pool the rest of the time. Who knows how that summer could have ended if I didn't have to take the mandatory two-week family vacation to Maine at the end of the first week of July?

That was the Maine trip where Spaghetti sealed his place in the McCarthy annals.

My parents went to the small town of Belgrade one Saturday to shop for the week. Posie and Bonnie went with them. Spaghetti was left to "mind the boys."

There were crab apple trees on this farm where we stayed, so we often would test our throwing arms by tossing them from the fields into the woods. At this point, The Ginger had sprouted a good six inches, so he was almost as tall as Eddie. Eddie and The Ginger's arms were the strongest given the leverage their length and size gave them. So, their throws always went deepest into the woods. Bored, the youngest, John, decided we should team up and have a crab apple fight just for the hell of it. Given that it was as good a reason as any, we all agreed. Out of fairness, Eddie teamed up with John and I teamed up with The Ginger.

John and I took to our respective trees and tossed the apples we pulled from their branches down to Eddie and The Ginger, who whipped them at the opponents as quickly as they caught them. It was pretty much a draw until The Ginger decided he would cut off the other team's supply chain and started pelting John who was vulnerable in his position half way up the tree. The Ginger, who went on to become an all-star pitcher and quarterback in High School, was deadly accurate, and knocked John off his perch, and he landed at the base of the tree with a thud. The Ginger then waited until Eddie ran out of ammunition and then raced towards him with an arm full of apples, their deadly thuds exploding off the back of his oldest brother. When The Ginger had closed to within feet of Eddie, my eldest brother ended the battle the way he went on to end so many more in his life.

Eddie spun around and hit The Ginger square on the left side of his jaw, sending the now unconscious brother spinning clockwise with his bloody mouth whipping a frothy crimson trail that landed across Eddie's face like a Jackson Pollack stroke on his canvas. It was pure genius. In that moment, I was more focused on the molar I saw fly out of The Ginger's mouth and disappear, after a few bounces, under a nearby shed.

Now Spaghetti had been sitting peacefully on the wooden stairs leading to the side of the farmhouse, a habit he developed sitting on the stoops of the 109th street tenements in Manhattan. He watched the melee unfold while firing his furnace of a pipe and petting his accomplice and confident, the border collie, Pepper. When he saw the knockout blow, he leapt to his feet and raced across the field, the billowing smoke adding to his image as a locomotive. When he reached Eddie, who was standing over The Ginger like Cassius Clay over Sonny Liston, Spaghetti spun my much taller brother around by his shoulder and struck him on his chin, knocking him right off his feet. While Eddie stayed conscious, a moment later he too spit one of his molars out of his mouth. Eye for an eye.

I didn't climb out of that tree until my parents returned from the store.

But that wasn't the worst event of my summer.

By the time I returned to Riverdale, Lara had moved on to Bobby Mazur, and my heart felt a little bit more broken.

CHAPTER TWENTY-TWO
(A RELIGIOUS EXPERIENCE)

Over the next few years, my body continued to process through human puberty, and I became even more attracted to the female form. That was probably explainable by the more accelerated development of the females around me. This wasn't as much fun as it sounds. I got taller, started adding muscle to my skinny human frame and my voice started to drop. I also sprouted hair where there never had been any, and I started to have very lucid dreams, which always ended as messy as they were exciting. I had to bribe my sister to teach me how to run the washer and dryer, and to keep her mouth shut.

The only one I confided this to was Robbie Maclaren, who had shared his own mixed experiences with his body and his girlfriends. As events would have it, our mutual inquisitiveness ultimately led to my last confession.

There was a small magazine shop down at the bottom of Mosholu Avenue, on the corner of Post Road, just a block off Broadway. One could find any magazine in print in this shop. Every hobby, indoor and outdoor, had its magazine propped on the high shelves along the seven rows that filled the shop's floor space. These shelves muted what little sunlight managed to filter through the years of grime that coated the shop's large glass windows.

The shop owner was sitting half-asleep behind his antique register, with its own side crank, right by the entranceway so he could spot the shoplifters. Way in the back of the store, at the end of the row, farthest from the owner, was a spot, where if you knew where to look, you could find girly magazines..

Robbie and I had heard rumors of this spot from BJ Delaney, a friend of my older brother, who served as the primary oracle of sex education among my group of friends. Rumor had it that he had reached third base with one of the older girls that lived down by Broadway, and while I wasn't sure what that meant beyond my own experience on a little league baseball diamond, I knew it was nothing to scoff at. Much of BJ's lessons, which all seemed focused on the internal trappings of a female, were lost on me, because all of my experience had been limited to mouth-to-mouth resuscitation, with the exception of an almost unintentional grind, and all of my body parts were external, which I fully appreciated whenever there was a grind.

But Robbie and I were definitely keen on getting a better look at the external features we were noticing on our female classmates, that, with the exception of summer swim wear, stayed well hidden beneath well positioned layers of clothing. Even in the summer, with all of the parents around, we really couldn't study the landscape, so we were left to our imaginations to fill in the blanks. We wanted to know what we would be working with should we be lucky enough to ever reach the promised land.

Our road map to the future was drawn for us during a Friday night group sleepover in our attic dormer bedrooms, where BJ, who was one of Eddie's guests for the evening, swore to us, "Lucky number seven boys. At the end of the aisle with the car magazines, they're stacked on a couple of wooden crates for all the world to see. But don't let old man Vinny catch you peeking at them."

First thing the next morning, Robbie and I pooled our money and headed down to Vinny's. We had it all planned out. We were going to go in there and place a couple of candy bars and sodas on the counter and then ask the proprietor where we could find the car magazines for a fictitious older brother.

It worked like a charm, as the old man didn't even look up as he called out "aisle seven."

We slowly ambled toward the aisle, stopping momentarily to look at a boating magazine to sell the ruse, and then, once out of sight in aisle seven, ran down to its far end. As I reached the sacred location, I almost mistook the Playboy for another car magazine, as the cover had a fully clothed brunette holding a chalkboard sign that said, "Grand Prix Racing The Ultimate Sport by Ken W. Purdy."

But Robbie was much more focused on our mission and flipped open the magazine to its pull-out centerfold page. There it was, as BJ promised, the beautiful blond Anne Randall, just as God had made her. Nice job, God.

Father, is this much detail necessary for this story? Stella interrupted.

You go right ahead, Dad, Apollo countered. *Feel free to show images if you'd like.*

Claire chuckled audibly. *You Centaurians are as bad as the humans.*

I promised you warts and all. I responded. *Now where was I?*

Anne Randall's boobs. Stella replied resignedly

Well, Robbie and I were so engaged by what we were looking at, we did not hear old man Vinny approach until he shouted out from directly behind us with a brogue that reminded me of Spaghetti's, "What are you two devils looking at that filth for?" He pushed passed us and returned the centerfold to its proper place beneath the Grand Prix cover, stopping only for a moment to make sure he had the crease just right. Then he turned to face us and waved his gnarly finger in our faces.

"I know both of your families," he sputtered, his spittle flying over us like a shower.

"I'll be sure to be stopping by the rectory tomorrow on my way to mass, to tell the Monsignor that you've been pleasuring yourselves while looking at naked women."

He pointed toward the front of the store. "Now get out of here, and don't let me see you again."

We were out the door before the spit on our hair had dried.

For the rest of the morning, we sat up by Matty's fort, wondering if Vinny would rat us out to the Monsignor. We had both been caught doing stupid things before, but this was new territory for us. For some strange reason, during this time of crisis, we reverted to our religious training, knowing that if this got back to our parents through Mother Church, we were certainly going to be martyred.

This now being Saturday afternoon, we knew that confessions would be running between one p.m. and three. I had been okay in the past with regularly confessing to the odd curse word and generalized impure thoughts, but I was resistant to sitting in that darkened booth sharing with the nasty old priest on the other side of the screen that I had my first good look at a woman's nipples earlier that morning. Robbie seemed convinced that our salvation was going to take an act of God, and that wouldn't happen if we didn't cleanse our souls.

We arrived at St. Maggie's church a little before three. The usual future seminarians and nuns were sitting in the pew outside the red-light confessional waiting to confess sins they were years away from ever committing. They all looked at Robbie and me like cult members at new recruits. We ignored them and took our place at the end of the pew. Robbie was first in line before me.

When Robbie finally entered the confessional, I sat there alone trying to think of a way to politely describe my mortal sin, wondering how much detail was needed for redemption. Since I was the last of the congregation in the church, the silence was calming. My concentration was broken by the sounds of a man's raised voice, and a moment later, Fr. Fontainebleau flew from the doorway of his center alcove in the confessional, moved over to the left side where Robbie had recently entered and threw open the curtain. He reached and grabbed Robbie by his collar and literally dragged him through the front side door of the church that led to the altar sacristy.

Knowing that there was nothing I could do for my friend, self-preservation kicked in and I hightailed it out of the church and ran all the way back to Matty's fort, where I then reported everything to the few of crew that had already collected there for the Saturday night festivities.

Matty had a strange smile on his face as he listened to the terror in my voice. When I finished, he pointed behind me, where Robbie now stood.

"What happened to you?" I stammered.

"The old bastard sat me down in the sacristy and lectured me for fifteen minutes about the evils of women, explaining in some convoluted way, that I did not follow, that the proper way to spell the word woman was F.I.S.H. He made me say 12 Our Father's and 12 Hail Mary's and ended it by kneeling beside me and accompanying me in an Act of Contrition."

"Do you think he'll tell anyone?" I asked.

"He can't," Matty said confidently. "First, because he has the holy vow of silence, and would go right to hell if he breathed a word of it."

Matty passed us two beers and waited for us to take our first sips.

"And second," Matty continued, "My mother thinks he's an old poof that was sent here after he got in trouble in another parish. He's not going to want to cause any trouble here. He'd probably get his ticket punched if anyone heard that he was alone with Robbie in the sacristy."

"Shit, that bastard kept putting his arm around my shoulder." Robbie complained.

"What about Vinny?" I asked. "He's going to go to the Monsignor."

"That old bastard hasn't stepped inside Church since they cancelled the Latin Mass." Matty said. "Don't worry, he's not going to make a special trip across Riverdale just to tell the Monsignor that you two were staring at the dirty magazines that he was selling to all the fathers of the parish."

And that afternoon I learned that whether it was a well sculpted nipple or a well-placed rumor, there was nothing more valuable than inside information.

CHAPTER TWENTY-THREE
(A GOOD DEFENSE)

My rising testosterone levels were also making me more aggressive. At first this manifested in more frequent fights and losses with my older brother over just about any slight, real, or imagined. Up until this point, I avoided any confrontation with him, given he was born with a propensity for joy during battle. It didn't help my cause that my older brother was ahead of my puberty curve, and his puberty had turned on his Viking genes, and he became a good five inches taller than me with a much bigger frame to build muscle around.

It was bad enough that I was forced to physically compete with my older brother, which was to be expected as part of the natural pecking order, but in no time at all my two younger siblings followed me through their puberty cycles, and that left me to be the runt of the litter.

The rule in the McCarthy house was to allow siblings to fight things out so long as the combatants remained conscious, and no bones or furniture were broken. Given that these fights often occurred while my father was off at work, and most of these battles took place around the house, it was left to Spaghetti to be the final arbiter in these situations. If one of us didn't surrender within a reasonable time, or the battle was getting too close to a vulnerable piece of furniture or other prized possession, he would intercede to break things up by grabbing the two by the scruff of the neck and hurling us in opposite directions. If the combatants tried to continue the altercation after he had interrupted it, he would end it with extreme prejudice by knocking the primary instigator right on his ass.

The one exception to this was New Year's Eve at the end of 1967. Spaghetti was working that particular doorman midnight shift so one of his younger co-workers could spend the night at home with his family. My parents were over at the St. Maggie's New Year's Eve bash with the rest of adult Catholic Riverdale. The boys were left in the care of Posie and my sister, and after a wonderful Posie dinner and sparkling apple juice, my two younger brothers finally retired for the night. Eddie and I went up to watch a movie in my parent's bedroom, because they had a portable television that wouldn't wake my brothers on the far side of the house.

We silently sat in our pajamas, eating some Jiffy pop, and drinking RC Cola while peacefully watching a John Wayne flick. Then we switched to WPIX, channel 11 to watch the Times Square activities. I am not sure what started that particular altercation, but as the aluminum ball began its descent down in Manhattan, a few loud "fuck yous" were exchanged. As we grappled to our feet on top of my parent's bed, I was doing everything I could to keep Eddie close enough to me where he could not land one of those right-handed haymakers that had blackened my eyes and flattened my nose in the past. Unfortunately, he already had twenty pounds of muscle on me, so the grappling wasn't advancing my cause. He grabbed my shoulders and went to toss me off the bed and as my body started to leave its feet I grabbed Eddie's shirt with both hands and hung on for dear life.

Eddie didn't realize his own strength but his tossing me off the bed was like tossing an anchor overboard with its chain wrapped around his neck. My momentum pulled Eddie right off the bed behind me, and our collective weight and force carried us the three feet towards and then through my parents splintering bedroom door.

The adrenaline masked the pain of the impact and we continued to grapple among the rubble on the floor of the hallway outside the bedroom as *Auld Lang Syne* played from the television. Eddie had managed to lock his hands around my throat, and I was desperately reaching for a scrap of wood to hit him with.

There is no way to fully describe the next feeling we were both subjected to. But excruciating pain flew through our interlocked bodies from the soles of our bare feet to the crowns of our heads, instantly causing our bodies to spasm like we had been electrocuted. The fight was over.

When I was able to bring my eyes back into focus, I looked up to see Posie standing above us. She was holding one of my brother's Rawling 26-inch wooden baseball bats that she had just laced across all four of our interlocked bare feet with a stroke that would have made Babe Ruth jealous. In that moment, I knew all of the family rumors about her role with the Irish freedom fighters were true.

Once she realized she had recovered our attention, she hissed, "Get this God damned mess cleared up before your parents get home."

She waved the bat over her head menacingly, before shaking in rage and shouting, "I'd finish you off, but I want to leave something for your grandfather to deal with when he finds out he'll have to replace this door." Then she flipped the bat onto her shoulder and disappeared down the stairs to her apartment.

"Happy New Year," she called behind her.

The one upside to always having to constantly punch above my weight class, is that it prepared me for altercations out in the street, because no one out there ever wanted to give me the beatings my siblings intended. So as my social group expanded and we continued to add alcohol and then other experiential enhancements to the hormonal tinderbox, fights inevitably ensued.

As it turned out, I was pretty good at it. I didn't get the obvious pleasure out of it that Eddie and The Ginger seem to draw and didn't have that explosive red line that my youngest brother could be pushed to. In fact, I hated confrontation. But I hated taking shit even more.

Defensively, I could take any punch and remain on my feet, so I was willing to sacrifice my face to get close enough to do my own damage. If you were close to my size, I let my counterpunching resolve the conflict. From fighting my siblings, I instinctively knew how to close distance on my larger opponents to lessen any size advantage and work their bodies before their chins. I didn't win them all, but the neighborhood learned that like a badger, I didn't back down or give in, and the damage I inflicted on my aggressors was not worth the battle. I was going to survive at all costs. So, most people left me alone.

On another front, given my increasing hormonal incitement, and my correlative fascination with the female form, I also continued to pursue the pleasure I felt through intimate, though innocent, contact. As I look back at those times, I realize I was searching for the same intimacy I had experienced with Erato, which, while blocked from my mental memory, still remained embedded in my heart, my emotions. I felt the desire to be wanted, to be connected to someone. But given my limited experience, which continued to follow the same pattern of easily invoked initial passion that always ended after the briefest of temporal interruptions, I came to accept my lot in life. Once out of sight, I was out of mind. I adapted accordingly.

I decided that while I may get my head bashed in by another boy, I was never going to let another girl hurt me.

CHAPTER TWENTY-FOUR
(GOT YOUR BACK)

Robbie Maclaren's family lived on the top floor in the oldest, most beautiful apartment complex in our section of North Riverdale. It was the first in the area to go co-op. So, they had purchased two adjoining apartments and knocked down a wall to make it a five-bedroom sprawl with two kitchens, living rooms and three bathrooms. It had views of Riverdale proper to the east and the Hudson River to the west.

Robbie's parents were both professionals. His dad was a lawyer, his mom was a teacher. Both had come from humble roots in the South Bronx and had worked their asses off to advance in the world. The dad, Robert Sr., served in the Navy and then went to City College and law school on the GI Bill, while his wife supported the family as a secretary. He then landed a one-in-a-million job in one of those mega law firms on Wall Street in Manhattan, and she went back and got her teaching degree.

Robbie's parents were also the perfect couple. Childhood sweethearts, youthful and gorgeous under any definition of the term. They looked like they belonged playing touch football in Hyannis port.

Their three children were equally genetically blessed by the combination of the best features of two perfect parents. Each had vampire good looks. Robbie's younger sister, Fiona, skipped cute and went right to beautiful, but had a good head on her shoulders, despite dating The Ginger from eighth grade through high school. Robbie's youngest sibling, Trevor, looked like Robbie with platinum hair, and was the perfect little brother to every one of Robbie's friends.

There were no airs about the family. The dad knew what he wanted and used all of his skills to get there, but he never lost his Bronx roots or his common touch. Despite his demanding professional schedule, he did all the things the other dads did. He coached baseball and football, took Robbie and his friends on camping trips, and in the early years, spent summer weekends with his family at the RNH pool, where he and his wife, Briana, used to make all of the other parents jealous by monopolizing the tennis courts.

As the family's fortunes continued to rise, Robbie's dad started renting summer houses out in the Hamptons in Long Island, to more readily engage with the financial class of New Yorkers that needed his expensive level of legal acumen. He bought a boat and became a salt water enthusiast, spending his entire weekends with his family on the water fishing and water skiing and scuba diving. In no time at all the parents were the top of the list of invitees to every Long Island social event of the summer.

At the end of the summer following seventh grade, Robbie's parents invited me to spend a few weeks with them in their West Hampton summer house. It was magical.

They treated me like one of their own. I got my own bedroom and received everything their kids got, including a set of top-quality snorkel gear. I got to order whatever I wanted when the family dined out and ate the haute cuisine Robbie's mother could effortlessly whip up in the house. Robbie's dad taught me how to drive his boat and didn't flinch when I almost ran over Trevor and Fiona when I circled too closely to scoop them up after an afternoon of water skiing. He just gently adjusted the steering wheel and calmly talked me through it. He actually got into the water to teach me to water ski, while Robbie manned the wheel. One night he took Robbie and me out night fishing for blue fish and snappers. I felt like Tom Canty in Mark Twain's Prince and the Pauper.

But it wasn't my exposure to the trappings of wealth that mattered most to me that summer. I got a first-hand lesson in what it meant to be able to wield true power to protect the underdog.

One night, the kids were all allowed to walk into town and attend the summer carnival. One of the Maclaren parents' friends from their old neighborhood were also out that weekend, with their children, including a daughter named Jillian, who was about my age. She was cute and on her way to being much cuter. They were child hood friends from back in their Fordham Road days, so Robbie took her along with us.

The carnival was as good as any I had seen every summer in Yonkers Raceway, with all of the usual rides and galleries, although the patrons were better dressed. It even had a freak show. But my favorite booth was the one with the air powered machine guns, where you had to shoot at a small square of hanging paper with a red star in its center. The goal was to obliterate the red square with the hundred worn and rusty bb pellets front loaded through a long metal tube into your machine gun. If you were successful, you got one of the big prizes. Nobody ever won.

I had spent the last five summers at Yonkers Raceway trying to master that gallery. It was the closest thing I had come upon to shooting real guns and there was something cathartic in firing rapid rounds at something with the intent to destroy it. The thing was that if you shot just at the center and tore away at the star from the inside out, you just shredded the star whose red remnants clung stubbornly to the white around it. After spending about half of the twenty dollars Mrs. Maclaren had slipped me when we were leaving on following my natural instincts, and losing repeatedly at fifty cents a try, I took my stack of losing star sheets and studied them.

I then came up with the idea that if I shot in a continuous circle around the red star, I would minimize the shredding and stood a better chance with a final barrage to knock out the circle in one piece, given that there was a continuous perimeter perforation that could give way before the unperforated center.

It took another ten tries before I figured out that by firing in five bb bursts, I could place and control the circle pattern I was building around the star. My theory was working, the center star was staying intact within the circle, but I just couldn't get the circle to pop out before I ran out of bbs.

By now Robbie, Jillian and the others had returned to cheer me on, which drew the attention of some of the other contestants and the worry of the carny working that booth, an old fucker who wore a bowler hat and had a gold front tooth.

Each time I reloaded, Robbie would start to chant "Jim-mee, Jim-mee, Jim-mee."

Each time I lost there was a groan of disappointment from the others.

"Why don't you quit for the night Champ?" The carney barked. "I'm beginning to feel bad taking all your money."

Had it been my money I probably would have quit after five tries. But that night I was sponsored, I was playing with the house's money. Plus, I hated to be called Champ ever since Monsignor Fitzmorris cast me out of heaven. I was all in.

I was down to my last dollar. Two more tries.

Each time I carved the circle with my bbs, and each time the circle held.

My last go round I thought I had it, the circle dropped from the center, and everyone was cheering, but when the carny drew the string forward, the circle clung to the back of the white square, and the carny proudly held the square flat horizontally so everyone could see it hanging there, fluttering in the softest of saltwater breezes. I wanted to knock his gold tooth down his throat.

I was beat, and humbled, and about to call it a night, when Jillian stepped forward and placed her last two quarters on the counter.

"Fuck this asshole!" she said in perfect Bronxese.

I slid the coins towards the carney. "You heard what the lady said."

"It's your money kid." He snorted as he slid the coins into his apron and loaded another tube into the machine gun.

This time I started from the six o'clock position and worked my way clockwise up to midnight, then I switched and shot counterclockwise from six to just north of one. The circle was free and hanging by the tiny bit of paper between midnight and one. The circle started to flutter with the strengthening breeze coming off the Long Island Sound. When it flipped up and out of the hole, I couldn't find my mark. I knew from counting the bursts, I had used about eighty bbs, but I was getting tired, and I could feel my hands starting to tremble just a little.

I watched the circle appear and disappear as the breeze worked its magic and after a few moments a pattern and timing developed. The circle disappeared and reappeared on one Mississippi counts. There-Mississippi, gone-Mississippi, there-Mississippi, gone-Mississippi, there-Mississippi, gone- fire!

As the circle reappeared, the last twenty bbs slammed into the final shred of paper holding it in place, sending the circle fluttering loose into the breeze and out over the counter.

The crowd went nuts. Jillian grabbed and hugged me, and we both hopped up and down with excitement. There was clearly more to her than met the eye. Trevor and Fiona started pointing toward the giant-sized pandas, dogs, and zebras along the top prize shelf in the back of the booth. Robbie called for the carney to retrieve the paper from its clasp, but before he did the old prick removed the magnifying glass from his apron.

He walked over to where I was standing and said, "Sorry kid, you left some red on the paper."

Robbie grabbed the paper from the carney and studied it. "No fucking way!" He shouted at the man. "Show me. Where?"

The carney confidently snatched the paper out of Robbie's hand and held his greasy old magnifying glass over the hole in the paper. "Right there," he announced under the dim light of the booth, "twelve o'clock, the point of the star, right at the top."

By now another family with an older granny in tow had stopped to see what the commotion was all about.

"What's going on here?" the feisty granny asked Jillian.

"This man is trying to rip us off." Jillian shouted so everyone within fifty feet could hear her.

"How?" demanded the granny, now very much interested.

Jillian snatched the paper out of the carney's hands and showed it to the woman.

"Do you see any red on that circle?" she asked her.

"No," replied Granny. "Why are you trying to swindle these children?"

"No one's swindling anyone!" the carney shouted indignantly. "You can see it through the magnifying glass."

"Hey, watch yourself, buddy," Granny's son responded. "That's my mother you're hollering at."

By now a larger crowd had formed, so the carney decided to cut his losses.

"Tell ya what I'm gonna do young man," he said to me, and the crowd, magnanimously. "Since you've been such a good sport, I'll let you pick something from the bottom prize shelf."

He displayed his hands in an arc behind him like he was the MC at a beauty pageant.

The crowd seemed appeased that small justice was some justice and started to move on.

I felt beaten again. I looked at the line of six-inch animals on the lowest shelf that couldn't have landed a sympathy spot on the island of lost toys. I turned to Jillian. "Your bet, your prize."

I could see the disappointment in her eyes. I felt like I let her down.

She finally chose a fluffy pink duck, and we all began to head towards the exit. I could feel the carney's eyes on me until we turned the corner.

The walk home didn't do anything to raise our spirits, and when we came through the door, Mrs. Maclaren met us with her warmest "How was the carnival?"

"The man at the machine gun booth ripped off Jimmy," Trevor announced.

"What?" came Mr. Maclaren's cry from the kitchen, in a tone that made me feel like I did something wrong. "Who ripped off Jimmy?"

"The old bastard at the booth," Robbie responded.

"Language, Robbie!" Mrs. Maclaren whispered.

Robbie's dad appeared looking pretty steamed. "What old bastard?" He looked over at me. "Tell me what happened, Jimmy."

I recounted the entire scene right up to the magnifying glass and showed him the crumpled red star card, which I retrieved from my pocket. He studied it carefully while I finished my story.

When I was done, Robbie's dad turned to Jillian and held out his hand for her stuffed pink duck. "Give that here," he said. She complied.

"I'll be right back," he said to his wife. "Jimmy, come with me."

We drove back to the carnival in his beautiful new Beemer. For the first few minutes of the ride, he was quiet. When we stopped at a red light about a block away from our destination, he turned to me and said, "Jimmy, never let the assholes in the world win."

I almost giggled when he said "assholes."

"I'm serious," he said, fighting back his own smile in response to my own. "The system is set up to screw the little guy—kids, poor, women, minorities."

A moment later, we pulled into a space on the road right outside the carnival entrance. Most of the crowds had cleared out as it was close to closing time.

"You must always stand up for yourself." He said, as he grabbed the pink duck from the seat behind him, "and for anyone else you care about."

I thought about that last bit for a moment and smiled when I realized that I fell within his circle of protection. I was used to my blood family stepping up in a physical sense, they knew the art of physical intimidation. But what I was about to witness was a completely different form of coercion.

The carney spotted me about twenty feet from his booth, and he immediately began to batten the hatches, as if he sensed the storm that was coming. He got one side of the hinged plywood down and locked just as we reached the remaining open side. He turned his back in the far corner and pretended like he was busy counting money from his apron.

"Excuse me," Robbie's dad said, calmly but firmly.

The carney ignored him.

"Excuse me, sir." He repeated.

Again, the carney ignored him.

"Hey asshole!" Robbie's dad said in the same tone I heard come from the kitchen ten minutes before.

That seemed to do the trick, as the carney looked over, like he just realized we were there.

"What can I do you for?" The carney said in his nicest tone. There was that gold tooth again.

"Remember this young man?" Robbie's dad placed his hand on my shoulder.

The carney removed his bowler and scratched his head while he stared at me and feigned like he was trying to recall my face. Shook his head, no.

"I see a lot of kids come through here each day," he responded. "Hard to keep them all in my head."

"Well, that's no surprise," Robbie's dad said. "Given the head."

"Maybe this will help your recollection?" He held up the wrinkled card and sad looking pink duck.

The carney now feigned a look of recognition, shaking his head, affirmatively. "That's right" he said as he pointed to me, "You're the kid who almost beat the star."

He turned to Robbie's dad and reached for the paper while he also reached for his magnifying glass in his apron, "But as you'll see here mister, there's a tiny tip of red –"

"—You can shove that magnifying glass right up your ass!" Robbie's dad responded, withdrawing his hand bearing the paper out of the older man's reach.

"Tomorrow morning, I'm having coffee with the Suffolk County commissioner." Robbie's dad continued. "We were in the same law school class."

Robbie's dad, turned to me, pointed to the carney, and shouted quite loudly, "Look Jimmy, a rat!"

He turned back to the carney. "By tomorrow afternoon, I'll make sure this entire carnival is shut down for health and safety inspections and will be sure to let the carnival owner know who he can thank for that."

Robbie's dad then held out the piece of paper and said, "You want to take another look?"

The carney waved him off, as beaten as I was a half hour before.

"Which one of those prizes on the top shelf would you like?" He grumbled.

Ten minutes later I proudly handed Jillian the Giant Panda.

I never forgot the lesson Robbie's dad taught me that night.

I also never forgot the first French kiss I received from Jillian on the back deck later that evening. I never saw the Panda or Jillian again.

PART TWO
A PROMISING OUTLOOK

CHAPTER TWENTY-FIVE
(BEGINNING OVER)

In seventh grade my mother insisted that I take all the separate tests for the Jesuit preparatory high schools in the New York area, as well as the broader based co-op exam for the remaining catholic high schools. Given that I never gave testing much thought, beyond those strange voices in my head that always appeared in time just to help me cheat, I ended up getting into them all.

However, when the time came to select my school in eighth grade, my father, Spaghetti and Posie overruled my mother's attempt to raise the family's academic profile by insisting that I follow my older brother into Archbishop Spillane High School in the Bronx. As the Irish often said, "We don't want to get above ourselves."

That was just fine with me. To begin with, all of the prep schools to which I had gained admission, were all boys schools. Seems the Black Pope Jesuits were only interested in educating male soldiers of God. Given my constantly evolving predilection for the opposite sex, the idea of spending four years locked away from them was not the least bit appealing to me. Spillane, at the time not completely coed, at least had the girls school sharing the same huge building. Close was good enough when you were dealing with hand grenades and women.

Spillane was, at that time, one of the academically strongest Catholic schools in the Metropolitan area. Indeed, it was the incubator for future Catholic professionals, with numerous teachers, lawyers, doctors, accountants, monsignors and even a future member of the United States Supreme Court among its student body. If you did not list it first among the four schools you wanted your co-op scores to be sent to, you probably didn't get in.

But Spillane's biggest selling point to the McCarthy side of the family was that my older brother had entered it the year before and was thriving there. No one had told the McCarthys that consistency was the hobgoblin of small minds. So, if Archbishop Spillane was good enough for Eddie, it was good enough for Jimmy.

And it would have been, had I given it a fair chance. Turns out it became my blessing and my curse.

On the very first day at my new school, in September 1970, I rode the converted "Special" New York City bus crammed with students from the western side of upper Manhattan and the Bronx. It ran from its collection center at a gas station in the St. John's Parish along Gun Hill Road to the east Bronx location of my latest bastion of education. My brother immediately abandoned me and assimilated into the crowd of complete strangers with his friends that counted a future priest turned lawyer and a future doctor. It also included his best friend, BJ Delaney, who ultimately became far more famous than any of the others. Indeed, BJ became mythic.

I stood as close to the back door of the bus as I could, knowing that was the quickest exit. In fact, I stood on the small stairway leading down to the doors, just to avoid the jostling. New Yorkers are hard wired for survival. That meant having an exit strategy from the moment you entered anything or anywhere, and included everything from relationships to buildings.

That lowered vantage point was quite a blessing, given that it put me at eye level of the chests of all of the older queens of the Spillane Special, a clique of the prettiest older girls from the St. John's Parish. Doreen McKenna was their leader, and the prettiest, with silken jet-black hair, a slightly upturned nose and porcelain white skin that had never suffered a pimple. The remainder of the bench seats were filled with her almost as pretty acolytes, each and every one of them out of my league. But it didn't stop me from looking at this assembly line of tightly uniformed tits and knees. It made the forty-five-minute trip to my new institutional home much more interesting, especially given that the old bus hit every one of the hundreds of potholes that littered those Bronx Streets. I almost got whiplash for my troubles, a small price to pay.

Once we all spilled out of the bus and in through the school's front doors, I worked my way to the edges of the flow of students coursing through the hallways and stopped at the first open space. There I dug my acceptance packet out of my school bag and located the listing of my homeroom class. Room 107.

Turns out, my home room was the Physical Science lab, where all the freshman who didn't test up into Biology, took their Introduction to Physical Science class. When I opened the door the first thing I saw was this black kid, whose name I later learned was Lonnie Jones, racing around one of the tall science tables, laughing hysterically, while being chased by a white kid who I had spotted earlier that morning on the Special Bus. The pursuer held the end of a long rubber tube whose one end was attached to the nozzle of an open gas jet on the lab table, and the other attached to a lit Bunsen burner in his hand.

"This man is crazy!" Lonnie shouted as he hid behind me, using my body as a shield. I kept my eyes focused on the flame from the burner, making sure it didn't get too close to my face.

"C'mon, get outta the way!" his pursuer shouted back, as the two danced around me trying to gain the advantage. "He dared me!"

"I was only kidding," Lonnie responded, before taking off down the left side of the classroom towards the back. "This boy is crazy!"

The pursuer was like a junk yard dog who realized he had run the length of his chain. The tubing popped off the nozzle and his burner went out. I walked over and shut off the hissing jet. Lonnie returned just long enough to grab his book bag off the seat by the lab table and retreat to another open seat in the back.

The pursuer went back and took his place at the other chair at that lab table and made himself busy checking a schedule of classes he had open on the first page of a notebook.

"Mind if I sit here?" I asked.

"Suit yourself." He said without looking over at me.

"My name's Jimmy. . . Jimmy McCarthy," I continued, as I pulled out my own schedule. I compared the two and saw we had the same classes, starting with Biology. The pursuer continued to ignore me. I glanced at the top of his schedule and spotted the name Charles A. Whittle, III.

"So, your name is Charles?"

"Don't call me Charles." He responded, still not looking up. "It's Chuck. Not Chas. Not Chucky, Not Charlie. Just Chuck."

"Well, Just Chuck. Nice to meet you." I said, extending my hand.

He finally looked over at me and studied me for a moment before extending his hand and briefly shaking my own.

"I saw you on the Special," I said, trying to continue the conversation.

"Fucking cattle car," he responded. "Sweated my ass off."

"You from St. John's?"

"Nah, St. Gabe's." He replied. "But I got a cousin who went there. Tough crowd."

St. Gabriel's Parish was a small affluent Catholic oasis in the middle of the predominantly Jewish "South Riverdale" that ran along the Hudson River from 242nd Street to Kapok Street. It ended at the point where the East River flowed into the Hudson. Manhattan lay across that quarter mile stretch of bridge over water directly to the south. Some of the crew used to go down to South Riverdale and try to hit on the Jewish girls that went to P.S. 24, but they never had much luck.

St. John's Parish was the next one east of St. Gabe's, and was made up of middle-class families that hadn't quite made the leap from apartment living to private houses.

St. John's also included the largest group of Public Housing Projects in the western Bronx, which made it far more ethnically diverse than either St. Gabe's or St. Maggie's. I had spotted a few very cute Latinas standing on the Special in front of Queen Doreen, so I guessed they were St. John's girls as well. The other west Bronx parishes that fed into the Spillane pipeline were Visitation, which sat wedged between St. Maggie's and St. John's. Then there were kids that rode the subway up to 225th Street from a couple of northern Manhattan parishes as far away as Washington Heights. One thing about New York City Catholic Schools, the nuns may have liked to torture their more unruly students, but they all beat a good education into the thickest of skulls whether you wanted it or not. I was living proof of that. So, no matter what your socio-economic status or what parish you hailed from, if you survived eight years of Catholic grammar school, you remained ahead of the academic curve.

"Have you done the tour?" He asked.

"No, but I have a map," I responded, lifting the diagram out of my packet of papers. My parents had bought my excuse to skip orientation because my older brother would look out for me. I knew all along that my brother would apply the same sink or swim mentality that defined every other aspect of

McCarthy philosophy. We swam in different directions the moment we hit the Spillane water.

Just Chuck looked over at my schedule and nodded. "My parents forced me to come for orientation. We have the same classes. Just follow me."

Over the next seven years, long after we left Spillane, I followed Just Chuck, or JC, as he came to be called, to hell and back and never once regretted it. And throughout those years, I never dared him to do anything I really didn't want him to do.

CHAPTER TWENTY-SIX
(RISE OF THE NONS)

Like any high school, Spillane was divided into cliques. As expected, you had the athletes and the cheerleaders sitting on top of the pecking order, then members of the student government, then participants in the theatre, AV, chess, and science clubs.

Turns out, JC and I were both competitive swimmers, so in a passing pique of school spirit, we joined the Spillane swim team. The only problem was that Spillane did not have a pool, so they rented time in the practice pool at a public high school in another part of the Bronx. The boys – there were no girls on that team as the girls' and boys' schools were still separate – had to make their way across the shadier sections of the Bronx on public transportation. We trained for a few hours each afternoon in an over chlorinated basement pool with a coach that spent an inordinate amount of time hanging around the locker room area. Then it was back onto the same public transportation to get home by dinner time.

Once the captain of the swim team, Benny Carbonara, strongly suggested that the team members had to shave their entire bodies and lessen water resistance in order to increase our swim times by hundredths of a second, JC and I were out. It had taken us way too long to gain the social respect our body hair provided just to throw it all away at the end of a razor. Indeed, by the time I entered high school, I had entered full blown puberty, and was already tired of having to shave every day to stay within the strict school regulations concerning facial hair. Given how many painful styptic pencils I went through on a regular basis just on my chin, I could not imagine using them on the more tender parts of my body.

JC and I quickly tired of all of the other regulations the school administration imposed upon us and decided we should use our time more beneficially by rebelling against those rules. Turns out, we were not alone. A lot of other students had fallen through the cracks in the high school social hierarchy and floated around in space like dark matter completing the universe. But they were really hard to identify in the shadows. Given their resistance to social conformity, they would not unite under one banner with any form of real structure. To paraphrase Groucho Marks, we wouldn't belong to any club that would have us.

JC did coin a title for this loosely formed alliance of underachievers – "Nons." We were the non-joiners, non-participants, and non-believers. There was something liberating in accepting our roles as outsiders, but it pretty much doomed my high school academic career from the very start. In the end I became a non-student.

One of the tell-tale signs of a Non was their refusal to conform to the school's grooming regulations. A boy's hair forelocks could not fall below the eyebrows, the sides could not touch the tops of his ears, and the back of the hair could not touch his collar. There was to be no facial hair, and the closely cropped side burns could not extend below the tragus, that little cartilage flap on the front of the ear directly outside the earhole.

The first thing JC and I did was grow our sideburns into muttonchops down to our jawline and allow the rest of our faces to sport a permanent five o'clock shadow. Over that first year we slowly grew our hair long, disguising it first with gel to keep it back away from our faces, close to our skulls and tucked down below our collars. Once it got long enough, we cut a thin back outer layer to collar length and then pulled back, folded, and tucked the illegal length of hair underneath the back flap with bobby pins.

During my final year at Spillane – I left involuntarily after three years - I took it to a whole new level, by sporting a short hair wig, but let's not get ahead of ourselves.

Surprisingly, despite her role as the perfect student and daughter, my sister Bonnie was an early sympathizer to my rebellion, and it was she who helped me perfect my duplicitous hairdo each morning before I left for school. Of course, I didn't realize at that time that Bonnie was keeping her own secrets.

It's always the quiet ones.

But being a Non was not just making a fashion statement. There were many other aspects of student life that had to be carefully considered and rejected.

For example, we decided early on that we were going to reject the rigorous class schedules that were imposed on us. So, each morning, instead of rolling off the Special Bus and proceeding right through the school entrance, JC and I would slip behind the bus while the crowd of students bottlenecked in front of the school, and then, use the bus as cover from the ever-watchful eyes of the administrators from their first-floor office windows that opened onto the front of the school. We would dart across the street, duck down and follow the row of parked cars down 229th Street until we reached Needham Avenue, and from there made our way to the Baychester Diner, to talk shit, drink coffee and smoke ciggies until we knew the first bell had sounded. Then we would return to School, go into the office, separately within a few minutes of each other, swear we had missed the Special bus and were compelled to take the sporadic public transportation to get across the Bronx, and be issued late passes. By the time we got ourselves situated in our lockers, we had missed half of first period. Given our classes were on a rotating schedule we could miss most of them by cutting first period every week.

It really didn't matter whether we attended all of our classes each day, because we were not going to pay attention anyway.

JC was incredibly bright. He liked to think deeply about matters that interested him. He was a voracious reader and always had a novel in his bookbag, which he would pull out and read whenever we traveled on public transportation together, in lieu of engaging in conversation. And he liked to read the classics. He had tested into the Riverdale private schools and, if his WASP of a father had gotten his way, he would have been enrolled in one of the big three Ivy league feeders located in the mansion-lined wealthy Fieldstone enclave of Riverdale.

However, JC's mother was a devout Catholic, who insisted, over her husband's strenuous resistance, that her only son would attend what she referred to as "the best Catholic High School in New York."

JC wasn't intuitive. There was nothing he could not comprehend; indeed, he could master any subject that he focused on, but he needed to study in order to absorb his lessons. He didn't have the ethereal life line that fed me information whenever I needed it. So, by the end of our first semester in Spillane, the chickens had come home to roost, and JC ranked at the very bottom of our freshman class.

He didn't stay there but he never forgot the honor.

CHAPTER TWENTY-SEVEN
(IDLE HANDS ARE THE DEVIL'S WORKSHOP)

The best thing about being a Non, was that for a short while after declaring our independence, at the end of school each day, I got to return home on the same Special bus that took me to school every morning, reuniting with those of our Riverdale crew who also opted out of their high school teams and clubs.

By this time, a Nicaraguan family had bought the local Mosholu deli from the old Irishman who owned it forever and they set about carving their slice of the American dream. Being an industrious family, the wife worked second and third jobs while the children pursued their education at St. Maggie's. That left the husband to run the deli alone during the late afternoon hours.

Since none of us could pronounce his real name properly, the father's name was shortened by the neighborhood to "Joe Bino." Joe was a short and stocky man with a permanent tan and thick black hair. He had a very youthful face with almost no facial hair. He was friendly to all of the kids in the neighborhood, and, as a result, no one shoplifted from his store. We weren't about to take money out of the mouths of such a nice and hard-working family. They were quickly adopted as Riverdalians.

That didn't mean we didn't take advantage of Joe Bino. You see, Joe's youth was spent working in the fields doing manual labor in his home country, so whatever education he was allowed was of limited duration and solely in Spanish. As a result, he relied on his wife and kids to help him sort out anything in this country that required him to read something in English.

Now at this time in our country, a store could not sell alcohol or cigarettes to a minor under the age of eighteen human years. The argument was that if someone was old enough to die fighting for their country, they were old enough to get drunk and have a final smoke before doing so.

It is a wonder how humans survived before AI was able to provide you with your daily needs and protect you from your stupidity. Apollo interjected.

It is a wonder how humans survived before the Great Galactic War finally sorted them out. Stella added.

Children, Claire responded turning to my offspring, *there is an ancient human proverb that I was always quite fond of – that which does not kill you, only makes you stronger. From my wise and eternal vantage point on both sides of the veil, that idea defines the human experience. So don't get caught up in the weeds here. Focus on the broad strokes of your father's story.*

Claire returned her head to my lap. *Continue Jimmy. Don't forget the ears.*

So, as I was saying, there were certain things that human kids could not legally purchase until they had reached the age of eighteen earth years. Alcohol and cigarettes were the two we were most interested in. To make sure kids could not get around the government's onerous laws, they required all shopkeepers to demand to see written proof whenever anyone tried to purchase those commodities.

Since I had more bodily hair growing from every part of my body than a lot of my friends, including on my face, I was often the one sent in to Joe Bino's to buy the beer and ciggies for the entire crew. The first time I did this Joe didn't even bat an eye given I looked older than most thirty-year-old Nicaraguans. But on my second trip to load up for a Friday night party up at Matty's fort, the size of the order must have spooked Joe Bino, so that when I tendered the stack of bills to pay for my haul, he looked across the counter and asked in his best Ricky Ricardo impersonation, "You have poof?"

"Poof?" I responded. "What's Poof?"

Joe Bino pointed to the brand-new sign on the wall behind the counter. "Under 18? It's the Law. We check ID."

Now I was quite certain that Joe Bino probably couldn't read that sign and that his wife told him what it said. However, given that I had been called on the issue, I had to do something. I went to my wallet and fished out the first card I spotted and flashed it towards Joe with as much authority as I could muster.

Joe Bino studied the document for a moment, in the same way I once stared at a wall full of hieroglyphics carved into Stonehenge. The symbols felt familiar, but I didn't have a clue what they meant. A moment later Joe Bino nodded and slid the large brown bag with my booty across the counter top. I slid my Library card back into my wallet and then exited the store.

By the time Joe Bino had learned to read enough English to make a difference, I had a copy of my older cousin Apple's draft card. It was close enough in physical description and old enough in age to put me across the finish line, until I got there on my own steam.

CHAPTER TWENTY-EIGHT
(GROWING ORGANICALLY)

High school was the first major evolutionary leap of the DNA pool of the Riverdale crew. By spring of our collective freshman year, everyone seemed to have brought in another crew member from their respective tours in high school. There was a certain symmetry to this process as the females also brought back new members. This system worked because the person who brought a newcomer into the crew from outside the neighborhood also vouched for them. There must be some theory in human physics to explain this, as the male to female count stayed relatively balanced. So, if a boy brought a new male member into the crew, one of the girls soon brought a female in to maintain the equilibrium.

Another way neighborhood stasis was maintained was when some of the more emotionally and physically mature girls from our crew were poached by some of the older kids. The girls were the only ones who could trade up in this fashion until we all crossed the eighteenth-year barrier. By that time everyone socialized at our local bar, Coaches II, and all bets were off. To compensate, some of the more advanced females from the grades below us were poached by our own crew. When that happened, the younger girl pretty much became an appendage of the male crew member until they were finally accepted by the existing female crew. Sometimes, during the interim, the new girlfriend brought some of her more emotionally and physically mature members of her original crew up to the new varsity with her. This kind of symbiosis, among the neighborhood age groups that gathered in close proximity of each other, for the most part, kept the peace. Nature abhors a vacuum.

You humans really were barbarians. Stella commented and chuckled.

I think it's kind of nice. Apollo countered. *Our system is so much more sterile.*

Do you two mind? I find this fascinating. Claire said impatiently. *Go on Jimmy.*

One of the primary poachers among the older crews was Magoo. Magoo was an athletic god, who from an early age broke every athletic record in Riverdale and beyond. He started on the St. Maggie's varsity basketball team in sixth grade and was its captain by seventh. He pitched for my father's baseball team every spring when he played for the North Riverdale Baseball League. His arm was so powerful my father had to recruit the strongest boys in the neighborhood just to catch for him. Only Keith Barber, who I always thought had the last vestiges of cave man vigor, could handle catching an entire game.

On offense, Magoo was the first kid in the neighborhood who could bat from either side of the plate. I remember watching him from the bench numerous times as he drove his home runs over the three-story P.S. 81 building outside of right field, deep into the woods above the rocks behind center field, and all the way to the sandbox in the children's park beyond left field. He also played quarterback and wide receiver for my father's football teams. There was no sport he could not master. He was the natural. Knowing what I know now, I would swear he was an alien hybrid.

Magoo won more athletic titles for my father than all of his blood children, who all played for him, combined. He was one of my father's favorite strays among the many who, throughout my human childhood, always appeared in my father's kitchen seeking counsel or paternal guidance. There were no locks on my father's door, or his heart.

And while older poachers were generally looked upon with absolute scorn by the younger males, no one hated Magoo. He was just too likeable, always inviting everyone in any age group to come play ball with him, and always generous in giving every teammate their moments in the sun. He'd even teach other players how to improve their respective athletic skills. And he had no problem sharing a beer with anyone, from anywhere. The kid was fucking Jesus to the rest of Riverdale, including me.

Indeed, there was no fault to assign. Magoo never intentionally went after a younger girl. They went after him.

Magoo would even apologize to the poached boyfriend and offer to break up with the girl if the boy wanted him to. No one ever took him up on his offer, because losing a girl to Magoo raised the ex-boyfriend's status exponentially among the other remaining females in the crew. It was a bittersweet win.

Seriously, father? Stella snorted. *What were these girls thinking?*

Don't blame the messenger. I responded. *That was human life growing up in the small part of my world during the mid-twentieth century.*

I could have been Magoo. Apollo sighed.

Could we move on here? Claire interrupted. *Your father has a long way to go in this story and while the Centauri day is a lot longer than earth's, it's still just a day and I would like him to finish before the end of this one. None of us is getting any younger.*

Claire looked up at me from where her head rested in my lap and, almost imperceptivity, nodded knowingly. I could not help but wink.

The last time I saw Magoo, was when I was a lawyer and came to visit my own father during his final days in the hospital. Emphysema had finally brought him down. I walked in to find Magoo sitting on the side of my father's bed, holding his dying hand, whispering to him. I couldn't bring myself to interrupt them, as my father had been as much of a father to Magoo as he had been to me. So, I gave them their time and waited outside the room until Magoo came out, wiping tears from his eyes. He still had all the youthful features that had long before abandoned me. He gave me a brief hug and left without saying a word. I heard from Bonnie that Magoo was in the back of St. Maggie's for my father's funeral, weeping openly.

*****

There was an additional surge in the crew membership as newcomers moved into the neighborhood and found their way to one of Riverdale's social oases. Walking onto The Courts during the afterschool afternoon was the most common way a neighborhood newcomer was absorbed into the group. This was where most of us still played outdoor games of basketball and football. If a person came along and proved themselves with their individual athletic prowess, they were usually first picked for one of the teams. Later they were invited back to that locale, or to the rocks just up off the baseball field, after dark, to participate in the neighborhood parties. Like water, they all rose or sank to their appropriate social level.

And that's where the reputations were really forged.

CHAPTER TWENTY-NINE (THE MORE THE MERRIER)

The Armstrong, Huggins and Horn families were a huge conglomerate of new kids that entered the neighborhood a few years earlier and took over the paper route business. It was a matriarchal clan led by three sisters that moved into a spacious corner house on Fieldstone and 259th Street. Bobby Armstrong was our age and attended the closest public high school, while his younger siblings and cousins finished their time at PS 81 or MS 141. The three sisters were close and dominant, from a long line of suffragette blood, and soon had their entire clan knee deep in all of the social and community programs being run out of the Riverdale Neighborhood House.

At that time RNH, which began when Grace Dodge, a descendant of the copper tycoon William E. Dodge, started a lending library for local workers, was in the beginning of its surging community activism era. The 1960s had stirred up the hearts and consciences of the wealthy donors from the toney Fieldstone and Wave Hill enclaves in North Riverdale, so money flowed for whatever social experiments its young transitioning hippy directors looked to implement. And that's where the "AHH" clan came into the picture.

The three sisters were the closest thing to the human embodiment of the early Celtic triple Goddesses, Anu – Danu – Tailtiu, whose governance included strength and endurance, movement and change, and finally sustenance and abundance. They immediately volunteered themselves and their small army of children to help start up and man the community recycling and a food collective.

As a result, there were a bunch of new faces milling around that section of the North Riverdale community.

Bobby Armstrong was the oldest of that clan's kids, so a lot of responsibility fell on his shoulders. But he quickly raised the art of delegation to a Tom Sawyer level, and soon had the younger members of his tribe assuming all of his responsibilities around RNH. That left him time to sneak up to The Courts where his killer set shot got him noticed and into the rotation of the constant full court games running during day light hours. That also ultimately landed him an invite to the after-dusk parties. I'm pretty sure Joe Marrero introduced Bobby, his younger brother Johnny, and his younger cousin Billy Huggins into the crew. That led Billy's younger in age only sister, Donna, into the crew as well.

The RNH also introduced another large Irish family that recently moved into North Riverdale. Dennis "Murray" Conley was the oldest boy in a family of twelve, who slipped into the mix at the same time as Bobby Armstrong. Murray was one of the freakishly bright catholic boys who attended Regis High School on the upper east side of Manhattan. Murray couldn't play basketball for shit, but he was fast enough with his feet to avoid any retribution that his equally fast wit and tongue garnered him.

The added benefit of the admission of boys from large families into the crew was that they also provided the ultimate introduction of, no longer little, sisters into the mix as well. By the time our class reached our senior year of high school, continuous cross-pollination of the high school classes had loosened the once stricter age borders of social interaction.

Robbie Maclaren brought in Brian Kelly from Fordham Prep in freshman year. That's where all of the brightest catholic boys went to be taught by disciples of the Jesuit Black Pope. I had tested into that school's "three-three program," but my family did not want me developing any airs about myself. My spot eventually went to someone more deserving, like Tommy Quirk, who I met years later at university. Turns out, the elder McCarthys did me a favor, but let's not get ahead of ourselves.

Brian Kelly was a tall drink of water whose laconic style of communication masked his commanding dry wit and perceptive eye. He also could play basketball better than most, so he made his bones with a corner jump shot that made up for his reticence to sacrifice his body in the paint. Don't really blame him, given that we played a rigorous "no blood, no foul" version of Sr. James Naismith's ball through the peach basket game.

Along with introducing JC, I brought my Manhattan cousin, Jimmy McEntee, into our crew. Jimmy was four years older than me but was small of stature and dressed like a greaser from the 1950s. He and his much younger sister were favorites of Posie and thus regular weekend guests at the McCarthy compound.

Jimmy was closer in age to my sister Bonnie and the two of them shared a brother-sister relationship as well. But given that I was more socially advanced than my perfect-child sister, and more likely to dabble in more entertaining adventures, Jimmy usually chose to tag along with me whenever I left the house. It was a symbiotic relationship. I got to use Jimmy's documents to purchase booze and ciggies, and Jimmy became a protected member of the crew that I ran with. Unfortunately for Jimmy, he quickly became my "conscience" (kind of like Jiminy Cricket to Pinocchio) and spent an inordinate amount of time trying to talk me out of doing the wrong thing. That full-time job might have destroyed a lesser man's soul (and he wasn't even a Ginger).

Unlike his McCarthy cousins, Jimmy opted for a more non-violent approach to life. This often forced him into the role of peacemaker between me and my older brother, Eddie, who never enjoyed hearing any lip from his younger brother and was more likely to match fists with wits should I force the issue.

Jimmy would often literally step between me and my eldest brother in an attempt to prevent an inevitable donnybrook. He paid a very dear price for that by intercepting black eyes, bruised ribs and swollen jaws that were meant by one angry brother for another.

One time near the Rocks above the baseball field Jimmy suffered a TKO for his troubles, as well as earned his nick name, Apples.

Now another inordinately large Irish Catholic family in our neighborhood were the Johnsons. Their father was a Captain in the FDNY, and they lived in a modest yet beautiful brick house on Fieldstone Road, just off Mosholu Avenue and just a half block South from Junior's Corner.

Peter "Poofy" Johnson was my age and rolled with our clique, along with his one-year older brother Raymond, better knowns as "Ray-Ray." Poofy was a smart-ass who honed his comedy act working the counter at Junior's Corner since he was able to see over it. He could make anyone laugh and no one was off limits. With the daring and timing of a Court Jester, he could get away with saying things that could get others killed.

Anyway, on the night in question, Poofy was entertaining a small crowd on the Rocks a few feet away from where my brother and I were arguing nose-to-nose - probably over which direction the wind was blowing at that moment - while the rest of the crowd was peacefully drinking beer. Cousin Jimmy, ever vigilant, was standing close by and directly to my left, putting him on Eddie's right. He kept turning from one brother to another - like a tennis match official - as we exchanged escalating barbs and threats, in an effort to get a sensible and calming word in edgewise.

Now in my defense, I have never thrown the first punch during arguments with my brother. That is because my brother Eddie was like Michael Meyers of Halloween fame, you just could not kill him, and I have honestly tried. Given Eddie's temper and my own very sharp tongue, physical confrontation was inevitable.

During this particular argument, I must have said something scathing about Eddie which led to the lightning launch of his favored nuclear, overhand right, just as Jimmy was making some completely logical and totally ignored point concerning the wonders of peaceful co-existence, and unfortunately leaned his head into the fist missile's pathway. I could hear its impact - like a pumpkin hitting concrete - and watched out of the corner of my eye as Jimmy's glasses were launched, spinning and air-bound, by his rapidly revolving head.

His body followed the torque of his head into that same spin cycle away from the two-man scrum my brother and I had now engaged. The obviously dazed Jimmy miraculously stayed up on his feet and chicken walked away, in a zig-zag pattern, in the direction of Poofy and his entourage, drawn to the peaceful sound of laughter. Ever the humanitarian, Poofy, clearly entertained by the combination of consumed alcohol and the McCarthy brothers floor show, did just the right thing and offered Jimmy a cold beer for medicinal purposes to be drank and/or placed on his now rapidly swelling jaw line.

For some inexplicable reason, at that moment Poofy also chose to inquire of the stumbling and dazed Jimmy, his family name, to share it with the coroner. Jimmy mumbled the word "McEntee" through his now blood-filled mouth, which sounded to one and all like "Macintosh." The now affably inebriated Poofy then declared to the crowd, "You mean like the Apples? I'm going to call you Apples." And just like that, the nickname stuck.

Poofy did me a favor that night, as I couldn't have my cousin coopting my name.

Like apples in general, things are always better when they are organic, including your social circles. So, our cast of characters continued to grow healthily, and it was just a matter of time before we reached critical mass. Then the real fun began.

CHAPTER THIRTY
(THE MAN)

One of the first lessons we learned at the knees of the older kids, when we were partying in the local parks or woods, was how to avoid the cops. Hold the high ground.

We weren't afraid of being arrested for underage drinking in public. The cops couldn't be bothered doing the paper work. The most they would do is confiscate your beers and ciggies and then drive you to the outside border of the 50th Precinct and drop you off, so you would have to walk home. If you gave them any lip, you would get a smack for your troubles. They knew they could get away with it. None of the truants in their precinct were dumb enough to complain to their parents about being mistreated by the cops while they were breaking the law.

The 50th Precinct was the place where street cops were transferred towards the end of their careers, to ride out their days in relative peace and safety. And each of these cops had earned this privilege from a twenty-year career patrolling one of the most exciting and dangerous cities in the world. No one shot at cops in North Riverdale, even at the worst of then Mayor Abe Beam's administration in the mid-seventies when the City almost went bankrupt.

The cops never even showed themselves after dark unless one of the nosey Riverdalians – who didn't have their own kid out on the streets - that lived close to the park called them with a noise complaint. We always made those locals pay afterwards by egging the shit out of their houses. At that point the cops would not respond to their frantic follow-up calls regarding the siege on their homes because their officers were still out on their public disturbance calls. In other words, they had stopped at the Broadway diner at 238th street to pick up coffees and snacks for their brothers in blue on the 4 to 12 shift.

If we were in the Mosholu Woods we didn't even bother moving from Matty's fort. We knew the cops weren't going to climb the rocks or take the long way around in the dark. On those few occasions where they were feeling a little ambitious, their flashlights dancing among the trees gave us plenty of warning, so we could stash our beers, cover the fort, and disappear out the Fieldstone side of the woods.

The only chance the cops had at catching us was when we were partying on The Courts. Every once in a while they'd pull a sweep and roll in with a show of force in a pincer movement, by pulling their squad cars into the south driveway of the PS 81 schoolyard, and also approach from the north along the wide park pathway that circled the baseball field. The only problem with that was that the schoolyard gates were locked by chains that were loose enough for skinny kids to slide through, but nowhere near wide enough for a cop in his mid-forties to slide past. So, by the time the cops got the cars to the openings and those chains off every kid that was present, boys and girls, had now cleared the fences to the baseball field or the RNH pool and were disappearing into the Mosholu Woods across the street, like cockroaches in a Manhattan kitchen.

The most athletic boys of the group would hang back long enough to toss the bottles and cans of beer over the fence and into the RNH pool, before scampering over themselves like gymnasts on a high bar. The cops weren't going to go into the water to retrieve them, so we would always swing back later and recover them, still cold from the night pool water.

The cops were usually good sports about it and often called out some of us by name as we raced away.

One particularly jocular cop, Sergeant Brian Gallagher, loved to call after me, "I see you McCarthy, and I'm telling your grandfather the next time I bump into him." He never did, or if he did, Spaghetti didn't grass me out to my parents. He was never a big fan of the *Gardaí*, as he called them. It could be that Gallagher didn't know my first name and guessing which one of the four male siblings was too broad a selection for a proper police identification, especially in the dark. Of course, by this point all four of us were drinking in the same area, so he was going to be right no matter which name he dropped.

Once we had enough beer in us, if we weren't attempting to lock lips with one or more of our female counterparts, we would do something stupid. One of the favorite pranks, developed by Joe Marrero, that we loved to pull on the local motorists, was for the group of boys to divide into two lines and crouch in the shadows on both sides of Mosholu in front of the Mosholu Woods entrance. As a car drew close, Joe would yell "Pull the rope!" The two groups of boys would stand in unison and pull the imaginary rope like a tug of war. It always caused the driver to slam on their brakes. Once they realized there was nothing there, they would leap out of their cars and start screaming all kinds of wonderful obscenities while the entire crew would race into the woods laughing our asses off.

One time I was the last to make it into the woods when this particular driver, a decent sized man in his thirties, unexpectedly chased us. As this was a first, I was totally surprised when this large hand grabbed my left shoulder just a few feet in from the road, spun me around and then countered that movement with a hard slap from his right hand. My ear was ringing, and I could feel the skin on my cheek swelling in the shape of his handprint, as I now lay on the pine needles looking up at him. Part of me wanted to cry. Part of me wanted to kill him.

"You think you're funny, dontcha, ya little prick?" he shouted. "Maybe I should haul you off to the 50th –"

He didn't finish his sentence. His face went pale in the faint glow of the streetlights coming from Mosholu. And then I heard the sound. At first it was just twigs snapping in the distant darkness behind me. Then the rumbling of many feet and the rising shouts of the twenty boys from the crew flying down the hill back towards our direction. I never saw fear in the eyes of a stranger before, but it was something I'd recognize many times afterwards. I didn't get too long a look because the stranger spun around and flew back in the direction of his car as the crew now hurtled past me carrying sticks and stones they picked up in the woods. By the time they made it to the street the assailant had reached his car and was now burning rubber as he raced past the arriving mob.

BJ Delaney and my older brother had been leading the charge, and just as I reached them, BJ, who had the build and strength of a Bornean Orangutan, hurled his large stone after the car, striking and shattering its back windshield, causing its occupant to accelerate past Mush Park and disappear onto the southbound entrance of the Sawmill River parkway.

"Go back to Manhattan you cocksucker!" BJ bellowed after him.

"You all right?" Eddie asked, examining the raised welt on my cheek. "He gotcha good."

I was surprised at Eddie's level of concern. I guess he didn't want anyone else painting his canvas.

"That's taking one for the team," BJ said approvingly. "Better get some ice on that or your folks will be asking about it."

BJ had been a fixture around my home since he came up together with Eddie as players on my father's baseball team. He was a star catcher with a gun of an arm, who could throw out even the crafty and swift Joe Marrero. BJ knew that the McCarthys only allowed family to put their hands on my siblings and me.

"Just tell them I did it." Eddie said. "And I'll just tell them you called me a fucking asshole in front of the girls."

"Just desserts then!" BJ said and laughed. "Perfectly believable. Sounds like a plan."

"We better disappear before that asshole stops at the next pay phone and calls the cops." Joe Marrero called out to us. With that the group broke into splinters and disappeared back into the woods, across the street and into the park, and around the corner through the side alley at the end of the woods towards Fieldstone Road. Another night in the books.

But I never forgot that slap, and I never again fucked with strangers, unless they had it coming.

CHAPTER THIRTY-ONE
(LEARNING TO DRIVE)

One of the truly inviolate laws of the universe, or at least of Riverdale, is six degrees of separation. It most commonly involves the sharing of knowledge or experience.

A clear example of its application among our crowd, was Matty Burns and learning to drive. Matty's older sister taught Matty to drive on their dead-end street. Matty then taught Danny Mo, who taught Joe Marrero, who taught Robbie Maclaren, who taught Brian Kelly, who taught JC, who taught me. Turns out we were fast learners. We had to be. We were fifteen years old, and we were learning on stolen cars.

In all fairness, it wasn't our fault. Blame it on vent windows.

If you are not going to share a visual, can you at least draw us a diagram? Apollo said in frustration.

Let me explain. Before the 1980s, most human automobiles did not have air conditioning. Given that a sealed car heats up very quickly, even during sunny winter days, the car manufacturers built tiny triangular glass vents in the front corner section of their driver and passenger windows. To release the heat from a parked car, the driver often slipped the slide lock and opened these glass triangles on their hinges which would then catch the passing air and force it inside the now moving car. If you cranked open the back windows just a crack, it cleared the heat from the car in a few blocks.

But given that most human men are distracted on their best days, and that most drivers at the time were men, who are naturally lazy, after any given trip those vent windows were rarely closed, never mind secured as they were designed to be.

Your mom really hated it when Jimmy left the toilet seat up, Claire shared and then broke into an audible Lurchy laugh.

And to make matters worse, a lot of the car ignition systems would allow the driver to turn off the car and remove the key without turning it that one final click to lock it, so that it could not be restarted without the key. Add the subtle sexually suggestive aesthetic design of raised lips along the key slot, and someone could turn the ignition on using just a small screw driver or a knife, or even a strong set of fingers, without damaging the auto.

All one needed was to gain access to the car, which is where the vent windows came in. If any of us got bored and decided it was time for a lesson, we would walk through the streets of the neighborhood at night, trying every vent window until one popped open. Given our youth we would then just slide a skinny arm in and grab the inside door handle and voila.

When you think about it, cars are very simple machines. One pedal makes it go, one makes it stop, and the steering wheel turns just like those on any toy you grew up with. The real trick was to be tall enough to work those pedals and see over the steering wheel. Everything else was intuitive, and after observing in the front passenger seat for a few joy rides, you graduated to taking the wheel yourself. Observe, do, teach.

We were not malicious criminals. We never actually "stole" the cars. We were more in a short-term borrower, joy-ride relationship with their actual owners. We were very careful when driving and we always returned the cars to within a block of their original parking spot on the side streets of Riverdale. Northern Fieldstone, Tyndall and Liebig offered the easiest pickings. Given the human male mindset, the car's owner usually just accepted that they had forgotten where they parked the night before, despite their wives strenuous arguments to the contrary. Never steal a woman's car.

And we only borrowed them at night, after most families retired to their homes to watch television and go to sleep. That way there was less chance of passing one of the pedestrian gossips, there was far less traffic on the roads and if someone saw you drive by it was dark enough to make legal identification almost impossible.

We usually took the borrowed car to Fieldstone Road, which was where the rich folks lived on private streets. You were only allowed to park your cars in the huge garages or long driveways, never on the street itself. That gave us plenty of roadway to practice our driving without the risk of sideswiping a parked car. Plus, the real cops didn't regularly patrol that area, and we only had the private toy cops to deal with. If one happened to spot us, we just left the area and returned the car to within spitting distance of its original home. We also liked to drive along the isolated river roads down by Wave Hill, but you had to be more careful, because the lighting was sporadic at best, and you risked going off into the steep drainage ditches on either side of the roads. In all fairness, none of my crew ever lost one car.

Those joy rides all came to an end for me one Saturday afternoon, when I shit too close to home and stole my sister Bonnie's Rambler to take Apples on his first observational driving lesson. Growing up in Manhattan, he had never actually ridden in the front seat of a car, given that most taxis only allowed you to ride in back. I probably would have gotten away with it if Apples' younger sister Christina, who was staying with us for that particular weekend with her older brother, didn't insist on coming along with us or she would rat us out.

It was, as most, a crime of opportunity. My sister was with my parents out visiting relatives in Queens. Spaghetti was working downtown, which left Posie to watch over the flock. She was cooking dinner.

I swiped Bonnie's keys from inside the kitchen door, and Apples and I pushed the Rambler to the end of the driveway before starting her up. It was a rather uneventful half hour ride until I made that return left onto Mosholu from Fieldstone. Just before I reached the family home, at the crest of the hill, I spotted a small woman standing in the middle of the street waving a dish towel over her head frantically, like someone stranded on a deserted island trying to get the attention of an overhead plane. It was Posie. And she was pissed.

It seems that when she went looking for Christina and found her missing, she realized that my sister's Rambler was also absent. My brothers were accounted for tossing a football around the backyard, so Posie put two and two together and came up with me.

Anyone who has ever experienced the rat tail snap of a wet summer towel will have some idea of the welts and pain Posie's dishrag inflicted as she laced into me before I had gotten both feet out of the car, which I had returned to its original position in the driveway. She almost took my eye out. I was just happy she didn't have the baseball bat.

She made me swear right there and then to never do something that stupid again on the threat that she would rat me out to my parents, and worse, Spaghetti, if I did.

Despite her histrionics, and her towel, I worshipped my grandmother, so I made and then kept my promise and never stole any car again. Whether I did anything else that stupid, I'll let you decide.

CHAPTER THIRTY-TWO
(WHEN WORLDS COLLIDE)

JC and I ended up safely in the upper level of the academic pack by the end of our freshman year, assuring our continuation the following year at Spillane. For me, that wasn't always going to be the case, and I blame that entirely on the powers that be at Archbishop Spillane. Screw it. It was all my fault.

You see, in 1971, social norms were relaxing, even among the Catholics, and, as a result, the progressives in the educational wing of the church were pushing for radical changes. The biggest change in Spillane was that the administration had decided to merge the boys' and girls' schools. I was doomed from the moment I stepped through the doorway on the first day of sophomore year.

Up until that point, my only contact with female Spillane students was brief interactions on the Special bus. But given that the girls were controlled by cliques, which had strict protocols and pecking orders, no girl dared to peel off from the pack to talk to a freshman boy, without the direct approval of Queen Doreen or one of her consorts. So, I basically accepted the male spartan life among JC and my other classmates throughout freshman year. It wasn't a total drought, as I was still experiencing the recurring date and dump scenario with different girls from the neighborhood. But as that solidified into the rule, I stopped waiting for the break up note or the phone call, and just assumed each new encounter would be a one off. No strings and no follow-up. Hot and heavy moments of passionate petting, and then move on before they could break my heart. After a while, I was running out of real estate.

In sophomore year we were all released into hallways full of rolled up blue skirts and matching sheer blue stockings, which might explain why my favorite color is blue. And don't get me started on the tight white dress shirts that were often accessorized like simple road maps by parallel blue striped suspenders.

I tried to distract myself by working with Eddie and BJ in their five-finger retail business of swiping books from the school bookstore. I would take the orders from classmates, and they would do the shopping. I always got a couple of bucks for brokering the deals. But for me, that wasn't a regular gig.

JC and I used to make some lunch money forging bus passes. The New York Transit system only had a limited color pallet on which to print the bus passes issued to the hundreds of thousands of students each month. JC went around collecting old passes from the students who would have tossed them anyway. We then stored and saved our stash by color until their color reappeared in a new month's pass with a different date and large capital letter appearing in a new color on its front center. For the costs of a handful of flair pens and a small ruler, we then carefully colored over the old markings to match the general card color and then copied the new dates and Capital letter in the right color on the card. If you put them behind the worn plastic of the bus pass holder, it was next to impossible to spot the forgery. We could turn out a really decent replica in about a half an hour, which we then sold for half the price that the school collected from the students. We weren't the only ones in the business as some of the boys from Manhattan, led by some kid called Yorg, had their competing forgeries out there on the market. Students tended to buy from the guys in their neighborhoods, because it was always easier to extract a refund should they be caught and have their fake bus pass confiscated. That was a rarity, given that bus drivers were driving under expired union contracts, and couldn't give a shit what a student flashed as they walked past them to the back of the bus. That side business kept us pretty busy for the first week of each month.

I never spent the money on lunch anyway. I had a slice in the inside of my school jacket through which I slipped the tuna on roll I ate every day at school, stopping only to pay for the carton of chocolate milk that stayed on my tray until I reached the cashier.

Given that I was no longer slinging newspapers to make money, every little bit of illicit income came in handy, especially in the colder months, when our crew often spent our afternoons back in Riverdale hanging around Luigi's Pizza shop. But Luigi, who bore a striking resemblance to the Italian bodyguard who betrayed Michael Corleone in the Godfather, insisted that if you wanted to sit in one of his booths, you either kept a fresh slice of pizza in front of you, or you accepted his challenge to match open hand finger strength in a duel to the death. Of course, even the strongest among us did not stand a chance against a man who spent every day massaging masses of gooey balls of pizza dough into the consistency necessary to deliver a perfect New York Pizza. But if you let him crush your hands in front of the girls in the group, he allowed everyone to stay another half hour without reordering another slice. I'm certain all of the microfractures Luigi administered to my still developing carpals and metacarpals during those years hardened my fists into the useful appendages I came to rely on as I got older. And it sure beat sitting in the park in the cold.

But back at Spillane, when I wasn't swiping stuff and hustling change, I was mesmerized by the smorgasbord of young blossoming women passing me in the hallways and sitting beside me in classes and the cafeteria each day. They were a broad collection from every race and economic background that gathered together each day to exercise the totally democratic concept of education, where the only thing that mattered for your future success, was how hard you hit the books. I, on the other hand, was just there for the sightseeing. But given the strength of the student clique system and the ever-watchful eyes of the teachers and administrators, my activity with the opposite sex seemed limited to a visual experience on a group level.

Father, is there a point in this story when you actually grow up? Stella interrupted. *I mean even on a purely human scale you appear to be in arrested development.*

We all weren't born fully formed from the womb. Apollo countered. *Even on Centauri, the women mature faster than the men.*

Why is it that young people cannot just sit back and enjoy a story anymore? Claire admonished. *I would have thought that your superior Centauri genes would have overcome any human ADHD.*

Stella, always the most thoughtful, considered that for a moment.

I'm sorry father, she apologized. *I keep forgetting that you were entirely human back then.*

It is a blessing and a curse. I responded and smiled at my offspring to show I took no offense. *But I believe it is worth sharing it all with you this one time. Because I don't want you to remember just this latest incarnation of your father. So much more went into getting me here. To making me who I am. To meeting Gina. The bad and the good.*

Proceed Jimmy. Claire instructed. *I'll keep the children in check.*

The tide turned that spring when Queen Doreen organized a schoolwide party in Bronx Park East. But before I can get to that story, there were freight trains to be ridden and robbed back in Riverdale.

CHAPTER THIRTY-THREE
(LUCK OF THE IRISH)

When things got particularly boring for us in Riverdale proper, we often migrated down to the Hudson River to find whatever mischief we could get ourselves into.

Danny Mo was my psychic twin, both born on the same day, in the same year, in the same city. Throughout our lives we were about the same size, even once, when we were older, sharing a dose of the same crabs by wearing the same suit. And while we were never able to determine who was the chicken or the egg in that situation, at least those crabs showed consistently good taste in their selection of bodies and couture.

But Danny Mo was born without the fear gene. A total adrenaline junkie. Throughout our youth, he would be the first to go and do what no one else would dare. And the worst part was that his craziness was infectious. He might have been the first to leap off the highest point of the 110-foot Columbia rock into the Harlem river, but once his blond hair surfaced in that murky water, the rest of the crew couldn't wait to follow him in. Danny was the canary in the coal mine. As long as he was alive, the rest of us were okay.

Now there were the natural draws to hanging down by the Hudson River. In the winter months we would tempt fate by leaping along the tops of clusters of river ice that got trapped in the small basins, that form along the sides of natural or man-made jetties. The one time I went through a large flat chunk of ice, that had just held the weight of my older brother, BJ Delaney was close enough to reach down and fish me out. I swear that the brief dip in those icy waters was enough to freeze my testicles into obsoletion.

In the warmer months, we would while away the time tossing stones at the floating white rubber whales whose pods seemed to surface most weekend mornings, having found their way through the thousands of miles of New York City sewer pipes into the highly polluted river. I once tried to fish by the Riverdale Tennis Club, just off the 254th Street Metro North station, but ended up losing my father's favorite lure when it caught on some trash below the surface. I never owned up to it.

But that pollution didn't keep some of us from swimming in that briny water. One day, while accompanying the Armstrong brothers, who loved to explore the area, we came upon a group of older men swimming in a small cove. It formed just below the bridge leading down from a local college, which sat on the northernmost border of the northwestern Bronx. One of those men was the father of Rocky O'Hanlon, one of the younger members of our crew. He later became one of our City's most heralded heroes when he led his team of firefighters into the South Tower of the World Trade Center, one beautiful morning in September.

But on that late spring day in the early seventies, Mr. O'Hanlon was holding court among a circle of older gentlemen, some sitting on large boulders along the edge of the small beach, while others floated and bobbed a short way out into the water. We waved to them as we passed. Bobby Armstrong shouted out to Mr. O'Hanlon, "Why aren't you afraid to swim in the river?"

"Because we're old!" Mr. O'Hanlon shouted back.

"Do you boys have your tetanus shots?" Another of the elders called out.

Now every one of the kids in our crew had more than enough tetanus vaccine flowing through their veins, given our propensity to do stupid things since childhood, so we all nodded yes.

"Then come on in." The old duffer shouted.

Bobby was stripped to his shorts and into the water before I got as far as the beach.

Just as I was about to follow Bobby into the water, I heard the short chirp of a cop siren coming from above and then spotted a police cruiser rolling from the college campus out onto the railway bridge. A moment later two young cops got out of their cruiser and made their way over to the edge of the bridge closest to where the men were swimming.

"Hey, you old bastards," the cop who was driving shouted, "get the fuck out of the river before I call for back up and take you all in."

The other cop laughed and lit a cigarette.

The old men turned to Mr. O'Hanlon, who held up his hand to calm them.

"Are you old and deaf?" The now impatient driver shouted. "Don't have me come down there or I'm going to crack some heads."

"Yeah," the other cop now chimed in. "You old bastards are trespassing on Metro North Property."

At this point, Mr. O'Hanlon, slipped on his loafers and fished his wallet out of the pocket of his shorts next to him on the rock. Then he slowly walked around to the far side of the hill on the river side of the bridge. A moment later he appeared on the bridge and walked over to the two officers. The driver had both hands on his hips with a "what the fuck" look on his face. The other flipped his cigarette off the bridge in our general direction and then joined his partner to face down the old man.

Their bravado disappeared the moment they both looked down at the wallet which Mr. O'Hanlon flipped open in their direction with the confidence of a black jack dealer. Both officers looked like they were about to cry and raised all four of their hands in supplication as they slowly backed towards their cruiser. The driver actually tumbled over his front quarter panel before crawling the rest of the way to his door. They threw the cruiser into reverse and peeled rubber as they disappeared back the way they came. The whole time Mr. O'Hanlon just stood there scowling at them until they were gone. Then he burst out laughing.

The older man who had invited us in for the swim, started to laugh as well and was soon joined by the rest of their crew. When he saw the puzzled look on my face he said to us all, "Boys, those two young cops just had their first introduction to Deputy Chief William O'Hanlon. I don't think that's the last they'll see of him."

I learned some valuable lessons that day. Never judge any book by its cover. Never let your enemy see you coming. And when you are in a jam, there is nothing more useful than a powerful friend.

* * * * *

The biggest draw to the Hudson River was the set of train tracks that ran down alongside the tributary until they crossed the east river and submerged into Manhattan's bedrock.

Every member of our crew kept a smooth, stretched, flattened disk that once was a coin he had placed on the tracks and then waited for a train to roll over it. It usually took a few tries because the train often propelled the disk like skeet in any direction, so you had to spend a good half hour circling the spot on the track where you left it in order to find it. And it always felt so warm when you finally picked it up.

As we got older our interests shifted from the imagined glamour of the speeding passenger trains, taking their successful occupants to and from the belly of Manhattan and the wealthier villages along the Hudson Valley, to the lumbering freight trains. Those trains made their trip south to the Highbridge freight yards past the Riverdale station every afternoon at around two p.m. and then made their return trip north at around four p.m.. We'd all seen the old movies showing the hobos and vagabonds hitching rides on freight trains cross country. We had no interest in leaving the area just yet. However, we certainly liked the challenge of running up along the side of the ladder of a freight car, grabbing hold, lifting our feet up to the lowest rung and then riding for a quarter mile before leaping off onto the next patch of wild grass and running the whole way back just to brag to our friends. Most times one of a daring duo would grab the front ladder on the freight car and his partner would grab the back ladder. You never did it alone because that would void the bragging rights, and your friends would say you're full of shit.

The most exciting part of the exercise was the moment you placed your grip on the highest rung you could reach and then lifted your body weight off the ground. For that split second before your foot found that bottom rung, which extended a foot below the body of the freight car, you were suspended in air, hanging on for dear life, and you never took a breath. It was pure adrenaline.

We only hopped southbound freights because they ran on the last track closest to the river which gave us a better running start and softer places to land. The southbound trip also had a set ending point just in case you weren't able to get off the car before it reached the freight yard. From there you could always walk to the nearest subway or bus stop and find your way back to Riverdale

The real trick when catching the southbound freight was hiding in wait so the freight engineer didn't spot you as the front of the train passed. If he did he would purposely speed up to prevent you from running fast enough to grab the ladders. To succeed, you would wait until most of the cars had passed which would lessen the chance you'd be spotted in the lead engine's side mirrors, given the gentle convex curve of the tracks that hugged the river along that area.

Even the dumbest among our crew knew that you only attempted this sober. Unless you weren't sober.

The last time I tried to hop a freight was St. Patty's Day of my sophomore year in Spillane. The one true social benefit of Catholic high school was that it closed for certain religious holidays. Since the Spillane Band always marched in the New York City Irish Parade, as we liked to call it, to take the holy out of it, the school gave the students off so they could attend the parade and support their school. I did neither.

However, a group of us were drinking on that holy day in support of our Celtic ancestors, in the woods that rose above the east side of the train tracks that we accessed by the Con Ed transformer on Independence Avenue. Danny Mo, who took the day off from public school in solidarity, was sitting with me on some rocks overlooking the Hudson River. We were drinking from a stash of Pabst Blue Ribbon that the crew had liberated a few days before from a freight car that was parked on a side-rail just above Kapok Street. Bobby Armstrong swore the freight car wasn't locked when he found it. Once the sun set, the rest of the crew formed a line and passed fifty cases hand-to-hand from the freight car, across the tracks, to the nearby woods where it was then divided up by the older kids and everyone got their piece. By then a crew from St. Gabe's had heard about it and came by to collect their share. The St. John's crew was not far behind. The key to peaceful coexistence among the parishes was to never be greedy.

We were drinking Danny Mo's share.

At around four p.m., well into our cups, we heard the northbound freight whistle. Danny was on his feet and salivating like one of Pavlov's dogs.

"Let's do this." he shouted.

"No fucking way." I responded.

Danny didn't listen, just hollered "C'mon," and took off down through the woods towards the tracks. I didn't have time to think about it and couldn't let him attempt it on his own. No matter how crazy the shit, you always had your boy's back.

Now this particular stretch of rails had about ten yards of sharp gravel between the edge of the woods and the inside freight track. The track itself ran along a raised bed that gently sloped downward towards the woods. Danny was a fast bastard and was already racing alongside the front ladder of a passing freight car. With an athletic leap, he grabbed the third rung of the ladder with both hands and lifted his right foot to its lowest rung. Then he leaned out facing south, holding on with just his right hand and calling back to me, "Come on, fuck head, leap."

I was too late to grab the back ladder of Danny's car and was going all out to catch the front ladder for the next car. But the freight engineer must have caught a glimpse of Danny Mo hanging off the car in his side mirrors, now that the train was following an inside concave curve along this north bound stretch, and just as I went to leap for the ladder the train accelerated, blowing my timing, so my left hand just barely caught the third rung and my right had dropped to the second rung. The train continued to accelerate, and I couldn't pull myself up to get a foot on the ladder. Worst still, my legs were extended behind me rocking with the movement of the train. Each second brought them closer to slipping below the undercarriage of the freight car. My arms were quickly tiring and all I could see were those rotating set of large metal wheels just feet away, waiting for me to let go.

"Kick off the car!" Danny shouted before he leapt from his ladder and rolled along the gravel. He shouted it again just as I reached the patch where he had come to a stop. With tears of desperation and pure panic, I propped the toe of my dangling left foot along the metal lip on the bottom of the freight car and propelled myself backwards with my arms just inches away from the ladder and train.

The landing knocked the wind out of me and sent me tumbling the entire ten yards down the decline towards the edge of the woods, during which the gravel made quick work of my sweatshirt and pants, shredding them in a way that would have made Edward Scissorhands proud.

When I finally came to a stop, everything immediately ached, and I could see blood in the scrapes and gashes along my hands, arms, and legs. But my head was unscathed, everything else on my body moved, and nothing seemed broken. By the time I lifted myself into a sitting position, the last of the train cars had passed and Danny Mo had arrived by my side.

"Are you okay?" he asked.

I wanted to smack the shit out of him, and would have, if I had the energy, but when I looked up at his face, all I could see was the absolute child-like joy that appeared there.

"That . . . was . . . so . . . fucking. . . cool." he said slowly, offering me a hand to lift me to my feet. "What a fucking great St. Patty's Day! C'mon, let's have a beer."

The most amazing thing about Danny-Mo was that he went on to live to a ripe old human age and passed naturally in his sleep. That is more than I can say for some of the others.

CHAPTER THIRTY-FOUR
(BRONX PARK EAST)

Bronx Park East is part of that great borough's green belt just east of the Bronx Zoo along Pelham Parkway. It falls approximately equidistant from all sections of the Bronx that fed students into Archbishop Spillane and also provided easy access by multiple bus routes and the No. 5 subway line for those coming from Eastchester or Manhattan. As such, it was the perfect location for the massive schoolwide party Queen Doreen decided to host one Saturday night during the spring of my sophomore year.

In all honesty, if I knew then what I know now, I would have set my sights on Doreen herself, given that she was the paragon of 1970s high school beauty. But, given my lowly status as an average underclassman, and a Non to boot, and the fact that I would have had to fight the long list of senior jocks who were vying for her attention, it was better that I kept to my place. As it turned out, by the end of that night, I still punched way above my weight class.

It was the common practice for young men of my stature to get lit in our neighborhood before traveling to other parts of the City for any serious partying. Since that Saturday evening's event was not to begin before dusk, JC and I started our festivities up in Mush Park earlier that day with a six-pack each from the last of JC's stash, of his St. Gabe's share of the beer train heist. At this point we were old hands and knew how to slowly pace ourselves so that we got enough of a buzz on to build our Dutch courage but didn't end up puking out before the night really began for us.

You must provide us with a visual for "puking out." Apollo interrupted.

I'll pass. Stella responded.

I've seen your father at his worst after a night of Macallan, Claire said. *It's not a pretty sight.*

If you keep interrupting, I'm never going to get through this.

Continue father. Stella instructed

Of course, we didn't expect BJ and Eddie to show up with a quart of Seagram's already cut with Seven Up. Nothing more deadly than a candy cocktail.

The only hard liquor I had sampled before then was Smirnoff Vodka the night of my grammar school graduation, when Jack Neville and I guzzled down half pints I had shop lifted before starting the graduation party circuit. The only thing I remember from that night was Nat Vacca showing me Kenny Albert's glass eye while I was slow dancing with Tracey Manning at her graduation party, and a random make out session with someone's older sister at another party that ended precipitously when I vomited on the floor. Talk about breaking a spell. Quite honestly, I wasn't sure about the make out session until I recalled it just now. She was the cute girlfriend of one of the older psychos named Demo from our neighborhood, so it was just as well it ended before it really started.

My graduation night ended when someone finally called my sister Bonnie, who retrieved me from the last locale and snuck me into our house through the basement, where I slept until my first real hangover the following day.

Since then, I had sworn off hard liquor and stuck to beer, given that the latter usually filled you up long before it could do any real damage.

But in this particular instance, Eddie and BJ insisted we graduate to their more sophisticated selection, through repeated infliction of the pejorative "pussies," and finally a friendly headlock by BJ while Eddie poured some of the sweet nectar into my mouth. That did the trick.

Once JC witnessed my capitulation, he readily joined in and soon the four of us had consumed the last of our combined stock. We were ready to party.

* * * * *

BJ was a beast. A freak of nature. He would have been a mountain man if there were any mountains in the Bronx. By the time he graduated from Spillane he had consumed every kind of alcoholic beverage known to man, including moonshine and poteen. He once took a Greyhound trip to Colorado, just so he could bring back a case of Coors Beer, which he shared with my brother and me on his return. And alcohol never seemed to have an effect on him, no matter how much he imbibed, beyond a growing gregariousness which sometimes resulted in inadvertent damage to anyone within reach. It was like being hugged by a gorilla. However, BJ was very protective of his friends, and was a definite asset in any bar brawl. You could not put him down. One of his many nicknames was The Party King.

Anyway, given that BJ's wits were the least affected by our tailgating, he herded the four of us onto the two buses it took to reach our destination. During that hour, I slept a little and sobered a little less.

Just before we got off the number twelve bus at our destination, BJ retrieved a box of Trojans from the pocket of his sweatshirt. He tore it open and handed one each to the three of us. "Here, in case you get lucky!"

I had never actually held a packaged condom in my hand before, and I wasn't quite sure of what "lucky" meant, so I studied the thin square, flipping it over to see if there were any directions I should know about, and trying to look like it wasn't the first time I had seen such a thing. I then realized that the source box BJ was holding was empty.

"What are you going to do?" I asked.

"Don't worry," BJ replied. He reached back into his pocket and removed an identical box, shaking it like a maraca to confirm its contents, just as the bus pulled into its stop.

Despite the waning light, we could see that the open fields of the park off Pelham Parkway were deserted. At first we thought BJ had taken us to the wrong location. And then we heard the distant sound of music coming from the wooded area on the southern end of the park. We followed it like it was coming from the Pied Piper.

Just beyond the tree line, crowds of high schoolers from all four classes were laughing and drinking as couples and in clusters like the world was coming to an end. It was hard to recognize some of them, given that when you take people out of their school uniforms and put them into street clothes, the visual context shifts as their individuality returns. Suddenly, the playing field is leveled, and everyone is left to work with just whatever God has given them. The skin hugging bell bottoms and tube tops that were in style at that time, even when supplemented by open sweatshirts or short jackets, put all the females on display. As expected, the Italian boys from the East side of the Bronx were all doing their

John Travolta impersonations with enough leather to keep the NFL in footballs for a decade.

The Riverdalian male dress code was that of the proletariat. Straight leg worn blue jeans, t-Shirts under sweatshirts, and construction boots. If it was really cold and you were getting fancy, you may don a blue or black p-coat and a skully. Gloves were for pussies.

We were all wearing our best sweatshirts.

But it was hard for a pigeon to stand out in a flock of peacocks, so after BJ and Eddie peeled off to find some of their classmates, JC and I walked through the crowds as if invisible. That is, until an intoxicated Joanna Skreegle raced up to JC with two beers in her hands and shrieked, "Chuck! So glad you made it."

Now Joanna was one of those smart girls from Eastchester in Eddie's class that looked cute enough in her school uniform without having to roll her skirts or wear tight dress shirts. She was one of the school's designated academic superstars, taking all AP classes, so we didn't have any interaction with her during the school day. Her free periods found her off in the library studying, while ours found the two of us up on the school roof smoking ciggies. There wasn't much overlap for socialization purposes. In fact, I had never said one word to her, or any other upper-class girl.

That night, we saw a whole different side of Joanna. Indeed, we also got a good look at the front and the back. She was a pleasant surprise from an aesthetic point of view.

"Have I missed something here?" I whispered to JC.

"She's been tutoring me in Chemistry after school." he whispered back.

Now for the last few weeks I had been wondering why JC was not riding home with us on the Special bus after school. When I asked him about it, he just shrugged it off, so I assumed he was doing a stretch in JUG – Justice under God, the religious version of detention - and thought no more about it. But going for tutoring meant that JC was trying to better himself, a bad look among the damned, and that could have led to a lot of ribbing, because I would have told everybody. It was no wonder he kept it to himself.

Joanna leaned in and gave JC a no hands hug, extending her right arm over his shoulder towards me and saying, "Here, a Bud for your bud." I gratefully relieved her extended hand of one of her Budweiser bottles and watched as she stood back and with her now freed hand, gratefully relieved me of my wingman, by grabbing JC's hand and leading him off into the crowd. I had to admire the pun.

"*Vaya con dios.*" I called after them, and then looked around, feeling very much alone.

I wandered through the bustling park hoping to spot my brother or BJ. I saw a friend named Billy Quigley - you'd never know the kid was a fucking genius - but he was well engaged with one of his female Spillane-St. John's parishioners over on a rock.

Being a committed Non definitely had its downside. If you don't give a shit about your school, you can't expect the school to give a shit about you. I finally wandered along a pathway that led to an open park bench and sat up on its top slat, with my feet on its seat. It was off by itself right on the eastern edge of the park, under a dim and flickering street lamp on Bronx Park East. I slowly sipped my bottle. At least I got a cold quality beer out of the deal. Joanna probably would have traded a Schlitz for me.

I stared up at the upper floors of the line of old limestone colored apartment buildings across the street. It was getting darker. Whenever I came to a window that was lit, I stopped and wondered about the inhabitants that lived there. I was distracted by a woman's silhouette behind a shaded window on the sixth floor. She was definitely animated, and I guessed that she was doing something in her kitchen, maybe at its sink or stove. I thought I could hear pots and pans banging. I got the sense that she was happy.

I didn't notice the presence sitting beside me until I went to flip my now empty bottle into a nearby trash can. I was so startled that I spun around, and half stood, dropping one foot off the bench so I could turn and face the person.

"Hi, Jimmy. Remember me?"

CHAPTER THIRTY-FIVE
(YOU TALKING TO ME)

It took a moment to register but there were those black eyes again.

The face was older than last time. So was the body. This was a full-blown teenager dressed in modern gear who could have just walked out of the park from Queen Doreen's party. She was fucking gorgeous.

She reached for my hand, and I pulled it away. She seemed surprised and then smiled.

"Forgive me," I said loudly, "but the last time we held hands I woke up on the floor of the woods."

At that exact moment another girl walked out of the park and turned when she heard my voice.

"Excuse me?" She said, surprised. She was one of those really cute northern Italian girls with shoulder length natural blonde hair, kewpie doll lips and porcelain skin. I couldn't be sure in the flickering lamp light, but her eyes might have been jade. She was wearing tight, straight leg jeans tucked in knee high leather boots, with a heel, and a matching short denim jacket.

"When were we ever in the woods?"

"Sorry," I apologized. "I wasn't talking to you."

The girl looked at me strangely. I pointed towards Eleni. The girl glanced in Eleni's direction but didn't seem to get it.

"Watch out for her, Jimmy," Eleni said, again with that smile. "She's trouble."

I seconded the once over I had given the blond. "Trouble! I'll take two helpings please." I didn't realize the words had slipped out of my mouth.

"Two helpings of what?" The blond girl responded. This time she smiled at me.

I gestured again with both hands towards Eleni, as if I was introducing her on stage.

Again, the blond looked in that direction but came up empty.

"You go to Spillane?" Blondie asked, with an accent that was just over the bridge from Queens. I was surprised and a little impressed that she was ignoring my beautiful companion.

"Yeah, sophomore. You?"

"Freshman."

She didn't look like a freshman, but then girls never do.

Just then a black, tricked-out 1970's Camaro pulled up to the curb with an older looking Italian male in a matching black ensemble behind the wheel. I could hear the Bee Gees "Lonely Days" blasting from his cassette player. He wore a diamond pinky ring on his right hand, which just caught the flickering street light as he fished a cigarette from a pack in the glove box and popped the lighter.

"C'mon Danielle, let's go." He called out impatiently without looking over through the smoke now exiting the half open passenger window. But you could tell this guy was a gentleman, as he leaned over and popped open the passenger door without taking his eyes off the lights on his dashboard. I could understand why I didn't warrant a second look, but I don't know how he could have missed Eleni sitting right there on the bench next to me.

"I'll see you around." Danielle half-whispered and smiled. Her teeth were perfect, and yes, her eyes were jade. Then she buried the smile, turned, strode over to the car, and slid past the now open door into the passenger seat. Still the gentleman, the driver leaned past her curves and pulled the door closed behind her by its elbow rest, giving her a kiss on the way back that unmistakably marked her as his girl. So, I guess he did see me.

She glanced out the window as the car started to pull away and I gave her a short finger roll wave. I thought I saw her smile return, but it could have been the flicker of the street lights reflecting off the passenger window. The same light disclosed that the Camaro had the words "Five Diamonds" stenciled in gold block letters across its black back bumper.

I turned back towards Eleni, "You could have said something—" but she was gone.

"Hey, fuckwad!" I looked back towards the park at the sound of BJ's bellow.

"Did you see a chick walk past you just now?" I asked, looking beyond him.

"Whatta ya talking about?" He asked. "What chick?"

"The beautiful chick with the black eyes."

"I'll give you black eyes." He said, grabbing me by the arm and pulling me after him like a child. "Stop fucking with me. Your brother's been looking all over for ya."

"Why?" I demanded.

"Time to go."

"We just got here." I said, digging my heels in and pulling my arm free.

He turned back towards me and looked at me like I was crazy. Then he held up his left wrist and pointed to his watch with the heavily scarred right index finger that barely survived an M80 explosion the summer before.

"It's ten thirty," he said. "The twelve bus stops running at eleven. I don't want to have to walk home through Fordham tonight."

"How's that possible?" I asked. "We just got here."

"We got here at seven and I had twelve beers, that's how that's possible." BJ replied, "now come on."

I wasn't going to argue with him, but I knew something was off. I could still smell that Budweiser when I cupped two hands over my nose and mouth. But the impact of the day's partying had worked its way out of my system. And I didn't even piss. I was completely sober.

The crowd had thinned and only the last of the lucky lovers were still hanging around the interior of the woods. I spotted JC sitting off on a rock with Joanna in his lap, her arms draped proprietarily over his shoulders, their foreheads touching. They were whispering and giggling between pecks, and he was running his middle finger up and down her stomach, coming very close to her breasts. I thought I spotted some leaves in her hair. She must have been one hell of a tutor.

"Just Chuck," I shouted. "We gotta go."

JC raised his lucky middle finger to simultaneously signal "one more moment" and "fuck you," so I turned away to give him some farewell privacy.

I spotted Eddie coming from the opposite direction. Someday I hoped to see a smile on his face, but not that day.

"Hey douchebag, where the fuck were ya?" He looked over my shoulder at JC and crooked his finger. "You too, asshole, let's go. You can mail her the engagement ring later."

BJ threw his simian arm across my shoulder and guided me in the direction of the bus stop on the other end of the park just below the subway station, with JC and Eddie following a few moments behind.

"So, tell me about this black-eyed chick," he said. I could smell all twelve beers on his breath. "Sounds cute. Do I know her?"

"I don't think so." I responded. "I'm not sure I do either."

Ten minutes later, as we each stretched out along the hard plastic benches of the last 12 bus out of Pelham Parkway, lighting up our cigarettes below the no smoking signs, JC pulled something from his pocket, crumpled it in his hand and tossed it across the bus at me, hitting me right on the nose. It dropped onto my lap. At first I thought it was a pack of matches. When I looked down, I saw the unfolding square cellophane with the word Trojan on it. It was torn and empty.

JC's eyes were closed, and he had a shit eating grin on his face.

The rat bastard passed the Chemistry regents exam that year with flying colors.

CHAPTER THIRTY-SIX
(GOOD GUYS WEAR BLACK)

Toward the end of my sophomore year in High School, I saw the film, *Billy Jack*. It was about an ex-Green Beret martial artist who prevents wild horses from being slaughtered and helps protect a school for native Americans, runaways, and the indigent. While I was impressed by the idea of standing up for wild creatures and the oppressed, I was really blown away by the fight scenes in the movie.

Does everything purely human boil down to fighting and fucking? Stella asked, quite seriously. Even during telepathy, those words felt cold and sterile.

You've managed to do enough of both over the last four hundred years. Apollo responded.

You should talk. You certainly held your own, brother, during the Great Galactic War. Stella replied with a smirk.

Do you two ever listen to yourselves? Claire interrupted. *You act like you were raised around the McCarthy Sunday table. Now if you don't mind I would like to hear the rest of your father's story. After all, he has evolved and while he might not have saved wild horses, he certainly saved my ass.*

I looked at both children, who nodded for me to continue.

Anyway, that movie offered new possibilities of learning how to defend myself. Given that I was always under threat from one of my siblings, never mind the older kids in the neighborhood and beyond, I thought that to be able to move like Billy Jack would be really useful. But martial arts training was in its infancy in the United States back then. And I had no idea how I was going to get to Asia to learn it home grown.

That spring, I was receiving my lifeguard certification from the YWCA up by Getty Square, a really rough area of Yonkers, which sat just north of Riverdale. One afternoon, while I was sitting on the front steps of the building waiting for my class to start, I spotted two older teens walking past me carrying their duffel bags. I recognized one of them as a classmate of my sister Bonnie back in the day at St. Maggie's, so I said hello.

Mike Mahaffey took a second to recognize me.

"McCarthy?" I nodded.

"Bonnie's little brother?" I nodded again.

He introduced the older teen standing next to him.

"This is my older brother, Bobby." Mike said.

He looked down at my knapsack.

"You take classes here?" Bobby asked.

"Getting my Lifeguard Cert." I responded. "You?"

"We teach Kung Fu a couple of days a week." Bobby responded.

I couldn't believe what I was hearing. I looked over both of these guys and my first thought was that they were a couple of college professors in training. They were wearing Khaki pants, loafers, and cardigans. There was nothing to suggest that they could perform the kind of movements that I had seen on the movie screen.

"You should stop by and check out the class." Mike said. "Tuesdays and Thursdays at 4 p.m. sharp."

I skipped my Life Guard class that afternoon, although I did pass the certification test that Saturday, and instead sat and watched the black-belted-brothers put a spartan group of Yonkers teens through their paces. There were no mats, no pads, no mouthpieces, and no headgear. Just a bunch of teens in black pajamas striking, blocking, and kicking with bare fists and feet. I watched the speed and repetition. I watched the fluid movements of kata and kumite. I watched the circular movements of the footwork. I watched as Bobby and Mike passed among the lines of students wearing an assortment of belt colors, stopping to adjust a stance or a fist. When the instructors called out the cadence it was like a game of Simon Says. If a student moved when they weren't supposed to, I didn't even see the brothers' leg before the student went down to a kick or a sweep. But that was the exception. These kids were disciplined. Even the white belts.

It didn't take much convincing of JC the next morning at school. He was in.

It wasn't hard to convince my father to finance the fifteen dollars a month it cost for classes. He had a healthy respect for Asian martial arts, having spent a large part of his tours during the Korean War in South Korea and the Philippines. But, he made me promise that once I turned seventeen, I would sign up for the Golden Gloves and see how Americans fight.

You see my father was the boxing champ of his destroyer in the Navy and took great pride in his stories of his exploits in the squared circle. Given that my seventeenth birthday was far into the distance, I gave the promise no thought at all. A lot can happen in a couple of years.

And I'm sure my father was secretly happy that I was going to get my ass kicked by someone else if I stepped out of line. Gave his knuckles a well needed rest.

That Thursday, JC and I showed up at our first class. Mike gave us our gis, those lightweight black pajamas the other students wore. Then he taught us how to properly tie our white belts and then took JC and I through a tutorial on stretching. That alone damned near killed me, especially when Mike stood behind me and pressed down on my shoulders as my body resisted dropping into a split. My balls had never touched wood before. They didn't like it.

Then Mike, who we were told to call *sensei*, showed us the basic lower, middle, and upper blocks, strikes and kicks. When he was satisfied that we were getting the hang of things, he took us out onto the main floor and allowed us to fall in at the back end of two of the four lines of students.

The brothers stood at the front of the class and called out their commands and counts over the next half hour. I thought I was going to expire. It was exhausting and hot. My lungs were killing me with each *kiai*, and I swore I was going to give up ciggies. I did.

Then the brothers started their rotations. As they called out instructions for combinations of blocks, strikes, and kicks, they moved among their students studying each of them for form, effort, and power. They would sometimes stop and make an adjustment, an extended fist or manipulate a leg so that the heel or the ball of your foot was positioned just right. But you had to wait for them to make the adjustment. You did not move after completing the commanded combination unless they told you to.

JC and I found that out the hard way. We were going through a series of three centered punches to the eyes, solar plexus, and stomach areas. By the tenth repetition, JC mixed up the order and had his ending strike pointed at the stomach level. As Bobby approached, JC made the mistake of adjusting his fist on his own. The hardened heel of Bobby's lightening hook kick caught JC right in his sternum. I thought I heard something crack and JC flew a few feet and landed on his ass, holding his chest, and trying to force air back into his lungs. But JC was no quitter. After a few gulps of air he staggered back to his feet and returned to his spot in the line beside me and assumed the latest position. By then I thought the brothers had moved on to the other rows, and since I thought I was safe, I turned my head just enough to extend my peripheral vision in JC's direction. The next thing I knew, my back foot was swept with such speed and force that it lifted both my legs forward and upward so that I was now staring at the old ornate tin ceiling tiles that covered the length of the dojo. I didn't get too good a look, because a moment later the air was blasted from my lungs from the impact of my full body weight landing on my back as I hit the hard wooden floor beneath me. I didn't even feel the back of my head slam into the wooden floor.

It took me a few seconds longer than JC to get back on my feet, and when I did, my first thought was to grab my clothes from the locker and never come back again. But if JC could stick it out, I wasn't going to be a pussy about it.

And we did. We both stuck with it for the next year, until part time work and full-time love demanded more of our attention. While we never got cold cocked again like we did that first class, we took many a beating from Bobby and Mike and a number of other advanced students. But as we improved the beatings diminished, and soon we were holding our own as green belts against even the blues and the browns. The blacks were light years ahead of the other students and always brought our egos back into check.

JC and I would put in extra time working out in my back yard on some weekends, and even though we were the best of friends, we'd go at it pretty hard. My technique was a bit better than his, but he had more of a killer instinct.

I didn't find my killer instinct until I was in my sixties once you three gave me a real reason to have one.

Amen to that. Claire responded.

And the best thing about our dabbling in the martial arts, was that the rumor quickly spread through the neighborhood, and then the school, and so the better we got at fighting, the less we had to do it. Even the older kids left us alone. Well, most of them.

CHAPTER THIRTY-SEVEN
(GRASSHOPPERS AND ANTS)

There is an old fable that is attributed to the Greek slave Aesop, which goes something like: there once was a grasshopper that spent the summer singing and dancing while he watched the ants beside him working to store up food for winter. When winter arrived, the grasshopper had nothing to eat and begged the ants for food. However, the ants told the grasshopper to fuck off and dance the winter away.

The summer after my sophomore year, my father decided that he wasn't going to allow me to waste away those summer months being a grasshopper. A friend of mine, Johnny Carey, hooked me up with some occasional cash work at Gaelic Park, manning the hotdog stands for that summer's concert series. I got to see bands like Deep Purple, Blue Oyster Cult, and Jefferson Airplane and made a few bucks for my troubles. During the years before that, my friends and I used to sneak into the park over the high wall on its Fieldstone side, and we caught bands like Three Dog Night, Humble Pie and Emerson Lake and Palmer. Where there's a will there's a way.

The rest of the time, my father made me work for spending money in his downtown offices, where I made copies, folded mailings, and ran deliveries. While I still hadn't a clue what it was he did for a living, I did learn quickly that there was no way I could spend the rest of my life following his footsteps. The work was so boring, that I was actually looking forward to our family trip to Maine just so I didn't have to sit in some claustrophobic high-rise building while most of my friends were hanging at the beach or partying in the woods. But my dad did put some money in my pocket, which allowed me to party on the weekends, and I made all of my Kung Fu classes, so I wasn't complaining.

JC had found some work at a local restaurant down in St. John's Parish, bussing tables and washing dishes for cash and a share of the daily tips. Brian Kelly was another hustler whose father hooked him up at an old hotel and restaurant called the Riverdale Inn. Joe Marrero made some cash running pizzas into the apartment buildings in South Riverdale while his older brother sat downstairs in the delivery car. Once Joe was old enough to drive, he turned the pizza delivery hustle into one of the more lucrative jobs in the neighborhood and bought himself a brand-new Javelin. He also started the Midnight Tire Company, where he borrowed hubcaps and tires from parked vehicles during early morning hours and sold them at a major cash discount. He even took orders.

By the end of the summer, I had scraped enough cash together to buy some new clothes and set aside a little extra to invest in my most important back to school acquisition, a short hair wig.

Towards the end of the prior school year, a rumor had spread that one of the graduating seniors, who rode the Special, had hidden a ponytail up under a dark brown wig. To the naked eye, it met the school's draconian male grooming rules. Before summer break, I had tracked the culprit down and negotiated a relatively steep price to purchase the wig he would no longer need. As the summer drew to its end, I met with that senior before he went off to college and acquired the wig. I then spent the last few weeks leading up to September learning how to wind my now ponytailed hair length evenly around the crown of my head, pinning it in place, and then carefully slipping the wig over the original. Voila.

The wig turned out to be the worst kept secret among my classmates, but it got me to the end of my Junior year, and my Spillane career. At that point, my life took its first unexpected detour.

But before I got to that milestone, Spaghetti called upon his Celtic connections and talked an old friend Pat Leary into hiring both Eddie and me as part-time stockboys, at a relatively new major supermarket known at the time as Daitch Shopwell. Pat agreed to take us on for old time's sake.

I liked and feared Pat in equal measures. I had no problem understanding his orders barked in the same Northern Irish brogue that I had been weaned on at Spaghetti's knee. Pat took no shit from us, and immediately taught me a few important life lessons. The first was the value of hard work. You never stopped working once you punched his time clock. And that was okay. I found I liked working with my hands and that the nonstop cycle of loading and unloading cases of cans and bottles from real trucks to conveyor belts to hand trucks to shelves was more of a work out than any gym membership could provide. And Pat never stopped working himself, so he led by example.

The second thing I learned from Pat was that there is a value to everything. The first time Pat caught me out back daydreaming, he pinned me up against the wall by my neck with a hand I could easily sit in and whispered through his spittle that I was there as a return on an old favor, but that if he ever caught me feckin' off again, he would gladly do a year's time in prison just to hit me once. I believed him. And I valued my life.

Pat also taught me how to MacGyver during medical emergencies. One week in, I made the rookie mistake of using a box cutter to open a case of mushrooms propped across my thigh. The razor passed through the cardboard, my jeans, and my flesh, opening what looked like a red eye on the front of the meatiest part of my leg. I called to my brother who was stacking soda in the next aisle, and he ran to get Pat. When Pat arrived, he grabbed one of the ubiquitous cloths the stock boys used to wipe down the shelves, tied it around the wounded leg and then carried me into the back area like I was a bag of chips. Pat told Ricky Cirillo, one of the three Italian brothers in the neighborhood who got their stockboy jobs through their mother, the bookkeeper, to get him the first aid kit.

A moment later, Ricky arrived holding a bottle of Peroxide, a roll of gauze, a roll of white medical tape and a box of Kotex, heavy flow. By then Pat had stripped me of my jeans and dignity and was wiping the blood as best he could from my bare thigh with the counter cloth, which he had soaked in the slop sink. Then with the dexterity and focus of a field medic, Pat poured a healthy dose of Peroxide on the wound, holding my writhing body stationary with his vice-like grip on my knee. Finally, he added insult to injury when he slapped the Kotex pad over the wound and pressure wrapped it in place with the gauze and tape. This wasn't his first rodeo.

Pat also demonstrated his skill as a seamstress when he closed the bloodied slice in my jeans with a few clicks of a stapler and told me to put them back on.

The last thing Pat taught me was that a real man never quits. He made me go back out on the floor and finish out my schedule that day.

I never lived down being the first McCarthy male to ever wear a Kotex.

Over the next year, I repaid Pat for his kindness and consideration, by relieving the store of a few cases of beer stashed in the garbage boxes going out the back door a couple of nights each week.

CHAPTER THIRTY-EIGHT
(A DHARMA BUM)

In our galaxy, and the others, there are millions of stars. About half of them, like earth's sun and our Proxima Centauri, have planets in fixed trajectories around them. In Riverdale, the neighborhood was our sun, and we, the kids that grew up there, were the planets fixed in a permanent orbit.

Mark Wallen arrived late in the day and was only passing through the Riverdale universe, like a comet. During his relatively brief time in our skies, he burned brightly, but then, like Icarus passed too close to our sun. And that was my fault.

I met Mark on a late September day, when he showed up to work at Daitch. After graduating high school, the spring before, he left a small town in upstate New York for the bright lights of the big city. He got as far as a one room basement apartment in the shady part of Yonkers, down by McLean Avenue. Before he left the hinterlands, he spent most of the money he had on a yellow 1970 Ducati 450 Desmo which brought him down state, and which he parked on the dead-end street behind the store during working hours.

Pat Leary liked the fact that Mark was a hard worker, and that he wasn't from the neighborhood, so he hadn't been infected by our bad habits. He also had a slight accent that stood out among the nasal voices of everyone else. He had no geographic loyalty to the rest of the employees, who, for the most part, were as thick as thieves, because thieving was a way of life. In fact, before any of us came to work at Daitch, we used to shoplift there regularly.

Mark worked full time on the day shift, so we usually overlapped for only a few hours on the three weekday afternoons I worked after school, unless he stayed late, which was pretty often. Unlike the rest of us who always had one eye on the clock and one foot out the door, Mark would grab whatever overtime Pat was offering. Mark kept to himself and did his job stocking the pet aisle. He took his coffee and lunch breaks alone usually out back by his bike or next door in the Jewish Deli. I remember once seeing him eating a bowl of some mush with torn pieces of flat bread. When I asked him later what it was he told me "hummus." You couldn't have gotten me to eat anything with a name like that.

Mark was the first Buddhist I ever met. I was completely indoctrinated by my Catholic upbringing, so I tended to worry about the eternal life of the few Protestants and Jews I had befriended in our neighborhood. They all seemed nice enough, but I knew they were in for a shock when they arrived before St. Peter, and they didn't know the password. Given that I wasn't too enamored with my own faith, especially after my humiliating dismissal from the altar boys, I wasn't out there trying to convert anyone. But I wasn't handing in my resignation letter just yet. I would let God sort it all out.

One Saturday morning I went down into the store basement to retrieve a few cases of canned goods and shift them from the pallet to the conveyor belt. The basement was as basements tend to be, dark, quiet, and eerie. I almost tripped over Mark, who was sitting quietly in the shadows, perfectly still in an open spot between the large boxes on the paper-goods pallet. His legs were folded up on each other and his hands were on his knees, which just extended beyond the edge of the pallet, with palms pointed at the ceiling. I thought he was dead, or worse, drunk, because if Pat caught him like that he would be dead as well. I was about to sound the alarm when his eyes opened, and he looked around like he had just arrived in a foreign land.

"What the fuck?!" I exclaimed to cover my fear and surprise.

"Sorry," Mark said as he popped straight up like a jack in the box from his seated position. "I thought I was alone."

"What were you doing?"

He looked really uncomfortable, like he knew from experience that his response was not going to go over well. He looked around to make sure that there was no one else in the area. Finally, he whispered, "I like to come down here on my coffee break and meditate."

Now I had some exposure to the concept of meditation from my martial arts training, as our senseis had shown us how to quiet our thoughts at the beginning of each class before we learned to kill each other. But I had never seen it practiced out here in the real world, as an end in itself, by someone in street clothes.

"Hey," I responded, "Your secret's safe with me, but don't let Pat catch you with your eyes closed, or he's going to assume you're fucking off and you may wake up in the cardboard compressor."

"Thanks," he said. "I'll keep that in mind."

Since I had grown up with everyone that worked in the store, and pretty much knew more about their lives than they did, I started engaging with Mark more during work hours just to hear a story that I hadn't witnessed or heard a million times before. Stockboys are used to talking to each other over the tops of the aisles, and you would often chat with your neighbors in the aisles on either side of you to make the day go faster. You just couldn't curse, so the shoppers didn't complain, and you had to keep working, because those shelves weren't going to stock themselves. That wasn't a problem for Mark, as I never heard him curse. Not once. At least not in the beginning.

If someone saw Pat entering their aisle they always shouted, "Hey Pat," so his neighbors knew to end their conversation.

Sometimes I would grab lunch with Mark on those odd Saturday's he was picking up overtime. I still wouldn't eat that shit hummus, but the Jewish Deli made a killer tuna on rye with a side of chips and a cream soda.

Turns out that Mark hailed from Jamestown, New York, whose only claim to fame was that it was the home of the Hollywood film and television star Lucille Ball. His parents had died in a car crash during a blizzard when he was fourteen. Mark spent the last few years of high school living in a foster home whose hosts treated their relationship with him, and the other foster kids that rotated through their home, as strictly business. He was happy enough, with food in his belly and a roof over his head. He even had his own room, but there was no emotional connection.

Mark had always been a worker. When he wasn't in school, which he really didn't care for, he was out shoveling snow or cutting lawns. In his junior year, he talked himself into a regular afternoon gig stocking shelves and working behind the counter in a small deli downtown that was owned by an old Vietnam veteran. The vet refused to share his war stories with Mark, but did share his practice of Buddhism that he brought back from Southeast Asia.

Mark told me that Buddhism was relatively simple in concept, if difficult in practice. He followed what he called the Noble Eightfold Path – eight "rights" – view, intention, speech, action, livelihood, effort, concentration, and mindfulness. That's why he didn't drink or smoke when I first met him. He didn't curse either. But he didn't seem to mind when I did, which was all the time. I was on my own path, he said. I would figure it out in the end.

But while Mark was a good influence on me, I was a bad influence on him.

When I first started to bring him around my crew he would easily socialize and yet politely refuse offers of beers or cigarettes. He enjoyed the comradery and was the perfect guest, who found everything any of my Riverdale friends said hilarious and was so passive that he deferred when he knew someone was drunk and talking absolute shit. He even kept me from getting into a few fights.

Mark got along great with my cousin Apples, who was just a little older than he was. They loved to talk about Apples' favorite topic, whether or not humans were alone in the universe. Mark explained that Buddhism has long understood that life is present throughout the universe, and that Buddhist scriptures depict Buddhas and bodhisattvas from many different world systems.

As kids, Apples and I used to spend warm summer nights camping out in our back yard. We would lay out on blankets and stare up at the stars. He liked to flash one of Spaghetti's flashlights at the stars, waiting for a flash back. If one came, I must have blinked. I was all in on anything magical and was raised with a healthy Irish respect for the Fae, but never gave what lay outside our world much thought. However, Apples was obsessed with outer space and refused to accept that this world was all there was. I just figured that was his way of coping with the shitty parts of life. We all needed a life boat.

"You know your cousin believes he's been abducted by greys." Mark said to me one day after a particularly long night partying up by Matty's fort. "And I believe him."

I laughed. Apples was like my brother, and I would kill for him. But sometimes he would come out with the craziest stories. I always listened patiently and never let anyone make fun of him. I was laughing at Mark because he was so trusting.

Turns out, I was the asshole, and Apples was telling the truth. But I didn't find that out until a human lifetime later, but you guys already know that.

Turns out that even the best Buddhists have their Achilles heel, and Mark was no different.

Girls seemed to like Mark's gentleness. He was naturally good looking and had an easy smile. And he never hit on them. Part of his eight noble "rights." And for a whole year he managed to avoid getting into a relationship with any of the locals.

I was beginning to suspect he was gay, which wasn't something I knew shit about. I just knew he didn't capitalize on the opportunities that kept presenting themselves, that some of the other guys would have killed for. I just figured he didn't like girls. But I didn't let any of the other guys even whisper that rumor more than once.

When Mark finally did find the wrong girl, during that New Year's Eve party at the end of 1973, she got him to go so far left, that in the end, there was nothing left of the old him to right. Mark was no Siddhartha Gautama, there was no nirvana beyond the sex. And once he lost his Buddha, he became just like the rest of us. Booze and ciggies were not far behind. And where that ultimately lead is on me.

But his long-term loss was my short-term gain, because by the end of my junior year Mark had gotten his lifeguard license at the WMCA. Since I still had a year left on mine, he scoured every country club in Westchester on his Ducati, putting our applications in until he finally landed us both a job, working the high chairs on weekends at a New Rochelle Yacht and Cabana club. Just so we could sit in the sun and check out the girls.

But a lot had to happen before we got there. And a lot happened afterwards.

CHAPTER THIRTY-NINE
(FEUGO MANZANAS AND PEGASUS)

When I returned to Spillane for my junior and final year, I did my best to fly under the radar. I had a nice pony-tail length of hair tucked under what was a relatively expensive rug, so I didn't want any teachers or the administration taking too close a notice of me. That meant avoiding JUG at all costs.

JC was doing a lot of "studying" during his free periods with his favorite tutor, Joanna Skeegle, so not having a wing man made it easier to keep on the down low. It just wasn't as much fun breaking rules by yourself, and I had quit smoking. Oddly enough, my own grades began improving even though I still didn't do any studying. Seemed like those voices were just getting a little clearer in my head come test time. My afternoons after school were spent equally divided between Daitch and the dojo, where I hung with Mark and JC, respectively, so the only time to party was on weekends.

On the female front, my love life seemed to ebb and flow through the repeated cycle of easy pick-up and painful break-up, as more and more of the local girls seemed to gain and lose interest with equal speed and intensity. I just assumed there was something wrong with me. That I wasn't delivering whatever the girls were looking for in a boyfriend. For a while I thought I had halitosis, but after subjecting my sister to repeated trials by literally blowing up her nostrils, she assured me that it wasn't my breath that was rotten. After a while, I stopped giving a shit, not because I was less enamored of women, but because I was tired of having my feelings crushed. And what sucked most of all, was that it wasn't something you could share with anyone. Big boys don't cry.

Most of the gang was now pairing off into couples, which just wasn't happening for me, so I started to shop elsewhere.

By now I was rocking a full five o'clock shadow by 2 p.m. most weekend days when I didn't have to deal with Spillane shaving rules. So, I could easily pass for 18 years old on looks alone. I started hitting the bars in other neighborhoods, just because I was feeling self-conscious about the rapid turnover among the local girls.

When I needed to fly under the radar, I could always rely on my cousin to have my back. That fall, on Saturday nights, Apples and I would walk up across the city line into Yonkers and hit this hole-in-the-wall dance club on Lawrence street called, The Pegasus Pub. Mark Wallen had driven passed it a few times on his way home from work to his place over by Saints Peter and Paul Church on McLean Avenue and said there always seemed to be a good crowd outside its door. But he still wasn't drinking, so he always turned down the invite to come along.

The exterior and interior of the club were painted completely black, including its windows, and a large silver Disco ball slowly rotated off the center ceiling. The only luminescence, besides the red exit signs, came from strategically placed black lights that made everyone's eyes and teeth pop, especially anyone with capped teeth, which gave you the feeling you were dancing in a room full of skeletons. But it did have its upside, because most the women wore sheer tops and their white bouncing bras kept time with the music. Could give a fellow whiplash if you got too caught up in the rhythm.

The crowd was mostly Latino with some blacks and Italians mixed in and it was hard to tell each week, due to the dark interior, if there were regulars. The bouncer didn't give a shit that two James McEntees with the exact same birthday were walking in together. As long as the money was legit. And none of the other attendees seemed to care that a couple of white boys were hanging around. Everyone was there for the music.

On the first night we went to Pegasus, Apples surprised the shit out of me by walking out on the dance floor when Willie Colón and Hector Lavoe's *Che Che Colé* started to play. He began dancing a *feugo* Salsa with a hot Latina, who first thought she was doing him a favor, while some of her friends looked on and giggled. Turns out that while his cousins were being raised playing every contact sport imaginable, the prick had been taking dance lessons as a young teen on the down low at the Park Avenue Fred Astaire Dance Studio. After that first song, the girls lined up to dance with *chico blanco*. And he never left the floor.

Apples was better than a cute puppy because he always got me noticed as well.

My dancing was much more limited and solely for an ulterior purpose. My sister Bonnie had taught me how to dance in the barn during our last summer trip to Maine. She had a Frankie Valley and The Four Seasons album and despite her best efforts, I was barely passable on my feet. I also had a problem with the slow dances because she insisted on leading. But I got by weaving in some slow-motion kata movements, which at least created a pattern of intentional movement on the floor.

Once in the club, I tried to scope out the potential single women who were there with their girlfriends, and then waited for a song that was slow enough to require body contact, which brought us close enough to hear each other's voices. That always led to a drink afterwards at the bar and then some flirtatious conversation for a while at one of the corner tables. At some point before the evening was over the girl inevitably leaned in for that kiss and then led me out into the alley beside the club for some serious action. And I was easy. I graduated from hickies to hand jobs out in that alley. I also touched my first breast. Black is beautiful.

TMI father, way TMI. Stella interrupted.

Will you just let him tell his story, sis? Apollo said. *You should have named me after your cousin, Apples, father, because I haven't fallen far from the tree.*

You know, it was bad enough listening to the flow of Jimmy's bullshit over all these years, Claire said, *but at least his puns were always good.*

Look, if you want the unedited version, I responded, undeterred, *you have to put up with the bitter and the sweet. Otherwise, you can just download it all sometime in the future. I'm calling it as I see it.*

Stella considered the latter option for just a moment, and then tossed her hands up in surrender, like I had seen Gina do so many times during our centuries together. You don't have to give birth to be a mother.

You were talking about black breasts, father. Apollo shared, the wicked glint in his eye matched in intensity by the grimace from his sister.

I probably would have spent the rest of my teen years dancing at Pegasus if Apples hadn't merengued with the wrong Latina one night, while her boyfriend was drinking heavily at the bar. I saw it unfolding and managed to stop the angry boyfriend from doing any damage to the bewildered Apples on the dance floor, but one teen with limited training wasn't going to stop the rest of his crew. Luckily, Frankie, a huge black bouncer whose college football career ended when he was stabbed in one eye as a teen, ran interference and escorted – yanked – my cousin and me off the floor and out the front door and then kept anyone from following after us. Always tip the bouncer. We ran all the way back to Riverdale.

In a way, my one-nighter dance floor dalliances kept me out of real trouble. There were no real commitments, and you could only go so far in an alleyway. I still had the same Trojan BJ had given me tucked safely and intact in my wallet. In fact, it had remained in that one spot so long that it looked like my wallet had ring worm. It never made it to Christmas.

CHAPTER FORTY
(BLOND AMBITION)

Every morning when we arrived at school during junior year, JC and I would head off to our lockers on the third floor, stash our bags and coats and then head down to the cafeteria for some bullshit with Eddie and BJ, and whomever else was available. Sometimes, JC would ditch me for a better offer from Joanne Skreegle for a make out session on the rooftop stairwell landing, which was totally acceptable, given I would have done the exact same thing.

But before I left my locker each morning, I spent a few extra seconds checking the mirror that hung on the inside of the top locker to make sure my dark brown wig was set evenly above both ears. Getting over on the school administration had become my *raison d'être*.

One morning in October, after JC's most recent ditching, I was so focused on double checking the hairpiece that I didn't notice the person standing beside me.

"You definitely look cuter in your natural shade of brown, and I miss the pony tail."

I spun so quickly that the wig shifted just a bit.

"Let me get that for you." A dainty set of hands attached to a very cute blond reached up and maneuvered the wig back into place. Funny how that bit of innocent intimacy instantly changed the dynamic between two strangers.

It took a moment more for me to place the face and body, now adorned in the respectable blue uniform, into the tight blue-jeans ensemble it sported that one-night last spring. But then I spotted the diamond pinky ring hanging from a thin gold chain around her neck. My eyes couldn't lie when the recognition occurred.

"I believe you asked for two helpings," She said and smiled.

I was instantly embarrassed all over again, and just a bit enchanted.

"I'm sorry about that," I stammered, then defaulted into the great panacea. "Would you accept the excuse that I was drunk?"

"I kinda figured that out given that you were talking to yourself." She said. "But I'm going to let you make it up to me by buying me a cup of terrible coffee in the cafeteria."

"And why would I do that?" I asked, knowing full well that I was going to do it, but distracted by her comment about me being alone that night on the bench.

"No offense, you are a decent looking guy and all, but I need you to explain to me why it was that I could not get you out of my head the rest of that weekend, like a bad song" she said, slamming my locker closed, and then taking my arm, "and then, poof, by Monday I completely forgot all about you. I haven't given you another thought until I spotted you ten seconds ago staring at yourself in the mirror. I never forget a face."

We walked down the hallway for a few steps and then she said, "And that wig is horrendous."

The coffee tasted a whole lot better than usual that morning

Danielle liked to talk. She quickly shared her biographical details of her very small Italian family going back three generations to a small city in Northern Italy, Bassano Del Grappa. They were a family of bakers. She was an only child, who was doted upon by her parents, and her grandparents. I could tell how close they were as a family just by the way she described them. She had a pleasant voice.

And while my sight line probably would have wandered south of her chin anyway, this time it kept stopping at that pinky ring around her neck.

"Hey buddy," she said with a smile, "my eyes are up here."

Those eyes were jade.

When you have been caught doing something wrong as many times as I have, you blush just at the accusation, even if you are completely innocent.

"Honestly," I stammered, "I was just noticing the ring."

This time, she blushed. She took a long sip of the coffee and then looked like she was about to say something, when the first bell of the day rang throughout the school, and the masses all started to shuffle in their seats and head out of the cafeteria.

"Saved by the bell," she said, with just a little less confidence in her voice. "I'll see you around."

I watched her until she was about to exit the cafeteria, when she turned and caught me staring. I gave her that same finger wave from the night at the park. She smiled, then turned and left.

"C'mon, fuckwad!" BJ's voice appeared right on cue, followed by the tremendous force of his paws landing on my shoulders from behind. I swear those impacts made me a half-inch shorter. "You're gonna be late for class."

"Who's that?" Eddie asked as he arrived right behind BJ, gesturing to where Danielle had been standing a moment before.

"Just a friend." I answered, as I got up from the table and followed them out into the hallway.

CHAPTER FORTY-ONE
(OPPORTUNITY KNOCKS)

In the late fall of 1972, Robbie Maclaren's dad earned his wings as partner in his mega law firm in the Wall Street area of Manhattan. So, the first thing he did to commemorate his legal ascension was to buy a huge house in the toniest section of Westchester, called Scarsdale, New York.

Mrs. Maclaren had moved the family to the new home within two weeks of closing, and had their co-op listed before the moving trucks left Riverdale. But she left just enough furniture behind for the realtors to build a staged apartment, including the queen-sized bed in their master bedroom. I heard they purchased an ornate king-sized poster bed to adorn their new master suite up north. As I said, they were both still young, beautiful, and athletic.

Robbie took the Metro North from his new home in Scarsdale to Fordham Prep each weekday morning and then grabbed the No. 20 bus from Fordham to Riverdale each afternoon after school, just so he could meet up with his steady girlfriend, Sally. You see, Robbie, like his dad before him, had fallen in love with his high school sweetheart, a beautiful and sensible middle-class girl from Yonkers, who proved the clone of Robbie's mother when it came to social engineering. And just like his parents, they married after college and Sally supported Robbie as he followed his dad into the legal profession.

But back in 1972, Robbie's mom would swing down each day to pick him up around six pm, and the cycle would start again the next school day. Robbie spent his weekends crashing overnight at his old apartment, having convinced his parents that it was better to have someone going in and out of the place, to keep potential burglars from casing and trashing the place on weekends.

Truth was that Robbie and half of our crew lost their virginity that winter in Robbie's apartment and were collectively very sad to finally see the apartment sold for a record fifty thousand dollars in March of 1973. A king's ransom.

Robbie was very democratic, as great leaders are, so he used a marble notebook to create a schedule that allowed his friends to access the apartment each weeknight between six and eight pm. One-hour slots, two opportunities each night. He left the notebook with Bobby Armstrong, who could always be found after school working some job at RNH. During the first month, a lot of these slots went unfilled, because let's face it, most of the boys didn't have enough game to find a willing partner, and most of the girls were too smart to waste themselves on the testosterone driven boys of our neighborhood. I don't blame them.

But some of the more serious pairings of steady couples at least took the opportunity to explore what it would be like to be naked with their steady in bed. Most of their physical fumbling's to date involved reaching past open zippers and loosened bras during some stolen privacy with the desperation and dexterity of Helen Keller learning the alphabet. Up until then, it was all a matter of touch. W-A-T-E-R!

And why were we all so much in a hurry to experience full blown sex? It's easy to blame it on the hippies from the sixties, with their "free love," Haight Ashbury and Woodstock. They were all young like us just one decade earlier and their perception of the world around them created this urgency to become complete humans, which meant entering that moment of ultimate intimacy. If only for that moment. We certainly weren't ready to be outdone by our predecessors.

I remember this Vietnam vet from our neighborhood, Johnny Peyton, who wasn't that much older than we were. Johnny was not a hippie, he volunteered for the army right out of high school and went to fight for his country. His valor was rewarded after his second tour "in country" when he returned to Riverdale with a chest full of medals and a permanent wheelchair.

One night during the summer of 1972, Johnny rolled up to the edge of the rocks with twelve beers and shared it with some of our crew. I could tell by the jaundice of his eyes that this wasn't his first round for the day. Towards the end of the night, I asked him what he missed most about his life before the wheelchair. Without skipping a beat, he said, "the sex, but not just the physical act."

At that point, I couldn't think of anything beyond the physical act.

"You're not going to get that just jerking off," he said with a mischievous laugh, "although I miss that too."

He went on to explain how, if the timing is just right, during the moment two people "climaxed," as he put it, they lost all sense of self. They became one with the other person, and no matter what they may have felt before, or even after that act, for those few seconds, as they were locked in each other's embrace, they were loved by someone. That other person. And nothing else mattered. Nothing.

"Most people haven't experienced a feeling like that since the moment they were born," Johnny said, wistfully, "and they spend all of their lives never getting back there." Then he guzzled the last of the beers and crushed the can with one hand on the only part of his body that hadn't failed him, his head.

"You know, the French speaking hookers in Saigon called orgasms 'little death'," Johnny said, and then laughed wickedly. I watched after him as he rolled off down the pathway and out of the park. Two weeks later he took his life.

I cannot speak for the rest of the crew, but from that moment on I knew I wanted to experience that feeling Johnny talked about, if only just once, before the universe put me in a wheel chair, or took my life.

Hence, the urgency.

But it wasn't as easy to get there as I thought, even if you found a willing partner.

CHAPTER FORTY-TWO
(PIZZA TO GO)

Murray Conlon got more action than any teenager deserved. I remember hearing in some movie that the brain is the sexiest part of the body so that must have given him an edge, because he was the smartest guy in our crew.

I remember being so jealous when he came back from his part-time job at a local nursing home one Saturday night and shared that had just slept with a full-blown woman doctor from the facility. Seems the young doctor had given him quite the physical. She even checked his prostate, wherever the hell that was. I begged him to get me a job there.

Late 1972 found Murray monopolizing Robbie's marble notebook. Sometimes he double booked. He never kissed and told, but rumor had it that he was steadily working his way through a series of young ladies he had left behind in his old neighborhood. And they actually paid the cab fare to come to him.

The deal was that the first person to use Robbie's apartment each night got the key from Bobby Armstrong, and after that first hour, left the key over the door jamb above the apartment entrance for the next guy. The next guy would wrap up his hour with a quick look around the apartment to make sure the beds were made and there was no food left in the kitchen. Then he would drop the key into a large milk can that sat on the far end of the Armstrong family's front porch, to be recycled by Bobby for the next day's lucky lotharios.

Not everybody got lucky every time they accessed the apartment. In fact, I'm willing to bet the real number was one in ten, if you remove Murray from the equation. I'm not even sure that Robbie reached home base back in the day. But most guys at least got a good look at the playing fields, and their girls got an equally good look at the sports equipment.

The members of our crew were notorious bullshit artists. So, as far as bragging was concerned, we all scored, each time and every time.

Joe Marrero may have been one that told the truth. He had been going steady with Lilly Tonelli since the summer of 1972, and he was the bad boy she was forbidden to see by her very Italian, and purportedly connected, family. She made it clear to everyone that she would never let him get away. She kept him well marked with neck hickies to warn off any rivals for his wandering eye or affection. Joe once showed me a dark purple hickey she placed just below his belly button. It was strategically brilliant, given that it was the first thing you saw when he opened his zipper. It looked like it hurt, and he swore she renewed it every time it started to fade. But Lilly had good reason to mark her territory. Like Murray, Joe was a player. And it got only worse when he formed a band and started playing gigs in back yards and house parties around the neighborhood.

JC was also an hourly border at casa Maclaren. Seems that Joanne Skeegle had gotten her license that fall and would make regular trips in her new car over to the west Bronx to make sure JC was keeping up with his studies. It must have been working, because by the end of the fall semester of junior year, JC was in the top quarter of our class.

JC wasn't a glutton when it came to reserving apartment time, for, as he explained, the bucket passenger seat in Joanna's Chevy Vega fully reclined, which allowed him to study the constellations while running the bases. However, he did admit that it was nice to have sex in a bed every once in a while. I always nodded like I knew what the fuck he was talking about.

Even Brian Kelly popped his cherry in the apartment that fall. Seems he reconnected with a crush from his grammar school years at Saints Peter and Paul named Trixie MacDonald. She was very impressed that he had not managed to get himself kicked out of Fordham Prep in three years, like one of his older brothers, and so assumed that he had a promising future before him. Some girls were ruled by their brains and not their hearts. Brian registered in the black in Trixie's cost-benefit analysis.

Given that I was staying busy with random weekly alleyway trysts outside that club in Yonkers, I didn't have the need or desire to enter the booking rotation back in Riverdale. I had given up the idea of having a steady girlfriend, and, quite honestly, given the indifference most of my neighborhood exes showed towards me, it wasn't like anyone was lining up to be the next one-night stand. So, I had pulled my line out of the local fishing hole. I preferred to land whatever physical intimacy I could easily get with pretty strangers, who wouldn't stick around long enough to break my heart. If you don't have any expectations, you can't be disappointed.

I did come close once. My sixteenth birthday fell in the middle of November 1972, and Robbie gave me the apartment for the entire night as his present to me. JC had a second cousin on his mother's side named Vickie Cariano who was a year older than us, who lived in Brooklyn but would party anywhere. And she drove. He swore she was a definite score, having seen her waylay more than a few waiters in the coat rooms at some of the family weddings. She was the blackest in his family of black sheep. But they were close, and they would make fun of the WASP side of his family every time they got together.

JC said that as long as I served her a meal and some wine she was ready to party. He would make the introduction as a special favor to me. Given I was a regular customer at all the local liquor stores and Luigi's made the best pizza in the world, I figured what did I have to lose. Hopefully my cherry.

On the Friday night in question, I waited patiently at casa Maclaren with my pepperoni Sicilian pizza and bottle of Chianti, presented as culinarily sophisticated as possible on the small round kitchen table by the one window next to the fire escape, which overlooked Mush Park. I checked to make sure I had BJ's condom in my wallet.

I watched the pizza get cold as the clock reached six-fifteen, with no sign of Vickie. I was feeling more and more nervous, and the building's heat was rising in the apartment, so I cracked the top of the kitchen window, and sat staring out at the local homeless guy named Circles. He sometimes slept on the benches in Mush, and was now having an animated conversation with himself under one of the park's street lamps. To calm my nerves, I popped the cork and sipped some Chianti. When it reached 6:30, I cursed JC and was about to call it a day, but then the downstairs buzzer rang.

When the apartment bell rang, I opened the door to find a tall, voluptuous Italian girl with long brown hair, parted in the middle, brown eyes, and very full lips. Her Romanesque nose did nothing to detract from a very attractive face.

"Oh, you're cute," she said, with a strong Bensonhurst accent. "Sorry I'm late, bridge traffic is a killer." She smiled and walked past me and into the apartment, and then removed and handed me her long leather coat which I then hung on the one open hanger beside my own parka in the otherwise empty hall closet.

"This is nice." she said, taking in the apartment. "Your's?"

"No, I'm house sitting for a friend." I lied.

Vickie was wearing a blue, V-neck, cashmere sweater that displayed a tight linear cleavage between what the close-fitting top defined as two very prominent breasts.

"It was nice for Charles to set us up on this blind date." Vickie said as she leaned in and pecked me on the cheek before making her way into the kitchen. "And you are far better looking than he told me."

"That's lovely, your perfume." I whispered. I was feeling extremely excited by her proximity. It had to be the wine.

"Diorella," she said. "Pizza and Chianti. You certainly know a way to this girl's heart."

"I'm sorry, the pizza is cold, but we can heat it up in the oven." I could not stop thinking about her breasts.

"What did you say?" She asked, distracted, like she was listening to another conversation at the same time.

"The pizza. . . it's cold." I repeated. "I can heat it up."

She stopped at the entrance to the kitchen and then turned back to me with a strange look on her face. I thought I had said something wrong. I was about to panic.

"The pizza can wait," she said as she grabbed my face in her hands and pulled me in for a very pleasant landing on her very soft lips. Her tongue slipped through and tickled the edge of mine. I was instantly hard.

"Bedroom?" She whispered.

I pointed down the hall. She took my hand led me down to the master bedroom.

I was fishing for my wallet from my back pocket with my free hand, thinking how I really needed to apologize for cursing JC. I kicked off my sneakers as I got closer to the door and as we entered the bedroom she released my hand and then released her body.

This wasn't like any quick fumble I ever had. This now naked woman literally tore my clothes off me and shoved me back on the bed. I didn't even get my socks off.

And she had a body to die for. She was full figured and powerful, and I felt her hard nipples pressing into my thighs as she climbed onto the end of the bed and used those soft full lips in a way I had only dreamed about. I was literally biting my lip to keep control of my physical response.

"Condom," she whispered.

I reached down to the floor and retrieved my empty pants, found the wallet, and with shaking hands removed the condom, and handed it to her. She tore the wrapper with her teeth and then expertly slid it over the end of my very happy penis and then unrolled it down the rest of the way with just one hand. I didn't even care how cold it felt when it first went on. I was in heaven.

And then I heard the loud crash, the sound of a bottle breaking and a heavy thud. By the time I heard "Mother fucker!" I had leapt off the bed and raced out into the hallway. The commotion was coming from the kitchen.

I turned the corner and automatically did what I had been training for the past six months to do, drop into fighting position, left leg forward and arms raised for striking. My eyes focused on the upended table, the flattened pizza lying on the floor beside it and the broken bottle of Chianti. The top of the window was fully open. I spotted the figure now rising up from the floor to his feet and I prepared to land the hardest kick I could summon. Then he spoke.

"Yo, dude, did I interrupt something, or are you just happy to see me?" And then he laughed in the unique way that only Murray laughed. He was covered from face to waist in the cheese, sauce, and pepperoni from my pizza, with some Chianti dressing. But he wasn't the least bit worried about his own appearance, as he was pointing at my still condomed and erect penis.

"You're not going to hit me with that, are ya?"

In that moment, with Murray now laughing hysterically, I understood the concept of absurdity. I joined in with his laughter because I didn't know what else to do. I had almost forgotten about Vickie until she flew past me as she tugged on the last of her clothes, grabbed her coat and headed out the apartment door. "Call me if you're ever out in Bensonhurst," was the last thing I heard before the door slammed behind her.

"Sorry about that," Murray said as he caught his breath. "I thought the place was free tonight and couldn't find Bobby Armstrong to get the key. I always leave the kitchen window unlocked so I can come in from the roof off the fire escape but slipped this time as I was climbing over the window sill." He reached over and grabbed the dish towel hanging over the side of the sink and tossed it at me. "Cover that thing up, will ya, it's gonna give me nightmares."

I suddenly realized I was still naked, although, my attention had now waned, and BJ's condom was looking sad and defeated. I threw the cloth back at Murray and ran back to the bedroom.

It took me a little longer to get my clothes back on, but then again I didn't have any help reversing the process. By the time I returned, Murray had gotten the kitchen back in order and the garbage all stowed away. He was cleaning the last of the pizza off his coat.

I was about to read him the riot act when the front door buzzer sounded. Murray looked at the clock. "Shit, that's Chrissy. I told her come by after seven."

He hung his coat over the kitchen chair and then hit the buzzer to let her in.

"Could you go down the stairs, Jimmy? No one knows I've been seeing Chrissy, and this is her first time up to casa Maclaren. I don't want you bumping into her in the elevator to put her off."

He opened the apartment door, and I could see the elevator numbers rising over its portal.

"You owe me ten bucks for the pizza and wine, you cock sucker," was all I could come up with as I grabbed my coat and headed over to the top of the stairs, just as the elevator reached our floor.

I could hear Murray's most welcoming voice as I raced down the stairway.

But I did get one bit of birthday revenge, because I had left BJ's deflated condom on the pillow in the bedroom.

Wait, so you didn't get laid? Apollo asked incredulously.

You are worse than a human! Claire admonished.

First dad and now my brother! Apollo has spent too much time with the Terrans. Stella said. *I'm going to need a warning the next time you are venturing into this subject matter.*

You're still not a virgin, are you? Apollo broke into laughter.

It's possible. Petrichor told me I was an immaculate conception. Stella added, then joined her brother in his merriment. Even Claire couldn't help but Lurch away with the others in that funny deep throated laugh.

You'd swear you invented it, I said with feigned indignation. But then I too had to laugh.

Can I move on? I asked.

Please, I have to get that last image out of my head. Stella said.

CHAPTER FORTY-THREE
(CHRISTMAS COMES EARLY)

"You owe me, after that shit you pulled on my cousin." JC said as he flipped his ciggie out the back window of the Special bus.

"Fuck that," I responded. "Blame Murray. He spoiled the party. I was all in." I couldn't help but recall those breasts.

"Well, she thought the two of you were weird, laughing like lunatics in the kitchen." JC said, "and you naked with wood."

He reached in his coat pocket and removed a piece of paper with a number starting with the 718-area code. "Here, she told me to give you her number."

I took the paper, slipped it into my coat, and never saw it again.

"So why are you going?" I asked. "We don't do school dances."

"Jo is on the Senior Dance Committee," JC said.

"So?"

"So, she wants me there with her."

"So?"

"So, I don't want to be there by myself with a bunch of nerds and jocks."

I hadn't been dancing for a few weeks since Apples got us banned from Pegasus. I missed that easy contact with girls.

"But that means I have to wear my wig." I said waving him off. "I'm not giving the deans a freebee at catching me."

"That means I have to wear my wig!" JC mimicked me but in a higher pitched voice. "Will you stop being such a pussy? You know I'd do it for you."

I hate when friends say that, especially when it's true. JC would do anything I asked him to do. He came with me to Kung Fu without making a fuss, and stuck with it, despite the many beatings we had endured on a weekly basis.

"C'mon fuck head! I'll buy your ticket."

"All right! If you are going to be such a fucking baby about it!" I shouted. "I'll go."

"Great," JC said, a big grin on his face. "Jo is picking me up at 6:30 Friday. We'll swing by and get you right afterwards."

* * * * *

Turns out that Eddie and BJ were also going to the dance, as BJ had his eye on a cute young girl named Ellie May Cavanaugh, and Eddie took his wing man duties very seriously. So come Friday December 15th, the three of us piled into the cramped back seat of Joanna's Vega and headed off with the happy couple to the Spillane gym, for its "Winter Wonderland" themed dance.

Joanna and her committee had done a wonderful job decking out the halls outside the gym with faux snow and mock up sleighs. There was even a huge inflatable Santa and a life-sized Rudolph, red nose flashing, as you entered. And when Joanna changed into her sexy-elf outfit to work the ticket counter at the front entrance, I got an instant epiphany as to why JC was totally whipped. There is nothing sexier than a hot nerd who doesn't know how hot she is.

One of the other nerdy seniors was working as the DJ for the dance, and I was really impressed by the mix and extent of the music he was playing. All the hits of the last three years with some early sixties' classics mixed in, often as a slow dance. It was nice to see the prettier alter egos of the many girls I had been passing in the hallways for the past couple of years, but all the really pretty ones were already paired up with their school boyfriends. The rest remained in clusters, either dancing with other girls, or just leaning in rows against the folded-up stands looking like they were intentionally choosing not to dance.

Eddie was standing off in a corner in the shadows, scanning the room before taking a quick hit from a silver flask he then returned to the inside of his jean jacket pocket. I know he had been dating one of the pretty cashiers up at Daitch named Linda Murphy, so I wasn't surprised that he wasn't chasing tale with BJ, who was out on the dance floor with Ellie May, dancing like no one was watching. But everyone was.

BJ was the ultimate character. He was everything you could want in a son, a natural athlete, a solid student, and one of the funniest guys you could ever share time with. Plus, he was a physical beast, not in the steroid athlete sense, but he had natural brute strength that made him an asset no matter what the setting. And despite his comical aura, he was always ready to throw down the first time one of his boys was in trouble. Eddie was one of his boys. That made me one of his boys, once removed. His presence always gave me an added sense of security.

I wandered the dark edges of the packed gym for a while, avoiding the roaming chaperones, including Bud Bosworth, the boy's dean of discipline. He was luckily such an imposing figure that I could spot his silhouette circulating through the dance floor like King Kong in order to maintain plenty of distance between us. He nailed me a few times in freshman year on the hair beef, before I got the hang of bobby pins and hair gel, and I didn't want to land in indefinite JUG for the spring semester, by having him take too close a look at my *cheveux*, as my French teacher would put it.

I used this migration to check out the female scenery, stopping along the way to say hi to a few of my other friends like Billy Quigley, who was working on chasing down a cute freshman he had his eye on. I made the mistake of seeking out JC, who was over with Joanna by the entrance. She was in whirlwind mode and went from one issue to another to keep everything running smoothly. He got to be her man. I finally got dragged onto the dance floor by one of Joanna's more nerdy friends, who was working the coat check and hadn't gotten to dance all night, but after faking my way through *Maggie May* and *Knock Three Times*, I realized that my wig was beginning to slip on the sweat that was now running in rivulets down my forehead and sideburns. I begged off a slow dance to *You've Got A Friend* by telling the girl I had to piss. Then I headed off to find my brother.

But the power of suggestion being what it was to most Irishmen, I ended up really having to piss, so I made my way past the accessible but packed locker room bathrooms and off into a west wing school hallway to find an open urinal. I had never had a school hallway all to myself before, and while I could still hear the pulse of the music in the gym, I was more focused on the sound of my boot heels clicking with an echo as I made my way to the nearest boys' bathroom.

Once inside, I locked the door behind me so I could remove my wig and wipe down my head, blotting my now soaked hair and resetting the pins. I went over to the window and opened it a crack, to allow the cold December air in to help cool me down. I watched in the closest mirror as the steam rose off my head and kept blotting my hair with paper towels until it became more manageable. I decided that I had done my good deed for the night and was going to find JC and tell him I was grabbing a cab. I was sure Eddie was ready to split as well. BJ would find his way home on his own. He always did.

As I returned to the foyer outside the gym, a pleasant female voice said, "That wig still looks ridiculous."

I turned and spotted blond Danielle standing by the coat check wearing a hip length rabbit coat, leaving to my view her very shapely legs extending from a tight short black skirt into an expensive looking pair of matching pumps.

"My eyes are still up here." She said, and a very white and even set of teeth escaped into a broad smile, framed by very red lipstick on her kewpie doll lips.

Why do I always blush?

"Coming or going?" I asked.

"Waiting for a ride." She answered. "You?"

"Heading out." I responded. "Way too cheerful in there."

"Maybe you can keep me company until my ride arrives."

Nights In White Satin started to play in the gym, just as the coat check nerd arrived back at her station.

"Jimmy," the nerd shouted excitedly, "come on, this is a great song."

I started to stammer when suddenly Danielle grabbed my hand and led me back towards the entrance, dropping her coat on the table and calling out, "Sorry, I've been saving my dance card for this one."

"Thanks for saving me back there." I said once we had gotten to the edge of the dance floor. There was that pinky ring hanging from its chain right at the apex of a very healthy alpine region.

"Shut up and dance," she responded, as she pulled me in close and started to slowly rock her hips in rhythm to the music. I spent the first two minutes of the song worrying that she could feel the same intense heat I was feeling where our bodies made contact.

When the flute solo began she leaned her head into my chest and rested it tucked under my chin. I could feel the ring between us.

"I just don't get it," she whispered.

"What?" I asked.

"Why it is I'm so attracted to you every time I see you?" She asked, looking up at me with those Jade eyes. "I mean, you're not even a great dancer."

"Shut up and dance." I said, pulling her closer and getting lost in the last refrain. When the song ended we continued to rock for a few more seconds, until she glanced at her watch.

"Shit!" She said, breaking free. "Gotta go, my ride's waiting."

She started towards the exit and then suddenly turned back, ran up to me and kissed me hard on the lips. "Merry Christmas," she shouted as she raced back through the exit as fast as her pumps would let her. I followed after her as far as the front of the school where I saw her slide into the passenger seat of that same black Camaro.

CHAPTER FORTY-FOUR
(BEER MUSCLES)

The Environmental Protection Agency was established by the United States government in 1970 to protect human and environmental health. But it wasn't the leaded gas, that automobile exhausts were still pumping into the air, that was going to do the most damage to my generation. The most dangerous chemical combination we were exposed to, in our environment, was alcohol and testosterone. And we loved its effects more than the enticing smell of galenic gasoline fumes.

By Spring of 1973, another lad had moved into the neighborhood and found his way into our crew. Steve Adamos arrived at the perfect time. The crews that both Eddie and I ran with started to socially merge on The Courts. This was a common event at the upper-class high school level in Riverdale, given the attrition rate and cross-pollination as the crews got older. Members of a crew were poached by the bar crowds, moved out of the neighborhood, or died. Steve's family had used their hard-earned money from a string of diners, to move to their comfortable brick house just off Fieldstone Road from their small apartment in the little Athens section of Astoria, Queens.

The local girls didn't mind Steve's arrival, as he was tall, dark, and handsome, with the thickest head of wavy, long jet-black hair that he wore tied in a pony tail. Of course, Steve made the rookie mistake of hitting on Eddie's then girlfriend, Linda MacDonald, the first night he rode up to The Courts on his ten speed and received a quick and decisive beat down for his troubles.

Having been on the receiving end of those beat downs since I could walk, I had to admire Steve's resilience in clinging desperately to my brother for a good five minutes. He even got off a few of his own futile punches, where had he gone limp after the first couple of blows, Eddie would have left him alone, like a grizzly with a dead camper. Eddie was a lot of things, but he wasn't cruel.

Once Steve finally capitulated by collapsing against a fence, some of the less popular girls exercised their Catholic upbringing by invoking the parable of the Good Samaritan. They raced over to administer cold beers to the rapid swelling of all areas of his pummeled face, that still bore remnants of its beauty. Patty Morin even offered Steve a swig from her own bottle of Bud to wash the blood off his teeth. She had a tendency of positioning her hands, and anything she held in them, directly in front of her ample bosom. Work those assets.

Steve was smart. He knew that if he hung around on the periphery of the group after his beating and showed the appropriate contrition, he stood a chance at redemption and acceptance, like a new wolf to an established pack. If he had turned after the beating and ran, he could never have come back. By the end of the evening, I had befriended Steve, if only to tweak my older brother's nose for all of those beatings he had given me. Steve was a naturally funny guy, and I like to laugh.

When he returned to The Courts the following Friday night, Steve proved his innate political acumen, that no doubt flowed through the veins of every Greek since the founding of democracy in Athens. He arrived with a six pack of Guinness which he presented as tribute to my brother. Steve became the third wheel to the Eddie and BJ tricycle from that moment on.

Steve proved to be a resourceful acquisition. He had an impeccable source for fake IDs back in Queens that held up to even the closest scrutiny in the most well-lit bar or liquor store. For twenty-five dollars and a passport photo, Steve could get you a photo college identification card to the school of your choice. Within a few months our crew defied the odds and received purported overnight acceptances to the best schools in the country. Most of the crew limited their choices to the schools in the area, but BJ Delaney was very proud of his Harvard ID and Danny Mo loved to pull out his Yale Blue Bulldog to impress the ladies. Eddie went with a more pedestrian Manhattan College ID, which was prescient, given that after many years and a few false starts, that school became his *alma mater*. I still got by using Apples' draft card, deep voice and my ubiquitous five o'clock shadow, and really didn't want to spend an extra twenty-five bucks, which was more than a third of my weekly salary at Daitch.

And Steve was game. That night he returned, bearing gifts, he proved that there was nothing he wouldn't do for a laugh or a thrill. He climbed the three-story drainpipe of PS 81 and then danced along the edge of its roof to the music blasting from BJ's boom box, below. Even though watching him triggered my vertigo, because any fall would have been fatal, I could not take my eyes off of him. He looked like the devil up there. If he had a stack of plates, he would have smashed them. He fit into our group, seamlessly.

When the crew road tested Steve's new IDs at the local Irish bars along the Broadway El, which crossed over into both the Visitation and St. John's Parishes, Steve's natural mischievousness, flirtatiousness and Spartan fearlessness could often spark full blown bar brawls.

Bar brawls tend to get a bad rap. But the truth of it is that once engaged, you are limited in the physical bodily damage that you can inflict or receive by the layout of your surroundings, furniture and the number of people that are involved. I know its counter-intuitive, but the more people that engage in a bar brawl, the less likely anyone can get seriously hurt, given that you are so busy fending off different assailants in close proximity that you can only land or take a few punches before someone else intervenes or distracts you. If you are fighting someone one-on-one, you fight with focus and intent until one of you is down, and that can result in serious damage, especially among the strong, stupid, and stubborn.

With a brawl, there is usually a quick cluster, like a rugby scrum, and after a few minutes a crew of well-trained bartenders and bouncers can usually herd the combatants *en mass* out of their establishment's doors and into the streets, where the pressure usually quickly dissipates, and both sides' leaders drag their crews in opposite directions. Then they return to their own neighborhoods to lick their wounds, brag to their girlfriends, and talk shit about their enemies to anyone who will listen.

Say what you will about the Irish's natural proclivity towards pugnaciousness, we never carried or used weapons of any sort, at least not as teenagers. If we were going to beat you, it would be with our fists. We didn't even mind losing once in a rare while, as long as it was a fair exchange. And there was always the next weekend to even the score.

Another interesting component to the concept of bar brawling was that it was never the real warriors of either crew that started the battles. I never saw Eddie or BJ start a fight with a stranger. It was always either the smallest man or the least physical specimen with the quickest tongue. But the code was that once the fight started, you were all in until it was over, or the cops showed up. Anyone who abstained was quickly marginalized, and soon abandoned.

Now some individuals were more flammable than others. Tommy Quirk, a diminutive intellectual giant who I met later, in college, was an exception. Tommy, who had a tongue like an adder, needed no encouragement beyond his second pint of beer, and could start a fight between Gandhi and Mother Teresa. But it usually took a combination of wit and recklessness to ignite an inferno, and that usually required two separate members of the crew.

Brian Kelly wasn't a warrior, although I did once see him shatter a bar stool across the back of an enemy brawler who was about to strike one of our own on the head from behind with a beer bottle. Brian had an unwavering sense of fairness and justice, which made him an absolute pain in the ass to have around when it was your goal to be anything but fair or just. While he had the tendency to drive me crazy on a regular basis, acting as my portable conscience, he proved to be far more of an asset than a liability when you were closing the books for the evening. He always made sure we all got home each night.

Once Brian got his license, he added an additional invaluable skill to his repertoire. As soon as his radar picked up on potential trouble, he quietly disappeared from the bar. But after the fracas, when we finally ended up outside the establishment, usually in a rush, there he was in his car, engine racing, passenger doors open, allowing for a quick getaway by the main instigators and as many of the other members of the crew that could squeeze into the car. Turns out we were better than clowns when it came to cramming a dozen guys into his mother's tan Impala. And no one caught Brian once his foot hit the gas pedal, braking optional.

But before Brian ever set foot in the DMV, he set foot in bars, preferably stocked with strippers. And he was just fine until the first time Steve Adamos joined him for an ogle through their beer binoculars.

CHAPTER FORTY-FIVE
(NICKELS, QUARTERS AND SILVER DOLLARS)

I'm not going to apologize for my human failings. We were born this way.

Human males' attraction to female breasts has been studied to death by human scientists in their twenty-first century. So, if either of you needs more of an explanation than the fact that I have always been attracted to them, I refer you to an old human book called The Chemistry Between Us: Love, Sex, and the Science of Attraction, *by Larry Young, Ph.D. , who does a much better job at explaining it than I ever could.*

My audience seemed surprisingly unresponsive. I was afraid I had shocked them into silence by the last few stories.

Go ahead father, Stella finally responded. *I'm not sure where you are going with all of this but speaking as a four hundred-and-forty-year-old female, in human years, there is nothing you can tell me about the sexual preferences of males of any humanoid species that will surprise me. I've seen it all. And I'm really not impressed.*

No offense to humans in general, and I love you all, Claire joined in, *but Stella may have a point.*

Will you just let him tell his story? Apollo responded. *This is just getting interesting. So primal.* Apollo audibly laughed. I continued.

Getting back to my "primal" human childhood, there wasn't one of us in the group who, after experiencing real female breasts, did not take every opportunity they could to revisit the experience as often as legally allowed. Sometimes that was from a distance.

Every once in a while, Brian Kelly would talk us into walking up to his neighborhood in Yonkers and hitting The Crow's Nest on a Friday night. It was a corner establishment on South Broadway just before it meets the beginning of McLean Avenue. It's beers on tap weren't any better than what we would find in every Irish bar along the Bronx Broadway, but it had something that the Irish bars never had. Viewable breasts.

The Crow's Nest was the only bar outside of Manhattan to have strippers perform every Friday night and their bouncers didn't do too close a check on our crews' educational IDs.

Brian Kelly liked to sit as close to the dance platform as he could and once he found a seat, he did not surrender it even to take a piss. The dance platform was along the side wall in the open space at the back of the bar, as far away from the prying eyes of passing pedestrians as the owner could place it. It was built of basic plywood construction and painted matte black. There was no curtain for the girls to enter from or return to. They arrived in a cargo van, and entered through the alleyway back door and then changed from their street clothes in the office behind the bar. Then they sat around the open back area getting free drinks from the excited and drunk male patrons, who were mostly old enough to be our fathers, until it was their time to gyrate on stage to the accompaniment of a boom box and a cassette tape.

Brian wasn't a perve. In fact, the first time I joined him for a show there, I learned that he was torn by our shared desire to enjoy live dancing naked women, and his equally unique desire to try to save them. It was part of his hardwired Arthurian code of justice and fairness. He couldn't really explain it beyond the fact that he always found at least one of the four or so dancers, that gyrated to music just a few feet away, who looked like she was there because life had dealt her a bad break. I couldn't argue with him, given that, the few moments I devoted to the thought, I was certain that life had dealt all of those women some misfortune that led them to that stage. But at that point in my life, I didn't have Brian's moral code. I wasn't thinking that far out of the box.

Given that the girls' regular handler, a very tough looking bastard that appeared and sounded Eastern European, a little like Boris Badenov from Rocky and Bullwinkle, was always sitting, watching the girls from his spot at the bar closer to the front of the establishment. I recommended that Brian keep his altruistic thoughts to himself and enjoy the flesh that was wobbling just a few feet away, a little above eye level. I even gave him a few singles to slide in their g strings to make him feel less guilty.

The talking Moose and Squirrel! Claire interjected excitedly. *I remember the first time one of those fat game hunters I had to carry over those mountains in Colorado let that thought slip. He also let the thought slip that he would love to shoot both of them. Imagine, he wanted to shoot a talking animal? Bastard. I almost bucked him into a ravine. Luckily his aim was as dull as his brain.*

Anyway, on that particular night Brain heeded my advice, and we both sat there long enough for Brian to get drunk enough that Eddie and BJ had to carry him the six long blocks, including a long winding hill, up to his beautiful house on Rumsey Road.

However, that next week, when a new foursome of slightly worse for the wear ladies paraded their parts on full display, and a lot of the crew made the trip north, Brian had Steve the Greek as his bar stool co-pilot. I was off watching BJ doing his best to get one of the dancer's numbers while she basically emptied his wallet of enough cash to buy her three over-priced margaritas. This woman was a prize matador to BJ's bull. Her flopping breasts were her cape. I was awestruck by her technique, as she touched his arms suggestively and leaned those large breasts on the table each time she laughed at his comments in the most flirtatious manner. I was as convinced as BJ that he was going to get laid as soon as she finished her shift. And he might have, if Steve the Greek didn't convince a very drunk Brian Kelly that he should act on his altruistic impulses and try to convince the youngest and relatively prettiest of the women that he could be her savior and get her out of this tawdry life. The Greek was like the Norse god Loki, anything to stir the pot.

Boris Badenov moved a lot quicker than anyone could have anticipated at the sound of the scream when Brian grabbed the young lady's wrist. Unfortunately for Boris, Eddie moved just as quickly and dropped the handler with a crushing blow that certainly did some serious damage to the man's orbital socket. I heard BJ shout, "wait here babe" to the old stripper as he yoked the first bouncer to reach my brother with one of his simian arms. That's when I saw Brian swing his bar stool across the back of one of the patrons who was about to strike BJ in the back of his head with a beer bottle. And then the scrum began.

Steve the Greek was locked in a duet with the bartender and handled him a lot better than he had handled my brother.

The next scream I heard came from another bouncer whose nose was clamped tightly in the teeth of Joe Marrero, whom he made the mistake of lifting in a face-to-face bearhug. I definitely saw Joe spit out a piece of flesh.

I was spun around and laced with a nice right hook directly below my left cheekbone, which gave me a bit of whiplash, and would have dropped me if I hadn't been struck there a thousand times before by Eddie over the last ten years. I wobbled for a second and then struck the very startled bouncer with three fast blows to the base of the nose, the solar plexus and then the throat, the last of which really surprised him as his air passages sealed and he dropped to the floor, eyes bulging. I didn't even have to kick him.

Brian grabbed me by the shoulder and tried to pull me towards the back door, but Eddie was in the middle of a circle of bouncers and customers who were very pissed off that tonight's titty show was over. I could tell which way Eddie was striking by the way the obvious recipient responded to his blows, some of them dropping.

I wasn't about to leave Eddie behind, although he looked like he was doing all right for himself. Luckily, BJ and the Greek started to peel off enough of Eddie's ring around the rosy team, to give him a fair chance with the stragglers. And my brother took full advantage as they now started to drop like wet blankets. I went over and relieved Joe Marrero of one of the two, blue-balled, customers working him over and after a few more well-placed blows, we all retreated out the back door and through the alley. BJ jammed a trash can against the outer door to give us a running start.

Brian Kelly took us through some neighborhood short cuts along the back streets to avoid the cops that we knew were coming. It was the least he could do, given that it was his well-intentioned conduct that just turned off the titty tap for our foreseeable future. But it wasn't the last time he tried to save a naked damsel in distress, and when the next opportunity arose, the woman actually wanted to be saved, and wanted to save him in return.

CHAPTER FORTY-SIX
(PORTRAIT OF AN ARTIST)

Junior year continued on autopilot. JC was still a daily school presence right through homeroom when Joanna Skeegle wasn't monopolizing his life. I was okay with that, given that she was good for him. We didn't share many other classes as Joanna had insisted that he test into the AP level courses. Sex was the ultimate motivator and JC continued to work hard at everything, including his school work and his martial arts. He even applied his work ethic to his passion in his employment, having worked his way up from being a bus boy, to server, to prep assistant, to sous-chef in the restaurant that employed him. He had a knack. Food was his pallet, and the stove was his canvas.

Speaking of canvases, back at school, I still enjoyed pulling minor capers with BJ and Eddie, who had made it their senior year goal to torment a really annoying art teacher, who seemed to have it out for them. Since that particular class was one of my electives, I got to join in the fun. But I stayed below the radar because my wig couldn't risk an up close and personal with Bud Bosworth, the Boy's Dean, in an afterschool session of JUG.

Eddie had taken art because he had an unexpected talent for it. When you slid a charcoal pencil or paintbrush into his ham hock right fist, it transformed it from *Mjölnir* into the most delicate instrument that created the most beautiful depictions of portraits, still life and landscapes. Eddie was like one of those four chimpanzees that helped write Shakespeare.

But the art teacher, Mr. Sphincter, as the students like to refer to him, was a once upon a time artist whose sole reason for living was to crush the hopes of anyone else with dreams, aspirations, or talent. And since he was a little man, he had the additional misfortune of suffering with a Napoleon complex. So, he really hated the big kids.

Eddie and BJ were now really big kids.

Despite running a successful back alley book store, Eddie and BJ were good students and limited their shenanigans to sophomoric enterprises. Eddie liked to paint watercolor murals of naked women along the third-floor school hallways – and given he had to do it quickly, with BJ always playing look out – my brother developed an impressionistic, almost cubist style that would have made Picasso proud. I'm pretty sure I recognized BJ's girlfriend from our night at The Crow's Nest, among some of his subjects. You never forget an areola.

Eddie was Banksy long before that was a thing. And in all fairness, Eddie knew that his watercolor art would be quickly wiped away by the maintenance squad, so he understood that it lived in the moment. *Carpe diem.*

Just look it up under human art history. Claire interrupted. *Go on Jimmy.*

No one in authority could figure out who the graffiti artist was, and it was causing quite the sensation among the student populace, half of whom had never gazed upon the naked form for any length of time. It was causing quite a stir on so many levels. The masses were becoming agitated and that was not good for the authoritarian regime.

While Mr. Sphincter's talent was now a memory, he knew how to recognize it in others. So, after Eddie's third rendition of twin peaks, the administration called upon Sphincter's services to try to uncover the culprit. Mr. Sphincter snapped a polaroid of the mural and pinned it to the cork board in front of his classroom.

Every Wednesday afternoon, we would enter Sphincter's class and find him staring at the photo, like it was porn. In fact, BJ began a cafeteria whisper campaign to spread the rumor that one of the female students had walked in unexpectedly and caught Sphincter choking his chicken, and that he needed only two fingers to do it.

When Sphincter demanded that we all turn in our sketch pads just before the Easter recess, we knew it was just a matter of time before the jig was up. I was in the clear because I could barely draw a stick figure, but there were too many tell-tale signs of genius throughout Eddie's work. BJ's art was humorously dark but not good. Eddie knew he was a dead man walking, so, in a daring response, late that Thursday afternoon, Eddie painted a grand mural of Sphincter buggering a sheep on the third-floor stairwell. A five-minute classic. He even painted a title, *The Good Shepherd.*

Now that's truly disgusting. Claire exclaimed. *I'm definitely having a word with your brother on my next trip across the veil.*

BJ scrawled a thought balloon in black water color above the sheep's head, "That's Bbbbbaaaaaaaddddd."

Sphincter was apoplectic when he pushed past the cluster of students and witnessed first-hand his public humiliation. I couldn't help but bleat like a sheep from the back of the crowd before descending the stairs to the tumultuous laughter of the remaining gawkers that quickly drowned out Sphincter's angry cries of "Who did that?!"

When I looked back up the stairway, I saw Sphincter glaring down the stairwell from the third floor. Our eyes met for just a moment, and as I quickly turned away, my wig shifted just enough for me to have to right it with one hand. I could feel his discerning eyes burning a hole though the top of my head.

Good Friday was a holy day of obligation which led us into a nice three-day weekend off from school. Once we had respectfully acknowledged the three pm end of the Crucifixion with our families at St. Maggie's Church, every Catholic student in the crew who wasn't working part-time met up on the rocks and respectfully cracked their first of many brews. *Confiteor Deo omnipotenti.*

The cafeteria was buzzing with rumor and excitement the following Monday morning, as the school year entered that final week of classes in May 1973.

When Sphincter arrived to get his usual cup of coffee and sweet bear claw, BJ tilted his head back and started to bleat like a sheep, which spread into a cacophony, sending the now very bright red Sphincter racing from the room.

When the Catholic hierarchy wants to inflict a serious beat down, they love to quote the Old Testament to make themselves feel righteous and just. Something told me that they were reaching back to the Hebrew Prophet Isaiah that week.

Behold, the day of the Lord is coming,

Cruel, with fury and burning anger,

To make the land a desolation;

And He will exterminate its sinners from it.

Isaiah 13:9.

The holy wrath fell upon us as we sat in homeroom and listened to the student pet of the week read the morning announcements over the PA system. The sweet lilting voice ended with the sentence,

"Will Edward McCarthy and Broderick Jameson Delaney please report immediately to the Dean's Office."

Now to their credit, both boys knew that the school couldn't prove anything beyond the circumstantial evidence of them both being enrolled in Sphincter's class and that Eddie had a knack for art. So, despite Sphincter's accusatory testimony before both the girls' and boys' deans, with references to sketch pads showing Eddie's artistic skills, including a skillful rendition of the Riverdale Junkie's Mule to show his way around the animal form, and BJ's handwriting in comically caustic thought balloons in his more rudimentary art, the boys held firm and repeatedly denied having anything to do with the mural. In the end, while Sphincter did not get the confession he was hoping would get them expelled, enough of his shit stuck to the wall to get them "indefinite JUG." This meant they would serve out the remainder of the School year up until their graduation, as the afterschool guests of Dean Bosworth. A small price to pay for mythic immortality among the student populace. They accepted their punishment without a whimper.

But Sphincter was going to have his pound of flesh.

CHAPTER FORTY-SEVEN
(A MOMENT IN TIME)

Eddie and BJ became quite the celebrities in the school cafeteria and a number of the students stopped by our table the next morning to buy them coffee and pastries in tribute for their daring deed.

This did not go unnoticed by Sphincter when he entered the cafeteria, and those cacophonous bleats began anew. You could see the anger in his eyes as he stared over at our table. I tried to ignore him because I figured he had done his worse to my brother and BJ and came up short. So why antagonize him? But when I looked over as he passed, with his coffee and bear claw, I could see he was staring directly at me.

It sent a chill down my spine.

That chill dissipated when Danielle stopped me forty-five minutes later in the third-floor hall way by my locker between classes. She was looking particularly cute, and there was no ring hanging around her neck.

"Your brother and his friend are heroes," She began. "But your bleat last Thursday in the stairwell was the icing on the cake."

I took a quick look around to make sure there were no idle ears.

"Were you in that crowd?" I asked, trying to sound as cool as possible. "I hadn't noticed."

She smiled, her Jade eyes popping against the black eyeliner. They looked suddenly inquisitive.

"What's your next class?" She asked.

"Physics."

"Not today." She said, as she took my hand and led me into the north stairwell that accessed the school roof. When we got to the roof landing she dropped her books and gently backed me against the wall.

"You can't dance for shit, and for the life of me I cannot remember anything about our Christmas kiss other than I desperately want another."

The kiss that followed was far softer and more pleasant, given that it lingered long enough for our tongues to touch and begin to dance. Her hands reached up to the sides of my face as mine reached around her waist and pulled her in closely. Her soft breasts pushed against my own, and this time I didn't feel the hard circle pressing into my breastbone.

As we came up for air, her fingers started to play with the edges of my wig.

"This really isn't flattering," she said, tugging on its left side above the ear. "And you need all the help you can get."

We spent the next half hour kissing the way teens tend to do, redirecting the passion that normally would be expressed through other parts of the body to our lips and tongues and grinding so hard that I almost came in my clothes. When the next bell rang, we took deep breaths to calm ourselves, readjusted everything that may have come askew, and gathered our books.

Danielle removed a pen from her purse and tore the last page out of her notebook.

"My parents are going away to my cousin's wedding in Pennsylvania this weekend. And I'm coming down with the flu," she said as she jotted down something and then handed me the paper. "There's my address. I'm planning to have some friends over, so if you'd like to stop by, maybe we can continue whatever this is in a proper fashion."

As much as I wanted to continue "this" I could not leave one question unanswered. Nor did I want to face the wrath of some fit twenty-something pissed off male who might have something more lethal in the glove compartment of his Camaro.

"What about your boyfriend?" I asked, gently tapping the spot where his ring had rested so recently.

"Carmine?" She responded, a dark look passing quickly across her brows. "We're over."

Just then the next bell signaling the beginning of third period sounded.

"Shit, I gotta go. I have to hand in a paper." She started to leave and then came back to me. "One more, just to make sure I remember this."

I cannot speak for Danielle, but, over five centuries later, I never forgot that last kiss.

CHAPTER FORTY-EIGHT
(THE PENNY DROPS)

Wednesday's last art class with Mr. Sphincter was memorable for a couple of reasons. The first was that Eddie and BJ were moved to the two seats directly in front of his desk in the room. The next was that Sphincter sat in Eddie's old seat directly in front of my own and spent the next forty minutes doing nothing but staring closely at my wig. The experience had the same intensity as when my mother would demand to smell my breath when I came in from a night of drinking. Only a handful of mints wasn't getting me out of this predicament and the nasty prick was so close I kept wishing he had popped a few mints before class.

The only good to come of it, was that BJ and Eddie took the opportunity to capitalize on Sphincter's distracted obsession with me. Eddie opened the large tub of glue on Sphincter's desk, while BJ dipped one of those oversized tongue depressors into it and then slapped it onto our class's page of Sphincter's open grade book before closing the book and sealing the final class grades for eternity.

Eddie also scribbled a smiling sheep onto the chalkboard before the class bell had sounded.

That sticky tongue depressor served as Sphincter's final straw that broke the sheep's back.

The next morning, as JC, BJ, Eddie, and me, sat around sipping coffee and laughing about their art class final "fuck you" coup, the double doors of the cafeteria flew open and both the boys' and girls' deans marched into the room.

I saw Bosworth scan the busy room from his giant's vantage, and then point over in our direction. I could have done a runner, but I was truly hoping they were after someone else. As the two approached they never took their eyes off me. Students in the surrounding tables started to pack their shit and leave to get free of the impact zone.

I stared into my coffee cup wishing I could disappear into it. I refused to look up when they arrived at my table.

"Jimmy McCarthy, on your feet!" commanded Sister Joan, the girls' dean of discipline.

I slowly complied, wondering if I should revisit fleeing to escape.

"Do you know what we're busting you for?" Sister Joan asked, just a little too gleefully.

"I glued the book!" BJ shouted. "Jimmy had nothing to do with it."

"Thank you for that confession, Master Delaney, but we're not here about any book." Bosworth said.

"No sister, I haven't a clue," I whispered.

She walked right up to me, reached up and tugged my wig hard enough to make it shift.

With nothing to lose I went on the offense, the voices in my head leading me into uncharted territory.

"My wig?" I said, pointing to it for emphasis. "You can't touch this wig. It's an invasion of my privacy. For all you know, I could be a bald cancer patient, and what you are doing now is exposing me to public ridicule and humiliation."

I couldn't help but smile as I listened to the bullshit flowing out of my mouth.

JC started to clap and soon others were mimicking his slow percussion.

"Save it counselor," Bosworth barked impatiently as he grabbed my arm and led me from the cafeteria. There was no sense in resisting, because the man was a physical beast with a grip like a vice.

"Dead man walking," one of the Eastchester Italians shouted out as we passed.

I spotted Danielle as I was passing the Parkchester table. She was the only one who wasn't staring in my direction. I noticed the ring hanging back around her neck.

When we entered the Dean's office, there was already a gathering of teachers standing around waiting for the show. I was surprised there wasn't someone milling through their crowd selling popcorn. Bosworth released my arm and spun me around by the shoulders, so I was facing the teachers, while he stood behind me and roughly relieved me of my wig. The teachers gasped in unison.

"Well, look at what we have here!" Bosworth exclaimed, with a whistle for emphasis.

The room was eerily silent, and I could hear each of the bobby pins he removed hitting the industrial blue carpet around my feet. As each section was unfastened, a lock of my hair would drop loose and hang in curls around my face and shoulders. When Bosworth was finished I could not help but give my head the defiant shake of freedom which allowed my hair to fall into place around my shoulders. I pulled it back off my face and stared at the smirks of every teacher I had offended over the past three years. They reveled in my final demise.

"You are immediately suspended until you get that hair cut in compliance with the school's grooming codes." Sister Joan read from a note card, not having the time to memorize her speech. "And then you will serve out the rest of this year and all of next year in indefinite JUG, with no Christmas reprieve."

I thought I heard Sphincter clap, and wanted to shout, "fuck you all," but realized that when I'm stuck in the bottom of a deep hole, I better stop digging.

"And finally," Sister Joan concluded with a flourish, "you will spend every free period of your senior year as my guest in this office. We will, of course put all of this in the letter we are sending home to your parents."

"Let that be a lesson to you and your friends," Sphincter finally shouted. "Glue my notebook, you little bastards."

Bosworth then handed me my knapsack and turned to escort me out of the office and then the building. I resisted just a moment so I could turn and look Sphincter directly in the eyes.

"Bbbbbaaaaaahhhhhh." I bleated, before Bosworth dragged me out the doorway. The last thing I heard behind me was the other teachers laughing.

"Don't come back without the haircut." Bosworth instructed as he opened the front door and ushered me through it.

I took him at his word and, much to my parents' chagrin, never set foot in Spillane again.

Never made it to that party either.

Well that certainly explains a lot about Apollo. Stella sighed.

I do love my long hair. Apollo responded, extending his chin upward and giving his shoulder length hair a shake.

I was talking about your rebelliousness. Stella countered.

Still, it is a nice mane. Your's too, Stella. Claire added. *But where did that burgundy color come from?*

Well, it didn't come from Proxima b. Stella responded. *Platinum blondes ruled until our lines reintroduced color.*

Given the way you two handled yourselves during the Great Galactic War, I'd say you both have a bit of The Ginger gene floating in your pools. I said, with a chuckle. *And that had its usefulness.*

Gangster! Claire exclaimed, with her own Lurchy laugh.

So, father, is there much more to your saga before we meet the youthful Gina? You've burned through most of our long Centaurian day.

If you guys are tired, we can pick this up tomorrow. I replied.

I'm good. Apollo chimed in. *If the rest of you are still on board. I'm finding the parts about your Terran sex life fascinating, so much more emotionally complicated than reproduction requires, but truly fascinating.*

Yes, but the emotional connection is the gold, the good stuff. I said, just a little wistfully.

I want to know what Spaghetti had to say about you getting kicked out of school? Stella added. *I'm surprised he didn't cut your head off with his shears.*

Claire studied me for a moment, and I felt her rummaging through my mind. *Maybe we should let your father press on.* She shared. *If that's all right with you, Jimmy.*

Go for it, father. Stella added, with a side glance at Claire. *You have our full attention.*

CHAPTER FORTY-NINE
(LEAVING THE FOLD)

There was something terrifying about leaving the Catholic school system. As I think back on it, I believe it has to do with the time Danny Mo was expelled from St. Maggie's in fourth grade for kicking Sister Alfred in the ass. Word went out to all of the classrooms from the Principal herself, that Danny Mo would never be allowed in heaven for his abominable act. But let's continue—

"No fucking way!" Apollo exclaimed aurally, "All due respect father, you don't get to drop that line and then just move on."

Was that a hint of a Bronx accent? He sounded just like his mother.

It's just that I didn't witness it first hand, I was in the other class. Bozzy MacDootz told me about it on the way home from school. Of course, Danny Mo proudly confirmed it later at Matty's fort.

Your boy's got a point, Claire added, *and given that it impacted your outlook on life, sounds pretty relevant to me.*

You might as well, father, or Apollo will never let it rest. Stella chimed in.

All right then.

Sister Alfred was a tiny little nun who had to be as old as a Centaurian and as tough as cat shit. She was a brilliant scholar and produced successful students, but did not accept anything but absolute submission to her authority. Anyone who disrupted her class was dealt a flurry of bantam speed blows from her oversized knuckles, then transferred into the other fourth grade class, to join your father and the other miscreants.

For decades Sister Alfred spent the first half hour after every lunch recess reading a chapter from her first edition copy of Uncle Tom's Cabin, a brilliant anti-slavery novel by the American author, Harriet Beecher Stowe. Rumor had it back then that Sister Alfred had been schoolmates with Ms. Stowe, which would have made the nun over a hundred years old, but no one could ever prove it to my satisfaction.

Anyway, Danny Mo enjoyed wandering the halls more than learning, so he was always the first to volunteer to take a written message by hand from Mrs. Fitzpatrick to any of the other teachers.

I just don't know how humans functioned with such archaic forms of communication. Stella said, shaking her head.

I thought about her comment for a second. It had been so long ago and such a relatively brief part of my existence, that it almost did not seem real.

I guess that it did slow our world down a little bit, I offered. *But in all honesty, our present ability to exchange entire lifetimes of information in seconds via binary telepathic transmission has robbed us of our ability to actually communicate with each other on a personal level. I think that has impacted our ability to empathize with others. That is why I am telling my story with my voice, in my human English, because I want you to experience each nuance, so you can fully understand who I was before you met me. That all would be lost in a ten second down load.*

Well, I like your voice, father. Apollo said. *Even if it sounds like you're talking through your nose. Go ahead.*

In this instance, Mrs. Fitzpatrick wanted to notify Sister Alfred about a change in scheduling for the upcoming fourth grade reading comprehension exams. She sent Danny Mo off with a note containing the new details.

As MacDootz later explained it, on the afternoon in question, Sister Alfred was sitting on the desk deeply engrossed in the tragic whipping to death of the good Christian slave, Tom, at the behest of evil Simon Legree, when there came a knock on the door. Drawing the Jesus analogy for this noble literary character was the high point of the nun's annual performance, so she was not about to stop. Sister Alfred ignored the first knock and continued to read on. But then there came a second knock. Again, she ignored it and read on.

That's when Danny Mo slowly opened the door just a crack to peak into the classroom. All of the students' eyes were on Danny, and he knew it. He opened the door just a crack more and began to make faces at his friends in response to the nun's reading. MacDootz swore Danny was on his game and before long muffled twitters turned into guffaws.

That's when the nun slammed her book closed and hopped off the desk with the agility of a gymnast. She crossed the room so quickly Danny couldn't get the door closed before she grabbed the indoor knob and yanked it open, with Danny still clinging to the outer knob. This pulled him forward and into the classroom bent over just enough for the old nun's claw to grasp his collar and begin to pummel his face mercilessly with her free hand like a speed bag. Danny was stunned, and after multiple shots, she reached over and tore the message from his hand, turned and headed back towards her desk without giving Danny another thought.

Danny stood shaking the cobwebs out of his head for a moment and the welts were already beginning to rise on his cheekbones. That's when MacDootz swore that he saw the devil in Danny's eyes. The students looked on in horror as Danny, an amazing athlete in his own right, closed the distance on the nun with one long stride and then followed it into an equally long kick which caught the nun right in the ass.

There have been different stories told about what happened next, but MacDootz swore that the impact of Danny's shoe mixed with the nun's own forward momentum lifted the tiny nun into the air and, as her arms extended outward, propelled her over the desk, robes flowing, like a large bat. It was said that she landed on her knees on the opposite side of the desk and then slid the rest of the way across the room, like a soccer player after a goal, until she came to rest against the radiators under the windows.

Some of the teacher's pets in the front seats reported that nun immediately began to speak in tongues. Rosemary McShane, who witnessed the event, told me she thought it was Latin. MacDootz swears the old nun was cursing.

Either way. The next thing I recall was seeing Danny pop open our classroom door, and with a look of absolute terror on his face, grab his school bag from the desk and race out of the room. He never returned.

Within the hour, the principal, Sister Rosalind, was making her rounds to the classes denying the rapidly expanding rumors that were spreading throughout the school. She explained that one of our students had chosen to voluntarily leave St. Maggies permanently, and attend the heathen-filled Riverdale public school, and that we should all say a prayer for his immortal soul, which was surely going to burn eternally in hell.

Sister Alfred, being the tough old bastard that she was, after surely praying for her assailant and for her safe landing, picked herself up off the floor, sat back down on her desk, and, without skipping another beat, finished her reading. There is nothing like religious fervor.

Anyway, at that time in junior year when I finally cut the religious umbilical cord to Spillane, I had just read Dante Alighieri's *The Divine Comedy* for third year English. I could not help but fear that, at some point, I would be doomed to joining my friend Danny Mo on one of Dante's rings of hell. Who knew at that time that, according to that great author, I was destined for a profession that assured me of a front row hot seat?

CHAPTER FIFTY
(THE SUN ALWAYS RISES)

Along with the crises of faith caused by my decision to leave Spillane, came the existential crises I knew was awaiting me once my family found out. I expected a slow and painful death.

My brother Eddie was cool about keeping it under wraps for as long as he could, and we would walk down the hill every morning dressed for school, wig in place, like we were going to catch the number twenty bus to take us to the Spillane Special. He would catch the first bus that had BJ waving from the back window, and I would stuff the wig in my knapsack and go hang out in Van Cortlandt Park for the rest of the day. I ended up reading all of the books I avoided reading for English class all year, just to distract me from thinking about how fucked up my life was about to become.

If it rained, I hung out in the local library and sat around the tables flipping through their collection of Addams family cartoons, and anything else I could find. I shared the room with lonely local pensioners who were reading the free daily papers while trying to distract themselves from thinking about just how fucked up their lives had already become. But they were stoics. Getting old sucked but the alternative wasn't any better.

What really sucked was that before the shit hit the fan, I was actually having a pretty decent year academically and could have cake-walked through the three Regents exams I was facing for my finals. It's not that I was working any harder than my first couple of years at school, in fact I put in even less effort than before, but I just seemed to test better. I just knew the right answers, even if I didn't really know the subject. Once I started accepting the answers that kept popping into my head, they flowed more freely, and I just went with it. If it was multiple choice, I selected the letter that felt right, even if it looked wrong. If it was an essay question, or a fill in, I wrote whatever streamed through my mind, like I was reading it off a chalkboard on the inside of my forehead. Physics was a bit more challenging, given I had a hard time interpreting and transcribing the strange symbols I needed to include in the responsive equations when showing the work. But I always got the final answers right. The only time I screwed up badly was when I second guessed my stream of consciousness. But I still didn't learn anything. It's not like the knowledge stayed with me. It was basically just copying off the smartest kid in class, only she was invisible, and inside my head.

After school hours, I still had my part time job at Daitch, where Mark Wallen did his best to try to find a bright side to it and I still met up with JC for our Kung Fu classes a couple of times a week. JC kept me up to date with what was happening at school and told me how he had been inundated with daily requests from other students to confirm the rumors about "the great unpinning." He was infamous by association. He only asked me how I was doing once, and offered to run away with me, like Huck and Tom, if that would make my life easier, but I turned him down. I may have been a fuck-up, but I made it a point of never sharing my misfortunes. At least back then.

I also knew that JC wanted to attend Joanna's graduation. She was going to be the Valedictorian of her class. It was bittersweet for JC because he knew Joanna would be leaving for Cal Berkley in August. And I really felt bad for him because I knew that he really loved her. And as much as I wouldn't want to share his heartbreak, I couldn't help but feel jealous that he had made that connection.

I also knew that Eddie and BJ would also get their sheepskins on the same day as Joanna. There would be no more hiding my secret come the first Saturday after finals.

Once I was home each day, I would take my dinner plate up to my room in the attic dormers and pretend to be studying, just so I wouldn't have to interact with my parents or grandparents.

Even without the stress, I could never sleep each night more than a few hours. Since the weather was getting warmer, I would find myself sneaking down the front stairs and sitting on the front stoop watching the last of the four a.m. bar stragglers stumble out of Coaches II, a long block down the Mosholu hill.

Then I killed time counting the seconds between the flashes of visible light from the top of the Dobbs Ferry Radio Station tower fifteen miles away in Westchester. The red light flashed every six seconds. The blue, every thirty. Sometimes I dozed off but would awaken as the commercial delivery trucks started to roll along Mosholu just before dawn. Then I would go back inside and pretend to get ready for school.

I was also moody with my younger siblings, which I might have gotten away with in the past, but now that they were outpacing me size wise, they weren't so ready to accept my shit. And after I yelled at them over some minor offense, The Ginger finally told me to fuck off, a mortal sin among Irish brothers that normally would have resulted in a physical confrontation. I still had the edge because of my training, but my younger brother was now developing into the brute he became, and there was no guaranty I would come out on top. Truth was, I just didn't give a shit, so I let it slide.

That didn't go unnoticed by the one sibling who always had my back.

As the day of reckoning got closer and closer, the pressure from my secret was causing me to have stress-related shortness of breath. It felt like someone had removed one of my lungs, and I could never get enough air in one breath. I felt like that fish on the beach, I was slowly suffocating.

For one fleeting moment, I felt like ending it.

In the early morning hours on the Friday before Eddie's graduation, I awoke on the steps to the sound of a passing backfiring delivery truck to find my sister, Bonnie, sitting quietly in her bathrobe beside me. She had arrived the night before from her private college in Purchase, New York, having just successfully completed her sophomore year finals, and to attend my brother's graduation. The star of the family was going to start her summer internship at the United Nations as a volunteer French interpreter the following Monday. But it was hard to be jealous of Bonnie. She didn't revel in her role of the perfect child, and humbly downplayed every academic accolade she had ever received. I loved her.

I hadn't seen Bonnie since the family got word of Nana Burke's passing in Ireland earlier that spring. My grandmother had returned "home" after she retired from the three jobs she juggled for thirty years, including being the first female superintendent of the buildings we lived in on Gerard Avenue in the Bronx. Bonnie had taken a week off from classes to accompany my mother to the funeral in Galway. The family couldn't afford to all go on the trip, so Bonnie took my father's place to represent the family. She was Nana's favorite.

My sister took my hand, and we sat there in silence, watching the eastern sky lighten from black to purple. Then the orange streaks began to peak over the horizon, hinting at dawn.

"You know Jimmy, there is nothing you have done that warrants the end of the world." She whispered. "No matter how bad you may think it is, that sun is still going to rise today, and tomorrow, and every day thereafter. And the world will wake up and go about its business. Five hundred years from now, no one will remember whatever it is that is troubling you so much."

I felt like I was four again, holding my sister's hand in front of the pram as we led the family caravan along Jerome Avenue in front of MaCombs park. I leaned over and rested my head on her shoulder and started to weep. She cupped my check with her other hand and started to make the soothing "musha, musha, musha" sounds that the consoling Irish in my family had made for centuries as she began to gently rock me. Now I was in full blown sobbing mode. There is nothing more cathartic than a good cry.

After a few minutes, she pointed to the top of the sun now peeking above the Mosholu woods. "There you go, right on schedule. We all have our secrets, and the world isn't going to end because of them. Let's just go inside, have a cup of tea, and tell the folks whatever it is you need to tell them, so we can all move on with our lives."

She stood and raised me to my feet with that powerful grip of hers.

"And besides, your life can't be over. Nana told me that you and I have great adventures yet to share."

I never asked her what she meant by that. But I followed her inside and faced my music.

CHAPTER FIFTY-ONE
(CAN'T WIN THEM ALL)

I was surprised at how well my father took the news. Looking back on it, at first I thought that Bonnie standing beside me when I blurted it out provided me with some mystical protection. But, I realize now that my father was just being philosophical. Given Bonnie was an all-star, Eddie was graduating and going on to college and The Ginger and my youngest were shaping up to be potential D1 college athletes, a four out of five record in child rearing wasn't bad. So, he was willing to take the bitter with the sweet.

Anyway, my dad hadn't forgotten my promise to sign up for the Golden Gloves come my next birthday, so maybe something useful would come of that. But I didn't escape unscathed. My father did pull his funding for my Kung Fu classes, so I had to give them up, and from that point on I had to make my own spending money. No more handouts.

My mother, on the other hand, almost took to her sick bed, and begged me to reconsider right up until the moment when I took her over to the public high school to register me for my senior year. She was so certain that I was about to sacrifice my immortal soul that she literally got down on her knees to plead one last time in front of the entrance way of the new school building that looked presciently similar to a prison. But by then I had grown in my beard and there was no way I was going back.

Spaghetti told me that he could hook me up with some work in the construction industry should I decide to just drop out altogether and Posie pulled me aside and said, "The last thing the world needs is another Irish laborer." She made me promise to at least get my high school diploma. I did and kept it.

That summer was spent working weekends with Mark Wallen as lifeguards at a Westchester country club and weekdays split between summer school mornings to make up the three Regents courses I walked away from and afternoons working at Daitch. Brian Kelly had gotten himself and Steve the Greek jobs as waiters in the fancy dining room at the same club, so we all rode together in Brian's car on the days our schedules over-lapped. Otherwise, Mark gave me a lift on his motorcycle. Sitting in the second seat of a bike is like letting your partner lead during a slow dance. It has all the same moves but just isn't as much fun.

Spaghetti did get Eddie and BJ summer jobs laboring for an Irish contractor, named Jack Sullivan, and they made great money even working as non-union. But each night the beers were their treat, so I wasn't complaining. Spaghetti eventually hooked me up with the same guy once I graduated from high school.

I slept through the morning summer school session and still aced the English, History and Physics Regents exams thanks to those voices in my head. I also got a wonderful tan sitting in the chair at the country club each weekend, thanks to my Black Irish genes. Fraternizing with the members was absolutely forbidden, so I kept to myself and still enjoyed the bikini eye candy that spent far more time roasting on the chase lounges than actually looking to drown in the water. Given this was the upper middle-class membership, even the moms looked good.

I was beginning to fill out, so I wasn't chopped liver, and a few of the women did ask me if I gave private swim lessons. I probably would have kept the lifeguard gig all the way to Labor Day if one of the pencil-necked husbands didn't lie to the pool manager that I encouraged his wife to invite me back to their cabana while he was out on the golf-course. Honestly, I had barely said two words to the woman the whole summer, despite the fact that she camped each weekend directly by my chair. I had only gone back there the one time at the end of my shift because she pleaded with me to carry back the full cooler she left by her chaise lounge. As soon as I realized by the discarded bathing suit on the cabana floor that she was showering in the back of the cabana - she had a pleasant singing voice - I left the cooler and took off. No good deed goes unpunished.

Mark Wallen immediately quit in solidarity. He was a lot more loyal to me than I was to him.

Steve the Greek didn't make it through the whole summer either, but his crime was to tell one of the larger bodied children that he wouldn't serve him his third requested order of pancakes one morning because he was a "fat bastard." Beware of Greeks serving shit.

Brian Kelly was the only one who managed to survive the whole summer at the country club. That's what Brian always did. Survive. Well, almost. On the Friday before the Labor Day weekend, he had words with the assistant manager about being purposedly left off the more lucrative tipping Saturday night dinner schedule, so, after telling his boss to kindly go fuck himself, he loaded two crates of prime rib from the kitchen into the trunk of his car and left. He was the hit of the neighborhood when he showed up at the annual Beerfest softball game barbecue Saturday night with his top flight addition to the menu. The country club served a lot of fish that weekend.

Come September, there was something liberating about getting off the religious version of the educational hamster wheel after eleven years. No more conformity, spiritual or physical. I was ready for something completely different. And I got it.

PART THREE
THE MIGHTY FALLEN

CHAPTER FIFTY-TWO
(PLAYING THE ODDS)

North Bronx Central High School was a fortress. It sat on a twenty-one-acre plot in the Bedford Park section of the Bronx, a block from the same Jerome Avenue that ran south past my childhood at Macombs Park and Yankee Stadium. The Number 4 IRT line ran along the elevated platform that ran that street's entire length in the Bronx. The Special bus passed NBC on its way to and from Spillane along the major east-west artery, Gun Hill Road, as a daily reminder of how far I had fallen. My new school sat at the heart of the Bronx Universe.

Once my mother accepted the inevitable, she went to the local library and dug up whatever facts about my new school that could give her some semblance of hope, like a long list of notable alumni, which proved to her mind that my attendance there was not my first step on the road to perdition. During the weekend family dinners, she trotted out the names of old actors, comics, and a host of other luminaries I either never knew or could not remember that had walked NBC's hallowed halls.

But this was the fall of 1973. Rome had fallen. New York City was in a financial crisis and facing bankruptcy. There was a hiring freeze that affected all of the Big Apple's work force and public services, including the police, fire department and teachers. Crime was rampant. The Bronx was burning, and public-school education was holding on by its fingernails. A perfect time for me to test those waters.

Luckily I wasn't alone. The Armstrong brothers and oldest cousin, Billy Huggins, had fed into NBC from their South Riverdale public junior high-school, and had the lay of the land. Joe Marrero had suffered a similar fate to mine when he left his Yonkers Catholic High School that June, so he also landed on the shore of the island of unwanted toys. But because my mother had left my registration to the literal last day, I was registered for the first of five overlapping schedules, with my first class, gym, at six o'clock in the morning. The rest of the crew didn't arrive until close to eight a.m.

Given that I had already successfully completed all of the state sanctioned regents' courses necessary to graduate, everything else on my schedule was electives. So, I took art, shop and surprisingly enough, music appreciation with the three oldest teachers whose tenure was the only thing that kept them in the system. I also took a creative writing class with my homeroom teacher, a crazy bastard named Jupiter Dorian, who was just too funny to ignore and the only class I never missed.

Gym was the only state mandated class you absolutely had to have four years of in order to receive your high school diploma. I was in pretty decent shape for a teenage human, so I figured it would be a bit of a cake walk for me.

My father dropped me off at the school on the first day, because the bus lines serving Riverdale didn't start running until after I had to be in class. It was still dark, and I remember watching the tail lights of his Caprice Station Wagon disappear south onto Jerome Avenue a few blocks away. I saw a couple of really big black guys heading towards the front door, so I followed them in. Turns out they were the defensive line of the perennial state powerhouse NBC football team, and the coach made them arrive every morning to lift weights and do anything else that would make them even bigger and meaner. It worked.

When I got into the gym locker room, I realized I didn't have a combination lock with me, so an older looking Spanish kid named Esteban Serrano, offered to share his locker.

"You don't want to leave your shit unlocked." He counseled.

Given that the only thing of value I had with me was my wallet, and that didn't hold more than a couple of bucks, I kept the twenty-dollar bill Posie had given me in my sneaker, I figured what did I have to lose so I paired up with "Stevie" as he liked to be called. Turns out Stevie was a "super-senior" who had ended up at NBC after a medical condition forced him to miss his last semester of his senior year over a year ago. Like me, he only had to get that gym credit in order to graduate.

When Stevie changed into his sweat shirt, I learned what caused his serious medical condition.

His entire chest was pock-marked with keloid scars the size of metal bbs that clustered between his belly button and solar plexus and diminished as it expanded outward. He saw me staring and laughed.

"Got into a fight over a parking space on Castle Hill Avenue and the motherfucker pulled out a shotgun." He said matter-of-factly. "Luckily it was bird shot or we wouldn't be having this conversation."

Stevie led me down to the huge gym floor where a group of about twenty physical freaks, of all nationalities, worked out with dead weights like they were trying to scare off predators in a prison yard. Stevie led me to the track lines that circled the floor and suggested I join him for a few laps in order to stay out of trouble. I did.

For the next half hour, I jogged along half listening to Stevie's life story while studying the collection of Italian gym teachers, sitting off in one corner, playing cards with actual chips and reviewing the daily racing form. I recognized the DRF from watching my mother's only brother gamble himself into bankruptcy. If he hadn't drank himself into terminal cirrhosis of the liver and the grave at 35, he probably would have lost what little he had left to the loan sharks that hounded him over his gambling debts. Broke Nana Burke's heart. I could recognize a habitual gambler when I saw one, and this entire crew would have bet on roaches crawling up a wall.

The head of the gym department, Salvatore Nardoni, was the tiniest of the crew. I heard him complaining to another one of the larger men that the Yankees had fucked him with his bookie again last season, and he was hoping that their new owners, led by some guy named Steinbrenner, would turn the team around. After the fourth lap around the gym, I peeled off from Stevie and walked over to the table where Nardoni sat chewing on the nub of a cigar.

"What do you want, kid." He asked, without looking up from his DRF, as he circled one of the horses in the sixth race at Belmont.

"I'd like to make you a bet." I responded.

Now just my saying the word "bet" in this area was comparable to saying the word "tits" in the back of the church. It got everyone's attention.

He looked up from his paper and one of his number twos named Felice, came over to the table to listen in.

"Okay, kid." He said with renewed interest. "What's the bet?"

"I bet you I can forge your signature and that you will not be able to spot the forgery."

Now I did not have Eddie's gift for drawing, but, over the years, I had trained myself to be able to forge anyone's signature by first forging those of my parents on tests and report cards throughout high school. I then expanded into forging the names of parents for some of my less industrious friends in Riverdale. It had gotten so easy for me that if you showed me a signature I could get it almost perfect in three tries.

Felice thought that this was a rather ballsy proposition and called out to the rest of the card players to come over.

"What's the ante?" Felice asked.

I took off my sneaker and tossed the sweaty twenty on his table.

Nardone sized me up to see if I was bullshitting. He reached for his wallet, and I stopped him.

"I don't want your money." I said.

"What do you want?" Nardone asked.

"If I win, I want you to sign off on my gym attendance for the entire year." I said.

"Can't do that." Nardone said, half-heartedly. He picked up Posie's twenty and shook it to air it out.

Now all of the gym teachers were excited, and some of them started to goad Nardone with their ball busting comments. There were lots of "C'mon Sal," and "don't be such a pussy," floating in the air.

Finally, he said. "Fuckit. How does it work?"

I told him that he had to sign three index cards and give me a fourth blank card. I would then take them over to their card table and after a few warm ups would sign the fourth card in front of Felice and lay the four cards on the table. He then had to come over and pick out the forgery.

Stevie had finished his mile and was walking over in our direction. I held up my hand to warn him off because I was afraid his presence would spook Nardone.

Now the men were excited and started making side bets among themselves on who was going to come out on top. The kitty started to grow. When I saw that this had taken on a life of its own I upped the ante.

"But if I win you also have to sign off for Stevie." I pointed in my locker mate's direction.

Nardone hesitated, and I was suddenly afraid I had overplayed my hand. Felice came to the rescue.

"C'mon Sally, this kid is never going to pull it off."

One of the other gym teachers came over with the four index cards and pen. Nardone looked at the cards and then the twenty. "All right, what the hell."

I went and stood by the card table and a moment later Felice came over and placed the three signed cards before me. I studied the three signatures and realized that this was going to be easy. Sal Nardone was a product of the Catholic school system and had the pretty cursive writing to prove it. I took the pen and, using the back of one of the DRF's, made only two trial runs and then signed card number four. I placed it in the number three spot on the card table with Felice watching me.

Nardone was the last of the gym teachers to reach the table. The others were all mumbling their own guesses as he studied each card. Finally, he smiled and reached forward.

"Sorry kid," he said with delight, "Thanks for your twenty. I'll be seeing you first thing tomorrow at gym."

And then he put his fat finger down with authority right on card number two.

I never saw the inside of that high school gym again.

CHAPTER FIFTY-THREE
(WHICH WITCH IS WITCH)

"I'm telling you, he's a fucking warlock!" Bobby Armstrong announced with more excitement than I had ever witnessed before. We all cut class, and had just hit the bagel shop under the El. We were now sitting along the benches on Jerome Avenue, eating bagels and talking shit while waiting for a decent amount of time to pass before we could all go home without our parents asking any questions. As long as we were there to call "present" in home room, the rest of the day was ours.

Joe Marrero took a drag from his Newport and followed it with a healthy bite from his bagel, chewing vigorously while the minty smoke flowed out his nose like a dragon. "I ain't buying it."

"Ask Billy!" Bobby challenged, turning to his cousin for back up.

"Mr. O'Connor, my English teacher, swore that he is." Billy responded. "They share the same classroom and Mr. O goes out the back door when Epstein enters the front during the break between classes. O is scared to death of him."

"Why?" I asked, fascinated by the idea that there was a self-avowed, adult witch roaming the halls of our school.

"O said that Epstein had been fired from his last school and at the exact moment the assistant principal handed Epstein his termination letter, the AP's car blew up in the school's parking lot."

"Epstein." Joe said. "That's a Jewish name. Are there any Jewish witches?"

"I never heard of one." I responded. "But what the fuck do I know?"

"I say we should come right out and ask him." Bobby said.

"What, walk up to him and ask, 'Mr. Epstein, are you a warlock?'" I said.

"Mr. O says he quite open about it." Billy said, as he tossed his empty grape juice container into a nearby trash can.

Joe flicked his cigarette under a passing cab on Jerome avenue.

"Billy, you are supposed to be in English class now, aren't you?" Bobby asked.

"Yeah," Billy answered.

"Let's go ask him then." Joe said, as he hopped off the bench.

"I'm down." I said, before following Joe down the path towards Mosholu Parkway.

Bobby and Billy followed us, but as we neared the school's front entrance, Billy pulled up.

"I owe Mr. O a paper so I'm gonna split." Billy said. "He's in Room 402. Catch you later."

We all waved as Billy headed off towards the Number One Bus. The rest of us entered the school, holding up our ID's as we passed the tall black policeman who functioned as the school's security guard. He barely looked up from his paper.

Sure enough, we got to Room 402 just as the change of class bell rang and Mr. O'Connor slid stealthily out the back door, just as a short, stocky but fit man in his mid-thirties entered the front of the classroom. I wasn't sure what I expected but this guy didn't fit any of the stereotypes. He looked more like an investment banker, clean shaven with his thick brown hair styled back off his face but left just long enough to show he was fashionable. He was wearing a tailored suit which was a disappointing light grey, not black. He had his nose in his Kelly book as we rolled into the classroom while his actual students were milling about trying to kill as much time as possible before class began.

Bobby Armstrong was never shy, so he walked right up to the desk and without even introducing himself said, "I hear you're a witch."

"And who told you that?' Epstein asked without looking up from his book.

"My cousin," Bobby said. "And he's never lied to me."

"Well, the good news is that your cousin maintains his perfect record." Epstein said, as he looked up from his book, first at Bobby, then at Joe, and finally at me. "But most of the men call themselves warlocks. I have no preference either way."

Bobby turned to Joe and me, vindicated. "What did I tell you?"

"Just because he calls himself a warlock, doesn't mean he is one." Joe countered. "Apples said he's been abducted by aliens. Doesn't make it true." He turned back to me. "No offence to your cousin."

"None taken." I responded. I wished I had believed Apples.

"You know," Epstein said. "Joe has a point. I could be just saying I'm a witch."

The other guys didn't seem to notice, but I strained my memory to see if I heard anyone mention Joe by name. We hadn't.

"And the fact that Jimmy here, has a small swirl circle on the palm below his left ring finger, and three squiggly lines below his pinky, doesn't necessarily make him a witch, either."

"Wait, what?" I stammered, blown away by this continued parlor trick. In that second, Epstein had grabbed my left hand and turned it palm upwards to show the others, who now stared at it in disbelief.

"Shit, you do have a circle and three squiggly lines." Bobby said, pointing.

"Sure enough." Joe added, looking even closer. "a ring finger swirl and three pinky lines."

"So, what!" I said defensively, as I pulled my hand away from the teacher and balled my palm into a fist. "I'm sure you both have the same thing. And I'm no witch."

My friends searched their own palms and showed me that neither had those same markings.

"No, you're a warlock," Joe corrected me, clearly enjoying my discomfort.

I was now studying my palm more closely. "That's a scar," I said, as I pointed to the swirl.

"Now you guys don't really believe I'm a witch, do you?" Epstein said, just as the start of class bell rung. "You can't be that gullible."

"See, I told you." Joe said. "Billy is crazy."

"Let's book." Bobby said, "I'm going to kick Billy's ass when I see him."

"I'm out." Joe responded, following Bobby towards the door.

Epstein smiled and held out his own left palm. There were those same markings.

"If you ever want to talk, Jimmy, you know where to find me."

This guy really creeped me out. I never went near the fourth floor of NBC again.

Apollo now appeared by my left side, flipped my hand over and smiled.

Our bodies don't scar.

There on my left palm, below my ring and pinky fingers were the swirl and the three squiggly lines.

You never went back to ask? Stella queried.

I was a human teenager, and while I believed in magic, I had only witnessed it practiced by the females of my clan. My interests at that age were focused on far more basic needs. Like sex.

A road not taken. Claire said. *Witchcraft, not sex,*

Truth is, I added, *I had forgotten all about it for the next fifty years and when magic finally came back into my life, I didn't need to rely on the old ways. I had Bobbi and Bonnie for that, and quantum physics after my evolution. But since I'm laying it all out for you I thought it was worth mentioning.*

Holy shit! Apollo exclaimed, holding out his left palm. *Look.*

There were those matching markings, and the remnants of a telepathic Bronx accent.

Well, it's about time you males got a little lucky. Stella said, with just a hint of disappointment. She held out her own left palm. It was sans swirl and squiggles.

Apollo has some homework to do. Claire said. *But let's return to the story at hand.*

As bad as her pun was, we all laughed.

Well since we are on the subject of hands, that leads me to another moment of human self-awareness.

CHAPTER FIFTY-FOUR
(PUNCH-DRUNK PROMISE)

On the night of my seventeenth birthday, along with the pair of bell bottom jeans I had been begging for, my father handed me an oversized birthday card. When I opened it, a cut out application for the 1974 New York Daily News Golden Gloves Tournament and my father's check in the appropriate amount made out to the New York Daily News Charities, slipped out onto the table. The application had been filled out. All that was left was the spot for my signature. My father handed me a pen.

To tell you the truth, I had forgotten my repeated promise and was hoping he did too.

But if there is one trait that has been consistently handed down through each generation of McCarthys, it's their tenacious stubbornness.

Tell me about it. Claire shared telepathically, following with an aural chuckle.

I signed the application and slid it back across the table and watched as he put it all together back into the envelope that my card had come in, jotted an address across its front, put a stamp on it and walked out the door. Five minutes later he returned from his round trip to the closest mailbox.

Then he served me my birthday cake and my family sang happy birthday. As usual, The Ginger was gone before I blew out the candles.

I was still in decent shape from my recently abandoned martial arts training, and I knew how to trade blows, given my family history, but I had never stepped into a boxing ring and didn't know anything about its rules. My father handed me a piece of paper with the name, address, and phone number for a boxing club in the Castle Hill Section of the Bronx. I looked at the address.

"And how the fuck am I supposed to get way over to the other side of the Bronx?" I asked.

"That's your fucking problem." He said with a smile. "A promise is a promise. Happy birthday."

To my surprise, when I later commiserated with Mark Wallen over a couple of beers, mine, not his, instead of supporting my recalcitrance, he supported my father's decision to hold me to my word and volunteered to help me train for the event. He even offered to drive me to Castle Hill on training days after he got off work if my father would lend him his car. So much for being a passive Buddhist.

I prayed that the owner of the gym, a Spanish guy named Joe Fernandez, would tell me that he only had daytime training hours. Nope, my bad luck held. They were open until ten pm every night of the week.

On Saturday November 17, 1973, Mark Wallen drove me to the address on the card my father gave me. It was a large dry cleaners. I thought my father had gotten the address wrong, so I called Joe from the pay phone in front of the dry-cleaning establishment, while Mark found a parking space. Joe told me to hold on for a second. A moment later a short, grizzly looking Latino exited the store front. His thick mane was shoulder-length and salt and pepper.

"You must be Jimmy." Joe said, sticking out his hand as an introduction. "I'm Joe Fernandez." He broke into a broad smile. "So, you want to learn how to box?"

I nodded. Just then Mark came trotting up beside me, stuck out his hand and introduced himself as my manager. Joe smiled at us, knowing we were out of our depth. He crooked his index finger and led me and Mark around the back of the building, where an entrance to the basement opened into a large fully equipped boxing gym, with speed bags, heavy bags, wall mirrors and a regulation-size ring in its center.

There were about a dozen boys of all shapes and sizes ranging from teens to their twenties working hard at various stations, and two smaller fighters were fully engaged in sparring in the center of the ring, while another older Latino was both refereeing and coaching them. A black midget was furiously massaging one of the fighters on what looked like a hospital gurney.

"You know, you're the first white kid who has ever trained here," Joe said with a wink. "I'm going to have to call you *chico blanco*. Assuming you stick it out."

I spotted his open palm snapping out towards my face and instinctively moved just out of its reach.

"That's good." He said with a laugh. I wasn't so lucky with the second snap, which caught me on the right cheek but didn't do any damage. That old fucker could move. "First lesson. There's always a second punch following the first one." Joe said. "C'mon, let's see what you can do."

For the next two hours, Joe put me through my paces, including teaching me how to jump rope for real and then how to throw punches from my shoulders, like a boxer, instead of from the chambers by my hips. He had me put on light leather gloves, and then mimic combinations he would show me, first slowly and then as fast as I could fire them at the hand pads he would also use to taunt me by cuffing the top of my head.

An hour into the work out, he wrapped my hands and put on the twenty-ounce gloves, popped a new mouth piece in my mouth, then put me in the ring with a Spanish kid named Rico who was a little taller and older than me. I immediately learned how fast this kid's hands were when he threw three quick jabs that caught me flatfooted and squarely on my forehead before the sound of the corner bell had stopped ringing. I didn't like that.

Rico danced around on his toes and threw a few more left jabs which I caught with my gloves. When I dropped my left glove, he made me pay with a right hook. I took it full blast on the cheekbone, as I had done with so many of Eddie's shots in the past. Then I surprised the kid when I closed the distance and punched him as hard as I could directly in his chest. I may have even kiai'd. He didn't see that coming. Neither did Joe, who leapt up into the ring and pulled me back into my neutral corner while the black midget, whose name was Johnny, slipped under the lowest rope and quickly attended to the fallen. Rico was back up on his feet a minute later with Johnny vigorously massaging his breast bone, but he wasn't happy.

I could feel my cheek swelling up, but luckily it didn't extend to my eye.

"So, you're a counter puncher." Joe said, his broad smile returning. He removed my gloves and started to unwind my wraps. "That will make for some great fights and an ugly face in a very short career."

"I'm not in this for the long haul." I said using my now free left hand to test the damage to my cheekbone. "And I wasn't born this pretty. I just need you to get me through this year's Golden Gloves without me looking like an asshole."

'I can sure do that much for you." Joe said, gently placing an ice pack Johnny handed him on my cheek. "Who knows, you may win a few fights. Welcome to the club."

As I pulled on my sweat shirt Joe added a final insult to my injury.

"You are going to need to lose the beard and cut that hair before your first fight." He said. "Dems the rules. Theirs, not mine."

I couldn't tell if it was pride or amusement I saw in my father's eyes after he spotted my swollen cheek when I walked through my kitchen door later that night.

Frankly, I didn't give a shit. But a promise is a promise.

CHAPTER FIFTY-FIVE
(TRAINING SUCKS)

For the next two months, I trained pretty much every day. My father hung both a speed and heavy bag in the garage, a building that I used to love to climb when I was younger, and bought me a leather jump rope. It was cold in the unheated garage, but I still worked up a sweat during each work out. If it snowed, I had to clear a spot in the back yard to jump rope because the ceiling in the garage was too low. The first time it snowed, I didn't account for the melt and freeze and when I went out the next afternoon I quickly slipped on the frozen sheen and fell right on my ass. Spaghetti, who liked to watch me train from the back porch perch, laughed his ass off.

Mark would swing by most evenings after work and drive me over to the Castle Hill Boxing Club, where Joe would match me up with whoever was around willing to spar a few rounds. I was naturally a middleweight, but Joe wanted me to drop down to the welterweight division where my punching power could do more damage. That meant more running, more sweating and no beers.

That also meant me sparring with fast smaller Latinos who would attack me like buzz saws. They couldn't hurt me, but it was frustrating as hell until I found my timing and could deliver the type of blows necessary to stop them in their tracks. But it was never pretty, and I never found the heart that came so naturally to every other fighter who wanted to take my head off just for daring to step in the ring with them. I just didn't like hurting people.

"Stop apologizing blanquito!" Joe would shout from the corner.

"That's it," Joe said to me after one practice. "I need to make you meaner. From here on out, no sex for you."

I laughed. I hadn't had a sniff of sex since the alleyway dalliances during my dancing days at the Pegasus Pub, unless you counted my last grind session at Spillane with the delightful Danielle.

"I'm not kidding," Joe said. "I don't even want you jerking off."

I cursed the promise I made to my father. I was feeling meaner already.

After that attitude adjustment, Joe kept putting me in the ring with his heavier fighters because he wanted to see just how well I could stand up to heavy punching power. This was a whole new level of frustration because while I was able to land more punches during these sparring sessions, I wasn't dropping these fighters like the lighter weights and I tended to stay engaged toe-to-toe, and not rely on footwork to get me out of trouble. The other problem was that I wouldn't go down either. A couple of these bastards rung my bell, but I would still stay up on my feet until the real corner bell sounded. Spaghetti had taught me that McCarthys only lay down when it was time to bury them, and not a moment before.

Of course, there was one sparring partner that didn't give me a choice. Joe had one superheavyweight in his stable named Hugo, who tipped the scales at 245. This guy was an Onyx mountain. But his problem was that he was even nicer than me. He could rock the two-hundred-pound heavy bags until they were swinging up against the ceiling like a pendulum, but if you put him in the ring with another giant, he would play patty-cake until the final bell rung. You couldn't hurt him, but you couldn't get him to hurt the other guy either.

The good news was that sparring with this guy made me look like a mongoose, and I liked being the guy avoiding the punches while landing my own. After landing a particularly solid right over his left eye, I saw that his eye was beginning to swell. I can only blame my autoerotic abstinence because I kept working that eye to see if I could bring this mountain down. I got cocky. And then I got my clock cleaned.

There is an old Looney Tunes cartoon where Bugs Bunny is in a boxing ring with a giant. That day, I was the rabbit.

I was so focused on snapping Hugo's head back with right hands to his left eye that I didn't notice the anger building in his right eye, or the right anvil of a fist that caught me in the solar plexus that literally lifted me off my feet and sent me hurtling across the ring into the corner, which, despite its padding, felt like landing against a steel pipe. I actually saw that rotating circle of stars as the blackness enveloped me. For the first time in my life, I was out for the count.

When I woke up, I was still slumped against the corner pad with Johnny the black dwarf lifting my arms over my shoulders to try to get me breathing regularly while Joe waved an ammonia ampule under my nose. Hugo stood over me apologizing for losing his temper. Joe looked thrilled that I had brought out the beast in his biggest beast. Mark stood just outside the ring, looking terrified, and kept asking me what day it was and who was the president of the United States. It was Nixon.

"Well, you were never out there to dance with him, were ya?" Joe said, as he helped me back up onto wobbly pins.

In that moment, all I could think of was how much I really missed the Pegasus Pub.

CHAPTER FIFTY-SIX
(THE BUDDHIST AND THE MAN EATER)

Even those intentionally celibate lost their virginity before I did.

Murray Conlon spread the word during the Thanksgiving party circuit of 1973 that a family of notorious Irish girls from back in the old neighborhood were throwing a major party for New Years. He could invite whoever he wanted as long as they would kick in twenty bucks each towards the party. According to Murray, the oldest of the sisters, Maggie Collins, was a true women's libber, in that she treated every man she ever met like every man had treated at least one woman in their life, badly. We were disposable goods, and she was a voracious consumer.

Murray said that Maggie was eighteen and didn't dip into the underage pool. But, if a guy was half way decent looking and could legally buy her enough beer, there was pretty much nothing she would not do to you to satisfy what survivors have described as an insatiable sexual appetite.

Looking back on it now, I feel bad that I talked Mark Wallen into going. I hadn't a clue at the time that he would become Maggie Collins' latest victim. But no one put a gun to his head, or that girl in his bed. I just didn't want him to feel like I excluded him from our social gatherings because he was such a straight shooter. Especially around the holidays.

Mark had stayed with our family over the Christmas holidays and in fact had slept on the riser bed in my attic bedroom from Friday the twenty-first right through to New Year's Eve.

It actually worked out for him. He could just walk around the block to Daitch every day and leave the fire engine red, with black racing stripes, 1970 Chevelle he had bought himself for Christmas in the driveway, if the weather was too poor to drive it.

That car could move. Mark took Eddie, BJ, and me for a ride down the Westside highway that first Saturday night of Christmas week and when I saw the speedometer hit 125 just as we shot past the Southbound cars coming in from New Jersey off the George Washington Bridge, I hopped in the back seat, where Eddie and BJ sat egging him on to go faster. I should have taken that sudden impulsiveness and recklessness as a sign that something in my always practical and sensible Buddhist buddy was changing. But, to tell you the truth, I was more worried at the time that he was going to kill all of us, and when he didn't I was just as consumed as the others by the adrenaline rush of cheating death.

Mark crammed six of us into his Chevy on the last night of the year and we drove over to the Bedford Park area by NBC, where Maggie and her sisters had rented a standalone building that housed a local Veteran's Group. Joe Marrero, his girl, Lilly Tonelli, plus a couple of newer members of the crew, Mike Austin and his girl, Delia Wolfe, crammed in the back seat. Mike and Joe had become friends over the past year working behind the counter in Knolls Pizza down in South Riverdale.

Eddie and BJ were driving over in BJ's recently acquired 1964 Mercury Midnight Marauder. They were bringing Brian Kelly, Steve the Greek, and another new acquisition, Rocky O'Hanlon, who had been hanging around the periphery of the group since he traded up and dated Becky Nugent, one of our classmates. Rocky had recently broken up with Becky and was hoping to have a shot with one of Maggie Collins' younger sisters, who were rumored to be not as exotic as Maggie, but weren't entering any religious order any time soon. Apples grabbed the last available seat.

When Mark's contingent arrived around ten pm, the party was in full swing and there were already a few people hurling their guts up between cars in front of the building. Murray was waiting by the door and signaled to the large dude collecting the money, that we were guests on Maggie's invite list.

Having made weight at the official weigh in, but still on my trainer's sex ban, my very blue balls didn't want to be anywhere near any available women, so I made a bee line to the series of kegs and cups lined up over against what normally served as this private establishment's bar and began to self-medicate. Then I took in the scenery.

While this wasn't the Pegasus Pub, there was still a strong contingent of lovely Latinas and a few smoking black girls, who had curves in all the right places, mixing freely with their friends from Murray's old neighborhood. On a boom box over by the open floor, Alison Steele was counting down 1973's hits on WNEW FM. I just prayed none of the girls asked me to dance or I wouldn't be worth shit the next time I was in the ring.

Of course, I hadn't factored in the fact that I hadn't had a beer in over a month.

Mark came over to where I was lurking with a big smile on his face and a coke in his hand.

"This is some party." He said. "I'm glad Murray invited me."

"Speak of the devil." I said and pointed to the approaching Murray who was leading an older girl towards us by the hand. Everyone she passed tried to catch her eye and say hello. I realized this must be the hostess of our soiree.

"Jimmy, Mark, I'd like to introduce Maggie Collins." Murray said with a nasally voice that even stood out in the Bronx. I nodded respectfully and hoisted my cup in salutation. I never said a word.

This young lady had a serious body with breasts so large they could smother a man if he wasn't careful. The top four buttons on her tailor-made shirt opened on a display of quivering cleavage, while the remaining buttons below struggled to restrain that which was hidden for only as long as she wished. I was afraid to gaze too long for fear that one of the buttons would pop and take my eye out. Her thick, reddish-brown hair was tied back in a loose pony tail with a bright red ribbon that looked like it had been commandeered from a Christmas tree. She had light skin and was well freckled, but they were faded enough not to distract you from the piercing blue eyes that were presently sizing up my unassuming friend.

"And how old are you, Mark?" She asked, her voice lyrical, with a whisky edge to it.

"Nineteen. Twenty this May." He responded, just a bit shyly. I could see that Mark was worried about losing an eye as well by the way he avoided looking in her general direction for more than a few seconds at a time.

"And how about you, Jimmy?" She asked, now leering in my direction.

"He's jail bate, like me." Murray volunteered before I could respond. "But if your standards have recently loosened, Maggie, I'd be happy to chaperone you the rest of the party and beyond. I can give you references from a satisfied doctor if you'd like."

"No, thank you Denis," Maggie said with a lascivious grin. "Mark looks like he will do just fine." Mark looked surprised and a bit tentative as Maggie slid her arm through the crook of his drinking hand and ushered him away, her breast slowly brushing his elbow as she maneuvered. No lie, I was hard just watching it.

Do you hear yourself, father? Stella interrupted. *You're like that schoolboy all over again.*

Will you please be quiet and let our father finish. Apollo countered. *This is his story and he'll tell it the way he wants.*

Or at least the way you want, Apollo, Claire said and laughed.

At that moment I was thrilled to be distracted by BJ and Eddie getting into it with the Big Dude at the door. Murray ran over and made the introductions before an ambulance needed to be called.

Apples spotted me as he followed them in and came over. I had his beer ready by the time he reached me. He looked anxious, took the cup from me, and drained it in one long pull.

"Jimmy," He said as he wiped his mouth on his sleeve. "I really need to talk to you about those Goddam aliens." The seriousness of his tone was matched only by the incredulity of my face.

"They grabbed me again Christmas morning." He said as I handed him a refill. "Each time it's the same thing. Me naked on a table and them probing me with all kinds of instruments."

Apollo burst out laughing. *I heard the anal probe was a 'thing' back in the day. Must have freaked the humans out. Those Greys did their homework.*

They were subcontracted by the Centaurians. Stella said proudly. *Petrichor told me that the Greys enjoyed getting their hands dirty doing the constant medical and evolutionary testing required to see how our great experiment was coming along. All for the greater good. They were very thorough.*

I thought about the image of my cousin Apples lying naked on a table in a room full of Greys getting his butt probed and couldn't help but laugh along with Apollo.

Claire had to have been peeking because a moment later I heard her Lurchy laugh join in.

And in the end, Stella continued, *it turned out just fine for cousin Apples. After all, when they finally did take him for good, they let him bring his woman, Connie, with him, and their family now rules Zeta Retuli the way our own family has risen on Proxima b.*

All's well that ends well, as the Bard said. Claire concluded. *And if we ever want your father to end his story, we better let him get back to it.*

Right. Well, I had no idea at this time that Apples was telling the truth. He was always on the nervous side and given that I never knew where he got to once he took that subway back into Manhattan, I just felt it was my obligation to humor him as much as possible and to keep everyone else from breaking his balls. But as he kept sharing his experiences with anyone who would listen, especially when he was drunk, this was getting harder and harder to do.

"They told me this time that they were cloning hybrids of me in their labs up on the ship." He said as he fished a Pall Mall cigarette from his shirt pocket and lit up, his hand with that slight tremor we were all so familiar with. I actually thought that he had taken one too many misfired shots from Eddie.

"What the fuck is cloning? And what the hell is a hybrid." He asked, a look of true bewilderment on his face.

Neither one of these words were on my last English Regents exam, so I had no answers for him.

The radio started playing "Message To You."

"Fucking Bee Gees! When are we going to hear some real dance music from them?" Apples said. He finished his refill, stamped out his cigarette and walked over towards the girls working the radio. "Can't we find some Spinners on that thing?"

"Here you go Poppi!" Called out a pretty Latina named Yvette, as Santana's *"Oye Como Va"* came on the radio. Apples walked over to the girl, took her hand, and led her onto the floor. Every Mick in the place stopped talking and watched as Apples guided the surprised Latina through her paces.

"Who knew that prick could move like that?" Eddie said as he walked up beside me and filled his beer cup.

"That's the Black Irish genes," BJ said, filling his own cup from the next tap. "Those strong Spanish swimmers from King Phillip's sunken Armada hit Irish shores and taught their ladies how to dance."

I didn't have the heart to mention the dance lessons.

"That must be it." Eddie said, watching Apples glide Yvette across the floor. A tall black girl cut in and the two gyrated their hips in synch throughout the instrumental section.

Joe Marrero and Lilly Tonelli joined them on the floor. Joe looked every bit as cool as Carlos Santana, and even lip synched the refrain as it returned on the radio.

Murray grabbed one of the other girl's hands and dragged her, laughing, out onto the floor.

Brian Kelly now came over. "Did you know these fuckers can dance?"

"Shocked as you are." I responded and refilled my beer.

"I can't dance unless I'm drunk." Brian added.

"Me either." Eddie said.

"Well, we better man up and start drinking then." I said, downing the rest of my beer.

Steve the Greek was deeply involved in a silent conversation with, it turned out, one of the younger Collins girls named Anne, and Rocky O'Hanlon had the rapt attention of another Irish girl over by the rest rooms. Mike Austin and his girl, Delia, were making out by the front entrance. All was right with the world.

I watched one of Murray's boys from the old neighborhood, a kid I only knew as Schwartz, guide his pretty girlfriend, Jaysree, around the floor like they were all alone. You could feel their connection, and the rest of the world didn't matter. I bet they found that elusive bond Johnny Peyton was talking about.

"Dancing babe at six o'clock," BJ said, pointing at the first girl that Apples led onto the floor, now dancing alone, lost in the music. Watching BJ approach the startled girl, doing his best imitation of Baloo the dancing bear from the Disney version of *The Jungle Book*, had me and Brian almost pissing ourselves.

When we caught our breath, Brian looked around to do a head check and came up one short.

"Where's Wallen?" Brian asked.

"Went somewhere with our hostess." I replied.

"The girl with the huge tits?" Eddie asked.

"Yeah, she certainly was a healthy girl." I responded.

"I saw her leading him outside about twenty minutes ago." Eddie said.

I walked to the front entrance and looked down the block to where Mark had parked his Chevy. It was gone.

I don't remember the clock striking twelve that night. Turns out I had drank myself into a stupor and Eddie flipped me over his shoulder and carried me back to BJ's car, where I slept for a few hours until everyone else spilled out of the party. I don't even remember the others all cramming into BJ's car, and he ultimately had to make a 2nd trip to pick up the stragglers left behind by Mark.

Mark didn't come back to the house that night, or the next. When I walked around to Daitch on January second to try to catch up with him at work, a very pissed off Pat Leary said that, "The fucker has called in sick."

I called Joe Fernandez and explained the situation and he told me to keep working out at home and get back there as soon as I could.

On Saturday morning, January 5th, Mark reappeared at my house like a feral cat returning from a walk about, looking exhausted. He actually laid down on the riser bed in my room and slept until Saturday night.

When he finally came to, he looked over at me sitting across the room on my bed, where I was reading an article about George Forman in the January edition of Ring Magazine. He smiled the goofiest smile I ever saw cross his face, and said, "Dude, I think she broke my dick."

CHAPTER FIFTY-SEVEN
(PROMISES KEPT AND HEARTS BROKEN)

I would love to tell you that I won my division in the Golden Gloves that year. Truth is that I made it past another Irish kid and a Jamaican. The next time I saw my father that proud, was the day I married Gina.

Funny thing when you are fighting in a ring. The lights above you extend their reach into the audience about two rows deep into the surrounding seats. That is where the rabid fans sit who like to leap to their feet throughout the fight and experience the blood sport vicariously. They love to hear the leather connect with flesh, muscle, and bone. They like to hear the grunts. They are thrilled when the sweat and blood flies off the fighters and sprinkles them like a brutal blessing. If a mouthpiece flies out, they are orgasmic. And they all know that the fighters can hear them when they shout, and they shout a lot. It is almost interactive.

The Irish kid was tough but ultimately dropped in the second round. The Jamaican was tougher and would not go down no matter how hard I hit him. He tied me up and hung on until the bell rung the third time. It was like slow dancing in prison. Exhausting. But it gave me a chance to glance over his shoulder at the audience who were all foaming at the mouth demanding that I kill this bastard. They didn't come to see a win. They came for an execution. Pure blood lust.

And no amount of sexual abstinence was going to make me want to kill my opponents. Turns out it would take a lot more than that, and I never found it in the ring. I'm pissed I wasted those celibate months when I was in my human prime and could have been out really trying to get laid.

My inadequate killer instinct became really apparent when I ran into my third opponent, a twenty-six-year-old man named Juan Carvallo, at some venue in Brooklyn. This guy was looking to make the Golden Gloves his entre into the professional boxing world. All of his eggs were in that one basket. And if that meant he had to kill me, so be it.

Now there is a big difference between a healthy seventeen-year-old and an equally healthy man in his mid-twenties. Two mountains can be at their peak, but one will always be larger than the other. Juan was more muscular than I was. And he was a south paw, which threw my timing and defense off completely.

The only thing I had going for me was my McCarthy forged granite jaw, and that was severely tested that night.

The first round we both ran into the center of the ring and just started banging on each other. Blow for blow. Mostly head shots. Ugly but the audience loved it. I didn't hear the bell for round one until the ref pulled us apart and sent us to our corners. I refused to sit on my stool while Joe wiped the sweat off my face and reapplied the Vaseline.

In the beginning of round two I did land a hard right to Juan's left rib cage that lifted him to his toes. He then tied me up for about thirty seconds while he caught his breath. Once the two of us went back to head-hunting, my right eye started to swell up. I knew I was in trouble when he landed two hard head shots in a row without me answering with a counter, so I tied him up for a few seconds to get my bearings.

The weird thing is that while this is going on your adrenaline is pumping so hard that you are not feeling any pain. It's more the pressure of the impact and the rocking of your head and body in response. But the salt from your sweat, and sometimes your opponent's, does burn when it reaches your eyes.

I glanced out at the audience again and this time they were calling for my opponent to finish me off. And that pissed me off enough to shove myself free and hit that fucker with a right overhand as hard as I could in his nose. It rocked him, but he didn't drop, and with blood now running out the edges of his nostrils he flew back at me with a flurry of head shots that had me on my heels. I was so distracted by trying to get my hands up to catch his blows that I didn't notice the white towel flying from my corner over the ropes and landing in the center of the ring.

Turns out that Mark and Joe almost got into a brawl fighting over that towel. Joe wanted me to fight my way out of it. The last remnants of Mark's Buddhism surfaced, and he wanted to keep me from getting permanent brain damage. Might have been too little too late.

Mark stopped the fight, and much to my father's chagrin, ended my boxing career that unexpectedly mild Saturday night in March. But he probably saved my marbles. I wish I put them to better use in the short term afterwards.

My one regret was not making it to the next round of the Golden Gloves, which would have been held at Madison Square Garden. Oh well, dems da brakes. Juan got to the Garden and went on to win my division. He had a pretty decent professional career for a few years afterwards. God bless him.

My father had driven me, my brothers, and Apples home after the fight, doing his best to console me with the usual bromides. He wasn't a man of many words, but when he said something, he meant it.

After the fight, Mark had taken off in his Chevy directly from the Brooklyn Gym to meet Maggie Collins, who he had been regularly seeing most weekends for the past few months, but he swore he'd catch up with me before the night was over. Given his plans, I hoped that he was wearing a metal condom and a respirator, and I didn't expect to see him anytime soon.

Win or lose, I had made plans to meet some of the crew back at The Courts, assuming I was still breathing. JC had cooked up some burgers and hot dogs at work and brought them along, in case, as he liked to put it, "anyone's feeling a little peckish." BJ, whose many nicknames included "The Party King," had brought along a liter of Jameson's in anticipation of a celebration, knowing it worked just as well for commiseration. I didn't like whiskey at the time, but coming from an Irish household I understood its ceremonial value to mark important occasions. It would have been rude to abstain.

I took my mandatory shot after Eddie said some entertaining words as a toast, summing up my brief boxing career, which ended with him wishing he could have stepped in on my behalf and actually won the fight. Truth is that he probably would have, but my father never asked him to try. Maybe my dad didn't need Eddie to prove he was an ass kicker.

This post fight gathering had special meaning for me, given that my two younger brothers had joined us all for the event. That was the first time the male siblings all shared a drink together. It wasn't the last.

The feeling of the whiskey burning in my throat had not yet subsided when Mark's Chevy rolled up into the outer driveway leading to The Courts, and he quickly slid through the opening in the chained gate and came directly over to the benches.

"That had to be the fastest lay in Riverdale history." I called out as he approached.

"Buddha, come and toast Jimmy!" BJ shouted and began to refill the dozen shot glasses he had swiped from his parent's house, along with the Jameson's. "Everybody drinks tonight!"

Mark walked over and, without saying a word, grabbed one of the shots and downed it. If I wasn't so shocked by the fact that Mark did not drink, I would have worried more about the faces he was making in response to the whiskey. He so quickly blushed that I thought his head would explode. What was even more surprising was that before he had actually caught his breath he grabbed another shot from its place along the wooden bench and tossed that down behind it.

Eddie told The Ginger to grab Mark's car keys and when my fierce red-afroed brother extended his large hand, Mark handed them over without a fight. Then he grabbed a third shot and tossed it down.

"What do you see in this crap?!" a very raspy voice then squeaked from between Mark's clenched teeth. His legs started to buckle and The Ginger and my youngest brother grabbed his arms and carried him over to where I sat on the benches.

"Better lean him over," JC counselled.

Just then Joe, Murray and Mike Austin showed up and as soon as Mark saw Murray, he bent over his knees, puked and then began to cry in his palms.

"What the fuck happened?" I demanded of Murray, with maybe just a little too much of an edge.

"Look, I warned you all," he replied, a bit defensively, before lifting and downing a shot from the remaining row on the bench. "Maggie moved on. That's what she does. It's nothing personal. Another lover, another notch on her headboard."

"Her sister dumped me New Year's day." Steve the Greek chimed in to commiserate.

"I've been nailing one of their cousins since that party," Rocky added, "maybe she's got a sister?"

"Shut the fuck up, little man," BJ bellowed. "Can't you see our boy here is heartbroken? He doesn't want to hear about your pussy-pounding!"

That BJ knew how to turn a phrase, even a filthy one. He was also dramatically at his best when he drank.

Steve the Greek applauded BJ's admonishment, then downed a shot in support of its gravitas.

" L'chaim, Jimmy!" Mike Austin said, raising his glass in my direction. He was the only one to sip his whiskey. He had been slowly civilized by spending a lot of time hanging with his girlfriend's respectable family.

"Nice shiner." Joe said to me, "I heard you were robbed." It was good to see that the Riverdale gossip circuit was fully functioning, even on a Saturday night.

Had Joe been one of us, he could have watched it happening in real time through father's eyes, Apollo shared.

Had they both been one of us, he could have watched father end the fight before the bell had stopped ringing. Stella joined in.

Well, they weren't Centaurians, and among humans, bad news travels best when it travels slow. Claire added. *No point in rushing disappointment.* She nodded for me to continue.

Joe tossed back two in a row, then did a full body shiver as the second shot kicked in. "Damn, that's good!"

My younger brothers soon called it a night and carried the still drunk and devastated Mark back to the house with instructions to put him to bed on the riser in my room. The rest of us finished BJ's Jameson's and the beers the others had brought with them. Boys with girlfriends then took off to check in with their better halves, Apples led the remaining underage bachelors off to see if they could find an open bodega over the Yonkers city line and buy some more beers before calling it a night, and BJ drove Eddie and me back to our house, leaving Mark's Chevy safely stowed in our driveway, before stumbling off in the direction of his own home.

Turns out, BJ took a little detour that night to a place he liked to retreat to when he needed to be alone to challenge the gods and set his world aright. He would sit fearlessly at the top of this man-made precipice and gaze out over the realm he loved. Eddie wasn't even aware of BJ's sacred space until it was too late. And when you are a teenager, it always is.

Promises kept and hearts broken. With every ending comes new beginnings, and then more endings.

CHAPTER FIFTY-EIGHT (GOODBYES)

There was no high school graduation walk, at least not for me. Since I barely spent any time within its actual walls, I never made any emotional connection with NBC or felt the need for a formal good bye. But my diploma arrived a few weeks later in the mail. The scarecrow got his sheepskin.

I did sit for and pass all my finals without attending class or ever opening a book. Joe Marrero and I handed in bongs made out of stolen Pyrex glass tubing and Chianti bottles for our final shop projects – there is a real art to drilling holes in glass - and Mr. Nardoni was honorable and true to his word and passed me and my locker mate, Esteban, in New York State's most important class.

Since I was no longer taking Kung Fu or boxing, I had time to take driver's ed and get my driver's license. My instructor, Mr. Grecco, was very impressed with my driving from day one and said I was a natural behind the wheel. I guess it's like riding a bike.

Mark Wallen substituted intense alcohol consumption for the loss of his intense sexual experience with Maggie Collins. He wouldn't listen to me or anyone else that there would be others who would actually give a shit about him. In the end, she broke more than his dick, she broke his heart. Every night after finishing his shift at Daitch, he would walk across the mall to the liquor store and pick up a pint of whatever caught his eye. Towards the end he had shifted to Vodka.

Mark was a sloppy drunk, but heartbreak will do that to you.

As we were rolling into the Memorial Day weekend of 1974, Robbie Maclaren decided to sponsor a communal graduation party in Tibbets Brook Park and invited all of his boys from Riverdale and all of his girl Sally's friends from Yonkers. Like Sally, all of Sally's friends were Italian and hot.

The party started on Thursday and was supposed to run the weekend. Man plans and the devil laughs.

Robbie and Sally were heading north to Boston in a few weeks. He to start his undergrad at Boston College, she to move-in with him and work as a waitress until they ultimately got married and lived happily ever after. They did. God bless them.

They weren't the only ones moving on. BJ had finished a year at Westchester Community College and decided he was finally ready for an academic break. He talked Steve the Greek into a hiatus from his job as a bike messenger and Apples into leaving his job at Barney's Men Store on Sixteenth and Seventh in Manhattan, so the three of them could take a cross-country odyssey together *via* Greyhound Express. Steve was the ultimate free spirit, and knew he could always find another job, even if it meant returning to the family diner business. Apples, who was absolutely determined to end the relentless cycle of alien abduction, that no one else witnessed, was more than ready to abandon New York. They were leaving the first week of June.

JC continued to work in the restaurant after being elevated to morning service chef and was enrolled for fall night classes in the Hospitality Management Program at Lehman College in the Bronx. He had managed to maintain a long-distance relationship with Joanna Skeegle through letters and the occasional phone call, so he remained a monk during his senior year at Spillane. She had returned from her first year of college and he was really excited to be bringing her to Robbie's party.

Joe Marrero had no choice but to remain monogamous with his girl Lilly, or her father would have made him disappear. He was crazy for getting mixed up with mafia types. He took BJ's place at WCC and found he had a knack for science. He followed his talents and ultimately moved to Florida where he was appointed the head radiologist in a major Ft. Lauderdale Hospital.

Brian Kelly got into some elite University in upper New York that bordered Canada. He became a bit of a coding genius and launched a successful company that sold video games. That school worked out for him on a whole different level, because in a town full of seedy bars, he finally met the Canadian stripper of his dreams, named Nanetta Concetta. In his senior year, he convinced her he could save her from her life of misery, and the two moved to Ottawa and made a very comfortable life for themselves.

Murray was the stand out. He blew away the neighborhood by gaining acceptance to St. John's College, in England's Oxford University where he read philosophy. At the time, I really didn't know shit about Oxford, or philosophy, or I would have been even more impressed. I heard he ended up staying on to teach. I wonder how he did with the doctors over there.

I sat for the SATs back in Spillane during the fall of my Junior year and scored in the high 1500s. I think they deducted a few points because I spelled my name wrong. I never engaged in the college application process beyond that because I couldn't give a shit about the idea of more education. One more thing that drove my poor mother crazy.

Eddie had toed the family line and was accepted into University where he had a decent freshman year. My mother had subsidized Eddie's education by going to work as a bookkeeper for the Jesuits over at the University, which allowed him to attend there for free.

Eddie even made friends with a whole new group of crazies, which he had started to bring around for the occasional party. While there, he also met and fell in love with the girl he would finally marry. A wonderful girl. They had a great run for many decades, until I managed to fuck that up too.

Once my mother made herself invaluable to her new bosses, without even asking me, she leveraged my SAT scores to talk them into admitting me into their School of General Studies. Basically, night school. At first I rejected it. But after my walking away from Spillane, she wasn't going to lose two in a row. She talked my father into kicking me out of the house if I didn't comply, I caved.

I was not planning to put any effort into it anyway. In fact, after the first month, I completely skipped classes and instead hung around with Eddie's new set of friends, until the Jesuits ratted me out to my mother. But by then, I couldn't give a rat's ass about anything.

Spaghetti secretly defied Posie and used his Irish connections to get me a job working construction during the day, with that local Irish contractor named Jack Sullivan. I was all scheduled to start on the first Monday in June. Eddie was going to work there for the summer, and then on weekends when needed. My younger brothers ended up going to work there during their summer breaks as well. By the time Eddie graduated college, he owned that company, and my brothers helped him run it.

But before any of this happened, this was meant to be a weekend of goodbyes. Turns out some of them were permanent.

CHAPTER FIFTY-NINE
(YOU CAN'T UN-RING THE BELL)

Once the Golden Gloves was safely in my rearview mirror, and I no longer had
to manifest my blood lust through abstinence, I was determined to lose my
virginity. The problem was that as Mark Wallen continued to spiral from his
breakup with Maggie Collins, he became an albatross around my neck. He was
so devastated by his romantic experience, and his loss of sexual ecstasy, that all
he wanted to do was to hit the local dive bars most nights and get drunk. His
eight rights of Buddhism had left him behind. The problem with those dive bars
was there were no young ladies, and the older ladies were almost as sad looking
as the men. I didn't want to lose my virginity to that crowd. I learned later that I
may have missed a golden opportunity. Experience counts.

I felt somewhat responsible for Mark's predicament. If I hadn't talked him
into going to that New Year's Eve party, he'd still be a sober and happy virgin.
Plus, he had no one else. My family had basically adopted him. He became one
of Spaghetti's favorites and Posie doted on him. Even Bonnie liked him, and she
never like any of my guy friends, even the cute ones. All Mark needed was a good
ass kicking by Eddie and he'd be all in.

But Robbie's Westchester weekend extravaganza was promising to be the
event of a lifetime, and I wasn't about to let Mark blow my chances with the
beautiful Italians Sally was bringing to the party. I volunteered to help Robbie
set up, and he loaned me his old car, a 1969 Dodge Dart, to pick up the kegs.
He had just inherited his grandmother's 1968 midnight blue grand prix, with

thirty miles on the odometer, so the Dart became his knock around car. I told Mark I wouldn't be riding with him, and to come along on his own after work.

Sally was good to her word, she brought lots of friends and they were all friendly.

Given that NBC was an all-boys school, and I had been on compelled celibacy for a chunk of my time over this past year, I really hadn't had much opportunity or inclination to pursue the opposite sex. My sexual fumblings with the dance partners outside the Pegasus Pub seemed a distant memory, and even the beautiful breasts of JC's cousin, Vickie Cariano, were getting harder to recall during those desperate moments of self-abuse. The last person I had kissed had been Danielle at Spillane, and while that had been exciting and memorable, it was an unfulfilled promise. The local girls were either taken by one of my friends or put-off by my one-off reputation, so I didn't even bother talking to any of them. I needed a win, badly.

"Jimmy," Sally said as I hoisted the last of the kegs from the trunk of the Dart and carried it to the designated spot in the clearing in the woods, "this is my friend, Gigi Califano!"

This beautiful brunette's smile was as dazzling as her perfect body, on full display in the Daisy Dukes shorts and halter top she was barely wearing. I might have pumped the keg a few times over my head to make my biceps pop just a little more. My post-fighting beard and hair were starting to grow back in, so I wasn't looking half bad either. I was staking my claim to this young lady right out of the gate.

For the next couple of hours, I only left Gigi's side to piss and refill our cups from the kegs. I couldn't tell you what music Danny Mo was playing from the boom box over by the kegs or even who else was around me, although I know I spotted everyone from the crew at one point or another. I wasn't there to get drunk, but I wasn't stopping Gigi from enjoying herself. I knew from the moment I met her where I wanted this to go, and she seemed fully responsive to me right from the start. In fact, before she finished her first cup, she leaned in for her first kiss, and it was all tongue.

When Mark finally showed up on his motorcycle, the party was in full swing. I was glad to see him riding the bike, because I wanted to convince myself that he'd be less likely to get wasted when he was flying without a net. Who was I kidding?

He parked his bike in the next clearing by some of the other cars, then immediately came over to where I was sitting with Gigi on a log, away from most of the others. I could tell from Mark's eyes that he had already started drinking and turned him down when he offered me a swig from his half-pint of vodka that he removed from his motorcycle jacket. I made a quick introduction, but Gigi barely acknowledged him beyond a half-hearted, no-look, "Hi."

"I saw the Greek and BJ over by the kegs," I said, clearly blowing him off. "You should go check them out. I'll catch up with your later." He hesitated until I shot him a look, and then he wandered off, like a spurned puppy.

I didn't see him again until darkness had fallen, although I was so distracted making out with Gigi that Bigfoot could have been standing in the woods behind me jerking off and I wouldn't have noticed. The evening had cooled a bit and Gigi and I had moved a little closer to some of the others, sitting around a camp fire, that was burning in the center of the clearing. One of the guys handed me a bottle of Budweiser from their private stash.

Mark staggered into the edge of the firelight. He polished off another half-pint of vodka and tossed the empty bottle into the fire.

"C'mon Jimmy," Mark said, his words slurring. "Let's get the fuck out of here."

"Can't you wait a bit?" I asked, just a shade impatiently. "I'm kinda working on something here."

My eyes went from Mark to Gigi, who smiled seductively.

"C'mon Jimmy," Mark insisted. "She'll keep. Won't you darling?" He asked, nodding appreciatively at my companion. "I'm too drunk to ride the bike home."

"Jimmy," Gigi said reaching over and placing her hand reassuringly on my thigh, "you said you were going to drive me home tonight."

I looked up at Mark who had been witnessing the exchange. "Just give me an hour," I pleaded. "I'll come back for you and take you home then. We can come back and retrieve your bike tomorrow."

Mark smiled and gave me a wink. He grabbed the half-finished beer from my hand, chugged the rest of it, then tossed the empty glass bottle into the fire.

"Sure thing, Jimmy," Mark called over his shoulder as he staggered back out into the woods. "I'm just going to take a piss and a nap. I'll be waiting for you when you get back."

A half hour later I lost my virginity to Gigi in the front seat of that Dodge Dart, on one of the side roads leading out of Tibbets.

"Don't worry," she said breathlessly as she pulled the string behind her neck and her halter fell loose, "I'm on the pill."

Gigi was aggressively athletic in her intensity and knew the best and quickest way to fully engage by shedding her shorts and straddling me in that front seat. Her salty, sweaty body was soft in all the right parts, and she was quite vocal in her appreciation of the exchange. She was also determined and kept at it until I finally released.

It all must have taken far longer than it seemed because by the time I had dropped her off about ten blocks away and returned to Tibbets, Mark and his motorcycle were gone. No one remembered seeing him leave. So, I left. I would track him down in the morning.

When I saw the series of cop lights just over the Bronx borough line on the Saw Mill River Parkway, I got off at the last Westchester exit onto McLean Avenue, and took the Yonkers side streets home rather than chance getting pulled over, at an NYPD holiday weekend drunk checkpoint.

That might have been the last night I ever slept peacefully, without a guilty conscience, and it wasn't because I never spoke to Gigi again.

CHAPTER SIXTY
(BURYING THE FALLEN)

I'm pretty sure I dreamt only of Gigi that night, and I know I woke up with wood, feeling pretty damn pleased with myself. I was finally a man in all material senses of the word, except those that actually counted, and I was hungry. My three youngest brothers were still asleep in their dormers as I passed their rooms, but Eddie's bed was empty.

No one was down in my parent's apartment, so I continued down to Posie and Spaghetti's place, where I found both the older generations, Eddie and my sister sitting around my grandparent's dining room table. Eddie looked like sleepless shit. My sister got up from the table and hugged me.

"Mark's dead," is all Eddie could say.

It didn't sink in. I stared around the table at everyone. No one made eye contact.

I had never seen Spaghetti cry - ever. At that moment, I spotted a tear run down his cheek. Then my knees buckled, and my sister helped me to the open chair at the end of the table.

"I was coming back from Tibbets with BJ around midnight and the cops had stopped traffic on the Saw Mill South to allow the Fire Department to clean up the wreckage. So, BJ asked one of the officers what had happened."

Posie brought me a cup of tea and shoveled three sugars into it. "Here," she said comfortingly, "get this in you, you've had a bit of a shock."

"He lost control of his bike just after the exit to the Mosholu parkway, sailed over the guard rail and struck a tree." Eddie continued almost clinically. "EMS said he had to be going fast because he died on impact."

That's when it hit me. My tears started and I could feel this deep sob, almost a cry, rise up from my chest and out my mouth. And then I felt the guilt strike me right through my heart and the pain was so intense that I was struggling to breath, as if the oxygen itself was shards of ground glass. My mother came over and began to rub my back with her "musha, musha. . . ."

Musha, musha, musha, Stella now repeated as she transported over to where I was sitting and began to rub my back.

Do you need a minute? Claire asked me.

I didn't understand what they meant until I looked over at Apollo and saw the tears now trickling down his cheeks. And then I reached up to my cheek and felt my own.

I took a settling breath and shook my head.

No, I'm okay. I shared. *I really want to finish this.*

They all nodded, and I continued.

By Memorial Day my parents had arranged and paid for the wake at Riverdale on the Hudson Funeral Home, where every Riverdalian had taken their final bows since my family had moved there. Mark's helmet had preserved his face, so he was able to have an open casket. There was an amazing turnout. He was buried next to the rest of my McCarthy ancestors in Gates of Heaven Cemetery, three days later.

The Ginger gave Spaghetti Mark's specifics, and my grandfather arranged for a headstone to be carved in the shape of a Celtic Cross.

"But he's not Irish," I said to him.

"He is now," was all Spaghetti would say.

A few days after the funeral, I cleared out Mark's rented room up in Yonkers. Among his personal effects I located the title to his Chevy, which had been sitting where he had last parked it in our driveway. I studied the signature on the license from his wallet that the police had given to my parents, and then filled out the transfer of title over to Eddie, pre dating it to April 30th and then I signed it perfectly as Mark F. Wallen.

Why didn't you take the car? Claire asked. *He was your friend. He would have wanted you to have it.*

I had taken enough. I responded. Everyone nodded.

I was desperate to lighten the heaviness that now had settled in the room with my children and closest friend. And then I found it. I continued.

Six months later, when all of my friends had returned to the neighborhood from their various points around the country for the Thanksgiving Holiday, Spaghetti held a special ceremony at Mark's gravesite to unveil the beautiful Celtic Cross headstone he had commissioned. My father had hired a bagpiper for the ceremony. My siblings were all standing by me as we gazed appreciatively at the six-foot grey head stone that would have made St. Patrick proud. It certainly had Spaghetti beaming as the crowd's compliments flowed freely.

Bonnie studied it for a moment and then leaned in and whispered. "I thought Mark was close to my age?"

"A few months younger." I responded. "Why?"

"They got the birth year wrong then," she said, as she pointed to the chiseled date at base of the headstone. Sure enough, it had his birth year as 1956. Three years off.

We all turned to The Ginger, who for the first time and last time since his birth had a look of terror in his eyes.

"Fuck it," was all he could stammer. "I ain't telling him."

With that, we all laughed for the first time in weeks. I knew Mark would get the joke. He was one of us now.

CHAPTER SIXTY-ONE
(VAYA CON DIOS MANZANAS)

My brother Eddie got the call from Colorado in late August. Apples had literally disappeared.

According to both BJ and Steve the Greek, they had left Apples sitting in a booth at a truck stop diner off I25 in northern Colorado, eating apple pie with coffee, and deeply engaged in conversation with Connie, their curvy Mexican waitress. Their Greyhound bus had stopped at dawn to refuel for this leg of the trip to Chicago. The passengers were allowed to stretch their legs and grab a bite to eat. BJ had just gone to piss so he was the first back to the booth. The pie, coffee, a pack of Pall Malls and Connie's order pad and pen were still on the table, so BJ ate the pie. Steve the Greek had phoned his mother from the pay phone by the front door, and didn't see Apples or the waitress leave. In fact, none of the other bus passengers noticed either friend or waitress move from the table. One moment they were there, the next, gone.

When the bus driver notified the passengers that it was time to board, the two boys finally became worried about their missing companion and demanded to talk to the someone in authority.

The manager of the diner was pissed to have lost his best night shift waitress. The lazy and laconic local sheriff finally made it out to the diner, and after taking a few statements, including from both BJ and Steve, concluded that the two just decided to run off together, probably down I25 towards Mexico. He called it the "Latina Lure". The sheriff ignored the fact that the waitress's car was still out in the parking lot, Apples' bag was still on the bus and that no one sitting around them actually saw them leave. The sheriff also rejected any suggestion by Apples' friends of alien abduction, saying, "That shit doesn't happen out here in God's country."

When Eddie phoned Apples' younger sister to report the news, all she could say was a cryptic, "Apples was always afraid this would happen." She promised to light a few votive candles and pray for his safe return.

When the two boys arrived home from the last leg of their cross-country odyssey, BJ delivered Apples' bag along with a case of Coors Golden Beer, which was shared among the crew as we toasted Apples in *absentia*. Steve the Greek had convinced himself that my cousin had decided to do a runner with the waitress, because Apples not only hit on every Latina they met on the trip, but also surprised the others with his fluency in Spanish. Steve finally admitted to us that he just couldn't get his head around the alternative. BJ, always one of the more open minded of the crew, just accepted the alien abduction theory, given that it was all Apples could talk about throughout their journey.

After gulping down his third beer, BJ leaned precariously on one ass cheek, ripped a thunderous loud fart then stood among the nosed pinched and teary eyed, held up his empty beer bottle to the heavens and shouted, "Let that be a warning to any alien considering abducting me for an anal probing. You will not escape unscathed!"

CHAPTER SIXTY-TWO
(BREAKING A DONKEY'S BACK)

Jack Sullivan knew from experience that the off the boat Irish had strong backs, and that he could work them as hard as he wanted as long as he paid them a decent wage. In just one decade, he built his small construction crew into a decent sized company doing just that. He called the US born Irish, "narrow backs," whose work ethic was suspect. As a rule, he never hired them.

But Spaghetti was from the same Northern county back "home" and vouched for his grandsons with the final sentence, "and if they give you one lick of trouble, just tell me and I'll see to them."

So, Jack hired me and Eddie on a trial basis.

Eddie was the bull right out of the chute. He outworked his broad back Irish cousins and when one of them complained during lunch at the end of the first week that Eddie was making them look bad my brother knocked him out. One shot. No one else said a word.

I, on the other hand, was the consummate narrow back. I didn't mind a hard day's work but didn't go out of my way looking for it.

But the boss thought I was funny, so while he put Eddie in charge of one of his crews, he let me drive him around in his Ford Bronco, checking on the different work sites and delivering emergency materials. It was a great gig. I felt like Scheherazade, the virgin in 1001 Arabian nights, whose tales kept her alive as long as she kept Shahryār the King interested in her stories each night. Sullivan liked to laugh.

On occasion, I was actually forced to do manual labor, especially if I got assigned to Eddie's crew. He didn't give a shit about my stories because he had lived through most of them. But he kept providing them as well.

We were a non-union crew of laborers. We often worked as a subcontractor alongside other union crews Sullivan had to provide on larger jobs. The union workers didn't like us because Eddie worked his crews harder than any of the union guys, and pushed jobs forward on schedule with little overtime. Delays and overtime padded the union workers' pay checks, so that loss made them unhappy.

Lenny Scavone, the head of the steelworker crew on this industrial boiler job out in Brooklyn, made the mistake of confronting Eddie one morning by placing his size twelve work boot on top of our crew's gang box, which prevented me from removing a badly needed pitch bar I was going to use on some demo work.

I politely asked him to stand aside, and he politely told me to, "fuck off." His crew thought that was very funny.

Lenny was a big guy. He had a bit of a beer belly, but when you work steel you don't need gym muscles. Yours get forged every day. He looked like he was a fit forty, and it just wasn't worth my pay packet to get into it with him. This wasn't a fight I was going to win on judge's points.

When I returned to where my brother was waiting, sans pitch bar, Eddie wasn't happy. So, I quickly explained the situation. Eddie thought about it for a moment and then walked over to where our gang box sat idly holding up Lenny's size twelve while Lenny smoked a cigarette. Seeing Eddie and me returning, the workers in Lenny's crew all started elbowing each other, waiting for the other shoe to drop. It did.

"Take your foot off my gang box." Eddie said. Eddie wouldn't know a smile if it bit him in the ass, and he didn't do polite.

"Fuck –" Lenny started to say before a flurry of Eddie's haymakers caught him in the center of his face, which literally exploded in blood as the skin on his nose peeled away and the cartilage disappeared in shards. Eddie probably hit him five times in that same spot with each fist before Lenny had the good sense to fall backward unconscious. Eddie looked around at Lenny's crew to see if anyone else had an objection. They didn't. In fact, they were busy carrying Lenny to one of their trucks to take him to the closest hospital.

"Get that fucking pitch bar." Eddie said to me as he wiped the blood off his knuckles. "I want that south wall down before lunch." It was.

Word spreads fast in the New York construction world, and soon Lenny's facial reconstruction and seventy-two stitches was the talk of every seedy bar in the five boroughs. Eddie never had another issue with his union brethren. And that particular job came in on time, and under budget.

Sullivan was sad to see Eddie return to college that fall and kept his promise to hire Eddie back on school breaks and the next summer. In fact, when Eddie returned to work the following May, he never left. He eventually brought my other brothers with him, first as summer employees, and ultimately full-time into the business as well. The Ginger quickly made his own name as a terror on the work sites, and was the youngest crew chief Sullivan ever let run a crew. My youngest brother had a touch of the Blarney as well, and learned he could price and sell jobs better than anyone. By the time I went to Law School, Eddie bought out Sullivan and built it into McCarthy Bros. Constr., Inc. He was very democratic and made his brothers partners. He even offered me a share in the business to return to the fold, but by then I realized I had the hands of a prince, not the callous mitts of my brothers.

I knew I couldn't stick around to join the family business because I suffered from vertigo. I hated working above four stories and if you were working construction in New York City, the basements were taller than four stories.

I found this out the hard way that fall. Jack Sullivan was on vacation visiting his family in North Carolina, so I was assigned to one of his crews working on what was to be a small twelve story building. I was one of the laborers on that job. One of my tasks was to carry a set of concrete tiles from a pallet in the middle of the building structure, on the top floor, out along the steel, to hanging platforms where the bricklayers were then using them inside huge metal hoppers. If Eddie was running that crew I probably could have begged off that assignment and gotten clean up duty. But as it was, the fellow running it that day was the asshole Eddie knocked out on his first week, so I wasn't getting any favors.

This one particular stretch of steel would have been bad enough to walk empty handed, but given I was carrying about six heavy tiles each trip in front of me using both hands, I couldn't even pull the tightrope move and use extended arms for balance. I thought I was having heart palpitations each time I stepped out to cross that steel, and it always took me ten minutes to get up the nerve to go back across it to retrieve more tiles. One time on the way back I kicked a soldering rod one of the crossing iron workers must have dropped, and watched it fall to the earth far below. There was a tiny cloud of dust as it struck dirt. It looked just like what you see in those Road Runner cartoons where Wile E. Coyote falls to his demise. Poof.

But the event that actually drove me out of the family business was that on the last trip across that I beam, an iron worker approached from the other side, blocking my path. Now I was carrying those tiles and was not about to turn around and go back. The stand-off didn't faze the iron worker, as he just stepped off the beam and dropped, catching himself with a very burley arm across the steel beam. He calmy waved me past him and then pulled himself back onto the steel and continued on his way. I literally had to change my shorts when I got down from that building at the end of shift.

Much to the family's shame, I quit at the end of the week, and never walked another stretch of steel. I never got to tell Sullivan all of my family stories. His loss.

But you never would have gotten to be telling us those stories now, had you stuck it out, Claire volunteered.

Yeah, you're right, I responded, smiling at my two children. *I took the path less traveled.*

Stella smiled back and Apollo winked.

And now I have a few more stories to tell.

CHAPTER SIXTY-THREE
(PWWC & PIE)

"What exactly is a PWWC?" I asked, pronouncing the acronym as I had been taught, like "prick " with a lisp.

"It's the Pre-Weekend Warmup Club." Eddie explained.

It was Wednesday night. I was supposed to be attending an English Lit class with Fr. Lombardi, a young Jesuit who thought my midterm paper "In Defense of Satan in Milton's Paradise Lost," showed I had a progressive mind. I got an A. It was the last paper I ever handed in at the University.

"We get together at Tommy Quirk's dorm room every Wednesday night and start drinking until Sunday." He continued. "By the time Friday night hits, we're all warmed up."

Eddie liked to park his car outside the campus on Southern Boulevard, by the gate closest to the Fordham Prep entrance. Car thieves preferred to hit the cars along the Fordham Road side of the campus, and there was always a chance that the guard in the security kiosk at that Prep entrance may actually see something. Eddie once caught a surprised scumbag trying to steal his car battery from that location and left the prick unconscious, propped against the exterior campus wall. He did mention to the security guard that the man looked poorly and may need an ambulance, before he drove off. No one ever touched his car after that.

Tommy Quirk was the titular head of one of the "societies" that provided extra-curricular social interaction among the student body at the University. Tiny in stature, he was an intellectual giant, who was one of the few to truly excel in a special academic program that allowed those that tested into it to attend three years at Fordham Prep and three years at the University, on scholarship. During school hours, he was industrious, friendly, and charming to one and all. But once that last class bell sounded, if you put a few beers in him, he would focus his discerning intellect on anyone who dared challenge him or his friends, and tear them to shreds with his sharp tongue and formidable vocabulary. That was always amusing to watch, and always ended up with Tommy's larger supporters getting into a fight to keep Tommy's latest victim from killing him.

The PWWCs were an unsanctioned subgroup of a particular University club. The PWWCs were started by Ralph Droz, a strikingly handsome and charming Puerto Rican from North Babylon, Long Island, who was attending college on an academic scholarship, and just happened to be Tommy Q's dorm mate. Ralph was charisma in a bottle. The women loved him, and the men wanted to be him. Eddie told me he met Ralph on the day my brother joined the club in question. Eddie arrived at the campus social building and when the lobby elevator opened, he found Ralph and another student, Mike Higgins, dressed in women's underwear, both handcuffed to the rails inside the elevator car. Turns out, Ralph and Mike were pledging for the society and their penance, as ordained by Tommy Q, was to ride in that elevator car, dressed in those matching red ensembles, for four hours straight.

When Tommy Q decreed that Eddie had to streak the campus as his initiation, Eddie politely threatened to kill him, and Tommy settled for Eddie having to go out and return with a case of Lowenbrau beer. Eddie more than made up for undermining Tommy Q's unchallenged authority by saving his life in many bars over the next few years.

While I was never an official initiate of the society, I was nonetheless treated by its members like a legacy, as Eddie's younger brother.

On this particular Wednesday, Eddie was bringing me along to my first official PWWC meeting. I had been introduced to Tommy and some of the other PWWCs during my senior year in high school, when Eddie would bring them around to party in our neighborhood. They were a fun bunch.

When we arrived at Tommy and Ralph's dorm suite, the party was in full blast, with music and a slide show being projected onto the side of the next dorm building. There was every form of consumable alcohol and one of the other PWWCs, Mickey McGlynn, working feverishly baking an oversized chocolate pudding pie in the kitchen area. I watched as he poured a sixteen ounce can of mixed vegetables into the concoction, a daring though interesting choice. Ralph was busy making out with his beautiful girlfriend Kathy Constantine – this girl was model pretty and equally brilliant – while Tommy and another PWWC, Kenny Billings were standing over a large hand drawn map of what looked like another college campus.

"Did you tell Jimmy the plan?" Ralph asked, as he came up for air.

"What plan?" I asked my brother.

"We are going to pie Kenny's ex-girlfriend tonight." Eddie reported.

"Sounds like fun." I responded.

"And you're the trojan horse." Eddie added.

Eddie went on to explain that Kenny's ex-girlfriend, who wore his promise ring, cheated on Kenny. When he discovered her infidelity she publicly humiliated him by spreading word among their friends that he was a kink. Liked to dress up in diapers.

This girl attended the same private college in Westchester that our sister Bonnie was attending. The plan was that I was to call Bonnie and explain that my friends and I wanted to come by her dorm for a visit, so she would leave word with campus security that they should allow us in.

"Why don't you call her?" I asked him.

"You're her favorite." Eddie said. "If I called her it would be the first time in her four years there and she would become suspicious."

Eddie was right. I was Bonnie's favorite. I was actually emotionally closer to her than to my brothers. We did stay in touch and would often hang together shooting shit when she came back to the McCarthy compound, for a Posie home-cooked meal and to do laundry on the odd weekend.

While no one else in the family knew it, Bonnie had recently come out to me as being gay, which was a whole different level of bonding, and trust.

"I don't know, Eddie." I hesitated. "There must be another way to get on campus."

"Nah," Eddie responded. "That's the school where the Kennedy's sent their girls. It's locked down like Fort Knox. Fifteen-foot walls around the entire campus. One way in and one way out. Right past the guard booth."

I thought about it over the next couple of beers, while the alcohol dulled my judgment and softened my moral code.

Ralph finally called over, "Hey, Jimmy, you do this for Kenny, and I'll make sure Kathy brings her hot cousin to the next party."

"And if she won't bang you, I will," Kathy added.

"Hey," Ralph shouted, "No one's banging you but me, darling." They both erupted into a wicked laugh and started making out like the world was ending. One more reason to want to be Ralph.

I made the call to Bonnie and told her Eddie, and I were meeting some friends after class in a bar on North Avenue in Westchester, to party with some Iona girls, and wanted to swing by and say hello. She was thrilled. I was guilty.

An hour later, Ralph's Camaro pulled into the entrance way for my sister's college with Ralph at the wheel, me riding shotgun and Mickey McGlynn in back, the chocolate pudding and veggie pie cradled carefully between his feet. I showed the guard my college ID and told him I was there to see Bonnie McCarthy. He checked his sheet for my name and waved us in.

Eddie was parked down the road with Kenny and Tommy Q in his car. They were going to run interference should we be chased out of the campus by security.

We parked directly outside the Tully Hall dorm, which was right across the circle from my sister's Wayne Dorm. Mickey and Ralph studied the photo of the target, Becky Stevens, one last time and Ralph and I walked into Tully and up to the reception desk while Mickey stood out front by the car, with the pie sitting on the open front passenger seat. He watched us through the large front glass windows that opened into the lobby.

The girl at the front desk looked up from her chemistry textbook and did a double take at Ralph. He met her gaze with his most seductive smile.

"Can I help you?" The girl asked, not breaking gaze with my friend.

"Is Becky Stevens in?" Ralph asked.

The girl checked her log, "Yes, I believe so," she said, looking up her room number. She lifted the phone off its cradle and punched in the numbers and covered the receiver with her hand.

"Who may I tell her is calling?" She asked.

I raised my finger to my lips to quiet her. "This is Becky's fiancé, just back from Harvard." I said as charmingly as possible. "I'm her cousin. We wanted to surprise her."

Suddenly the girl's attention was focused on me, and her smile broadened. "You're not engaged, are you?"

"Not yet," I said flirtatiously. "But the night's young." She giggled and blushed. Ralph looked over at me like he had never seen me before.

The girl took her hand off the receiver as a voice could be heard on the line.

"Becky," the girl said. "There's a handsome stranger here to see you. No, he won't give me his name, but I wouldn't keep him waiting, or someone else may run off with him." She looked back over at me and winked.

"She's on her way down." The girl shared as she hung up the phone.

Ralph tapped his forehead. "Shit, I left the flowers in the car."

"C'mon, I'll go out with you and wait there, give you some privacy."

"Are you coming back?" The girl asked me, hesitantly.

"Sure," I said, "I'll be back Saturday to take Becky to lunch for her birthday. I'll stop by and say hello. And your name is? "

"Janet." She said excitedly.

"I'll see you Saturday, Janet." I turned away just as the elevator door opened and Becky exited and walked over to Janet. They exchanged a few words and Janet pointed after me.

Ralph was holding the outer lobby door open, and I held the interior door, as Mickey waltzed past us, the pie in his hand behind his back, and headed directly towards the waiting Becky. Her focus was so intent on where Ralph and I were standing she didn't notice Mickey until he was close enough to whisper, "I have a special delivery for you!"

The pie landed on the top of Becky's head with enough force that its chocolate contents splattered in a circle around her, painting the lobby walls with enough droplets to make it look like a crime scene. Janet was lucky enough to be beyond the impact zone. Ralph was already in his Camaro as Mickey flew by me and leaped past the front bucket seat and into the back. I could hear Becky cursing in a way her dainty appearance never suggested possible. Live and learn.

I barely got the door closed before Ralph was racing across the campus heading towards its exit before any alarm could sound. He slowed as we approached the guard booth. The guard was on the phone and half returned my wave before his face registered what he was being told and he stood up and shouted "Wait."

But Ralph was gone and flashing his headlights, and as we passed, Eddie pulled out behind us and followed us onto the Merit Parkway south to freedom.

It was the perfect crime, until the head of security matched the get-away Camaro to my college ID.

I never gave up the others to the Dean of Students during the subsequent investigation, who in return decided to make an example of me for embarrassing the University. My mother was not pleased when I was expelled.

My sister took my duplicity in stride. She swore to her Dean of Students that she knew nothing about the caper and was shocked that her little brother would be involved in such shenanigans. Since she had a spotless record in the school and was one of their top students, they let it go.

When she came down to the house a few weeks later, Bonnie pulled me aside and said, "That bitch had it coming. She called one of my friends a 'rug munching dike' the other day in the quad."

My mother was good to her word. The week after she received my formal notice of dismissal, I was told to go find another place to live.

CHAPTER SIXTY-FOUR
(AUNT VIOLET'S FLOP HOUSE)

I had been sitting on a bit of savings from my time working for Sullivan, so I put the word out among the older kids in the neighborhood that I was looking for a cheap place to rent. Butch Sorrentino, a friend of Joe Marrero's older brother, said his Aunt Violet owned a huge Victorian up along the Riverdale-Yonkers line, she rented rooms, and that the entire attic apartment just opened up. He said that it was partially furnished. He used the word "eclectic." He said he would put in a good word if I could find two others to go in on it with me.

Joe Marrero, who, while still going to school, was working enough hours at the radiology department at a local nursing home to cover his nut, immediately offered to come in with me. JC had plenty of cash from working steadily at the same restaurant since forever and saw an opportunity to take that next step towards independence. Plus, he was looking for a place, besides Joanna's car, where they could have sex during her breaks from school. I fronted the security deposit and Butch made the deal for us.

Aunt Violet's house was something out of Puccini's *La bohème*. It was four stories high if you counted the basement and attic, and its structural footprint covered a third of the large Bronx block it sat on. The attic apartment was accessible through the back of the building up a dark, narrow wooden stairway, whose every second flight accessed a door for each of the floors. Butch said the stairway was once used by the family servants. At the attic level the eighth flight opened on a tiny landing with two doors. The left accessed a bedroom. The right, the entrance hallway to the apartment.

The layout of the apartment reminded me of the old railroad flats in the brownstones Posie and Spaghetti lived in on 109th street in Manhattan. It had a series of rooms connecting to each other in a line. The bathroom sat along the back of the house. The bedroom that accessed the stairwell, also accessed the bathroom off to one side. The bathroom then opened towards the front of the house into another bedroom, which opened forward into the main hallway, which then led into a large living room that overlooked the front of the house. Off the center hallway was a small kitchen, and off the living room was another bedroom that also overlooked the front of the house.

There was a deep interior stairwell off the center hallway that led to the floor below. The hallway sconce light was so dim you could never see more than a few steps down those stairs without a flash light. It led to the floor where single rooms were rented to single adults, who, for whatever reason, decided to live monastic lives of peace and solitude. I only used that stairway once during our time there, and only in one direction.

Joe took the bedroom off the outer, access stairwell, given that his girl Lilly would be living there with him on a regular basis, and she wanted the privacy of her own entranceway and direct access to the bathroom. JC took the next bedroom off the bathroom, which was the closest thing to a large square room, and I took the bedroom at the front of the house, because it had this cool antique desk that sat beneath the front windows.

Given this was an attic apartment, some of its exterior walls, like one side of my bedroom, sloped outward. It reminded me of those tintype photos of a Parisian artist's garret.

Aunt Violet was actually Butch's great-aunt, which made her old for a human. She was short and squat, with a round face bordered by silver-blue curls and accented with pearl rimmed glasses and a gold thin chain which allowed her to hang them around her thick neck. Her jawline had long ago taken on the shape of a frog's jaw pouch. She lived on the first level off the back stairway, and we were instructed to slide our cash envelope of rent under that door on the first of every month. She always rewarded our timely payment by leaving a pan of lasagna, with a nice note, outside that door on the second day of every month. Violet's son, Richard, lived with her. He was like Boo Radley, I never actually saw him, but he would sometimes leave notes from his mother pinned to our front door.

Aunt Violet had a deep but pleasant voice, which she liked to use by shouting up the stairway whenever she wanted to speak with us. The longer we lived there, the more we heard it.

During our first weekend there in November 1974, we sponsored an open house where everyone was asked to bring at least one extra bottle of vodka as a house warming present.

I woke up the next morning with a brutal hangover and my left ear pierced.

But the first image I had was of one of the older sisters of one of my crew members making a coyote exit out of my bedroom. Unfortunately for her, my bedroom door creaked. When I looked up, through my painful haze, I spotted a rear view of her nicely shaped ass peaking from beneath a t-shirt as she carried her clothes out the door. I must have had a good time because there was a used condom on the floor beside my bed. I never heard from her again. Well, at least the room was baptized.

Turned out Joe, JC and I were just a few of the male victims of one of our female visitors, who had a large baby pin in her purse and a lighter and alcohol available for sterile technique. My earring was actually a bit of twisted wire, so I went out the next day and replaced it with a gold hoop from the local jewelry store.

Not the one you are wearing now? Claire asked incredulously.

Yep, it's held up for over five centuries. I responded, flicking it with my left index finger. *The salesman was right when he told me gold would last forever.*

There was also a note pinned to our door, explaining in beautiful cursive penmanship, that the party kept a number of the second-floor lodgers awake, that someone had puked in a corner of the basement landing, and we were not allowed to climb out on the front roof to smoke.

We were off to a magnificent start.

CHAPTER SIXTY-FIVE
(PAGING DR. WONG)

"Smokey, you only turn eighteen once!" Joe said. "Snapper, four martinis for me and my friends."

It was Thursday night, November 14th.

"Technically," Snapper said, as he set the martini glasses in front of us, "according to the fake proof Jimmy's been flashing for over a year, this is at least the second time he's ridden the earth eighteen times around the sun."

The bartender's comment made me think of cousin Apples. I still carried his draft card in my wallet and him in my heart. I wished he was there with me, and hoped that he and Connie were happy, wherever they were.

He was up on Zeta Reticuli 1 & 2, teaching those greys the cha-cha. Apollo shared, then aurally laughed.

Stay in the moment, Claire admonished him.

Yes, we know all about where Apples landed. Stella responded. *Let father get on with it, you can see he's getting tired. Go on, father.*

I gazed at my legacy, blood, and friend, and secretly thought of how lucky I was to have traveled this path. I mentally lifted a martini glass in toast to the three of them, then proceeded.

Snapper was one of the older kids that had followed the path from St. Maggie's school yard to the Coaches II bar, where we were all now sitting. His family was one of the few that had lived in Riverdale longer than my own. Hands down, he was absolutely the nicest guy that ever breathed Riverdale air, and could console a crying drunk with more compassion than Mother Teresa. But he was also a big bastard and knew how to clear a bar if he had to. It made him the perfect bartender.

When Joe went to pay for the drinks, Snapper waved him off and rapped his knuckles on the bar. "Happy birthday, Jimmy. First round on me."

Having sworn off vodka after the earring episode - I didn't want to wake up with a Prince Albert piercing – I allowed Joe to talk me into experimenting with a gin-based drink. Since I had only seen adults drink martinis growing up, I thought it was perfect for the night I became legal.

Joe handed the glasses to me, JC, and Mike Austin, keeping the last for himself

I waited another five minutes for the clock to hit 7:45 pm and then raised the glass in a toast, and as the other's impatiently shouted "happy birthday" and tossed down their drinks, I took my first long sip.

It tasted better in my head. But as the night proceeded and my brothers and remaining friends, who weren't off at college, came to join me at the bar, I acquired a taste for the sweet gin and dry vermouth they kept plying me with. I even ate the olives, which was a first for this Irish pallet.

The gin kicked all of our asses.

By eleven p.m., we were a mess. We were all weeping as I toasted Mark Wallen for our last round. Of course, we did the stupid thing and after a circle of sloppy goodbyes, the four originals piled into Joe's new car, a silver Javelin, and headed back to the apartment to continue the party on the cheap, with the case of beers we had cooling in the fridge.

Luckily, Delia Wolfe had trained Mike Austin not to get too sloshed, so he was the closest to sober and drove us home. Thank God for small miracles.

Really stupid father! Stella admonished, as she shared her memories of riding in our family Toyota. *You were human, you could have been killed.*

I'm with sis on this one. Apollo responded. *Think about it, you never would have had me!*

I think we can all agree that Jimmy has done some questionable things in his lives, human and Centaurian, so let's move on. Claire counseled. *Go ahead Jimmy, you were all drunk in the Javelin.*

That's right. We were all drunk in the Javelin. But Austin got us home safe and sound.

I let those words sit for a moment.

Wait, that's it? Apollo shared.

I smiled for a heartbeat longer. Then proceeded.

Austin carried Joe up the stairs, got Joe's door open and left him on his bed. Then he returned to help me and JC, who had only made it as far as the landing directly outside Aunt Violet's doorway, up the rest of the stairs, one of us at a time. I was fixated on a chip in the paint on Violet's brown door while I waited for Mike. The chip looked a bit like Jesus.

Anyway, by the time we all got up the stairs, JC and I agreed that the beers didn't seem that good an idea. Austin, who had his own Firebird parked out in front of the apartment, was about to head out when we all heard Joe calling from the back of the apartment.

"Ssssmmmmmooooookkkkkkeeeeeeyyyyyy!"

It was coming from the bathroom.

I was drunk tired, lying on our couch in the living room, and didn't want to be bothered.

"Ssssmmmmmooooookkkkkkeeeeeeyyyyyy!" Joe's voice called again.

"That asshole's going to wake Aunt Violet," JC said.

"Smokey, c'mere I gotta show you something," Joe's disembodied voice sounded a third time.

"Maybe he's got you a gift." Austin said.

"Mine was the second round of martinis." JC added.

Austin helped me to my feet, and we all walked through JC's bedroom to get to the bathroom, JC dropped onto his bed as he reached it. I could not believe what I saw.

Joe was standing on the windowsill in the frame of the now open bay window that overlooked the wooded back yard, four stories below. When he saw he finally had his audience, Joe stuck his arms out shoulder high and proceeded to hesitantly walk the windowsill, much like one does during a field sobriety test.

"Look, I'm Philippe Petit!" Joe said. "My birthday trick for you! Happy—"

There are times in one's life, when one really cannot trust what one's eyes are seeing. This was the first of many that I remember. Everything seemed to flow in slow motion.

Joe started to lose his balance, and by the time Austin and I could reach the window, he was gone. I looked out after him and watched as he fell like a diver off a high board in a perfect swan position, those arms still extended.

"Ssssmmmmmooooookkkkkkeeeeeeyyyyyy!" he called as he fell.

Luckily he only traveled about fifteen feet before his exposed chest struck the railing in the wooden French balcony on the floor below us and flipped him backwards onto the deck, where he landed in the crucified position, facing upward. His eyes rolled back white into his head.

"I'll get JC!" Austin cried, while I stared down at Joe to see if he was still breathing. He moaned.

The martinis in me told me what I needed to do. Despite my vertigo, I leapt out the window after him and was a bit surprised as my feet landed on the ancient deck of the French balcony and proceeded through the wood, my body safely coming to a stop when my hips wedged into the hole my feet had made. I was too far away from Joe to offer any assistance and could barely reach his foot by leaning forward at my waist. I looked up and saw Austin's horrified face poking out our bathroom window.

And then I heard a blood curdling shriek as the lights in the room off the balcony came on. I could see through the now luminated French doors into a bedroom, just as JC passed through its doorway. Its very surprised occupant, a heavy-set spinster woman in her forties, literally wearing a full-length formless white nighty with an anachronistic head cap, acrobatically leapt up to her feet on the bed and cried blue murder. JC did a double take and then rushed over and threw the French doors open. Well almost. They jammed against Joe's unconscious form, causing JC to have to shimmy through their abbreviated opening. In full MacGyver mode and with surprising strength, JC reached over and pulled me free from my hole, and then lifted Joe into a fireman's carry position across his shoulders and carried him back into the room. This set off a second series of shrieks from the woman, who had now returned to a sitting position and pulled her blankets to her chin. As I followed JC and Joe through her room, all I could manage was an apologetic, "nice view."

When I reached the hallway outside the bedroom, I saw JC, still carrying Joe, fumbling with a number of doorknobs on identical looking wooden doors, until he found the one that opened onto the interior stairway that led up to our apartment.

As they disappeared upstairs, I spotted Aunt Violet at the end of the long hallway. There was nothing sweet looking about her now. In fact, she would have looked right at home as an extra in a horror movie, so I was through the stairway door before it closed behind my friends. I turned and threw the lock bolt before I followed them up the long dark stairway.

When I reached the living room, much to my surprise, Joe was lying on the couch, awake and listening as Austin filled him in on what had just transpired. Everyone was surprisingly sober, but adrenaline will do that to you.

JC appeared with a couple of beers in his hands, just as Joe burst into laughter at the end of Austin's dramatic recital. The laughter didn't last long.

"Shit," Joe cried sharply, taking the offered beer from JC, and placing it against his chest. "I think I broke my ribs."

Back in fire drill mode, JC carefully lifted Joe back into the fireman's carry and followed Austin out the door of the apartment. By the time I had reached the second floor behind them Violet appeared looking every bit as angry as I had witnessed in the hallway.

"You better look into providing window guards in the apartment. And that balcony is unsafe." I bluffed as I passed her. "My friend could have died tonight."

I didn't wait to hear her response.

Joe and JC were in the back seat, and Mike behind the wheel when I slid into shotgun position. Mike burned rubber and headed north towards the closest hospital, Yonkers Memorial. It felt like I was riding in the Batmobile as we ran every light on South Broadway. Luckily, due to the hour, traffic, pedestrian and auto, was minimal. We were there in five minutes.

When we arrived at the emergency room the intake nurse asked for our moaning's friend's name. Given that none of us had medical insurance, and no way to pay for Joe, we weren't sure how to respond until Joe whispered though clenched teeth, "Carl La Fong."

Mike, the most sober of us, then explained how Joe had fallen on the stairs and cracked his ribs. The nurse gently sat Joe in a wheel chair and took him off towards an examination room. She directed us to the surprisingly empty waiting room.

Moments later, the hospital intercom system announced, "Dr. Wong, exam room three. Patient Carl La Fong." I know this was bad form, as we didn't know what was happening to our friend, but we couldn't help but laugh at the rhyme.

It is kinda funny. Claire shared, then followed with her Lurchy laugh.

With no word for the next half hour, we amused ourselves by having wheel chair races along a nearby hallway. Then finally a nurse appeared and informed us that our friend, Carl, was all right, with just two fractured ribs, and that the attending doctor was now wrapping his chest with a compression bandage. We would be able to take him home in a few minutes.

"Would that be doctor Wong?" JC asked.

"Yes," the nurse replied deadpan. She gave us a quizzical look as we all burst into laughter, then left us to our merriment.

A moment later Joe appeared walking very gingerly but determined as he carefully finished buttoning his shirt.

"C'mon," he said. "Let's get out of here. The nurse just went to get the financial forms she wants Carl La Fong to sign."

We arrived back at the apartment to find a note written in beautiful cursive penmanship tacked to the apartment door, threatening us with immediate eviction should we ever put our co-tenants through that fright again, and notifying us that her son would be by first thing in the morning to put up window guards. He also replaced the French balcony.

The four of us watched the sun rise on the first morning of my nineteenth human year from the front rooftop ledge of the apartment. We were wrapped in coats and blankets, sipping coffee. Joe and JC enjoyed a communal buzz from splitting one of the narcotics Joe had gotten from the nurse at Yonkers Memorial. All's well that ends well.

I hadn't a clue of what the rest of my life was going to be like. But I was happy in the moment and had my friends around me. And that's all that mattered. Ignorance truly is bliss.

CHAPTER SIXTY-SIX
(YELLOW SCHOOL BUS)

My savings from Sullivan were beginning to dwindle, so I needed to find gainful employment that didn't require me standing on top of a tall building shouting, "Look ma, no hands."

BJ had landed a gig driving those small yellow school buses that are no bigger than a regular cargo van. Since it was a weekday gig while school was in session, and could work around Eddie's class schedule, BJ hooked him up, leaving my brother free to work construction on weekends and holidays. Now that I was eighteen, the two went into the boss, a fresh out of college young man named Zach Gilbert, and talked him into hiring me as a sub. This meant I would pick up runs for anyone who called out sick. Given that most of the drivers were from around my neighborhood, they were prone to alcohol induced flus, so there was pretty steady work available for a fill-in. The hourly pay was decent, but the added bonus was you got to keep your buses overnight and got free gas.

Now these runs were not to collect the riffraff of society. No public-school peasants rode in these yellow boxes. Neither did the kids going to Catholic School. These runs were for the students that attended the private schools in Riverdale. Most of these kids were brahmans, descendants from the upper echelons of the top professionals in the metropolitan area. And each of these kids innately knew they were special. None of them lived in Riverdale.

The runs either went North into the toney towns of Westchester, or South into the monied canyons of Manhattan.

Zach Gilbert explained, my first day, that it was best if the drivers didn't fraternize with their riders. It was easy while I subbed because the kids from Manhattan who boarded the buses didn't even notice I wasn't their usual driver, and the Westchester kids were too polite to ask why a new guy was behind the wheel.

First, I had to take a test to add Class D to my New York State Driver's license. Easy-peasy. Didn't even study. The voices in my head came through as usual.

Then I had to perform ride alongs for a couple of weeks with different drivers to learn their routes. BJ's route was the upper east side of Manhattan. I felt a strange sense of *déjà vu* when we pulled up in front of the building, where Spaghetti worked the door, to pick up one of the little Lord Fauntleroys that was on his way to success.

Eddie picked up kids from Rye, Scarsdale, and New Rochelle, who had a little less starch in their clothing than their Manhattan brethren. I think having massive back yards to play in softened their edges.

My favorite ride along was with an older kid named Brendan Murray, who, after we dropped off the last child on his Westchester route one afternoon, fired up a blunt that would have made any Rastafarian weep in envy. I didn't need to accept his generous offer of a hit. I felt just fine inhaling the secondary smoke in the enclosed yellow box we were riding in. My first contact high. Good shit.

Overall, most of the young kids were really nice and respectful. However, when you got to the high schoolers, their sense of entitlement began to show.

There were no high school seniors on the bus. By then their parents had bought them their first foreign car to ride to school in. That was fine with me because the juniors were tough enough to deal with since they all took their SATs and already knew which Ivy school they would be attending.

In the morning, most of the older girls sat in the last row in the back of the bus and busied themselves applying the makeup their parents would never allow them to walk out of the house with. I'm not going to lie. Most of the juniors were good looking, especially after they had their first encounters with plastic surgeons to correct whatever minor flaws their generations of beautiful genetics hadn't already resolved. But jail bait is jail bait whether it's sirloin or hot dogs. So, I never engaged with them. They were never on the bus ride going home, as they usually had extra-curricular activities that may have included a senior boyfriend. They didn't let that makeup go to waste.

The younger high school boys were friendlier in their own way. Once they realized that I was a talking monkey, some of them would ask me about my background, if only to kill time during the boring ride from house to house to house to school, or the reverse.

When I finally took over my own route, after Brendan Murray packed it in and moved to California, I landed a crew of Westchester kids that I actually started to like. There were three best friends, Jonny, Rusty, and Dave, that had come through their lower school together and were now mighty high schoolers. They were beginning to feel their hormonal oats although their voices had not yet broken.

One day, as I was waiting to collect them from school, I spotted an older boy, obviously a senior, giving Rusty shit over something, while the other two friends stood by looking terrified. When I saw the older boy shove Rusty on the shoulder, I hopped out of the bus and walked over to them.

"Everything okay here?" I asked the older boy, who in all fairness was only a few years younger than me. He looked like an athlete, fit and large, but I could tell just by how he tried to position his body towards me that he had never been punched hard in the face.

I would never have thrown the first punch. I knew this kid's father, mother, uncle, aunt, or grandparent was probably a lawyer, so I wasn't about to set myself up for an arrest on an assault charge. But I did get up close enough to his face to make him either walk away or kiss me. Luckily for both of us, he walked away, but not before he shot me that defensively condescending look, that generations of social inbreeding cause superiors to bestow on their purported inferiors, who scare the shit out of them.

By the time the three amigos got back on the bus, I was their new best friend.

Over the next few weeks, these kids grilled me with every question imaginable, often innocently crossing the line into my private life. And I was okay with that. I shared what I cared to and told them to "fuck off" when they pushed the boundaries. And they loved it. They even started to mimic my nasal rendition of "fuck off."

They actually started sharing their own lives with me, and I learned that all three of them were the children of trophy mothers from second marriages. They told me of their lives with nannies and half siblings and vacations to Europe or the islands. They all went to the same sleep away camp every summer while their parents went off on their separate child-free adventures. Turns out, they all knew someone who belonged to the Yacht club I had worked at with Mark Wallen, and told me all about the private clubs they belonged to, and all of the great gossip they had heard there about this important personage or that politician. I learned that, despite all the private school education and the trappings of success, they all had an innocence about them that I realized I never had.

Tennessee Williams once said that, "friends are God's way of apologizing to us for our families."

These three boys had formed their own crew, like I had formed mine, to find some semblance of security in their lives that can only be forged from true friendship. These kids had each other's back. And now I had theirs.

I even showed them some defensive moves, with hand and arm locks, that could help them out if they ever got into a jam on their own. They had a great time trying them out on each other. One Friday afternoon I relented to their repeated requests that I let them all attack me at once on Jonny's front lawn. When I gently left them all sitting on their asses, they looked like I had just shared the secret of great sex.

They called me "The Mick." And I was just fine with that.

I'm not sure if their infatuation with their Irish bodyguard would have continued beyond a few months, given that all new toys ultimately lose their shine. I never got the chance. My job as their chauffer ended abruptly due to bovine intercession. I couldn't see this coming.

CHAPTER SIXTY-SEVEN (EASTERN RUSTLERS)

"Cows, Smokey!" Joe cried, his voice quivering. "Fucking cows!"

Joe never called to me through his bedroom door before, so I was a bit surprised to hear his disembodied voice as I stood on the apartment landing, locking the door, leaving for a morning bus run. Given that the old wooden stairway acted like an echo chamber, I wasn't surprised that I woke him when I dropped my keys.

"Are you tripping again, Joe?" I asked his bedroom door. When the door was unresponsive, I just assumed I had caught Joe in the middle of a night terror and headed off down the stairs. It was an early spring day in March. The weather had been unusually warm, so I was dressed in my usual T-shirt, hoody, and jeans ensemble. No coat necessary.

When I threw open the basement door and stepped out into the back end of the driveway, my momentum from flying down the stairway carried me right into the black and white face of a life-sized replica of a dairy calf, pointed directly at the basement door. It literally gut punched me. From this uncomfortable vantage point, I got a great look at its life-sized mother, staring happily, with a plastic smile on its face, standing directly behind her calf. They were both affixed, in line, to a set of heavy metal rails.

Anyone who had lived more than five minutes in Riverdale, would recognize these two cows as the mascots of the Happy Dairy Ice Cream franchise, that sat on the roof of their original Riverdale Avenue store, just over the Yonkers city line.

I raced back upstairs and started banging on Joe's bedroom door.

"What the fuck are the Happy Dairy cows doing in the driveway?" I demanded.

The bedroom door opened just a crack, and the face of Lilly Tonelli appeared. I could hear Joe somewhere in the dark behind her mumbling, "cows."

"They were there when we got home from my family's engagement party." Lilly said, shoving her well-manicured left hand through the crack in the door. I couldn't help but notice the large emerald-shaped diamond ring Joe had recently bought at a major discount from one of the diamond stores that paid tribute to Lilly's father, Sonny Tonelli. "Joe was really drunk, so I drove the Javelin."

Joe had been "really drunk" on a regular basis since Lilly made him the offer he couldn't refuse. Marriage. In exchange, Sonny would pay for the wedding of the century, the rest of Joe's schooling and set them up afterwards with a beautiful home in the Florida town of Lilly's choice. Sonny had recently expanded his Westchester family's operations to the Miami area. Sonny was at least looking forward to warm winters of his discontent, after having to cave to his only daughter's decision that would bring Latin blood into his Sicilian gene pool. Lilly got whatever she wanted. And Lilly wanted Joe.

"Keep July of next year open." Lilly said, withdrawing her hand and slamming the door.

I ran into the apartment and tried to wake JC, but he was out for count and could sleep like the dead.

By then I was running late, so I raced back down the stairs, and, this time avoiding the calf's muzzle, made it out to my school bus and headed off on my morning run.

Later that morning, after dropping my charges safely at the doors of their private schools, I arrived at Junior's Corner to grab my usual coffee and bacon and egg on a roll. BJ was sitting at the counter gobbling down a massive breakfast and intently reading something off the cover page of *The Herald Statesman*. He was laughing as I sidled up on the spinning stool next to him.

"Check this out," BJ said, holding up the paper. "Eddie made the news."

There in the first, above the fold, quadrant of the area's local paper was a large photo of the Happy Dairy bovines below the headline "Holy Cow! Stolen Icons An Udder Disgrace."

After a brief history of the Happy Dairy Franchise and its mascots, the story went on to recite the eye witness testimony of a retired artist who lived in a second-floor apartment in the building directly across Riverdale Avenue. He witnessed the crime and purportedly told the Yonkers police that at three am, after hearing a loud crash, he saw a yellow school bus towing the pair of bovines in the direction of the Bronx, a rope around the calf's neck, and sparks flying from behind their metal runners. The paper reported that the artist was distraught, having painted numerous renditions of the bovine pair over the past twenty years, which he would gladly sell to anyone that was interested.

"How do you know it was Eddie?" I asked.

"Who else would do it?" he replied.

Just then another school bus pulled up in front of Junior's and a very proud Eddie and Steve the Greek appeared in the doorway, both wearing cowboy hats and kerchiefs around their necks. They had obviously not slept.

"We are not worthy!" BJ shouted, as he slid off his stool, dropped to his knees and started bowing at the two knuckleheads, who both started laughing.

"It was the Greek's idea." Eddie said.

"But my boy tore it free from the roof, rivets flying." Greek replied with unbridled admiration at Eddie's herculean endeavor. "I don't know how the fuck he managed to drag those things across that roof and drop them into the alley."

"Where Steve sat waiting with the rope." Eddie interrupted.

"We dragged them all the way to Coaches II." Steve continued. "Man, we took photos and everything."

"Are you two fucking nuts?" I shouted, rhetorically, waving the newspaper in Eddie's face. Eddie took a second to decide whether to deck me for cursing at him in public or read the paper. The photo of the cows on page one probably saved me a trip to the emergency room.

"Holy shit." He said, grabbing the paper from me. The Greek started reading over his shoulder and whistled when he spotted the reference to the school bus.

"Now what are you going to do?" BJ asked.

"You mean, what's Jimmy gonna do?" Eddie replied, smirking. "Last time I checked, those cows were sitting where I left them at the end of a driveway, at the house where Jimmy lives, and Jimmy drives a yellow school bus."

"Are you fucking kidding me?" I shouted, this time expecting an answer, and when it didn't come, I continued, "I swear, if I get nailed on this, I'm giving you up."

"Sgt. Nathan," Eddie shouted to the proprietor, who respectfully and politely always ignored his customers conversations. "I'll have two BLT's and a coffee to go."

Then he turned back to me and patted me gently on the cheek directly below his favorite spot to park his knuckles. "Jimmy," he said. "You're my brother. You're never going to rat me out."

I wanted to kill him, but I knew he was unkillable, at least by me. I also knew he was right. McCarthys don't rat on their own.

Eddie tossed a few bills on the counter and grabbed the steaming brown bag that Nathan placed there. "Thanks, Sarge, keep the change."

As my brother followed BJ and The Greek out of the shop, he stopped and turned back to me.

"You'll figure it out, Jimmy." He said with a smile. "That's what you do."

CHAPTER SIXTY-EIGHT
(THERE ARE NO COWS IN RIVERDALE)

By the time I had gassed up the bus and returned to Aunt Violet's Flop House, a number of the crew were hanging out around the back of the driveway. The Riverdale gossip lines must have been burning up their wires that morning. Bozzy MacDootz had a measuring tape out and was measuring the height, length, and width of both the calf and the mother. Then he was measuring the dimensions of the basement door leading up to the apartment. Matty Burns was sitting on the back of the mother cow, faking like he was riding a bull, one arm waving over his head while he dug his imaginary spurs into both sides. The Armstrong brothers were snapping photos of the cast and crew with their Polaroid camera.

JC sat in one of the beach chairs he brought down from the living room, and was writing furiously on some correspondence paper between sips of coffee and stares at the cows.

"Wait until Joanna reads this!" He shouted to no one in particular, before he folded the paper and slipped it into an envelope. "She's gonna piss herself."

Lilly Tonelli came through the basement door in her usual huff, shot the cows and friends a dirty look, stormed out the driveway and hopped into an arriving Miles Cab. A moment later Joe appeared looking equal parts contrite and relieved.

"Trouble at home?" I asked.

"Nah, I just won't commit to a set date for the wedding." Joe said. "I'm hoping for a lightning bolt to strike me before next summer."

He circled the cows, shaking his head in disbelief, and then came back over to me.

"What are you going to do with them?" Joe asked, removing something from his pocket and handing me a piece of paper with beautiful cursive penmanship. "Pay the rent and get those God Damned Cows out of the yard. Violet."

MacDootz came over and said, "Don't worry, Matty and I have it all figured out. I'm going home to grab my dad's chain saw. We'll cut these suckers up, carry them up to the apartment and reassemble them."

I was willing to try anything at that point. But I was more for dumping them in the Hudson.

"You can't cut those up!" Bobby Armstrong said. "Those cows are over fifty years old. They are on the Yonkers Historical Register. You damage them and it's a felony."

"Matty," I shouted," Get off those fucking cows before you scratch them."

Just then, Eddie's school bus pulled up at the end of the driveway, and Eddie, BJ and Greek rolled out, followed by the PWWC's Ralph and the little genius Tommy Q. Eddie was carrying a large tarp which he then threw over the cows.

"Let's go upstairs, Tommy Q has a plan." He said.

* * * * *

"The plan is rather simple in its elegance." Tommy Q began, "We wait until dark and then we carry the cows up the block to the Yonkers city line. "

"Why don't we just tow them?" Steve the Greek said. "That's what got them here."

"We need to be a little less obtrusive." Tommy Q counseled. "You don't want any of the neighbors spotting us this time."

"Then what?" Ralph asked.

"We get some law-abiding citizen to call the cops and tell them they just spotted the stolen cows."

"Who?" Eddie said. "Can't be one of us, we're knee deep in it."

"Snapper will do it." Bobby Armstrong said. "He can call the cops from the bar."

"Why would Snapper do it?" I asked.

"He's fucking our cousin." Bobby said. "He wants to stay in our good graces."

"Sounds like a plan," JC said. "What do we do until dark?"

"We gotta do our afternoon bus runs." Eddie said.

"I'll go down to Coaches and clear the call with Snapper. " Bobby said. "He comes on shift around two."

"The rest of you hang here, and make sure no one fucks with those cows." I said. "The whole fucking neighborhood probably knows about them. Ralph, please make sure no one touches them."

"Don't worry." Ralph said. "I got this."

* * * * *

I prayed the whole afternoon run that I wouldn't return to find a host of squad cars circling the driveway. Luckily, it was quiet. Ralph sat beside the shrouded cows at the end of the driveway in JC's beach chair reading the paper. Leaning on the side of the chair was a Louisville Slugger. There were no other buses parked in the area, so I worried that my brother and BJ had bailed.

"It's been quiet." Ralph said, looking up and spotting my approach. "The Armstrong brothers just got back and are upstairs with Tommy Q and the others. Joe just went out for pizza and brews."

I went upstairs and waited for sunset.

Eddie and BJ arrived a half hour later on foot, having parked their buses in my family's back yard so they couldn't be spotted from the street.

When the clock ticked six, we were all upstairs having a blast, finishing off the pizza and beers and laughing about how much trouble this could have gotten us into. I almost got into it with Eddie an hour earlier when I mentioned what a cock sucker he was for dropping me into it. Luckily BJ and Greek were there to hold him back. But we had forgotten all about our troubles when zero hour arrived.

Tommy Q went out first and walked to the northern end of the block where the Bronx ended, and Yonkers began. Once he was sure that there was no one on the streets, he signaled with a flashlight and then Eddie, BJ, Ralph, and the Greek lifted the cows by their rails and, with lots of grunting and groaning carried them down that long Bronx block and set them safely under a street light on the corner. Tommy then pulled the tarp off like a magician and they all raced back to the apartment.

I then drove the Armstrongs to Coaches in my school bus, and we watched and listened as Snapper made the call to the Yonkers Police Department's Third Precinct, which just sat a few blocks north of the Happy Dairy store.

"Yes," Snapper began in his most grown-up voice. "I was out walking my dogs this evening and I spotted those missing cows I read about in the papers. On the corner of Tyndall and 263rd street. Yes, that's right, there were two of them. Thank you Sergeant."

Then it was a second call to the Fiftieth Precinct in the Bronx. Belt and suspenders.

Snapper started with the same script.

"Yes," Snapper began. "I was out walking my dogs this evening and I spotted those missing cows —" Snapper pulled the phone away from his ear and I could hear shouting coming from the receiver. "What do you mean there's no cows in Riverdale?" Snapper shouted back. "I just saw fucking two of them on the corner of 263rd and Tyndall. I think they're the ones stolen from Yonkers." Snapper listened and smiled. "No, I won't give you my name" he said, laughed and hung up.

"You owe me." He said to the Armstrongs.

I parked the school bus a few blocks away from the apartment and we all ran the rest of the way. When we arrived upstairs Tommy Q was leaning out the window, off the ledge on the front of the roof, watching the cows through a set of binoculars. We got there just in time.

"Holy shit." Tommy Q began his play-by-play in his high-pitched voice "The Yonkers cops arrived ten seconds before 50. Both of them have large flatbed trucks with them. Sergeants from each team seem to be arguing and both are pointing at the cows with one hand and towards their respective territories with the other."

Tommy stopped and did a double take through the binoculars.

"You're never gonna believe this." He said with just the right tone of astonishment. "They're fucking flipping a coin. Wait it's hit the ground; they've got their flashlights out looking for it. Hold on, now the Yonkers cops are cheering. The Bronx Sergeant just waved off his truck and the New York cops are all returning to their vehicles and driving away."

He watched for a few moments more, then turned to us with the greatest satisfaction.

"Gentlemen," He said with a dramatic flair, "the Yonkers cops just left with their cows. There will be no cattle rustlers hanged today."

We all then moved the party back to Coaches II, making sure to leave Snapper an extra-large tip at the end of the night. The following day I drove my school bus back to the main bus depot and slid the keys through the office door slot with a note to Zack Clifford, that said "I quit."

That was just too close a call, and I couldn't know if one of the more ambitious detectives decided to follow up on the school bus mentioned in the Herald Statesman, which indeed heralded the cows' recovery with that morning's headline: "Stolen Cows Recovered, Investigation Ongoing."

But it turns out that wasn't the last time I had a brush with either the law or large live stock.

Tell me about it. Claire said with that Lurchy laugh.

CHAPTER SIXTY-NINE
(FOX IN THE HENHOUSE)

"Call Robbie Stanton, he'll hook you up." Joe said, tossing me a crumpled piece of paper with a phone number on it. Now that I was gainfully unemployed, JC had offered to land me a job bussing tables at his restaurant, but Joe had countered with something literally within walking distance of Aunt Violet's Flop House.

Peter and Robbie Stanton were a couple of older Riverdale brothers that ran the campus security for a small Catholic college nestled in the upper Northwest corner of the Bronx. It was originally run by the Sisters of Charity, as an all-girls school that primarily produced teachers, nurses, and more nuns. It had recently gone co-ed, but most of the men on campus were crossovers from its brother school, an engineering fortress on the opposite end of Riverdale.

The 200-acre wooded campus was a bucolic anachronism, with winding paths through its most serene thickly wooded sections. Many of the local mothers took their young children to wander there during its most beautiful seasons of fall and spring, when the trees were at their aesthetic best. Many of the buildings on campus were hundreds of years old, as were all of its nuns. Not too far off its Riverdale Avenue border, sat a beautiful, bridged grotto in the center of a large pond stocked with koi fish and turtles, and the occasional water fowl in the warmer months. Children used to love to go there and toss bread to the fish and fowl. The elders used to go there and leave candles and flowers at the statute of Mother Mary in the center of the grotto. The campus' natural beauty brought nothing but serenity to those that were searching for it.

The college's hundreds of female students brought bliss to the red-blooded males in the geographic area. Especially when they ventured out to the local bar scene.

* * * * *

The student body concentrated around the southwest part of the campus with a large quad of dorms and the academic buildings. They were stationed along the steep hill that overlooked and led down to the Hudson River, where many of us partied during our youth.

Billie Joel had just released his hit single "Only The Good Die Young."

Who is Billy Joel? Stella asked. *And what's a single?*

I'll fill you in later. Claire said. *The short answer is that he was the greatest troubadour in your father's human lifetime.*

I thought for a moment about how music wasn't a major thing on Proxima b. In fact, the hybrids had first reintroduced it when Petrichor saved all our asses. Thank God I had Jayney download every song I ever loved from Earth's Internet shortly after our forced emigration, which was definitely an Irish thing, but over time I just stopped playing them. As I thought back on it now, I hadn't played anything since Gina had passed.

Having stopped made me feel a little less guilty over all the song royalties I owed for the past four hundred years. Still, the pure Centaurians didn't seem to have that musical passion gene. Which is a shame, because a good song can capture the best moments in a person's life forever.

Anyway, Billy Joel had suggested that Catholic girls were a little late out of the sex gate.

He obviously hung out in the wrong parish.

Indeed, just the prior fall, a group of twenty-one of the local lads, followed Steve the Greek in a midnight campus wide streak of this quiet little college. It had the girls all hanging out of their dorm rooms, cat calling and tossing various assortment of underwear at the passing string of healthy young men, wearing nothing but Zorro masks. I caught a very bad cold that weekend.

What's this streaking you're talking about? Apollo asked.

If I told you, I'd scar you forever. I replied.

That space ship has flown. Apollo shared and laughed aurally.

Anyway, I called Robbie Stanton, who told me that there was an opening coming up for the graveyard shift right after Easter break, and if I wanted it, just come on down to the campus security office and fill out the paperwork. The only downside was that I had to cut my hair and shave my beard.

I was tired of fighting that last fight, especially now that I was just fighting it with myself, and this time I was being paid to do it. So, I lost the locks and the beard but kept my moustache, which were still in style in the latter half of the seventies. If Burt Reynolds and Tom Selleck's mustache had a baby, it would have been mine.

Who?

Shhh Stella, I'll explain later. Claire shared.

I did a few trial tours as a ride along with the guard who was retiring, an ex-cop who luckily didn't recognize me from the prior fall, when his 1965 Mustang that served as the campus security vehicle, just couldn't take the curbs to follow our naked group into the woods where our clothes were waiting. Our collective quick hop over a short iron fence on the Riverdale Avenue side of the woods left him waiting in frustration for our return on the campus roadway, listening to the continued catcalls of the aroused student body. I never forget a face.

Mostly my new job meant I would sit from midnight to seven am in the main guard booth by the southern entrance to the campus, which also provided a clear view of the four main dorms, and make sure the local trouble makers didn't infiltrate the campus. That was the easiest part. I was the fox in this hen house, and I knew all the other foxes in the neighborhood. No one bothered the chickens during my tours.

Once an hour I would get in the car and tour the campus, checking doors and making sure the buildings were all locked down.

You can get into a lot of mischief during those hours.

Robbie Stanton warned me that the one thing the nuns would not tolerate was fraternizing between the security team and the students. Given that I was running out of employment options, I took those words to heart, so I kept to myself. It was pretty easy, given that I arrived on campus after most of the students were asleep. They had a campus curfew of ten pm, so I only saw the occasional straggler, and if they were a female, I didn't even leave the guard booth to check their ID, I just waved them through. So, I didn't even have to speak to anyone. The early birds that were up before my shift ended were the industrious types with a purpose, so they were up and out towards the cafeteria or classes and didn't do much more than wave out of politeness in my direction as they passed.

I spent the overnight hours sucking down coffee from a thermos, which reminded me of the thermos Spaghetti took with him every night working as a doorman. Thermos coffee just sucks but it was a necessary evil if I didn't want to fall asleep.

To keep me distracted, I played with the CB radio in the security booth.

Human communication just sucks. Apollo volunteered impatiently. *I don't know how you could stand living like that. Handwritten notes, radios, telephones, how did you get anything done?*

Truth is, we hid in the down time. I responded. *There is something to be said for being unreachable, which I haven't experienced for over four hundred years. There's no hiding from thought.*

Are you boys finished with your bitch session? Stella interrupted. *Some of us would like to hear the rest of the story. I'm quite enjoying father's voice.*

Here, here! Claire shared. *Get on with it, Jimmy. You're not getting any younger here.*

I would spin the dials on the CB listening to the overnight truckers speeding up and down the nearby Major Deegan Expressway, or east and west on the Cross-Bronx Expressway, calling out to each other in the darkness by their recognizable handles – like a game of Marco-Polo in a pool - and when they finally connected it was like listening to old friends bumping into each other in passing. A few shared sentences of recognition between two isolated people where you just didn't expect to find it. I was living through them vicariously. I found joy in their connection. It made it a little less lonely as you crossed the witching hour and headed towards dawn.

The big problem with working midnights was that you were going into work when all your friends were getting wasted in the bars, and even on your days off you had to keep to the day sleeping schedule or you felt like shit on your first day back on duty. And my two days off were usually during the middle of the week so my communal social life sucked.

`Sometimes Joe and JC would make the effort to hang with me, but they worked with the living, and they had their own lives, so they eventually crashed while we were sitting around the apartment watching TV, listening to music, and drinking beers. Eddie and BJ were good for a rare late night, but I tried to make that the exception, because they were still driving those school buses.

When I came home to Aunt Violet's Flop House most weekend mornings, I had to step over my friends sleeping in the chairs, sofa and floors. They had made the better choice of staying put rather than chance driving home. Once in a while I found one of the luckier ones crashed with some girl in my bedroom, so I took the couch and tried not to peek when the girl did her coyote exit though the living room. Rocky O'Hanlon was a repeat offender. Charming prick.

Beggars can't be choosers, and so it was with my love life. I hadn't had a steady girlfriend since Chrissy Dosela in grade school, so there was no one waiting for me back at Aunt Violets. On my midweek nights off I would often leave the Bronx entirely, and walk into the closest bar to whatever random subway station I exited, in whatever borough I was in. I would sit around drinking beers and watching the muted television off in the corner until a decent looking woman looked lonely enough for me to go over to talk to. And there was always a lonely woman. Bars are where the lonely people like to go, just so they don't feel alone. Just like me.

I really wasn't after sex. Sometimes I just wanted to talk to a girl. They are just so much more interesting than men.

But the sex always arrived. And it didn't matter how old the woman was or how pretty they thought they were, or their race, or how fat or skinny, or tall or short. The sex was always good. Because, for some reason, they were always really into it. I guess it was because I was younger than most of them. They were the initiators. They did all the work, and I was always responsive and appreciative. It was like I was their last shot at feeling that physical connection, so they were going to leave their mark. The older the woman, the more, new things, I learned. Unlike formal education, I actually liked these lessons.

But I never felt that emotional connection that Johnny Peyton talked about. It was always a physical sensation. Wonderful, yes, each time.

After a while I just assumed I would never find it. Maybe that was good. Maybe after finding it just once, you can't live without it. Maybe that's why Johnny killed himself.

After each encounter, I always waited for my partner to fall asleep, you could hear it in their relaxed breathing, and then I grabbed my clothes and left. And that's the beauty of New York City. There's always a cab looking to pick up the shame-walkers just as the sun starts to break over Long Island.

I never went back to the same bar twice, no matter how much I liked the woman. I didn't want the rejection that always came if I waited around long enough.

Luckily, I don't think even a Centaurian can live long enough to hit every bar in New York City once.

So, I didn't need to shit where I ate, and I left the college coeds alone, until I covered that one Friday evening shift for Robbie Stanton, who had a wedding he had to travel to. No good deed goes unpunished.

CHAPTER SEVENTY
(THE TIME TRAVELER)

Now, the fact that I was willing to engage in meaningless sex did not mean that these women meant nothing to me. As I said, I always enjoyed talking with women. But I was a better listener, loneliness will do that to a person. Every one of the women had their story to share, and I was willing to hear it. Some stories involved their ex-boyfriends or ex-husbands, or soon to be ex-whatever. Some involved other choices, good and bad, they had made in their lives. Some involved ancient wounds instilled by family members when they were younger, or more recent ones instilled by some present asshole in their lives. I honestly felt for each of them. By sharing their pain, I forgot some of my own. And had I gotten the chance, I would have given those that had inflicted those emotional and physical scars a good old fashioned Irish welcome.

Indeed, it was usually after listening to their stories, when I was just trying to offer them my heartfelt emotional consolation, that the tide always turned, and their interests turned amorous. I guess they felt an emotional connection. I always ended up feeling the physical. Except once.

And maybe that is why, after hundreds of years, I remember only one of the women's names, the one that got away. Madison Taylor.

It was about 5 pm on a Wednesday in May. I was sitting in a dive bar in Hell's Kitchen at the corner of 55th and 8th, on the west side of Manhattan. I was feeling nostalgic for the area where Spaghetti and his brother, Barney, used to drink and carouse when they first came over from Ireland. The generations of brogues that once sat at these bars had morphed into a sound that newcomers to the city had labeled a Clinton accent. Except for the bartender, an older, powerfully built son-of-a-bitch with a Northern Irish brogue and kind eyes. He introduced himself as the proprietor, Kyle Dooley, when he poured me a welcoming shot of Bushmills.

I must have missed the woman when I first came into the place, which was strange because I always made it a practice to scan the room. But it was dark, and my eyes took a bit of time adjusting to the blackness. All I saw were the old timers quietly sitting at the bar sipping shots of whiskey through their little red drink straws, like ancient hummingbirds, because their hands suffered from delirium tremors. When I finally did spot her, while I was trying to locate the bathroom at the back of the bar, she was sitting alone at a table, fixated on some strange little translucent square she was holding in her palm. When she saw me glancing over in her direction, she slipped the square into her pocket, and turned her attention to the drink that Kyle was bringing over to her at that moment. I didn't get the sense she was looking for company, so I went about my business and returned to the bar.

"Is she one of your regulars?" I asked Kyle the next time he returned to my spot with a beer. He glanced over in her direction and shook his head. "Nope," he said removing my empty and tossing it in a bin below the bar. "Must be another tourist. We get them sometimes. Like you."

"Fuck you," I said, "I'm no tourist."

Kyle smiled. "No," he said, "But you're not too far removed from back home. Where are your people from?"

He was thrilled to learn that my family was from Tyrone, as he was from Derry, which made us instant co-conspirators. After that I got more bar knocks with unrequested shots, as I shared some of the stories I knew about my grandfather's middle of the night escape on a fishing boat from a time before the Troubles, and Kyle shared that he too could never return home for his much more recent transgressions.

I was feeling a buzz when I first heard that woman's voice.

"I said, no thank you!" While the sound of her voice was pleasant, its tone was firm leaning into harsh.

"Calm down. I'm just trying to buy you a drink, sweetheart." said an Irish male's Clinton brogue in response.

"And I'm just trying to finish the drink I already have," She responded confidently. "Alone."

"Sean," Kyle barked over my shoulder. "Leave that woman be."

"Feck off, Kyle. Mind your business."

I turned to watch the drama unfold and spotted a man who looked to be in his thirties, obviously drunk, as he clumsily sat down at the woman's table. He looked like every mick construction worker I had ever met. He had two tumblers of whisky and was now sliding one into the woman's space across the table.

She wasn't having it. She picked up her own drink, downed it in a gulp, flipped her glass over on the table and stood up to leave.

And that's when he grabbed her arm in a way a man never should.

Now, I would love to tell you that I walked over and said something cool, or terrifying, which caused Sean to cower and slink out of the bar. But real fighters don't talk. My now drunk body just slid off its stool and moved the way it had been trained to as I crossed the floor quickly and then hit Sean square on the chin just as he rose from his chair to meet me. I must have been channeling Spaghetti, or at least Eddie, because Sean dropped like a wet blanket. My hand hurt like hell. My pinky knuckle showed an obvious boxer's break. And that's why you wrap.

"Fook!" came the exasperated voice of Kyle over my shoulder.

"Lad, you better take this lassie and get out of here." Kyle said as he lifted Sean from the floor and gently put him back in his chair. "You don't know who you just hit, and because of your fine grandfather, I'm not about to tell you. But you both better be gone when boy-o wakes up."

The woman grabbed my arm and started to lead me out of the bar.

I started to resist.

"Hold on, " I said, and turned back to Kyle. "That fucker had it coming."

"True," Kyle said, checking Sean for signs of life. "But I can't tell him that. But I will tell you that you'll be in for a world of shit if you're here when he comes to. His cousin is Jimmy Conlan."

"We better get out of here," said the woman, obviously recognizing a name that meant nothing to me. So, I followed her out into the late evening dusk.

By the time I reached the curb she had already hailed a taxi. That moment was the first chance I had to actually look her over. She was attractive.

Five foot six with light hair that hung to her shoulders in a loose wave, like someone who gets out of the shower, or the beach, and just lets their hair dry on its own. She dressed like money, but her clothes had a vintage look to them. And she wore sensible flats. Her youthful face masked a toned body that could have been in its early thirties, and she moved with the confidence of someone who has fought for whatever she has and won.

When the cab pulled up she held the door open and called to me. "Come on, Sean will be waking up any second."

I slid in the back seat behind her, and the cab headed north just as Sean himself staggered out of the bar looking very pissed.

"Take 57th towards the Park." She said to the driver, an older black man with the nub of a well chewed cigar dangling from his lip. It was then that I noticed the absence of a New York accent. She was clearly a transplant from somewhere out west.

She turned back to me and extended her hand. "Madison Taylor," she said, "but now that we're such good friends, you can call me Maddy."

"Jimmy," I responded. "Jimmy McCarthy."

When I took her hand I winced from the pain of the broken knuckle." Maddy took a closer look and sucked her teeth, like she had seen this before. She gazed along the street and called to the driver.

"Pull over there, driver." She pointed. "Right in front of that drugstore."

She hopped out and entered the store while the driver eyed me suspiciously, like I was going to do a runner and beat him on his fare. I took a ten out of my wallet and gave it to him. He paused the meter.

She reappeared after a few minutes carrying a small bag, but then entered the delicatessen right next door. This time the bag she appeared with was the size of the six pack she was carrying.

"Central Park West and 60th," she instructed as she handed me the bag of beer. Then she started to go through the pharmacy bag. And before she had finished her check list the cabby pulled over on the park side of the street.

"How much?" she said glancing at the silent meter.

"It's covered," the old driver growled. "Have a nice day, mam!"

We slid out and she walked through a narrow entrance in the wall and onto a path I had taken many times in the past. It led to Umpire Rock, a great place to sit and people watch. It also gave you a great vantage point to spot the skells that may be wandering the park, looking for trouble. Dusk was heading for darkness.

She climbed the large stone like an old friend. She certainly knew her way around the park.

She sat at the peak of the rock and motioned for me to sit beside her.

"Let's see that hand," she said.

She gently placed her left thumb and finger above and below the broken knuckle, while holding my wrist in her right hand. Then she said,

"This is going to –" she pulled the knuckle towards her with more strength than she looked like she had.

"Ffffffuuuuuuuuuccccckkkkkkkk!" I screamed, trying to pull my right hand free from her grip. But she held on and pulled the hand by the wrist back into her lap area, where she studied the knuckle and ran her fingers gently along the throbbing but realigned metacarpal.

"As good as its going to get," she declared with a smile. It was a nice smile.

She tore open some of the packages with her teeth and began to wrap the now free ace bandage firmly, but not too tightly, around my right hand from mid fingers to my wrist, and then sealed it off with some thick white medical tape.

She studied the finished job with a critical eye, then gently released my hand. I didn't pull it back right away.

"You a nurse?" I asked, now looking over my bandaged hand. It was still sore as shit.

"No," she replied. "But I've seen a few broken bones in my day."

She reached into the brown bag and removed two beers, popping the first and handing it to me.

I instinctively looked around to make sure there were no cops or parkies patrolling the area to ticket us for drinking in public. It was getting dark, so the park was clearing out.

She held up her beer for a toast. "To drunken assholes, and chivalrous men."

I tapped cans and took a sip. It felt weird drinking lefty, and, being called chivalrous.

We finished those first beers in relative silence, just watching as the last of the natural light handed off to the streetlights, and the distant glitters from the taller apartment buildings that surrounded the park.

As I popped my second beer one handed, I got a little nosier.

"So, what were you doing by yourself in a Hell's Kitchen bar?" I asked. "You're no Mick." The beer was cold and good.

"Research," she responded. She seemed to look at me funny, and I couldn't tell if she was drunker than she looked, or I was drunker than I felt. I had a few beers and shots with Kyle before breaking my knuckle on fiddlefuck's chin, but I was pretty sure that buzz had passed with the adrenaline rush.

"What kind of research?" I asked. I was really feeling Maddy's voice, so I wanted to hear more of it.

"I study criminals." She replied.

"You're not a cop." I said. "I know cops when I see them."

She laughed and shook her head, her hair swinging gently as she did. "Nah," she said, "it's more of a hobby."

I heard a strange noise coming from her pocket. She reached in and removed that little square thing she had been looking at in the bar. I couldn't get a good look at it, but there was definitely a glow coming from it, like from a color TV.

I'll explain the ancient technology later. Claire shared before the siblings could ask.

Maddy cupped it and turned away from me while she did something with her other hand, then slid it back into her pocket. "Sorry about that." She said.

She finished her beer and dropped the can back into the bag.

"Well, Jimmy McCarthy," she said as she rose to her feet. "I've got to be some place in exactly ten minutes."

I stood and grabbed the bag with the last three beers. "I'll walk you."

"Not a good idea." She said, a little anxiously.

"Shit, don't tell me you have a jealous boyfriend." I said, smiling. "I'm really not hitting on you, I swear it."

"No," she said, returning the smile. "Nothing like that."

"Look, its dark now and the park is a dangerous place." I countered, "let me just walk you wherever you gotta go, and then I'll leave. Promise."

She thought it over for a moment. "Okay, but when I tell you to turn around, you must promise that you'll do it."

"If you let me walk you wherever," I replied, "I'll stand on my fucking head."

She took my left hand in her right and began to lead me off the rocks. She never said a word while she walked, and I spent the silence trying to work up the nerve to ask for her number.

When we reached the Pine Bank Arch, she led me down to the path that ran beneath it. I could barely see ten feet in front of me. I heard that sound again, and she reached into her pocket and removed the glowing square, which illuminated her profile. Then she released my hand, turned towards me, and stared up into my eyes.

"You are a good guy, Jimmy McCarthy." she said. "Thanks for the knock out." We stared at each other in silence for a few seconds more.

"Now turn around." She said.

I hesitated.

"You promised." She said.

I finally turned in the direction she was pointing, away from the underpass below the arch. I could feel her leave and then quickly return, walking around me until she was facing me again. Without saying anything she grabbed my face and pulled me into a kiss, but before I could wrap my arms around her, she pushed away, and had the most magical smile as she said. "Don't know why, but I had to do that." Then she raced past me toward the underpass.

As I turned to call after her, she was gone. Vanished. I thought I saw the faintest outline of a portal, like the ones we can travel through, disappear into the darkness underneath the arch.

Was she one of us? Apollo asked.

No, she was definitely human. I responded, feeling a little more wistful than I expected.

Do you ever see her again? Stella queried.

No, I replied. *I was back to being alone.*

CHAPTER SEVENTY-ONE
(WHY KINGS DIE)

The knocking on my bedroom door hadn't registered beyond being incorporated into whatever REM dream I was having, so when I felt someone's hand on my shoulder shaking me, I sat up abruptly, sending JC and Joe leaping a few paces back away from my bed. My friends knew I hated having my daytime sleep disturbed, so I was afraid Aunt Violet's Flop House was on fire. I started to stagger to my feet.

"Smokey, hold on," Joe said, steadying me with his hand on my shoulder. As my eyes cleared away the last of my sleep, I saw that they both had been crying.

"BJ's dead." JC whispered, as if the words themselves were hurting him.

They hurt me.

This couldn't be real, so I shook my head violently, trying to clear my cobwebs, to force those words right out of my ears.

The young aren't supposed to die. We all believed we were immortal. I immediately thought of Mark Wallen.

Then panic set in as the obvious associations registered and I pushed myself to my feet. "Eddie?" I asked, fearing the worst. "Is Eddie all right?"

"Eddie wasn't involved." JC said. "Although The Ginger said he's taking it bad."

"What happened?" I asked, guilty over the twinge of relief I just felt.

"No one knows for sure." Joe said. "He went off Skyview. First building"

Death is death, and how one gets there is irrelevant, but given our lifestyles and the odds, a car accident was the expected response. Bar fight would have been a close second.

Skyview had three of the tallest buildings in the Bronx, and given that they sat on top of the highest natural landmass overlooking the Hudson River, they could be spotted from pretty much anywhere in the surrounding five-mile radius. They were to the Bronx, what The World Trade Center was to Manhattan. Our fortress. Iconic. New York City didn't have mountains to climb or worship. We had skyscrapers. I walked over to my bedroom window, lifted the shade, and looked out at them now.

Given my vertigo, I was one of the few Riverdalians who hadn't played on top of those buildings at some point in their youth. Many of the crew, like the Armstrongs, had raced down their eight interior staircases with abandon as part of their newspaper routes. A few of the more daringly stupid would race each other down the outside of the buildings, by climbing down from floor to floor, along their exterior hallways that lined the eastern side of the buildings, like a long set of shelves.

The only security in the buildings were concierges in the large front lobbies, and some random security cameras in the huge underground parking complex that ran underneath all three buildings. The building maintenance staff was busy enough dealing with real problems this little city caused for them on a daily basis, to care about whether certain kids were citizens or interlopers. The locals knew where the building cameras were and that the main basement door on the first building, leading out to the hill that took you down to the Riverdale Avenue shopping center and the rest of our community, was always unlocked, for the convenience of the residents.

"When did it happen?" I asked, not wanting to piece together the visuals that were now running through my mind.

"Dog walker found him at seven fifteen this morning." JC responded.

That was approximately the same time I was walking back from work that morning. The college sat just north of those towers. If I just happened to look to my right at just the wrong time, I might have witnessed it. I shuddered at the thought.

"Do you think he killed himself?" Joe asked no one in particular.

I thought about the kid who pretty much grew up in my house, like my older brother's twin, and couldn't find one memory that suggested he would take his own life. Everything about life brought him joy. He was The Party King, the first and last to celebrate anything that could warrant a toast. He enjoyed all the alcohol that flowed between those two points. He loved his family. He loved his friends. He loved his life. He was a freak of nature who could play any sport and fight any man. And he would never intentionally cause the pain we were now all feeling. Not BJ.

"No," I whispered back, to no one in particular.

But I knew that the Riverdale gossip mill would speculate that he had. Because that gave the worst of them something juicy to share, and make themselves relevant at a time before the Internet replaced them.

I also knew that I had to go home. My brother would be devastated. My parents, who loved BJ like one of their own, would mourn his loss accordingly. Spaghetti and Posie would set about making sure that everything a family needed to get done during this time, got done. Irish families wake as one. We're good at it.

"Any news on a wake?" I asked as I started to get dressed. Everyone who died in Riverdale was waked in the Riverdale On Hudson Funeral Home, which sat in the shadows of the three monoliths that set the scene for this tragedy.

"Nothing yet." JC said. "But I'll let you know when I hear something."

* * * * *

As horrible as it sounds, there is something to be said for being the immediate family of the deceased. The universe forces you to keep putting one foot in front of the other so that you don't spiral into a catatonic state. You have to make all of the arrangements, and there are so many to deal with. There's the wake itself that needs to be scheduled, the funeral mass, the grave site selected and the post cemetery gathering catered, and everything in between down to the type of wood, handles and trim on the coffin, and the songs and readings at the mass. You also had to decide who would do those readings and who would carry the dead that final time.

And once that's done you have to present yourself to the community, and watch for three days and nights, as the members parade past the deceased and say their quick prayers. During those moments, they mentally assess how well the undertaker performed the makeover, or comment quietly on just how bad things were that it compelled a closed coffin. And you have to be nice to everyone, as they take your hand in passing and offer their condolences.

No matter what the reality, there has never been a rat bastard buried in Riverdale. All the sinners are saints in the end.

And no one does a wake better than the Irish.

Our perennially persecuted ancestors carried their black humor across the Atlantic and saved it for just these kinds of occasions, because if you don't laugh at Death, Death wins. The Irish shed their tears in private. And so, you can never be sure there is a dead Irishman in the front of the room until you hear the laughter in the back.

Hell, if you sit around an Irish table long enough, you'll hear more entertaining stories about the great wakes and funerals of the Riverdale families than you will hear about their weddings. After all, you can be married more than once, but only one person can comfortably fit in an open coffin. It is a one-time only, sold out, solo performance.

It seemed like we had just gone through it all just yesterday, when we buried Mark Wallen. Those wounds always feel fresh.

But while the family of the deceased are blessedly busy with all of these details, the rest of us who love and mourn that person who has passed, can only wait, and worry about the family in the middle of it all. And that sucked. But that's what we did.

CHAPTER SEVENTY-TWO
(BACK TO THE NEST)

Why is it that parents never empty a child's room after they move out?

My attic dormer bedroom was pretty much just as I left it when I moved out to Aunt Violet's Flop House. I could tell that The Ginger had made tiny incursions into my space because the bed wasn't made, and I found an empty condom wrapper on the nightstand. Only The Ginger would have the balls to sneak his girlfriend up into the attic, and since my room was the farthest from the one staircase that led to our common space, it gave him time to hide his guest under the bed should anyone else come up those creaky stairs. I knew for a fact that Eddie never crossed that line, because his sex life had been limited to front seat fumbles in Mark Wallen's Chevy down by the river, and the occasional use of my bedroom in Aunt Violet's on the weekend nights when I was working. My friends hated when Eddie was there because it rendered the adjacent living room a no-fly zone for their parties. Eddie was very private, and his girl was determined to maintain the plausibility of virginity right up until her wedding day. Eddie would sooner pitch a friend out the front window than listen to his upset girlfriend.

But Eddie wasn't thinking about sex when I found him that morning. He was sitting on the rooftop ledge of the front porch, just outside the front window of his bedroom, staring out at Mosholu Avenue and the Mosholu Woods beyond. He was smoking one of our Dad's Marlboros, its half empty pack sat next to him. I poked my head out the window, ever conscious of my vertigo and reticent to leave the safety of the four attic walls around me.

"Are you okay?" I asked.

He took a long drag on his cigarette and slowly exhaled to give himself time to think before answering.

"He was perfectly fine when I dropped him off home this morning." He said as he chain-lit the next cigarette and flicked the first one off the roof onto Mosholu below.

"We were planning a road trip to Colorado this summer." Eddie continued. "BJ wanted to show me the Coors Brewery in Golding."

Eddie turned to look up at me. I could see that his eyes were red from crying. I had never seen Eddie actually cry, even when he got hurt as a child. He'd shout and bellow and curse the gods. But no tears. Just wasn't in him.

"And before you ask," he added, "No, he didn't kill himself."

He turned back away from me and stared down Mosholu. A cleaning crew was going in and out of Coaches II down the block, cleaning up Friday night's mess and getting it ready for Saturday's version of the same.

I carefully slid my body through the window and sat next to my older brother, my back hugging the wall behind me, never getting any closer than three feet from the ledge.

"I'm sorry." I whispered.

He sighed but didn't respond.

His body was so much larger than mine that I was completely blocked from a sudden gust of wind, that literally snatched the glowing tip off his cigarette, and sent it flying like a tiny meteor in the direction of the park to our south.

"Any word on the wake?" I asked, just to fill the silence.

"His sister told me Monday afternoon and evening at ROH. Funeral Tuesday, 11 am. Internment in the family plot in Gate of Heaven. I'm guessing The Riverdale Steakhouse afterwards."

A one day wake was unusual, but after all, he went off a building.

The Steakhouse had been the first real restaurant in Riverdale since we had moved there, and did a great business because the locals could walk there and stagger home. The meals were solid American fare with different variations of meat and potatoes, thick sandwiches, and any kind of alcohol you desired. It was a good choice to celebrate life or commiserate over its passing.

"You going to be okay out here?" I asked, my vertigo beginning to get the better of me.

"Yeah," he said. "Go ahead back in."

I practically leapt back into his bedroom.

My mother was on the second floor back porch, hanging out laundry on the line that ran across the yard to the giant tulip tree that Spaghetti maintained like a prized orchid. My grandfather was down in the yard, at the moment, watering the tree and the plants that surrounded it. Pepper was watching him from a careful distance, always ready to race away when my grandfather, laughing, turned the hose on him. But Spaghetti didn't want to play today. I could smell Posie's cooking wafting upstairs from her kitchen below. My father was out picking up the two youngest boys from their Saturday athletic activities at Fordham Prep. My sister was now living in Manhattan with her roommate, while teaching at an elite private Catholic girls' high school on the upper east side. Everything was as it always was. And yet it wasn't.

"Do you mind if I crash here for a couple of days?" I asked my mother.

She put the last of the sheets on the line, turned, and wrapped her arms around me. As she pulled my head onto her shoulder. I don't know what came over me, but I suddenly lost it and burst into uncontrollable sobs. My defenses were shattered, and I was four years old again.

"Musha, musha, musha," she cooed as she rubbed my back until the sobbing subsided.

I finally caught my breath and pulled back from her.

"Stay as long as you like." she said. "This will always be your home."

I went into work that night and arranged with Robbie Stanton to take the next few nights off. It was fine, given that the spring semester had ended, and the students for the first summer school session were not arriving until that Friday. But he needed me to come in Friday, for that early shift I had promised to cover. Then I went back to the Mosholu house and slept until Sunday dinner.

Bonnie arrived just in time for dinner, and while enjoying one of the best meals Posie ever served us, we all sat around telling family stories and laughing and ball breaking, and occasionally cursing each other out, like we were trying to show Death that it wasn't welcomed in our home.

But that didn't stop the ghost.

CHAPTER SEVENTY-THREE
(MARLEY WAS AN AMATEUR)

I could feel the wind on my skin, and off in a corner by a brick wall, a crumpled brown paper bag danced energetically until another strong gust lifted it upwards and over the wall. I could see glittering lights from the entire northern Bronx, fading like the stars above in the transitioning night before me. I knew I was up high but didn't suffer any vertigo. I struggled to spot a rooftop down on Liebig Avenue just a few blocks away from the St. Maggie's Steeple, and for some reason it felt like home. I knew everyone below me was still asleep. I was sitting now on the edge of the brick wall, my legs dangling over into the last of the darkness. I could see the bottle of beer in my hand as it raised to my lips and emptied. But, it wasn't my hand. It was much larger, and I never drank with my left hand. I felt so tired and struggled to keep my eyes open, just as the sun started to peek over the horizon of the Long Island sound in the distance. I tossed the empty beer bottle over my shoulder, but the sound of its shattering glass was stolen by another strong gust of wind. If I could just keep my eyes open. If I could just make it to another day. But I am so tired. Just let me rest my eyes a moment more. It will all be okay. Just one more moment.

It was one of those restless sleeps that always occurred when I tried to transition from my inverted night-day work schedule to acclimate to the real world. I knew I had to get some sleep in if I was going to make it through the next few days of mourning with friends and family. I had a lot of beers at dinner and afterwards, which was a little strange, because I had never drank alcohol with my parents before. My parents and grandparents finally made their excuses and retired for the night, and left the kids sitting around the table in the backyard. Eddie left to go visit his girlfriend and asked if he could borrow my bedroom at Aunt Violet's for a few hours. We all seek consolation in different places. When Bonnie and my younger siblings finally called it night, I went upstairs and lay in the bed for what seemed an eternity before I must have fallen asleep.

I'm not sure what woke me, and for the first few seconds I lay there in bed trying to get my bearings, trying to make sense of that dream I just had. The room was black, and the radium hands on the windup clock on my side table signaled three am. I was about to turn over and go back to sleep when I sensed that I wasn't alone in the room.

I glanced down towards the foot of my bed. A soft light from the streetlamps on Mosholu permeated the straight hallway leading from Eddie's room, at the front of the house, to my room at the back. There was a large figure partially obscuring that light. I thought it was Eddie coming in from a night of commiseration.

"Just leave the keys on the dresser," I said as I tried to maneuver into a more comfortable position under the light blanket on my bed. But although I had turned away, I sensed that the figure was still there. After a moment I lifted my head and glanced towards the open doorway. The figure stood quietly facing in my direction. Hard as I tried to focus, I couldn't make out the facial features in the darkness.

"Eddie, you're drunk, just go to bed." I said, feeling instantly guilty over how pissed I must have sounded.

But the figure just stood there. Now I really was getting pissed. Eddie had a history of getting so wasted he was almost catatonic. This had a familiar feel to it.

"Fucking Eddie, please go to bed," I pleaded.

And that's when the figure turned to its right and I could see the baseball mitt sized hands in silhouette, open like they were pleading for something. And then I remembered the dream, and the hands on the beer bottle, and I knew.

"BJ?!" I whispered.

The figure turned back in my direction. I never took my eyes off its right hand, which still displayed open as a shadow on the figure's hip.

Then I felt the word more than heard it. *Accident.*

Now I was completely awake and had raised myself into a sitting position leaning back onto my headboard, pulling the blanket on top of me as I tried to cover my body up to my chin. I never took my eyes off the figure, and I could see the fingers on the silhouetted hand move. Then the entire figure just slowly expanded, its shadow form blocking out the last of the light as it expanded beyond the confines of the room, like a shadow wall had cut me off from the rest of the house.

I panicked. I stood up on the bed and threw the balled-up blanket towards the ethereal membrane, and followed the opening it created out of my room, down the hallway and down the stairs. I didn't even stop to check and see if my brothers were safe in their rooms as I passed. I was terrified.

When I reached the second floor living room, I found my mother sitting peacefully in an armchair doing some sewing. I leapt into the first armchair I came to and sat, knees tucked before me, silently rocking like a basket case. My mother continued working on an intricate stitch before tying it off and looking over at me. The whole time I struggled with what I was about to say to her.

"You saw BJ, didn't you?"

All I could do was nod.

She smiled.

"I've felt him around us quite a few times this weekend." She said as she packed up her sewing kit. "I'm sure he just woke me a half hour ago. I couldn't go back to sleep."

She stared at me for a moment as she carefully thought about her next words.

"I think he's trying to tell us something," She said.

"It was an accident." I whispered before I realized what I was saying.

She looked at me and smiled.

"Yes," she said, nodding. "That's what I was getting to."

She stood up and returned the sewing kit to its place on top of the bookshelves in the living room, then she turned back to me and said, "Well, I'm not going back to sleep anytime soon. Let's put the kettle on."

As she headed out of the room, I called out to her. "Mom, why tell us?"

She stopped and smiled as she thought about her response.

"That's easy dear." She said. "Because he knew we'd listen."

I never told any of my siblings about that night. I guess my mother didn't either.

Gate of Heaven Cemetery, in Hawthorne, New York, is the only place any Bronx Irishman worth a damn would want to be buried. Such New York luminaries as Babe Ruth, Billy Martin, Sal Mineo, The Mara Family, Condé Nast, Mary Higgins Clarke, Mario Biaggi and James Cagney, call it their final resting place. So, if you are sharing acreage with them, you have already risen seven rungs on the New York social ladder. The McCarthy's made sure to lock up an entire section on one of the rolling hillsides, that gave our family an unobstructed view of the rest of the cemetery. Spaghetti actually lay on the ground where he wanted his grave to make sure of the view he would be having. He always said that no matter how hard we try, we all go to earth in the end. So, plan accordingly.

BJ's family had their own mausoleum on the top of one of the oldest sections in Gate of Heaven, so we took some comfort knowing he'd be hanging in the same section as his hero, Billy Martin, who would have been right at home growing up in Riverdale. The crew were on our best behavior throughout the wake and funeral, out of respect for the family, but once we left the funeral afterparty, the gloves came off.

Eddie insisted that we leave the Bronx so we could cut loose without worrying about the Riverdale gossip machine kicking it into high gear. We chose a place called The Candle's Wick, a hole in the wall type of establishment, that sat right across the Major Deegan from Yonkers Raceway. This gave us an easy exit strategy should the need arise. Along with the regulars, there were representatives of the PWWCs and even our younger siblings came along, having gotten their own fake ID's as they acquired a taste for beer.

The evening was going along just fine. Then Eddie, feeling a little maudlin, decided that he wanted to repeatedly play "Dream On," by the popular band Aerosmith, on the bar's jukebox, while singing along in his terrible tenor. To give him his due, the bartender was very patient once we explained that my brother had just buried his best friend.

But some of the other patrons were not as empathetic, and when one of the bikers decided to pull the plug on the jukebox, the tenth time Eddie was belting the title refrain, the place went deadly silent, and Tommy Q, turned to the man and said, "You shouldn't have done that."

Brian Kelly grabbed my youngest brother and Rocky O'Hanlon and went to start the cars. Eddie turned to The Ginger and said, "Lock the door."

What started out as a one-on-one vicious pummeling of the biker by Eddie, became a ménage à trois, with Eddie beating the biker and his friend. That then quickly escalated to an all-out brawl among anyone who decided to align with one combatant or the other. In fairness, the Riverdalians all observed the Marquis of Queensbury rules, as no new combatant entered the fray on our side unless someone jumped in on the other. While I had witnessed many horrific beatings bestowed by my older brother, this was the first time I got to see The Ginger in action, and quite honestly, it scared the shit out of me when I saw him lift another biker over his head and toss him over the bar. He was good.

JC and Joe were the first two off the bench and gave as good as they got. The Greek dropped a huge bastard with a well-placed kick to his groin. Beware of Greeks bearing gifts.

I didn't engage in the battle until Tommy Q saw the bartender get on the pay phone and called out to the rest of us that it was time to go because the cops would be there shortly. At that point, I stepped in to subdue a few tenacious opponents who were hanging onto other members of our crew in hopes of preventing our immediate escape. I was about to make my exit, when the large eunuch, that The Greek had dropped a few minutes before, got a second wind and yoked me from behind, almost snapping my neck. Luckily Ralph Droz was standing behind him with the fifth of scotch he had snatched during the melee from the top shelf behind the bar. The large fucker took a second dive with a decent head gash for his troubles while Ralph and I exited stage left. I was surprised that the bottle didn't shatter. That really was quality Scotch. Ralph took the bottle with him.

Once the last of us were safely in the three running cars in front of the bar, our caravan hopped on the southbound Major Deegan and disappeared into the Bronx, exiting by 242nd street and taking the side roads back to our neighborhood, leaving the Yonkers cops to clean up the mess we had left behind. I'm certain that BJ was with us that night.

The next morning, his head now cleared in the best way he knew how, Eddie packed his Chevy, withdrew his savings, promised his girlfriend his unending love upon his return, then headed out of town. Said he was first going to Golden, Colorado. Then he was going to climb the highest mountain in the state, toast his old friend with a case of cold Coors, and a long pee off the peak. At the last second Steve The Greek arrived with a knapsack and hopped in the Chevy with Eddie. Said he was going to find Apples while he was out there.

I returned to work for my next shift. After struggling to switch my body back to vampire hours, I took that extra early Friday night shift I promised Robbie I would cover, with the intention of working a double. It turned out to be a lot more challenging than I expected.

CHAPTER SEVENTY-FIVE
(ERATO-ELENI)

I've always loved Fridays. In the human world they are filled with such potential for fun and excitement - especially in the summer.

This particular Friday started out promising, at least for my friends. It's all about relationships.

I awoke from my vampirine sleep to learn that JC received a letter at Aunt Violet's Flop House from Joanna Skeegle asking him to move to Paris. He would live with her in the Fifth arrondissement on her parents' dime, while she completed her senior year abroad studies at the Sorbonne. It seems she could no longer live without him. JC openly thanked BJ's condom, shared those many years ago, for his stroke of good luck, no pun intended, and started planning his trip.

Joe had finally relented and picked his wedding day after his future father-in-law made him that unrefusable offer, so the rest of his now extended life was falling into place.

Brian Kelly had returned from college with his ingenious plan to salvage a stripper named Nanetta Concetta, who he had been following in a series of bars along the Canadian Coast. However, the success of his plan required two full time jobs this summer to bankroll. He stopped by the apartment to let us know he had just landed that critical second job, working as night security in a White Plains bank.

Robbie Maclaren returned from Com Ave in Boston with big news. He and Sally had decided to marry that following summer before he entered Law School. Out of all of my friends, I believed this pairing had the most potential for success. But what the fuck did I know?

While I wanted to sit around and share in the joy of my friends, by cracking that cold case of beer waiting in our fridge, I had to go earn my keep as the sheep dog for the summer flock of students a few blocks away. It was time to work that summer double I had promised Robbie Stanton, so he could go off and attend a weekend wedding in Pennsylvania. Seems love was everywhere I turned.

Given this was the move-in weekend for the first of two summer sessions, and my first shift was the 4pm to midnight, I couldn't just pull my usual hide in the guard booth move that the graveyard shift had allowed me. I had to play concierge, as well as protect and serve. Some of the students had already completed a year or two and were just accelerating their studies, so they knew where they were going. Some were first timers getting ahead before their freshman year actually began, who needed that additional gentle touch. I wondered where they all found their drive and discipline. I felt like that lazy grasshopper watching those industrious ants working away towards some goal I just couldn't visualize.

Seventy-five percent of the students arriving were female, and while I couldn't help but note and catalogue those physical packages that were more aesthetically pleasing, I limited myself to checking their admission packages and pointing to the relevant dorm they would be staying in. I realized that most of the arrivals looked upon me as an automaton, and barely made eye contact with me during our exchanges. My position as a security guard stamped me with a "Lacks Potential" tattoo on my forehead. I didn't need them for that, I was pretty self-aware. Smiles were optional on both sides.

All of the students were supposed to arrive no later than six pm, so their move-in would be completed no later than eight pm. But there are always the stragglers.

One particular straggler stood out. At around nine pm, a beautiful blue Caprice Classic rolled up with its rag top down, and a blond woman in her late thirties behind the wheel. Lynyrd Skynyrd's "Free Bird" was blasting from her top-of-the-line speaker system. Her sun-bleached hair made the tan on her angular face look that much deeper. She was wearing a fluorescent yellow tank top, which accented an unusually full bosom, on what otherwise looked like a taught runner's body. She appeared too old and confident to be a new student.

"Hi," she said, throwing the car in park, standing up and leaning over the top of the windshield. "Sorry I'm late. Just drove up from Florida."

I walked around to the driver's side of the car, just because I wanted to get a better look at her.

She handed me a card that identified her as Melissa Gunderson, PhD, and held out her Florida license with her other hand confirming that fact. There were no rings on either hand.

And then she smiled with a set of large white teeth, that were naturally straight and seemed to glow from her very tan face.

"I'm Doctor Gunderson," she said. "I'll be teaching Advanced Biometrics to all of these hungry young students this summer."

I hadn't a fucking clue what Biometrics was and didn't care. This woman was hot, and I was instantly attracted to her. I was struggling to keep my eyes from lowering to the nicely sculpted breasts pressing along the top of the windshield.

"I'm supposed to be bunking in Alumnae Hall for the summer." She added.

"Well Doctor Gunderson," I responded, handing her back her card. "I'm Jimmy McCarthy, the night watch dog. Pleased to meet you." I extended my recently repaired right hand in greeting, which she took and held for just that extra second. I felt her pinky rub along the slight bump on the knitted metacarpal.

Once free, I pointed with my right hand across the quad to the dorm in question.

"That's your new home for the summer." I said, with my most grown up voice. "If there is anything I can do for you to make your stay here more pleasant or productive," I now pointed back to my guard booth, "I can be found most nights from midnight to dawn, sitting right over there."

I could not help myself. I was hitting on this woman. And quite honestly, at that moment, I didn't give a shit if I got fired for it.

I had seen enough looks from lonely women to recognize a spark of interest, and spotted that flash, so now I smiled back at her with my fully natural and slightly crooked set of choppers.

She looked over at the guard booth and then back at me and smiled again.

"Good to know." She said with just the hint of seduction. "I feel safer already."

She dropped back into her driver's seat and this time I couldn't avoid watching her chest rebound as she threw the car into drive and sped off into the quad towards Alumnae. I wondered if there was a biometric for that.

* * * * *

Midnight found me reading a worn student's copy of The Odyssey that someone had dropped off at the lost and found at the end of the spring semester. I had started using the lost and found as my own personal library, just to keep the boredom at bay, and found that reading kept my interests better than listening to the truckers on the CB radio. I wasn't a big fan of the poetic form, but I certainly felt bad for the title's protagonist, who seemed to be in a world of shit. I also felt bad for Calypso, who fell in love with Odysseus but had to let him go. It really must suck to piss off the gods.

This late-night reading had also reawakened my interest in learning new things. JC had mentioned that Lehman College was having an open house for its second summer session in July. If I was interested, I should stop in and meet with his guidance counselor, Anna Hillman, and that she could hook me up. I jotted a reminder for me to give her a call the next morning and stuck it in the Odyssey as a bookmark.

But duty called so I hopped into the old blue mustang and made my midnight rounds, checking all of those doors and windows, and making sure the nuns weren't having a rave. When I returned, I found a folded note taped to the door of the guard booth.

"Anywhere an adult can get a drink around here after midnight? Room A 23. Knock 3 times. I may be sleeping. *au naturel.* M"

Even the print looked sexy.

It is amazing how easily I can get lost in my own thoughts, especially with a trigger like that note. I don't know how long I was sitting there contemplating that walk across the quad, before I heard that soft rapping on the glass of the booth door. I looked up almost expecting to see Dr. Gunderson.

Instead, a beautiful brunette gazed at me with jet black eyes. It took me a moment before I recognized her now older appearance. Eleni.

I slid open the door. She was now in her twenties and even more gorgeous than the last time I saw her, sitting with me on that bench outside of Bronx Park East.

"Give me that note." She said softly. Her voice made me instantly forget about Dr. Gunderson's breasts.

I handed it to her, and she stood back from the booth and held it above her head between her left finger and thumb, and it suddenly ignited, its ashes floating off into the night sky.

"Now give me your hand!" She commanded.

"You're not going to burn me, are ya?"

She smiled while she thought about it.

"Not in that sense of the word." She responded. "Please, give me your hand Jimmy."

I extended my hand. "Well, since you asked so nice—"

I awoke lying in a field. There was ambient sunlike light and warmth, with no evident source. The sky above was azure. I could see a lake with woods beyond it. It felt familiar.

"Hello Jimmy."

I leapt to my feet and spun around.

Before me, stood the most beautiful woman I had ever seen in life, film, or art. She wore a diaphanous tunic that seemed to float along the curves of the body underneath. The material seemed sentient. There was a glow that framed her silhouette. The golden gown ended right above two perfect legs that completed the ideal. While I wanted to continue to study this body, my gaze was drawn to her eyes, whose blackness did not invite, but commanded my compliance.

"Remember me?"

The sound of her voice, which at first seemed to come from all around us, now emanated from between her two full, glistening lips. I was only now able to break the gaze and stepped back just as her form seemed to change right before me.

"Eleni," I whispered.

"In my human form, yes."

This form had lost the aura that was there moments before. The skin was less translucent. The face was less symmetrical, less perfect, but equally beautiful.

My mind tried to recall the changes I had witnessed in her over the years, but the face before me forced me to concentrate only on what was before my eyes.

"Where are we?" I asked.

She thought about that for a moment as she reached for my hand. I recoiled just enough to make her smile, and what a smile it was.

"Elysium." She responded. "Heaven to some. Whatever you want it to be."

She slowly continued to reach.

"You are not going to knock me out again, are you?" I asked, still holding my hand teasingly just inches away from her own. "I kinda like it here."

"No," she said, and then she looked a little sad, pensive. "If it were up to me, I'd keep you here with me forever."

"Can we do that in our dreams?" I asked, feeling suddenly comfortable with the idea that I must be dreaming. This time I reached for her hand, and it felt so warm, so soft, so real.

"This is a dream, right?" I looked for confirmation.

"Does this feel like a dream?" She pulled me close and kissed me. I smelled the lavender on her breath and felt disoriented, like I was leaving my body. The last thing I felt was her tongue, touching the end of my own. Electrifying. I tried to reach for her, to pull her close to me, but I no longer had a body, it was just my conscious thought.

Don't worry, I'm here. Eleni shared. It was similar to the way we Centurians communicate but far more enhanced. I could hear her, feel her, still smell the lavender. It wasn't just thought.

And then I was feeling her emotions, like they were my own. Desire, comfort, love. They increased in intensity, overwhelmed me, but wouldn't let me free. It was orgasmic, pure ecstasy. It had no focal point, just repeatedly washed over my consciousness, and carried whatever I had become along through the darkness. I wasn't breathing or thinking, I was just feeling. I was just the voice in my head, and she was with me, and I loved what she was doing to me. I would have stayed in that form forever.

Suddenly, I was back in my body, lying in the grass in Elysium. I was naked, locked in Eleni's naked embrace, her face buried in my chest. She was real. She was perfect. I could feel her heart beating rapidly beneath the soft round breast pressed tightly against my own. She looked up at me and I could see tears on her cheeks. In that moment I did not care about her physical beauty. I wanted to go, wherever it was I had just been and feel that connection, the love that those tears now represented.

"Please don't cry," I whispered. And I went to kiss her again. To go back.

But she turned away, and then reached up and caught my chin in her hand.

"I'm sorry, Jimmy." She whispered back. "I'm not your forever. You need to go back. She's waiting for you."

"I'm not going anywhere." I said. "Do you know how long I've waited to feel what you just did to me?"

"You'll feel it again," Eleni said, her voice trembling. "With her."

"Her?" I stammered. "Her, who? I want you. I want to stay here."

"When you awake, there will be no memory of here, or of me," she whispered. "Women will love you only for who you are, or not at all. And with this final kiss, I take back the gift I first gave you."

I felt her body rolling over on mine. I could feel every inch of her against me as she took my face into her hands and pulled her own lips towards my own. I was aroused. I thought I was going back there with her. I smelled the lavender, felt her tongue, and then it was dark.

* * * * *

What is that sound? Rapping.

"Hello."

More rapping.

"Excuse me," came a nasally female voice. "Mr. security guard."

I rolled my neck and slowly opened my eyes. I felt so disoriented. What the hell was I dreaming? Gone. I was in the guard booth, slumped down in my chair. I must have fallen asleep. I still hadn't changed circadian rhythm back over completely to nocturnal after the funeral.

"Hey, asshole." Came that nasally voice again. "Are you going to sleep all fucking day?"

I looked up and saw the cutest smile, on the cutest Italian face, with the most sparkling brown eyes I had ever encountered, peeking through the glass of the locked guard booth door. She placed the cover sheet of her admission packet up against glass, and I read the name at the top. Gina Buccola, nursing student.

"Oh good. You're alive." She said. "Now get off your cute little ass and show me which one of these fucking dorms is mine."

It was love at first sight.

EPILOGUE
(SUNSET)

What? That's it? Apollo responded.

What? You want to hear about Jimmy and Gina's sex life? Claire responded. *Not me, and I've caught them at it in the barn. Eternally traumatized.*

Okay, that's just gross. Stella shared. *A hard pass from me.*

No, not the sex. Apollo responded. *The connection. Did you have that same connection with mom?*

I thought about it for a moment before answering. *Yeah,* I responded, *not all the time, and not just when we made love. But it was always there when I needed it.*

Claire winked at me. The two kids smiled as they considered my response.

I miss Gina. Stella finally shared. Apollo nodded in agreement. I thought I saw a tear in his eye.

I quietly studied the last three of the closest beings with whom I had shared the last five hundred years and I couldn't feel any more love than I felt for them. But I was tired. More tired than I ever felt before.

If I think of anything else worth telling, I'll let you know. I shared. *But we've been at this for a full Centaurian day, so I need to pack it in.*

Claire looked up at me from where her head still rested in my lap.

You feeling okay, Jimmy?

Yeah, I'm good. I responded. *Just tired.*

Why don't we give your dad a rest? Claire shared with the others.

They each came over to where I was sitting. I was happy they had maintained the human practice of hugging and I hugged them both now maybe a bit harder than they expected. Neither complained. Stella kissed my cheek.

Well, we better get back to ruling this planet. Apollo said.

Watch and learn little brother. Stella replied, and she winked at me.

See you Claire. Apollo shared.

See you soon, father. Stella shared.

They grasped hands, and just like when they were kids, they smiled at each other and disappeared.

I looked at my closest friend, who hadn't taken her eyes off me since I finished my story.

"I'm just going to close my eyes for a few." I said aurally.

"Yeah, you do that." She replied in her deep whisky voice.

* * * * *

Jimmy, c'mon, we gotta go. Claire was back in my head in what seemed like seconds. *They're waiting for us.*

I stood up and tried to get my bearings. I felt a little disoriented. I couldn't understand what I was looking at. The room was so bright.

"Jayney, dull the lights." I said aurally.

"Jayney can't hear you." Claire responded.

I tried to focus on the room, but it wasn't a room. It looked like an expanse leading out in front of me. There was a mist which captured and reflected the light. I thought I could see some figures in the distance moving as a group in our direction. But they were lost in the brightness.

My knees were wobbly as I tried to take a step. I steadied myself on Claire.

"Where are we?" I asked. "Is this Elysium?"

"Home, Jimmy. Elysium was just a stop along the way." Claire said. "C'mon, lean on me until you get your legs under you."

We walked up what seemed to be a slight rise with no definable boundaries. When we got to the top, Claire stopped, and turned to me. "Go ahead, Jimmy, I'll catch up."

I nodded and took a few more steps forward. The group approaching from the other side stopped and allowed one of their number to continue towards me. It was a female. Her stride was familiar, athletic, confident. As beautiful as the first time I saw her.

"You certainly took your fucking time, Jimmy Moran."

And there was the feeling of oneness I had been missing, again.

NEVER THE END

ACKNOWLEDGEMENTS

First and foremost, I must thank Eileen Cotto (who embraces how her character appears in FJM), Anna Hillman (the fictitious college guidance counselor in FJM), Anne Rifenburg (née Collins, one of the sisters at the party) and Yvette Benson (Apples' dancing Latina character partner. Were we siblings in a past life? Absolutely love the shit you have given me during the edits.) You all make an appearance in this novel. Also, Mark, "Lenny" Lenahan (appearing here as the character JC) and Joe Serrano (appearing here as the character Joe Marrero). Your collective careful eyes and attention to detail kept me from looking like a right mug, instead of just a mug. Thank you.

To my lovely wife, Lisa, children, Luke (& Georgie), Jackie (& Zach (Mc)Gilbert – who appears as the head of the yellow bus company) and Mark (& Sara), and grandchildren, Lucian, Scarlett, Savanna and Stella, I love you all. There is magic in this world. I really mean that. May all of your dreams continue to come true forever.

To the McCaffrey Clan, especially my siblings, Veronica, Eddie, Bernie ("The Ginger") and John, and all of your respective spouses and children, their spouses, and grandchildren, with a special mention of Barbara Frank, I couldn't have written any of this without you all. Thank you for keeping me alive this long and for putting up with my bullshit. Thank you Eddie, a true artist, who created the Irish American Alpha and Omega symbol on the cover page and back story of this book. Bbbbaaaaahhhhhhh.

Special shout out to my cousin Jimmy "Apples" (RIP), his wife Connie (RIP), and to his sister Christina Jubak (who hid in the back seat of the stolen car during that last joy ride – which never happened), and to all of their respective and collective descendants. I love you guys. Apples, you not only played a major role in my life, but I could not have survived my childhood without your continuous intercession. We had a lot of laughs.

To the amazing writers Christy Cooper-Burnett, Ivy Logan and Colin Broderick, thanks for the cover blurbs. May all of your books sell millions of copies.

To Lonnie Bell (fine Celt), Jennifer (cute and tough little Italian), Tamber (cutest voice ever), Mari (cute and compact), Tina (pretty eyed bartender) and the rest of the staff and regulars including Jeff & Krista, Pete & Jen, Randy & Katrina, Dan & Beth, and Barry & Christine, at Mike O'Shays in Longmont Colorado. Cannot wait until this book sits on your literary shelf. Special shout out to Kyle Dooley, a dear friend who reads all of the books being placed on the MOS shelf and knows *The Claire Trilogy* better than I do. He also is one of my inner circle of readers that reviewed *Finding Jimmy Moran* as I wrote it. Oh, and he appears as the bartender in the Hell's Kitchen scene. And shout out to his daughter, Shelby, who also is a fan of TCT. Special thanks to Chris "Wolfman Jack" Goldenberry for being such a great local supporter.

To Greg Schumann and The Longmont Theatre group, including without limitation, Dwayne, Zander & Hanna, thank you for maintaining the cultural vanguard in NoCo.

To the Wallen Witches and all of their family members, thanks for the continued support. Thank you Dina for reading my FJM draft. And thank you my BIL Lori Buccola for giving Gina your family name.

To Everett and Michelle, my favorite extraterrestrials. Never leave this earth.

To the OFC—Brian "BC" Corry (and Nan), Joe "Bam-Bam" Serrano (and Donna), Mark "Lenny" Lenahan, Mike "Stein" & "Disco" Augustyni (and Delia) and Eileen "Bubbles" Cotto (née Collins), I brought you all back in some form or another in this book, although I could not begin to do any one of you justice without getting us all arrested. We had a hell of a time growing up. So happy we all made it this far. Love you all.

To Ralph and Debbie Droz, Jackie and Sue Vaughan, Robin and Peter Vaughan, Big Jack (RIP) and Connie Vaughan, Tommy (RIP) and Ann McQuillen, Ed McCarroll, Chuck Quigley, Mary Moran (my dear SIL), Tom Delaney (RIP), Dr. Martin Stransky, Terry Collins, Eddie and Larry Clause, Tommy O'Hagan (RIP), Sergeant Brian Gallagher, Peter and Raymond Smith, Johnny Carey (his lovely wife Helen and kids and grandkids), Eddie (RIP) and Joanne Ganz, Terry Ganz (RIP), Steve Charleton (RIP), Jimmy, Stevie, Peter and Matthew Betz, John Hughes, Denis "Murray" Collins (RIP), Jimmy "Schwartz" Whitelaw (and wife Jaysree), Peter "Snapper" Lee, the nicest guy in Riverdale, and wife Pat (née Hughes) and the whole Lee family, Karen "Cruiser" Anderson,

Steve "The Greek" Athineous (RIP), Matty Burke (and older sister Katy), Danny "Mo" Moriarity, Mike Daley, Mike Higgins, Chrissy Pompa, Claudia Panatiari, Chrissy "Pee Wee" Lebovich, Keith Bartlett, Laura Bunting, Luigi from Ken-n-Ed's Pizza, Chrissy and Kathy T, Doreen Flanagan, Bonnie Hogan, Nina Zingale, Mary Jane Dougherty, Rev. Gregory McNeil, Peter and Robbie Sexton, Rosemary McBride, Leslie Romani, Teresa Cariano, Patty Perratini, Elaine Staltare, Nat Vacca, Kevin Amberson, Laurie Richardson, Terry Daley, Sue Woebke, Tracy Jennings, Melissa Guerin, Maurice McGrath, Marty "Magoo" McLaughlin (RIP), Phil "Flip" Cunningham, Frankie Cannataro, Tommy Tracey, Tommy Jennings, Kenny Bielik, Keith Bartlett, Willis Carey, Regina and Rosie Lambeau, Tommy & Mike McBride, the Teifer Brothers, the other McCaffrey brothers, Kathie Mazzarulli, Bob Baisley, Jimmy Bridenbach, Sal Linza, Diane Viale, Joe Fernandez, Mark Wallen, Joe Freyer, Annie Torrez, Bob and Mike Mahoney, Marissa Banez, Mark Lafayette, Brian Egan, Margaret Flynn and Denise Menard, Pete Neary, Mike McLaughlin, the rest of the Collins' Clan, Dr. Lenworth Johnson, the DiNome Family, the Sammartano Family, the DiLullo Family, and anyone else that may even in the slightest way possible resemble any of the characters mentioned herein, I thank you for your past friendships and the roles you have all played in my very selective, imaginative, and extremely questionable memory. Any resemblance in whole or in aggregate to any of the characters was completely unintentional – undoubtedly *scènes à faire* - and all of the stories relating to those characters are completely fictional. Never happened, none of it. I swear it. *Confiteor Deo omnipoténti* . . . .

To St. Margaret's School and Church. I loved my time there and I would not have been a lawyer or a writer without the discipline and fine education you provided (and continue to provide to others to this day). The priests, nuns and lay teachers were always professional and Saints to put up with me, my siblings, and anyone I associated with. None of the fictional stories that appear in this book in what anyone may suggest was a similar setting - undoubtedly *scènes à faire* - ever happened. Never laid a hand on me (and if you had, I would have deserved it). I swear it. *Confiteor Deo omnipoténti* . . . .

The same holds true for any high school or university that may have a record of my attendance (absences or dismissals). It never happened. None of it. Completely fictional. I swear it. *Confiteor Deo omnipoténti* . . . .

To my close circle of dear writer friends Colin Broderick (thanks for the cover blurb), Christy Cooper-Burnett (thanks for the cover blurb and loaning me the cross-over character Madison Taylor - Passport To Terror - in the Hell's Kitchen chapter) and Margaret Reyes Dempsey (Mind Games is a must read), thanks for the continued support and comradery. Also, a shout out to the young writer Ivy Logan (Broken) for the cover blurb. I strongly recommend all of their books.

To Richard Lamb. Your covers are amazing. Thank you for continuing to make my novels look good.

To the real Jimmy Moran. Love you brother. Love to Liz and all of the family. RIP Frances Mahoney.

To Bob Kunisch, my invaluable accountant and dear friend. I would be totally lost without you.

To all of my writer friends and other artists in the Twitterverse Writers Group and the NoCo Writers Group. I wish each and every one of you nothing but success. There are plenty of readers out there that we need to keep busy. Keep supporting each other.

To Jimmy and Kathy Fronsdahl, I appreciate your continuing support. Stay well. Love you both. Claire sends her love.

To the rest of my inner circle of readers, including, without limitation, Joe Serrano, Mike "Mikey" Abramson, Kyle Dooley (yes, the Hell's Kitchen Bartender), Kirsten Williams, Yvette Benson, Ralph Droz, Mary McCaffrey (née Moran), and my wife Lisa. I could never do what I do without your real time feedback. Love you all.

To Dan Pearson and his family. As always, with all due respect.

To my dear friend and law partner, Robert "never Bobby" Meloni. I love you, no matter what.

To Helen (BFF), Bobbi, Eddie, and Kim and Anthony Russo, and the real magic you continue to share. Love you all.

To every friend and family in Riverdale (Bronx), I know you all appreciate what a magical place it is. Keep rocking it.

To all my Berthoud friends and neighbors. Pay attention to those Ley Lines. You are the best.

To Reagan and Minna Rothe and the entire production, sales, and PR teams at Black Rose Writing, here goes number 4. Thanks for this continuing opportunity and all of your patience and support.

To all members of the Military, Police, Fire, and EMS departments throughout the country, thank you from the bottom of my heart for your selfless service. You are all loved and respected.

Thank you Tommy "Rocky" O'Hagan, Bill McGinn, Orio Palmer, and all of those first responders and other men and women who sacrificed their lives on 9-11-01. You will never be forgotten.

To Claire, who continues to share this amazing journey with me. I am forever in your debt. You, of course, will ultimately continue to carry the sequel in your latest incarnation. Just can't keep a good mule down, or silent.

And much love to my mini-mule, Claire's PA and little sister, Honey.

Finally, to every female, real or imagined, that ever shared a kiss, thank you for your kindness.

photo by Michael Daley

I expressly incorporate by reference every person mentioned in the prior acknowledgments in *The Claire Trilogy* that I may have missed here. Each and every one of you have played your role in getting me to the completion of this book as well. So, thank you all from the bottom of my heart.

For those present readers who have not read *The Claire Trilogy*, go do it now, if only for the acknowledgements.

ABOUT THE AUTHOR

Tom McCaffrey is a born-and-bred New Yorker who, after a long career working as a successful entertainment attorney in Manhattan, relocated with his wife to a small town in Northern Colorado to follow a road less traveled and return to his first passion, writing. Both Tom and Claire and the gang are thrilled that *The Claire Trilogy* continues.

NOTE FROM THE AUTHOR

Word-of-mouth is crucial for any author to succeed. If you enjoyed *Finding Jimmy Moran*, please leave a review online—anywhere you are able. Even if it's just a sentence or two. It would make all the difference and would be very much appreciated.

Thanks!
Tom McCaffrey

We hope you enjoyed reading this title from:

BLACK ROSE
writing™

www.blackrosewriting.com

Subscribe to our mailing list—*The Rosevine*—and receive **FREE** books, daily deals, and stay current with news about upcoming releases and our hottest authors.

Scan the QR code below to sign up.

Already a subscriber? Please accept a sincere thank you for being a fan of Black Rose Writing authors.

View other Black Rose Writing titles at www.blackrosewriting.com/books and use promo code **PRINT** to receive a **20% discount** when purchasing.

CPSIA information can be obtained
at www.ICGtesting.com
Printed in the USA
LVHW090713160423
744468LV00007B/785

9 781685 131746